# WHERE THERE'S A WILL

Robert Cox

Published by Jaromin Publishing
Bough Beech, Kent, England

Cover design by Patricia Le Baudrier (c) 2014

ISBN: 9780993106514

All characters and situations are entirely fictitious.

Printed and bound in Great Britain by
www.printondemand-worldwide.com

# PREFACE

As an author putting his head and first attempt at a novel on the chopping block of public scrutiny, the idea of a preface felt slightly uncomfortable. Is anyone interested in what an unknown writer has to say about his own work?

I decided not to bother. That was until checking through my own book collection and reading Tom Hughes' preface to 'Tom Brown at Oxford,' his sequel to 'Tom Brown's Schooldays.'

*"Prefaces written to explain the objects or meaning of a book, or to make any appeal, are in my opinion, nuisances. Any book worth reading will explain its own objects and meaning, and the more it is criticised and turned inside out, the better for it and its author. Of all books, too, it seems to me that novels require prefaces least - at any rate on their first appearance. Notwithstanding which belief, I must ask readers for three minutes' patience before they make trial of this book."*

Three long minutes of patience. That was 1861; probably the equivalent in today's whirlwind of about ten seconds. In my copy of 'Tom Brown's Schooldays' there is no preface, so whilst not altogether heeding his sound advice I'll let Tom Hughes' finish all that remains to be said.

*"I have only, then, to say, that neither is the hero a portrait of myself, nor is there any other portrait\* (of anyone I know) in the book......with these remarks I leave this volume in the hands of readers."*

R. Cox

---

\* *"Except in the case of Dr Arnold, where the true name is given."* (T.H.)

# CONTENTS

*For my mother who, contrary to what the reader might assume
from the content of this story, was my constant, loving friend.*

*Also for my father who died when I was sixteen
and left his quiet reassuring voice never far from my mind.*

## Chapter One

## HENRY'S DAY OF RECKONING

'Thank you God, for nothing!'

Henry Winston Scroggins lay on his back in bed directing his hushed verbal salvo through the pre-dawn gloom at the crack across his ceiling. His sparse covering was a once white sheet and a once bright orange silk eiderdown which he gripped between two sets of podgy fingers and tugged as close up under his several chins as was possible without self-asphyxiating.

The ceiling was less a ceiling and more a precariously sagging expanse of plaster that bore a large brown stain from an attic water tank leakage many moons ago, the crack growing longer and wider and the stain browner and uglier in dismal sympathy with Henry growing older and unhappier.

On this particular morning, as if to enhance the depressing scene and Henry's woeful state of mind, a baying wind lashed relentless torrents of rain against his window, sending the rattling, rotting wooden frame into ominous paroxysms as if it were about to burst in and shower him with glass. And it was a sad fact that at times like this, his lowest, that Henry often wished the window would burst in; but then his bed wasn't quite close enough for death to be instant and painless - and that really wouldn't do.

Born during an air raid forty years earlier on a still, cloudy night, Henry owed his first and last name to his father, his middle name to the Luftwaffe and nothing at all to his mother, the old witch in the next room who was starting to clatter about in irritation at her tea not being delivered on time; her thin, rigid head and roman nose cocked like a pet shop parrot, listening for signs of life through the wall.

It was the 23rd December 1980, one month into Henry's forty-first year. John Lennon had been murdered in New York two weeks earlier and the novelty of England's first female Prime Minister was beginning to wear off - she who lived and worked just a hundred yards or so from Henry's Whitehall office.

Elsewhere, a joyful fawning populace was whipping itself into a frenzy at the prospect of a shell-shocked prince and shy, pretty kindergarten teacher (yet to publicly demonstrate the faculty of coherent speech) marrying the following summer.

But what did Henry care? What possible interest or reason could he have for celebrating *anything*, let alone the happiness of two young people pampered from their first breath.

Progress and Happiness had forgotten all about Henry. On a graph of Life where the rise and fall of the curve illustrates each success and failure, each high point and crisis, Henry's forty-year mark displayed an almost unwavering straight line with just the odd blip here and there at a vague sniff of promotion before hopes were dashed and life went on as before. The greatest drama in his mundane existence occurred when the eight-thirteen from Lewisham to Charing Cross arrived late, forcing him to waddle and weave a little faster through the human traffic across the concourse and left down Whitehall.

'Henry!'

The word gripped his skull like metal pincers above the ears.

'Oh, God help me,' he muttered, with a touch of hypocrisy.

*'Henry!'*

He rolled over and fumbled for his spectacles on the bedside table. As his fingers folded around them he felt the Evening Standard racing-guide pages on which they rested. The racing guide, what a laugh. He certainly didn't need any help picking out the losers. Why did losers always pick losers, he thought? What came first, the human loser or the perverse horse? It hardly mattered for he bought the paper every night all the same, kidding himself it was for the front page headlines and crossword.

Anyway, there was always his thoughtful mother. She made sure a copy was delivered to the house every evening in case Henry forgot to buy one; always had done since Henry's first interest and lack of expertise in the sport had become obvious. Such a good woman, so thoughtful, and when it seemed that every horse he'd ever backed had stopped, like Ferdinand the Bull, to smell the flowers along the track, there she was with the same sympathetic grimace that he always wanted to punch.

Heaven forbid if any of his colleagues in The Department ever found out his betting weakness. At least that was one place, the only place, where he felt he earned some vague form of respect. But if they ever found out! No, that was a step beyond which he could see no possible return. But she was different, his mother. She encouraged his little weakness; she, who despised every vice in the world with a venomous passion, encouraged him, for whilst the majority of Henry's horses crossed the line sniffing the backside of another, or preferably several, Henry was hers. There was no way out - apart from her death.

'Henry! Where are you!' Pause. '*Hen*-ree!'

Henry peered at the lenses of his spectacles to check their cleanliness which had always occurred to him a silly habit in so much as he could never see any smears until he had them on, but it was one of life's pointless rituals, of which he had many.

'*Henry!*' This time screeched and inducing a choking fit.

'Go on, choke you old cow,' he whispered, huffing on his lenses and rubbing them on his pyjama sleeve to prolong the agony in the next room and bring the fury to a suitable crescendo. Yes, he would certainly need his specs this morning. He always felt so terribly vulnerable without them and heaven knows he needed all his faculties to tackle her today of all days, the day he'd decided for the first time in his life - to fight back.

'*Henry!*'

She banged hard on the wall behind him, vibrating the framed sepia print of Constable's 'Haywain' above his head, to which he instinctively jolted forward in case it fell.

'Henry! *Tea!* It's late!'

'Well get up then you lazy old bat,' he hissed under his breath, as he always did in these moments of true togetherness.

Chapter Two

# A MALEDICTION CALLED MOTHER

'Coming Mother! I won't be a moment!'

But Henry wasn't moving. He wasn't ready to move and he smiled with childish glee at not being ready to move, spectacles now polished and in place and fingers knitted across his chest like the effigy of a once portly bishop. His shrunken cotton pyjamas, the blue and white stripes melded into one shade of 'smoke' through endless dark washes, no longer served the distant extremities of hands and feet so he kept his jacket buttoned up tight under his hamster jowls on these winter nights in a vain attempt to repel the cold and damp that permeated every inch of the drab, comfortless room.

He thought about his little grumble at The Almighty when he had waited his customary few seconds for a post-blasphemy thunderbolt to arrive through the ceiling. It never did of course, but was always worth a try and probably a safer option than shards of glass. Despite the ceiling representing the rough direction of where God was supposed to live, Henry didn't have a religious bone in his body. It just allowed him to open a pressure valve, a perfectly innocent venting of his spleen over the tragedy of his existence and the malignant presence that lay twitching and listening to his every movement through the wall. A malediction he called Mother.

Despite lacking religion Henry knew his gospels pretty well and had a sort of bloke'ish affinity with Jesus, a brave but stubborn chap in his opinion, who refuses an offer of clemency and then has the nerve to complain when it's worryingly obvious God's switched his day off from Sunday to Friday. Poor man, up on the cross gasping 'Eli, Eli, lama sabachthani' and not a sign to be had of the Heavenly Father.

Good Friday? Henry had never figured out what was so good about it, but fearing it was something obvious missed only by himself, had never liked to ask. He had many unanswered questions about life, the main one lying a few feet away. Why was she still breathing?

So yes, he knew his gospels fairly well and he mainly knew them because a worn black leather bible constituted twenty percent of the book stock in the house which, over the years since ceasing to act as a cudgel for his God-fearing mother to apply randomly to his small head, he'd thumbed through many times. This was more often out of boredom but also to reassure himself that it wasn't a bad blueprint for the world if only certain members of the human race didn't choose to ignore or distort the valuable teachings for their own means, causing centuries of indiscriminate suffering mainly to the meek and mild. The meek and mild like himself that is. It was certainly a sad fact that from where he stood, or lay, he had to look no further for a working microcosm of his theory than the four walls of his own house. How terribly, avoidably tragic it all was.

The Old Testament stories he thought mainly a load of tosh; fairy tales by depressed beardy hacks without the meteorological knowledge to explain why things went bang and flash in the sky. But even despite this easy dismissal, there remained indelibly imprinted on his brain the terrifying thirty-year old image of fire and brimstone spewing forth over the pulpit of St. Michael & All Angels Church as the fearsome, bushy eye-browed vicar singled out the quaking Henry, smallest choirboy, for demonic threats of thunderbolts and lightning, very *very* frightening, that to this day still braced the forty-year-old man for the arrival of one. A thunderbolt he was certain he wanted but might later regret; not unlike when one's head's in a gas oven but a little too woozy to reach the 'Off' tap as the thought suddenly arrives that life's maybe not so bad after all, and your winning lottery numbers are read out on the kitchen television as you slip into permanent unconsciousness.

With a deep sigh Henry turned his head towards the window where the faded green curtains failed to meet through years of reduced circumstances and, bringing one hand slowly up to his face, scratched his nose. He smiled lovingly at the rain.

'Ah, Hollywood rain,' he purred, barely audible against the howling, rattling attack from outside, 'dear old Hollywood rain.'

Whenever rain fell in such relentless waves that it seemed impossible for a sky to throw so much down and still be taken seriously, there was Gene Kelly in Henry's head being hosed down by fifty firemen. Dear old Gene Kelly singing, dancing, splishing and sploshing in and out of the gutter with his twirling umbrella and perfect white teeth; happy, hopping, handsome Gene Kelly singing, just singing in the rain.

Henry used to do that on his way home from school when it rained; hop in and out of the gutter in his Wellington boots holding his satchel over his head as an umbrella, singing the song tunelessly, breathlessly, almost happily. It was the only film he'd ever seen at the pictures, a birthday treat from his father's father, a small, light-footed, friendly man with a black pencil moustache and flat oily hair who tap-danced on their lino when he visited, which wasn't often. Henry smiled, remembering him and his vaudeville voice and the walking stick he'd grab as a cane from the hallstand, and thought there must have been times when he, Henry, was happy. It was just people made him miserable, children at school who called him 'loony', 'four eyes' and 'fatty', his mother waiting at home with her ever ready stinging palm who always - but no, this wasn't a day for giving her one morsel of credit for his misery.

Having scratched his nose he unbuttoned his jacket and dispatched the same fingernail on an exploratory trip to his naval, a neat and tidy little orifice buried in white fat and a whirlpool of black hair. He glanced down at it with an effort, due to chins and belly fat, and thought it was something of a shame really, his belly button being buried, in view of it originally being one of his better features. A boy in gym had once told him this and because he was a kind sort of boy and meant it, it had stuck in Henry's mind as the only compliment he could ever remember being paid; physical compliment that is. And it had come from a boy, a kind thoughtful boy who had probably never given him another thought.

He didn't ever remember a girl seeing or complimenting his belly button. So as he dug at this part of his body once connecting him to the body now ominously silent in the next room, he considered the changes that had taken place in the world during his forty unhappy years.

World War II ended when he was five, the last year he saw his father; Man had landed on the Moon when he was twenty-nine; cars now cluttered the previously barren, safe gutters of streets making it impossible for him to do his Gene Kelly dance (even if he wanted to); and in 1962 whilst his mother was in hospital for a week - a sad quick recovery - he'd papered over, in a rebellious fit of lunacy and wasteful excess of paste, the dismal Victorian dark crimson velvet embossed wallpaper of his vapid sanctuary.

He'd spotted several rolls of a tissue-thin green and white ivy creeper design on offer at Woolworths and buoyed with ecstasy and bravado the first day of her absence had, on an impulse, created a hideous mix of velvet red roses and green-brown ivy, churned together with the paste he'd bought and felt frugally obliged to use up. A fearsome but short fit of vitriol on his mother's return was followed by a prolonged period, almost a month, of deathly silence.

His first and last rebellion was therefore quickly over, but that was eighteen years ago and with forty now ticked off there welled fresh rumblings, a sort of now or never feeling. Not caring a jot about life or death can turn a lamb into a wolf. Twenty years ago he couldn't even grow a moustache but now he'd a fair covering of body hair, which at least looked wolfish.

His naval exploration now completed, Henry lay flat-out with hands flopped beside him on the grey, grimy, threadbare sheet. He was indeed a man tired of life. He told himself often; remonstrated with himself for carrying on the same monotonous, debilitating routine day in day out with no hope of any change remotely in sight.

But in these moments of solitary despair he sought small crumbs of comfort in the knowledge that he was now on life's home run, hopefully with not too many more decades to endure. Being a man whose only diversion outside work was a flutter on the horses, he was prone to using racing analogies when at work, annoying little expressions like 'home straight (or run)', 'final furlong', 'spurred along', 'starting-line' and the most irritating of all 'gee up' which were repeated too many times to too many colleagues in the Department, giving the expressions their own name of 'Scroggisms' when arriving on the memos he incessantly sent around the office. But memos being memos and his time and motion memos having such a nauseating effect, Henry's attempts at literary gems, as he thought they might possibly be received, always fell badly and had to be destroyed.

He lay and thought about the horses; those damn horses! Oh, if only they *were* a flutter. If only he'd learnt years ago to flutter in moderation, or better still, not to flutter at all. Would he still be there trapped within those same four drab walls on that same thin grey sheet, waiting for that same hideous voice to penetrate his eardrums? Fluttering; the one meagre indulgence he permitted himself as a young man when all those around him were dating, jiving, drinking, or even studying, and it had consumed him, consumed his wages, and in doing so any chance he ever had of ridding himself of the only known relative he had in the world.

Irma Scroggins sat up hunched in her bed listening and biting her lower lip with little impatient nips, like a rabbit expecting its breakfast to be interrupted. It was a bed that forty years and ten months earlier had apparently supported a whole seven minutes of unbridled feigning on the part of Henry Scroggins senior as the valiant man closed his eyes, gritted his teeth and thought of Vera Lynn. Only he knew the true identity of Henry junior's spiritual mother. That was, at least, the story his father liked to tell, for he, Henry junior, was sometimes a little eaves-dropper into his father's chats with wartime A.R.P mates.

In fact it was a small miracle that Henry lay on his bed at all, for just seconds after the deed was done by Henry senior, the future father had been forced to leap from his bed, grab tin helmet, boots, gloves and pistol and rush to the wailing siren's call to tramp the burning streets and claw bricks from broken bodies. Oh yes, even the horror of war on the doorstep had its compensations, saving Henry senior the ritual of any post-coital 'pleasantries.' But not so for Henry junior; no compensation whatsoever for the downtrodden product of this pre-bombing dalliance who had always mentally replaced the last word of the cliché 'life's too short' with 'long' whenever he heard it.

He'd listened once through the banisters, crouched in the shadows on the stairs after bedtime, as his father related in the kitchen the story of his son's conception to his friends whilst sharing a drop of home brew after a bombing raid, and wished - oh how Henry wished, like his laughing father - that the Luftwaffe had arrived just a few minutes earlier.

So there in bed sat the butt of the joke, holding her breath, nipping at her lip, listening intently for signs of life through the wall. She squinted at the large oak clock ticking loudly through the silence on the black iron mantelpiece at the end of her bed. Six-forty-seven. She scowled impatiently. Her tea had to be on time, Henry knew that, otherwise her day of monotonous regularity was thrown entirely out of order; six-forty-seven indeed and not a stirring to be heard.

Henry the antagonist lifted his head slightly off the pillow, imagining with schoolboy glee the state of intense agitation he was creating with the evil one unable to detect any signs of activity because of the noise of the weather. She'd be angry at the wind and the rain because that's how she was, angry at anything she couldn't control, and the noisy elements were currently an impediment. She was rarely angry with Henry.

Oh how Henry hated her! He hated her to the point where he would constantly fantasise about her funeral and today, slumping back on his pillow, inhaling deeply and smiling vacantly at the crack in the ceiling, he once more pictured the glorious day, should it ever come before his. There, amidst all the false sorrow, the odd hypocritical tear falling down the cheeks of the few remaining acquaintances from whom without exception she had alienated herself over the years with her spiteful, hateful manner. But they'd be there 'grieving', as is done at funerals whether the corpse means anything to you warm or cold, and he, Henry, would turn around to them grinning triumphantly from the front row as if a 100-1 shot he'd backed with his whole week's wages had romped home just moments before.

Then, as the vicar poured wasted words on top of wasted tears, Henry would stride towards the cheapest coffin money could buy - even so, still a total waste of stake money - and taking out a piece of chalk from his mackintosh pocket, would write with an impudent flourish the words 'Good Riddance!' on the side. Then, and this was his favourite part, he would turn again towards the black-shrouded faces amongst the pews and a dazzling shaft of sunlight would suddenly pierce the scene from a high window. Smiles would break out from the frowns, hats would be thrown in the air, flowers snatched back off the coffin and rammed into buttonholes, and a rosy-faced brass band would strike up outside the chapel led by an extremely boisterous conductor playing something wonderfully up-tempo like 'The Archers'.

Henry lifted himself onto one plump elbow and leaned across to flick on his bedside lamp. He squinted at his watch, noting with satisfaction that it was now three minutes past seven, and methodically scratched his fat, hairy belly up, down, around. Offering another little dig at the naval, a pat to say 'that's it for the day', a yawn - and he was ready to rise.

He felt a chill race through his body as bare feet came in contact with cold lino before slippers were located and slipped on. Not a carpet, rug or warm radiator graced the room, or any room come to that; the whole place divest of home comfort, everything hard surfaced and hard edged like the hard heart that beat - more's the pity - in the room next door.

But what was the point? He only had himself to blame. He was the one who'd allowed not only the human race but six or seven generations of racehorses to trample all over his life and consign him to a life of penury. But as the wind howled ferociously outside he thought of the tiny wind of change that had lately been welling up inside him. He wasn't sure where it came from or whether it was anything more than a harmless breeze that would soon fade and die, or perhaps just an unconscious restless gesture to mark his fortieth year. Whatever it was, something had been nagging away in his head telling him for the first time in his life -

to fight back! For whether imprisonment and degradation are chains in a tyrant's rat-infested dungeon or the entrapment of debt and a despotic parent, the fact remains there are bounds to human endurance.

So as he sat on the edge of the bed, pulled his crumpled grey suit trousers over his feet and hauled his braces over his pyjama jacket, Henry knew he had probably reached that boundary of endurance and with life offering not a grain of hope for something better he stared vacantly at the lino and imagined her sitting there erect and stiff just a few feet away through the wall, her paper-mache face and wisps of grey hair protruding out of the maroon and blue crocheted shawl pulled tight around her head and shoulders; red rims circling cold, sunken, watery eyes; mouth mumbling and chattering some critical oath or other; yellow talons gripping the shawl, those revolting hands that reminded him of a chicken's lower leg - dry, empty skin hanging from bent bones. How she revolted him, his mother.

If only the stroke had killed her off last year instead of breathing fresh life and energy into her and a renewed bitterness to oppress him still further. What possible use was she to humanity? What minute contribution did she make? Did her presence on this earth make anyone's life a little more bearable? Did it hell! She was a wicked old lady and gave nothing, absolutely nothing! But then Henry suddenly reminded himself she did give something; she gave him the will to cling on to life until after she was gone. Yes, that was a real plus. Not that he would change his lifestyle in any particular way - oh no, that was positively unthinkable - but he could enjoy her not being there, he could wallow in her permanent absence, her not being part of his life. And more than anything else, he would be free of that *voice*.

'Henry! *Henry!*'

He assembled the cups, milk and Arrowroot biscuit that she insisted upon but only ever nibbled or sucked, and practised how he was going to announce the news to her.

She would of course be hurt, deeply; she would also be in fear of her life what with all the break-ins lately in the district, and without any shadow of doubt she would feign tears.

But most of all - and this was the most satisfying part - she would be furious; furious to the point of rage. And what would make it even worse for her was the fact that she had to look hurt and neglected when she felt nothing but absolute and uncontrollable rage inside, an uncontrollable rage that she had to control otherwise Henry would think that his abandoning of her for three hours that evening was making her angry instead of just upset; and deeply hurt - of course.

'Morning Mother!' said Henry as he pushed open the bedroom door with his backside and shunted in sideways, clutching a tray, as he had done now for some ten years.

'There you are,' he said kindly, presenting her with her cup and wishing, as he did every morning, that he could pour it straight over her head, 'drink it up while it's just right.'

Irma Scroggins peered stony-faced into the cup to check, as usual, for colour and content. Henry was forbidden to buy teabags but also severely chastised if one, just one, grout was found floating on top. He had his own supply of teabags secretly hidden in a cupboard that the old dragon couldn't reach, even with the help of a stool, and when she wasn't around - only ever when she wasn't around, which wasn't often - did he permit himself the luxury of dangled tea.

She held the cup up to her crack of a mouth. Henry watched breathlessly and felt his own mouth turn up into the disapproving sneer one makes when an unwelcome smell hits the nostrils. The vertical creases above her top lip closed together in a pursed slurp and closing her eyes in pain she withdrew her mouth quickly, exclaiming:

'Ugh! You fool! Too hot! More milk!'

Oh joy, it had worked. Henry released his breath and composed his mouth back into one of surprise and distress, jumping forward to take the steaming tea.

He really had been naughty, had Henry, but it was how he felt. Instead of waiting until the tea was the right drinkable temperature for her, he had deliberately rushed the boiling water from kettle to teapot to mouth in such haste that his only fear had been rejection on the colour factor, or maybe an errant grout.

But the extra steam from the unusually cold morning air had aided concealment of the colour and allowed him his small sadistic moment. And by golly it had worked a treat and the pleasure was indescribable. He once more wiped the grin from his face that arrived back quite uninvited and shaking his head apologetically, carried the offending tea downstairs, added a morsel of milk and cold water, and returned.

'Mother,' he said, picking his moment when her mouth was full, 'Mother, I'm going to be home later this evening. I'm going to the office Christmas party you see. I'll catch the nine fifty-five from Charing Cross so I'm home well before midnight.'

In regard to Mrs Irma Scroggins only contribution to the conversation so far that morning being exclamations limited to 'Henry! It's late! You fool! Too hot! More milk!' she suddenly found the most amazing reserves of vocabulary and pathos. In fact the rendition that immediately followed Henry's selfish announcement - and her swallowing her mouthful - even took her battle-scarred son by surprise. So much so that Henry, for a while pre-occupied with his mother's latent acting talent, was temporarily lost for words.

But temporary it was. For this morning *Henry* was in control, and being in control he soon joined in the charade, playing his part to the full. In fact he even went so far as to place a consoling arm around his mother's shuddering shoulder and add a few 'there-theres' whilst admiring the dramatic scene in the mirror behind the clock on the mantelpiece. He stared at the reflection of the top of his mother's shaking, cowed head and realised for the first time that she had a bald circle, like a monk, or a moon, and suddenly an explosion of laughter erupted from his nostrils which he had to quickly turn into a spluttering, coughing sneeze.

In twenty years with the Department, Henry's absence from the office Christmas party was as traditional as the decorations, the drink, the mistletoe and the pinching of secretaries' bottoms, an act of festive generosity they permitted on this special day but resented the rest of the year.

So Henry had finally made a stand but would it be like Custer's, he wondered; his last?

For the time being anyway, he'd made it, and the charade was over. His mother's 'hurt' had completed a rapid metamorphosis and was nicely settled in as rage; white rage.

At precisely seven fifty-seven Henry stood before his cracked, rectangular swivel mirror, examined the shiny baldness of his high-domed head - not unlike his mother's he sadly noted - pushed the knot of his tie into his chin fat, buttoned his suit jacket, picked up his yellow scarf, grey woollen gloves, mackintosh and racing guide, decided he cut a not unreasonable figure for a chubby forty-year old, listened to the cursing and crashing about next door, took a long, deep breath, and thought, 'Henry, what on earth have you done?'

Finally he tiptoed from the room and along the landing, holding his breath as he passed his mother's door, down the stairs (avoiding the creaking step) until gingerly turning the handle of the kitchen door that led to the back yard. Peering through the four panes of glass in the top half of the door at the raging tempest whipping up the garden's flotsam and jetsam, he made his exit, fearing that if he opened his umbrella he might, like Mary Poppins, soon be sailing over the glistening, sodden rooftops of south east London.

Chapter Three

# THE OFFICE CHRISTMAS PARTY

'He-llo Henry! How very good to see you dear boy!'

The voice was laced with all the warm sincerity of a gas-chamber guard. Peregrine Spencer, as Department Head and thereby Henry's boss, was one for maximum social participation amongst his staff outside office hours and Henry's twenty year abstention from anything remotely smacking of 'social' was bitterly resented. Spencer took it as an affront to his authority and good nature but had long ago abandoned any hope of persuading Henry to join in.

So Henry's contribution to office hanky-panky remained on a par with Nero's to the Rome Fire Brigade and Spencer took great pleasure in fostering this image on behalf of his reticent subordinate at every opportunity. But the nods, the winks and the nudges were not for Henry's eyes and he went his sober way in blissful ignorance. The joke therefore, among the remaining forty-six staff members, remained strictly private.

'Good evening Peregrine,' replied Henry, trying not to wince at the pungent smell of alcohol and white blobs of expectorant that flew from the moist rubbery lips of the face much too close to his.

'Got a few lined up for you tonight old chap,' grinned the red-nosed, pin-striped bull of a man, wrapping one long ape-like arm around Henry's shoulders and whacking him on the chest with his other hand.

Henry involuntarily expelled air from his lungs and pushed his dislodged spectacles back up to the bridge of his nose.

'A few what?' he gasped innocently.

Peregrine Spencer clutched his drink and peered around the large open plan office with dramatic surreptitiousness pretence.

'*Crumpet* old chap! You know - slap n' tickle!'

Henry said nothing but peered over his lenses in horror at the revelry that was at that moment gathering rapid momentum further down the office.

'I shan't be stopping long,' announced Henry, nervously tugging his gloves further up his wrists to emphasise the point. 'Just the one barley wine,' he added with a limp chuckle, 'that's me at Christmas.' This was a lie as he'd never touched a drop of alcohol in his life but Henry had decided that he'd not give Spencer any opportunity to feel this was the occasion to break his abstinence. And he'd deliberately chosen barley wine as his preferred drink in the hope that it was one of the most unlikely beverages to be found at an office party and he could instantly revert to his number one choice of orange juice.

Peregrine Spencer threw back his head and bellowed with laughter, reminding Henry of the Laughing Policeman at the end of Margate pier that had once terrified him as a child on a rare day trip. He also had time to examine Spencer's tonsils that had obviously been there throughout their twenty-year acquaintance but until this evening he'd never had chance to study. He also noted the thick growth of hair protruding from Spencer's nostrils and the white blobs in the corner of his mouth and wondered whether they'd also always been there and why he'd never noticed them.

'That's what you think!' slurred Spencer into Henry's ear, lurching a little unsteadily and nudging the shorter man with a knowing elbow and wink to match. 'That's what *you* think Henry!' And without any doubt it was exactly what Henry thought.

As it was, Henry smiled wanly, then dutifully followed the beckoning figure of Peregrine Spencer as he made his way back into the fray, making one or two polite gestures of conversation with colleagues before retiring to his own desk with a glass, small, of barley wine, which to his great disappointment they had in plentiful stock - a favourite with one of the ladies apparently.

His desk, which was partly hidden by a section of beige partition some distance from the core of the party outside Spencer's office, made him feel reasonably safe. He also still had on his dark grey mackintosh and slightly paler grey gloves and yellow scarf in order to radiate a distinct lack of permanence should any unwanted attention be focused upon him. He shuffled a few papers on his desk, thought how different the office looked after hours, sighed, moved his glass two inches to the right, lifted a burst balloon from his in-tray as if it were diseased, dropped it into his waste bin and sliding his mackintosh sleeve an inch up his wrist, peered discreetly at his watch and whistled softly.

He noted with some dismay that it was still only eight-thirty, precisely the same time as when he last looked, so he proceeded to check his watch with the office clock. This action only brought further disappointment by registering eight-twenty-nine but then the clock was notoriously unreliable as he of all people could verify. Only if it had been showing eight thirty-one would he have been prepared, on just this one 'social' occasion, to place some trust in it.

At this precise moment of concentrated time-checking, his solitude and concentration were suddenly and violently interrupted by the arrival of a body on his desk, which sent the trays, desk-tidy and other assorted items crashing to various parts of the floor and the contents of Henry's glass down his mackintosh. Now the fact that Henry no more wanted the drink than fly in the air and that he was suitably dressed for such an accident, in his mackintosh, were no compensation for the extreme shock inflicted.

The body squirmed and an inverted face contorted itself into the just recognisable features of Richard Gaines, post-room supervisor and inveterate occupant of a coveted barstool in The Carpenter's Arms next door.

'Henry you ole' wanker - 'ow are yer mate?' slurred the face, eyes currently out of control and rolling through the top of his head.

It was apparent that he'd taken it upon himself to start the Christmas party rather earlier than the rest of the staff and had been seen, by Henry no less, slipping out of the building at approximately eight minutes past eleven that morning with Sun newspaper tucked under his arm and relighting half an inch of bent roll-up during the thirty yards journey to his barstool. Where the post was going to end up that day was anyone's guess.

Henry couldn't be absolutely certain what a 'wanker' should look like (he'd never liked to ask) so replied that he was 'fine thank you.' The face then became as upright as it could manage in its current condition and in unison with the eyes rolling back down into place, a trickle of saliva followed in the same direction from mouth to lower chin. The eyes, having now resumed their normal position, invited the mouth to join the party, this twisted orifice proceeding to make several more unsuccessful attempts to speak. These attempts, valiant under the circumstances, were aided and abetted by a finger wagging roughly two inches in front of Henry's nose, a finger that would have helped emphasise a point if in fact that point could have been prised from the gullet of the drunken orator.

Finally, did the words that Richard Gaines had fought so well to expel, fall upon Henry's virgin ears.

'Henry - f'fuck sake mate, let y'self go! Join the f...'

'Fun?' finished off Henry as the man disappeared over the edge of the desk. Henry leant forward slightly and peered at the muttering, crumpled mound trying to co-ordinate its limbs into rising from the floor, like a freshly born calf or foal. He then proceeded to carefully pick up the items scattered around his desk as if tidying at the end of his normal day. This was all too much for Henry, he'd made a bad mistake in joining the party just to teach his mother a lesson and now decided it was time to leave and find some other venue to delay his return home, maybe the Wimpey Bar in Coventry Street. He did love a Wimpy and, apart from William Hill's betting shop, it was the only place with enough magnetism to draw him off his normal route.

'Time I was on my way,' he said, directing his message to the hand that had just risen from below and groped the desk for support, 'I'll finish this and be getting off home.'

'Going?' said the head that popped up behind the hand. *'Going?'* repeated the head, now joined by half a torso as it rose to nothing like its full height. 'Like hell you are mate!' And with that the whole dishevelled package, combining an alarming feat of gyroscopic meanderings with a finger wagging in the air, lurched off to the mainstream of the party spreading the news that Henry, who everyone had either forgotten about or had no idea had actually arrived, was thinking of leaving.

To the utmost horror of our sober paragon of virtue, heads turned his way, glasses were placed on desks, secretaries were reluctantly put down and a posse of shirt-sleeved deputies, tie-knots in various positions from mid-chest to armpit, followed the one and only Sheriff Peregrine Spencer in a determined march towards the panic-stricken Henry who instantly rose with heart beating louder every second and eyes transfixed on the advancing lynch party.

He lifted a hand to adjust his spectacles, placed the other gloved hand on the back of his chair and moved around in order to place himself in a position where he could run away if required, and it was looking fairly much that way. He glanced away briefly in the direction of the fire escape, his closest exit point, and wished, oh how he wished, he'd decided to discreetly pass through it a few minutes earlier. But it was too late.

'Henry…' came the distinctive spurious tone of Peregrine Spencer.

'Yes, P-Peregrine,' stammered Henry.

'You're not leaving us old chap?'

'Yes.'

'No.'

'Oh.'

'Henry, now come on. The fun's just about to start for goodness sake!'

'No really. You see, my mother…'

'Oh, stuff your mother!'

Henry thought how much he would like to but shook his head and peered nervously at the array of menacing leers that were now fixed upon him.

'No, honestly Peregrine, I promised her faithfully that I'd catch the…'

And with that he lifted his eyes to the office clock and declared in plain astonishment, 'Oh, good heavens above! Is that the time?' He then checked his watch with an exaggerated spin of the wrist and a horrified elevation of the eyebrows to verify his statement for any who were in doubt, and proceeded to take a step towards the door. Now this door, whilst only twenty or so feet to the left past a row of filing cabinets, may just as well have been in the Great Wall of China for all the progress he was about to make. The iron hand of Peregrine Spencer descended on Henry's sloping shoulder with the delicacy of a sledge-hammer and promptly rammed him back onto his chair with such force that the poor escapee felt sure his four coccyxes had just been compounded into one large, single vertebra.

'Just one for the road then eh?' whispered Peregrine in such a smoothly persuasive manner that Henry himself now began to believe that his stay would be extended.

'But I came by train,' said Henry, attempting humour.

'Ha-ha. Get the man a drink!' ordered Peregrine.

'Just a small one if I must.'

'Large!'

'Just the one then, and then I really must be....'

Peregrine Spencer clipped his fingers, crying out 'A drink for Henry!' whilst smiling around at the others and declaring 'and an honour for all of us dirty socialites! Eh, Henry?'

Henry had a strong feeling that Peregrine wasn't being entirely sincere but he smiled and took a deep breath of resignation. Peregrine Spencer, stunned by the lack of action that his clipped fingers had generated, did it again, but this time with a matadorial flourish.

'Drink! Drink! Drink!' he shouted, 'the poor man's thirsty for Christ's sake!'

'No I'm really not thirsty at all,' said Henry.

'You are,' corrected Peregrine with a broad toothy smile.

Henry realised he obviously was thirsty and watched as a flurry of underlings scurried away after turning several full circles to get their bearings and getting a little entangled with each other. The remainder of the group, bedecked in colourful hats, streamers and various other ingenious ways of looking ridiculous, resumed their merry ways. Drink continued to be consumed in large quantities at high speed, balloons popped to female screams and male howls of laughter, normally upright figures lurched haphazardly and destructively through a melee of desks and expensive office machines, male bosses became silly and increasingly familiar with female staff, and juniors became increasingly cocky and familiar with their seniors. In other words, in this Whitehall office not a hundred yards from the very spot where King Charles lost his head in 1649, everybody but Henry seemed to be losing theirs and Christmas was being celebrated in much the same fashion as it had been in that same area for centuries, apart from the ten years following the loss of the aforementioned royal head when a certain Mr Cromwell decided to be a party-pooper - and banned it.

Only one diminutive, oddball figure sat in miserable isolation from it all. Isolation in spirit that is, for poor Henry was blessedly surrounded with as much conviviality as he could wish for in a thousand lifetimes. Someone shouted 'Turn it up!' and Bing Crosby's 'White Christmas' crashed hideously distorted upon the assembled eardrums before being reduced to a bearable level of decibels whereby every frenzied impersonator (for that's the effect the song had on the men) could, with knees bent, heads thrown back, glasses waved demonstratively and cigarettes waved dangerously, enjoy the sound of his own voice in the dire hope that the female they were at that time trying to impress would recognise their hidden talent and suddenly regard them with fresh and dewy eyes as the most attractive man present.

Henry watched. Blank-faced, he watched. And as he watched he wished with every aching bone in his body that he was at home 'snug' around the few coals permitted on the fire with his slippers on, cocoa on the table beside him and his racing guide open on his lap. His mother wasn't in this picture; he needed a picture of comfort and security and happiness right at this moment and she was no part of that. Every night when she went to bed, dead on the stroke of ten o'clock, he had his happiest half an hour. No evil presence, none of the brutal outside world to contend with and every horse at that stage, a winner.

'Henry, good to see you smiling old chap. Hold on! Here comes your drink. This'll put some hairs on your chest alright. Here! Henry's having his drink! Everyone gather round please! It's initiation time for our one and only beloved time and motion man, Mr Henry...' Peregrine frowned and whispered so everyone could hear clearly, 'whass y'middle name Henry?'

'Winston,' muttered Henry, wishing at that precise moment that it was Matthew, Mark, Luke, John, Peter or even Jesus or Gabriel - anything but Winston.

'Winston? *Win*-ston? *Winston!* The crowd could not have asked for a more perfect excuse to erupt into delirium punctuated by multifarious deliveries of 'We'll fight them on the beaches' and 'Never befores'. Tears were wiped from eyes, heads were shaken, arms clasped around new best mates' shoulders, and amongst all this sat the passive, bespectacled countenance of the least festive person in London.

'Scroggins!' cried Peregrine Spencer above the din, triumphantly bringing Henry's full name to completion. The cheers that followed were tumultuous, the look of satisfaction on Spencer's face indescribable, and the knot in Henry's stomach - unknottable.

The tortured and the torturer smiled at each other but not a warm feeling passed between them. Peregrine Spencer was having his finest hour, a true Churchillian moment with even a Winston thrown in for good measure. What more could a sadistic bully ask for! He turned, glass raised to the assemblage, many of whose heads were now swaying as if their neck bearings had gone, and pronounced with an affectionate gaze back at Henry, 'To an insti-choo-shun....within this Insti-shoo-stun!' And with that, for those present who may have been rather too far gone to respond on cue, he waved his glass in a circle to show he meant the Department and all those worthy members privileged to dwell within.

The slightly delayed response arrived and was as tumultuous as the first but now embellished with a few 'Hoorays!' 'Bravos!' 'Get it down you's' and 'Good ole Henry's!'

Henry swallowed as he watched the glass of light brown liquid slopping around above him at the end of Peregrine Spencer's extended arm, clearing his oesophagus for the inevitable. In his infinite naivety he desperately clung to the belief that it could be ginger ale or perhaps watered-down Coke but in his very limited experience of the sad, debauched society that he shrank from, something told him it could be whisky. Oh, Heaven forbid!

He recoiled as the glass came closer to his face across the table. Suddenly, Peregrine pulled the glass away from him. 'Thank heavens' thought Henry; he'd known all along it was only a joke.

'I've got a better idea!' shouted Peregrine, 'June my love, come here my dear. Administer the medicine to our patient. I'm sure he'd much sooner have a lovely sweet nurse than a wicked old doctor. Eh, Henry?'

Now it does well to remember that female staff in offices, like their male counterparts come in shapes, sizes, styles and demeanours that are manifold. June Catchpole in her two brief but devastating weeks with the Department, had been personally responsible for so many dry-cleaned suits, straighter backs, tidier hairstyles, deeper voices, carefully-chosen witticisms and Steve McQueen walks amongst the generally sloppy male contingent, that unless the wives, girlfriends, partners, bits-on-the-side, were blindly devoted, just blind, or totally disinterested in them, suspicions of late would had to have been aroused.

June Catchpole was large. At this stage nothing more need be added; nothing that is apart from to mention a trifling point that Henry Scroggins was without doubt the only male member of the staff who during office hours was unaware of exactly what cast the shadow across his desk when she stood beside him. He would only have been interested in the manila folder clutched tightly against the shadow-makers and once that folder was handed to him, he would then have been the only person failing to follow the shadow-makers and their carrier back from whence they came.

Now he sat noticing only the glass that the popular Miss Catchpole held enticingly in her hand as she leant across the desk towards him. He was completely oblivious also of the style of sweater that she had quite unwittingly (for all we know) selected for the party, a style that could not have failed to gain the attention of even the most taciturn, polite, male heterosexual. But not Henry - he bit his lip.

'Come on then Mr Scroggins,' coaxed his blonde temptress, responding to the whooping catcalls by moving round and trying to sit on Henry's lap, 'or can I call you Henry, Henry?'

'Yes. I mean no! You may call me Henry but not, that is to say I'd prefer it if you didn't, you know, if you see what I mean, Miss Catchpole.'

'See what you mean Henry? What do you mean, "see what I mean" Mister Time and Motion Scroggins? Winston!' A smile of sudden inspiration spread across her face as she looked around at the assembled crowd and leered, 'I've got the *time* Henry - if you've got the *motion*!' And with this fabulous impromptu crowd-pleaser she turned her attention back to Henry who got as far as uttering, 'Please Miss Catch...'

Whether it was the shock of the vile, burning sensation as it was dashed onto Henry's taste buds, or whether it was the fact that when one is talking the windpipe has a tendency to be more open than the food-pipe, or whether indeed it was an unfortunate combination of both these things, we shall never know; but the direct effect that the introduction of an alien liquid had on Henry's system was a sight to behold. Clutching his throat with both gloved hands like a garrotted snowman, he shrank from his chair with scant regard for the lady who had made herself comfortable on his lap and proceeded to choke and gasp for breath with eyes that were positively frog-like.

'There! That's the spirit!' shrieked a gleeful Peregrine, not always a man with the right word, 'give him another one! I think he likes it!'

Ah yes, this was sport - good old medieval sport. If only Peregrine had available to him a post-horn and a recording of *D' Ye Ken John Peel* so much more authenticity could have been added to the whole scene, but this would do for now.

'Come on Henry! Up you get!' encouraged the executive court-jester, 'jingle bells, jingle bells, jingle all the way...' and as they all sang heartily, Henry choked privately. But if the poor man, as he made an attempt to rise, thought that this was the end of his ordeal, then he was much mistaken. Pulling at his scarf, still wrapped tightly around his neck, with one hand, he raised the other in submission. For his pains all he got was a demolition job on his spine as willing colleagues, interpreting his gesture as a plea for a few pats on the back, rained a mass of blows on him that would make any future visit to a chiropractor seem like a fly landing on his shoulder.

'That's it!' shrieked Peregrine Spencer, turning to snatch the glass from the lips of the man closest to him, the previous owner staring blankly at his hand still curled round the space the glass had just vacated, 'get this down him chaps! Only the first few that hurt, what! Ha-ha-ha! Happy Christmas Henry!' And passing the glass to the Department's latest and most noticeable acquisition he turned and grabbed yet another from the hand of an equally unsuspecting junior male, and with one throat-jerking gulp, swallowed the lot.

'Happy Christmas Henry!' he repeated, drawing a pinstriped sleeve across his mouth, 'Happy Christmas to you and your lovely ole mother!' And with that last innocently misguided statement he lunged into action, enveloping the closest female, who being rather short, disappeared inside his jacket, screamed and dropped her glass.

Yes, it was just another office Christmas party but for the thoroughly dismal Henry Scroggins whose countenance could only be compared with a depressed bloodhound, it was a nightmare of the worst possible kind. Dazed and dishevelled and with the whisky now having a slight affect on his brain, he sat submissively in his chair as once again the buxom Miss Catchpole settled herself on his lap to the rhythmic clapping and chanting of the drunken horde - 'Go Henry! Go Henry! Go Henry! Go!' - to which the lady responded by pushing back a few long, wayward strands of blonde hair, wriggling her backside into a comfortable position on his lap, and with a knowing grin to the others that was guaranteed to bring - and the lady was not disappointed – louder, lecherous screams of encouragement.

Smiling into Henry's face, her massive pneumatic crimson lips only inches away and pursed Monroe-like as if they had any faint chance of tantalising her victim, June Catchpole brought the glass dramatically in an arch around to his mouth. Henry felt hands grab his arms and pin them behind the chair, rendering resistance impossible. He felt his spectacles removed to a mighty applause and smelt the now familiar vile pungency of the drink beneath his nostrils. On reflex he jerked his head back and into the chin of his tormentor, bone against bone, teeth 'clacking' to a curse and gasp.

'Oo you little bugger!' he heard her rasp, 'that 'urt! Now do as mummy says and drink yer medisin' up like a good boy!'

At these words and maybe due to the illusionary effect that the whisky and lack of spectacles were having on him, there descended upon Henry a vision of his mother. She was leaning over him with a spoon outstretched towards his mouth as he shrank back, lips clamped together like a vice and head turned desperately away. He felt her rough hand on his chin, wrenching his face back towards her ugly glaring features and uneven yellow teeth, parted menacingly. He smelt the fried onions on her breath as she rammed the spoon repeatedly into his teeth, trying to part them. Regrettably for the young boy he was suffering from a blocked nose and in order to breathe had no choice but to open his mouth and provide a momentary opportunity for the sudden thrust and insertion of spoon and medicine. So vile was the taste that he also had no choice but to spit. And as he spat and the spoon clanked to the floor and spun into the skirting board, a shadow fell across his head a split second before the arrival of his mother's bony hand. The blow was heavy and her wedding ring pierced the top of his ear, causing him to scream. He peered up, holding his hand to the side of his head, she walking away wringing her hand in pain and cursing. He sat and watched as she ripped off her faded floral apron, screwed it into a ball and threw it fiercely at him, swearing something incoherent and storming out, slamming the door as if all the pain in her life was caused by one small boy. The apron opened and died like a butterfly long before it reached him, and lay on the floor looking as dead as him.

A balloon exploded in Henry's ear and he felt something warm and soft against his face, a human balloon, one of June Catchpole's breasts as she squeezed it against his cheek. Then it was gone, replaced by glass and whisky and his nose was being pinched, allowing the option of swallowing or suffocating. A blinding flash lit the scene followed by a slow whirring sound, one that seemed familiar though he couldn't quite place it. The cheers were now louder but at least the pressure of the woman's bottom was released from his lap and irritating wisps of hair gone from his face.

'Here it comes! Here it comes!' cried a shrill voice and the screams and hoots and bellows reached a crescendo as a pale grey Polaroid photo developed before Henry's misty eyes. He watched and listened in silent stupor and, amidst all the pandemonium and noise, couldn't help thinking how beautifully Bing Crosby sang 'Silent Night'.

## Chapter Four

# THE POLICE STATION -
# WHERE HENRY MEETS MILLICENT

In the darkness of a small back garden, or yard as it should more appropriately be described, a yard sandwiched like the rest in Viola Street between a two-bedroom terraced house and a dimly-lit back alley, two cats had chosen a duelling ground of dustbins to attempt to settle a dispute in an extremely high-pitched and spiteful manner. As this feline fracas reached a level of noise that could only signal the disembowelling of one, or possibly both, a light in the bedroom above them turned off. And so did the cats. Now for those raised in the country this opera amongst the clattering dustbin lids would in all probability mean little or nothing, but to the dedicated town dweller it was a typical synchronised display of suburban orchestration to which they were frequently treated. The Last Night of the Toms!

Within the bedroom and sitting bolt upright in her bed, was Irma Scroggins. We can only ever thank the lamplight filtering from the alley into the room and shedding its soft amber sheen, for the illuminated roman profile that stared fixedly ahead like the bust of an emperor planning his next genocidal jaunt at the Coliseum; a profile listening, waiting, hardly daring to breathe, oblivious of cats, ears tuned only to the sound of the back gate and shuffling, guilty feet down the concrete path, fumbled rattling keys at the back kitchen door marking a vain attempt at an unheard entry. But none of this came so she sat there a motionless study in bitter fermentation.

And as Irma Scroggins sat, at one with Lot's wife save the rise and fall of her punctured old chest, her breath came quickly and laboured by the sheer frustration of it all. Her mind raced with not only the anger inside spinning out of control but with the travesty of the whole dreadful situation. After forty years without a murmur of rebellion, the son for whom she had sacrificed everything, the son whom she had showered, yes showered, with love and singular devotion since birth - had betrayed her! Judas Scroggins went through her mind. It had a certain ring to it. The grandfather clock, with cruel timing, chimed out twelve midnight in the hallway below and pierced her like a knife.

In a police-station some ten miles or so north, the sole reason for this sweet old lady's torment sat smiling peacefully on a high-backed wooden chair, hands gripped together between legs that swung backwards and forwards in time with the owners singing of 'Jingle Bells', shoes just able to swing without impediment but now and then scraping the floor. If a model of contentment and self-satisfaction was ever required by an artist then this would have been the moment to capture it. The fact that Jingle was heard more to sound like 'shingle' and Bells like 'belch' also denoted that the rotund, bespectacled vision beaming its way around the dimly lit holding cell in which he sat, taking in all the new and exciting sights and sensations, might have taken too much drink that night.

Henry Winston Scroggins had never before in his life had the privilege, if that's the word, of stepping inside a police station anywhere, so to be a 'guest' now in one of the most famous police stations in the most famous city in the world, was something to write home about. If, however, the reasons for his being there at just past midnight on a cold, wet December night were of an honourable social nature, then the jocund bearing of the little man in mud-stained grey mackintosh, with gloves stuffed in pockets and scarf dangling loosely to one side, could be easily understood. After all, it was the time of year for goodwill to all men, which of course should include policemen - but he was under arrest.

So, why the happiness? By way of explanation it should be pointed out that Henry's partaking of the demon alcohol had not ended where we left him last. The second drink forced upon him by the amply-endowed June Catchpole had served not only to numb his lips, pallet and senses but - far more dangerously - to nullify his powers of resistance. A third drink had been rapidly followed by a fourth, a fifth, and almost certainly a sixth and seventh but by that stage nobody was in any fit state to count, least of all the greatest counter of the Department himself.

Now alcohol, as anyone who has imbibed to excess well knows - or anyone who knows anyone well who imbibes to excess well knows - has a tendency to colour the world a little lighter or darker depending on the individual's general character, or particular mood at the time of intake. The black get blacker and the gentle ones tend to drift peacefully off to sleep. Henry, new to the game, had been through both. After a warming up period, stoking up the flickering fire in his belly with a succession of whiskies, rums, beers and various ingenious cocktails, he had embarked upon a dark period commencing at Peregrine Spencer's head with the aid of a black onyx Buddha paperweight. This was followed by a sleepy period ending on the floor of a police-station cell, but had now emerged into a third period - a lively period and in exceedingly good humour - on a high chair in the company of a fur-coated lady beside him and a police constable at a high wooden counter just beyond the blue metal bars and door of his area of confinement.

Strange as it may seem in view of his personality, Henry was basking in a sort of 'voyage of discovery' feeling which being clouded by a brain not yet sufficiently compos mentis to appreciate the seriousness, had placed him in this state of euphoria whereby he was desperate to lavish affection on someone. He smiled through the blue bars at the constable who, having only just recently been one half of Henry's arresting party and wishing to retain the appropriate distance between felon and lawman, coughed and dropped his eyes back to the form he was studying on the counter.

Undeterred, Henry turned his attention to the fur-coated lady who, had all the way through his rendition of Jingle Bells, been trying to read a book. She, seated on a chair of normal height, was approximately a foot to the left and six inches below Henry's gaze. He peered down at the top of her head, still softly singing the one line of his adopted Christmas carol, and noted the curly chestnut hair, too curly not to be permed he decided.

He could smell the sweet odour of her perfume that he liked and thought was more than likely French although he really hadn't the foggiest idea. The fur coat looked expensive but then they all did and he was not expert enough in that field either, to know real from imitation. The fur coat, being the padded shoulder, half-length variety, rested on a dark brown pleated skirt that would normally, he guessed, have hung slightly below knee level when standing up, but with her legs crossed to support her book it was exposing a very shapely nylon covered knee. Apart from the foot of the same leg poking forward shod in patent brown leather, the only other item of clothing for him to study was a rather large cream, silk bow that protruded at the neck of the fur coat and was obviously part of a blouse.

Henry had already, within the ten minutes spent in her company, tried twice to make conversation. He was not a conversationalist at the best of times, least of all with members of the opposite sex, and so the lady should have been honoured but if she was she was concealing it very well. So failing that and to relieve his boredom he screwed his neck around almost horizontally in an attempt to read the cover of the book, to which the lady without any movement whatsoever of her head, raised the book cover to within six inches of his face.

Henry, taken aback by this helpful gesture, leaned back to focus and read out loud.

'Lady Chatterley's Lover.'

'Happy now?' asked the lady, surprisingly unfriendly but all the same, very well spoken, by Henry's reckoning.

'Yes thank you,' replied Henry, undaunted by what he vaguely discerned in his dizzy state as a form of rebuff. 'Good book eh?' he enquired, pushing his glasses back up the bridge of his nose and sniffing.

'Yes' came the curt reply, 'when I get the chance to read it.'

Henry, completely missing the point, shook his head in an expression of wise sympathy and chuckled. 'Yes, it's a busy old world alright - it is that - oh yes indeed,' and finished with another chuckle to emphasise his broad view on life.

The lady continued to read but Henry had broken through and was not to be put off.

'What's it about then - the book?' he asked politely, nodding towards it to help identify it from the complete lack of other books in the room. The constable coughed again and studied them from beneath a furrowed brow, which expression Henry amiably returned, momentarily distracted from his literary conversation. The lady sighed tiredly and turned her book face down onto her skirt.

'If you must know, it's about a lady who screws her gamekeeper,' she remarked casually, as if it were an everyday occurrence. This instantly conjured up a vision in Henry's mind of a somewhat manly woman in khaki overalls brandishing a screwdriver. He wasn't quite sure what a gamekeeper looked like.

'Sounds painful,' observed Henry.

'At times it was. Very painful.'

Henry had now exhausted his questions and so continued singing Jingle Bells and swinging his legs to fill the pregnant interlude. But the book, still being cover-up in her hand as she sighed impatiently and looked towards the counter, now presented him with the author's name which to his delight he recognised and was thus able to re-ignite the conversation.

'D. H. Lawrence, eh?' he remarked enthusiastically, snapping his fingers twice in the air to help recall an Evening Standard article he'd briefly scanned through in the train a few weeks previously. 'Wrote The Seven Pillars of Something or other. Lawrence of Arabia! That's him! That's the chap! Ha!'

The lady shook her head slowly. 'He was T.E, *this* is D.H', she said and turned the book over to read, still shaking her head in condescending disbelief.

Just then a commotion broke out in a room down the corridor from the counter; shouting, swearing, scuffling and the scraping of furniture. Henry just had time to flash a 'should we panic?' stare at the constable when, as quickly as it had started, it stopped; and silence. Henry then darted a glance at the lady beside him who was already staring at the constable who had taken two steps towards the room and now stood listening for a re-commencement of the trouble. Satisfying himself that whoever was dealing with the situation had performed a fairly deft act of finalising it, the constable shook his head and threw a nervous glance at the odd incarcerated couple.

'Takes all sorts,' offered Henry to his fellow inmate in a loud confidential whisper, grinning widely and completely forgetting that he was currently one of the sorts. The lady rose, killing the impact of Henry's philosophical gem and strolled two steps to the door of the cell, high heels clacking on the concrete floor.

'David, how much longer?' she asked.

The young policeman smiled shyly.

'I don't think we'll be long now Millie, just waiting for my colleague and then we'll be with you. After Mr Scroggins, that is.' And then, lifting a form in his hand, added, 'Third time this month Millie. What's going on?'

'Needs must,' she said with the faintest of smiles. 'Most of Fleet Street were camped outside my flat for weeks after the last fiasco and now the poor old blighters in Westminster and the Law Courts are scared out of their wits. So, as I say, "needs must" and when one is forced to show one's face for business, one can sometimes get noticed by the wrong people.'

'We have our job to do Millie. If it was up to me…'

'If it was up to you and I, David, we'd probably be settling the problem in a far friendlier manner in a far better place.'

She grinned at him seductively, causing the young constable's small elephant ears and plump cheeks to burn red with embarrassment at Henry's open-mouthed attempt to concentrate on the conversation. The officer blew out a deep breath and instantly became overly inquisitive about how long his colleague, currently dealing with the boisterous new arrival - the man now subdued to an occasional moan and pleading of his innocence - was going to be. He strode manfully to the door of the room and listened.

The lady, Millie, turned towards Henry. The latest addition to London's crime figures, who was studying the ink on the inside of his thumbs with a look of distinct curiosity, noticed a wry smile on her lips, not unlike the one on the constable's.

Henry, who between listening intently to their conversation whilst equally intrigued by how the ink had got onto his thumbs, instinctively joined in the smiling as their eyes met. He didn't want to be left out. They were all in this together, whatever it was.

For the first time he saw her face-on. She was very pretty in a made-up sort of way; early-thirties he guessed, and more glamorous than pretty, in the film star mode with her fur coat and all; the type you see on the television walking into film premieres with a young male partner on their arm. Her lips were small, pert and cupid-like, perfectly painted with red lipstick. He suddenly thought of June Catchpole's red lips and the Polaroid photograph, and as the blood surged up the back of his neck he placed a hand to his mackintosh pocket and felt the stiffness of the card.

He'd forgotten about the photograph which had been somehow stuffed in his pocket; forgotten about the party, or what he could remember of it. He felt a sudden need to divert his thoughts and so spoke to the lady, who had resumed her seat and her reading.

'What - um - what are you here for if you don't mind me asking?' he enquired, peering over his spectacles at her.

'Soliciting,' replied the lady without looking up, or a moment's hesitation.

Henry thought about this for a while and on hearing a small splutter from behind the counter, decided to act nonchalant.

'Ohh, soliciting,' declared the knowledgeable one, happy at last to be in on the secret, 'what a stroke of luck.'

'Luck? What are you talking about?'

Suddenly much relieved to be in safe hands with the effects of the drink beginning to wear off and the unwelcome effects of reality creeping in, Henry elaborated.

'Well,' he said, 'the trouble it seems I might be in, I think I'm going to need you before the night's out.'

The lady frowned. Henry continued unabated.

'Yes I seeee now,' elongating the 'see' to indicate the depth of his extraordinary perception, 'very clever, veeery clever indeed.' And with that he thumbed his nose twice at her, winked, tapped his head and added, 'Business brain - clever - like it.'

'I'm sorry,' said the lady, staring at him with the slightest shake of her head, 'what exactly...is clever?'

Henry put a hand on the lady's shoulder, winked at the constable who was now trying to control another bout of coughing that had come upon him, and spoke quietly in her ear.

'I get it, it's okay. You sit here, right - you sit here all evening, and then as all the people come in under arrest, you convert them to clients! Veeery enterprising. I *like* it, oh yes!'

At the conclusion of this startling observation, the constable's fit seemed to get further out of control whilst the lady buried her face in her book. Henry looked from one to the other and his face fell.

'Am I right?' he enquired.

'No,' said the lady, 'you are quite wrong. In fact I find the insinuation rather offensive. Now please, if you have nothing more sensible to add to the conversation, stimulating as it is, I would like to read my book.'

And that's precisely what she did, with the heaviest sigh and most pronounced shake of the head, as a finale to the many assorted smaller ones that had preceded them during her short acquaintance with the strange little man.

Henry scowled quietly to himself. 'I'm the one who ought to be offended,' he thought, staring out of the side of his spectacles at the set jaw and pursed lips beside him. It was a nice jaw as jaws went. He had never really studied features on people. People were people; they did jobs of work and they were either nice or indifferent to him and that's how he judged the human race - the depth of Henry's anthropological study.

Physical attraction was not a feeling he ever experienced. He'd trained himself at an early age not to let it impinge on his life and was proud of this, one of his few strengths, he believed. It seemed to him that the more people delved and dabbled in relationships, either sexual or platonic, the bigger fools they made of themselves and the more miserable they became - not that he could get any more miserable himself, which rather thwarted the theory - but anyway, he felt it was one less thing in his life to worry about and he therefore remained detached from anything resembling a serious friendship; in fact he was detached from just about everything, apart from his mother. And horses.

His stomach knotted for a moment until he pushed her image with a giant yard-broom out of the side of his mind. This was how he'd got rid of all nasty thoughts since childhood, a broom sweeping them out and happy ones gushing into the void. His happy ones were on his father's knee feeling safe and sad as his father sang in his soft baritone 'Johnny's won your marbles,' and the other was the first walnuts he ever cracked on his own at Christmas and his father laughing and crying out, 'Well done Henry m'lad!' She, his mother, was always in the background, a menacing presence but not interfering in these moments.

Unsettled as Henry was by the lady's admonishment, he felt a compulsion to look at her. Her hands were very white, almost transparent, and the tracking of the fine blue veins fascinated him, mainly because he noted that they were the exact colour of his blotting paper at work. One hand was extended across the book holding down the page and he noticed how long and slender her fingers were and how immaculately manicured her nails. But then that's what you'd expect from a solicitor.

A solicitor; a lady solicitor. He didn't think he'd heard of a lady solicitor before. No wonder she spoke in such refined tones. He might have guessed it, but then never having met one before it probably wouldn't have entered his head, certainly not in the state it was in at the moment. He stared vacantly ahead and thought of the word. Soliciting; was it ever used as a verb? Hello, I'm a solicitor; I solicit, he solicits, you solicit, we solicit, they are soliciting...*she* solicits? It sounded familiar but somehow - not quite right. In the midst of this deliberation the subject of his thoughts, the solicitoress, spoke.

'What's your name?'

The words were now addressed to Henry in a milder tone, taking him by surprise.

'Henry,' said Henry.

She smiled. 'That's nice. I had a dog called Henry when I was little.'

A dog. Henry wasn't too sure about being called the same as a dog, especially not knowing the breed.

'What sort?' he asked.

'A poodle - a little toy poodle.'

A poodle. Henry was hoping for at least an Alsatian or a bulldog. A poodle, and a little toy one at that, was rather a disappointment.

'I thought they were usually called Fifi or…Lulu,' he said, hoping maybe she'd suddenly remember that Henry was the Alsatian her parents had bought later.

'Oh no, she was definitely Henry,' purred the lady in affectionate remembrance.

'She!' exclaimed Henry, 'A girl toy poodle called…*Henry*?'

'Short for Henrietta.'

'Oh,' said Henry not absolutely certain whether he should be pleased or not, 'yes, in that case, I suppose so.' And he sat there trying in his mind to call a poodle 'Henry' and make it sound right. He threw it a stick and shouted 'Fetch Henry!' but it didn't move which was an indication it didn't like its name. So he tried again throwing the stick, shouting rather more encouragingly 'Fetch *Henrietta*!' and this time the dog shot off like a rocket and came back panting for it to be thrown again. This was reassuring.

'Where do you live?' continued the lady softly, her lips hardly parting as the words passed by them.

'Lewisham,' answered Henry.

'Lewisham,' repeated the lady, frowning into a void that Henry imagined had a tube map in it that someone of her standing would never stray beyond - apart from perhaps Paris to buy her perfume.

'South London, near Catford and…Greenwich. Main line, no underground there,' he added helpfully.

She nodded.

'Do you live alone?'

'Oh…no.'

'Married?'

'No.'

'Children?'

'No.'

'Gay?'

'Pardon?'

'Doesn't matter.'

Henry's head was now all but clear with just the odd cobweb in the odd corner. He looked around the bare cell with its bare whitewashed walls and bare concrete floor, at the low wooden benches stretching along the two walls opposite to where he and the lady sat on the only two chairs, and for the first time realised it was actually what it was; a cell. A cell with bars between him and the outside world, between him and the constable who was at that moment reaching up carrying out running repairs to some dangling decorations.

He noticed the sturdy, steel, army green filing cabinets in the corridor that looked as if they could at one time have housed Churchill's war plans underneath Whitehall; at the array of almost toppling documents piled high on them; at the glaring strip-lights overhead; at the counter with its Dr. Barnados tin, a few Christmas cards and a shell ash tray; at his raincoat smothered with dirty, damp marks and finally, at the face of the angel beside him.

Fear and elation gripped him, both emotions strangling each other at once. What a radiant smile, what a face of absolute compassion. He had never experienced true fear or any form of tenderness and how strange that they should both, in their extremes, come upon him all at once after forty years of nothing.

'Where's your...office?' he whispered, swallowing.

She smiled at the euphemism. Nobody had ever called her place an 'office' before. She liked it. How unusual this little man was. How sweetly inoffensive and desperately sad he looked.

'Just ten minutes by taxi,' she cooed back, close to his face, and as her sweet breath flowed into Henry's nostrils the rarest sensation filled his head as blood coursed through his neck and cheeks like a raging fire.

'Scroggins! Henry Winston Scroggins!'

The tranquillity of the moment was indefinably shattered by the harsh, raw voice of a second constable who had appeared from the room where he'd recently been gainfully employed with the shouting, scuffling man. He marched military fashion down the corridor towards the cell door, resting one hand on the counter for support and peering at a clipboard in the other.

His square head and cropped grey hair were as harsh and hard as his voice and after a swift glance at Henry and Millicent, the latter to whom he gave a brief wink, he twisted his neck towards his colleague, jutting his jaw to emphasise his obvious authority.

'Is this Scroggins?' he barked, nodding sideways at the diminutive figure seated on the stool, one inky hand timidly half raised in reply to his name-call.

'Yes!' snapped the junior constable. 'Bring him in shall I?'

'Well I'm not going to sit on Millie's lap and charge 'im, am I now?' replied the abrasive elder man, nodding at the lady and adding, 'evening Millie, you'll 'ave your own bed in here soon love, if you keep this up.'

'Thank you Constable Jennings,' answered the lady, 'you're too kind,' with a sarcasm that even Henry may have detected but for the acute panic that had suddenly seized his whole being. The officer, having now lightened the proceedings - or so he thought - with his own brand of delicate police station humour, proceeded to unlock the cell door. He frowned at his clipboard.

'Blimey Scroggins, what gets into you blokes? Few drinks and you go rampaging around like a wounded bleedin' bull.' He read: 'Assaulting a Mr Peregrine Spencer, thereby occasioning actual bodily harm; drunk and disorderly; lobbing a brick (he frowned at the young constable here and was about to ask whether lobbing was correct police vocabulary, but declined)...lobbing a brick through Ladbroke's betting shop window; resisting arrest by trying to wriggle out of his mackintosh (another glance at the constable)...whilst singing Jingle Bells...out of tune.'

There was a sudden splutter of laughter from the lady who clapped her hand over her mouth and muttered, 'My apologies. Do carry on PC Jennings.'

Henry looked at her in terror. This wasn't funny. And neither did the senior office think so.

'Is this your idea of a joke, Constable Steele?' he demanded.

The blushing constable straightened both his expression and his back and nervously cleared his throat into a cupped hand.

'Just a bit of...Christmas spirit.'

'A bit of what?' snapped the other, still frowning in some disgust at the charge-sheet.

'Christmas spirit!' came the official constabulary reply.

'Oh, we're all highly amused I'm sure,' replied the military man, looking up at Henry who was as far removed from amused as a human can possibly be. 'Ok, Scroggins, let's be 'aving you. Fingerprinted and photographed I assume, Constable Steele?'

'All done Constable Jennings.'

Henry, now standing near the open cell door ready to exit, looked down at his hands, palms up, and suddenly realised the reason for his inky fingers. A vague image of being propped in a chair in another room soon after he arrived, and a burly woman trying to hold his hands and his head straight, appeared before him - then an unexpected blinding flash. Henry thought of this and then the earlier flash with June Catchpole on his lap. Having never been intentionally photographed in his adult life, here he was with two 'portraits' in one night.

Constable Jennings, now joined by Constable Steele at the cell door, turned on his heels and strode back to the far room, singing out breezily, 'Fetch 'im in. And mind he don't wriggle out that raincoat!'

Henry's nervous state had advanced during this exchange to gibbering hysteria. His hands were shaking and his lips quivering uncontrollably as he stood distraught and lonely in the middle of a nightmare. Then something touched his back and he heard the lady's voice, soft and soothing.

'Relax. Don't worry Henry.'

He swivelled to face her and was greeted with the most wonderful benign sight he'd ever witnessed. An outstretched white hand, a beautiful caring smile and a radiance of such brilliant intensity that his fears, in that brief instant, seemed to drain completely away. And then rapidly return.

'What will they do with me?' he asked. He needed the benefit of her professional advice as a small comfort to go in with.

'First offence?'

'Yes - of course.'

'You'll get bail. Court tomorrow. Bow Street probably.'

'My mother…'

'Pardon?'

'It doesn't matter.'

'Mr Scroggins please! I 'aven't got all night!'

'Will you wait for me?'

'I've no choice.'

'Promise?

'Promise.'

'Can we go to your office? I mean - this late at night.'

She smiled sweetly into his misty eyes.

'Of course we can. We'll talk about it over a drink. What do you drink?'

'Constable Steele! Mr Scroggins!'

'Cocoa.'

'Cocoa?'

## Chapter Five

## BARELY LEGAL

Millicent Carter, a woman of some vision, had long ago reached a conclusion that men had been placed on Earth to play games of different sorts and that women had been provided in order to mop up their mess, dry their tears when things went wrong and oddly enough, keep producing more men. Whilst she neither condoned nor willingly accepted these facts, they were there, they existed, and they were unlikely to change. She had looked around and seen intelligent, highly capable women, mostly friends of her mother, pandering to the whims of insensitive male partners almost without question and invariably with little or no return of affection. Her parents were no exception.

But then there was Cleopatra, Mata Hari and other inspiring immortals from whom Millicent quickly perceived that she, like most other women if they so desired, held the omnipotent key - their sexuality - to combat this male dominance. But far from jumping on a soapbox, beating her breast and burning her bra, she quietly studied the weakest of man's many Achilles heels and contemplated the possibility of capitalisation. And so it was, early in her blossoming maidenhood, on waking up to the fact that she possessed a beauty and femininity surpassing most of her friends, an attraction that made her a very special rose in a garden of very busy bees, she took stock and made a decision.

After having completed three years at Oxford University gaining degrees in Economics and Human Biology, she would diligently try to pursue a career, no doubt one that her parents were at that stage deciding upon; she would also make every attempt to settle into a comfortable relationship with a nice young man, one of whom her parents had at that time neither selected or approved; and if, at the age of twenty-one, her parents, whom she loved and loathed with equal intensity, were still trying to orchestrate every line, scene and act of her life (as they always had), then she would take matters quite coldly into her own hands and trade in the one market where she knew success was guaranteed, with the one product that would never go out of fashion and one that she just happened to thoroughly enjoy, to a degree that if degrees were handed out for Promiscuity, then she would no doubt have sailed through with honours.

After all, she resolved, was supply and demand - or rather demand and supply - not the one thing that kept the modern Merry-Go-World turning? And wasn't hers, long-regarded as the oldest profession, not fulfilling the greatest and most natural demand of them all? Of course it was and how utterly fatuous of the high and mighty to pour scorn and pontificate, as they did, on not only the 'business' but also on the poor customers, many of whom but for her and her fellow philanthropists, would quite possibly forever be denied the undeniable pleasures of the flesh.

It seemed it was only the exchange of money for services rendered that touched their sublime consciences so much and so with her sweet conscience carefree and clear, a youthful spring in her pretty young step and a precocious twinkle in her dancing eyes, the young Millicent had set about fulfilling needs and supplying demands with as much freedom of spirit and dedicated zest as a very contented butcher, baker or candlestick-maker.

She knew her goods and chattels were of the highest quality; she would provide them with the utmost impunity and, barring biological restrictions on trading hours, always deliver on time. She saw herself not as a 'femme fatale' but as a doctor or therapist (wouldn't Daddy be proud), with the treatment she administered far more salutary than anything gained through the NHS. For sex, as any regular exponent will testify, is extremely good for the health. It is however, rather like credit - you either get it, or you don't.

Working on this simple premise, Millicent Carter at the age of thirty-five in the early hours of Christmas Eve in rain-spattered London, was currently hostess to what could arguably be described as England's unhealthiest forty-year-old.

Henry Scroggins, bereft of any dignity that he may have once possessed, terrified of what the daylight hours were about to bring, and desperately clinging to a belief that Millicent Carter's

49

soliciting wand was in the same league as King Arthur's Excalibur, sat nervously perched near the dangerous end of a chaise-longue. As one unaccustomed to such an incomplete item of furniture, his one gloved hand could be seen clutching a steaming mug which every so often travelled in an arc towards where the arm of the chair should have been, and then, thwarted in its intention, travelled all the way back again to the cradle of its ungloved partner.

Then there was the dog. As if Henry didn't have enough to worry about, this hairy little monster masquerading as a Yorkshire Terrier had grabbed the loose glove from his lap, scurried off under a nest of cabriole-legged tables and lay crouched and peering out excitedly with its woollen hostage under one paw and a huge pink bow flopped ridiculously down across its squat forehead, an expression of angry defiance on its face that dared its latest adversary to retrieve at his peril.

Henry wasn't daring. Henry was waiting for the nasty little thing to grow bored or until its mistress decided to return from wherever she had disappeared five minutes ago into the multi-door labyrinths of her flat, after handing Henry his cocoa. He peered vacantly at the creature, a rather pre-occupied stare that the animal was watching intently, waiting for any irregular movement and any slight hint of attack. Henry then made the mistake of scratching his nose, and the dog, misinterpreting this as imminent retaliatory action, barred its teeth and growled a long, low, menacing, grumbling growl from deep down inside its hairy little belly. If Henry had been a regular visitor to Millicent Carter's 'office' he would have known that supplying George with something tasty from a tantalising, rustling bag was par for the course, but of course Henry didn't know and was being punished for his forgetfulness.

So with one eye on George, another gazing around the dimly lit opulence of the lounge, and a head throbbing into the early stages of his first ever hangover, Henry sat in miserable dejection. He'd been trying desperately to claw his way out of the deep morass of self-recrimination that he'd plunged into since leaving the police station and with the help of his temporary guardian had briefly managed to lift his heart on the taxi journey to her flat, but now in these few moments alone with his thoughts he had slumped quite miserably backwards.

He, Henry Winston Scroggins, the epitome of staid conservatism, the most uninteresting person he knew - had committed a crime. No, not crime; *crimes*. He pondered on the word. It sounded so awful, so unbelievably awful. It was a word that conjured up visions of striped jerseys, furtive looks and bags over shoulders; of open windows, curtains fluttering in the moonlight, bloody daggers and wide-eyed bodies spread-eagled across beds staring at ceilings; visions of gaunt-faced, white-wigged judges peering over half-glasses and solemnly lifting black hats. He shuddered, suddenly feeling cold, and wished desperately for the warmth of Millicent to waft confidently back into the room.

She had gone to change, so she said, but that was an age ago and Henry needed her smiling face and reassurance. She would make everything right; she knew exactly what to do; she'd been through it all so many times. She'd told him that, and the way that the policemen treated her, and she them; so familiar, so self-assured. How lucky she was, not to have the fear that was wracking him, to be able to talk to the police on their level and have the respect, albeit a little flippant, that one in her profession automatically drew from lesser mortals such as himself. She was to be envied, but at least he had her on his side. Still though, even with her as a formidable ally, he could see no way out. He had committed assault, occasioning bodily harm, and on Peregrine Spencer of all people.

He had, although he did not remember any part of the incident, demolished the window of Ladbroke's betting shop close to the Department building, the shop so convenient for his fluttering habit but one which he'd been forced to ignore for twenty years and walk a mile every lunchtime to place his bets with William Hill, and even then remained forever petrified that a colleague would do the same and meet him eye to eye across the betting-shop floor. Despite living in mortal dread of this, a sense of self-preservation had some time ago devised a plan whereby his mother, just once a week (whichever particular day he might ever be caught out) permitted herself a small flutter and he was merely placing the bet for her. As with her funeral, the plan was very real in his head and well rehearsed; he would stress to his 'discoverer' that because his dear mother now had so few pleasures left in life he would never, never, deny her this small trifle just once a week after all she'd done for him. He tended to mentally choke on this part but it was all for a good cause, that being of his own small pleasure. He even had several embellishments at the ready to add credence to his story by stating that the smile on her sweet face the night before her 'flutter day' was worth his speedy lunchtime walk, and if questioned why he didn't use the very convenient Ladbrokes opposite the office, then here he was also prepared.

It was a sad tale. Her first boyfriend back in 1928 was a young man called William Hill who, though he'd left her broken-hearted, was forever etched upon her fragile soul. Yes a strange sentimental loyalty indeed, some might say perverse, but William was her first love, and, even if his name was associated more with losing than winning - still to this day he remained her one and only true love. So having lost her beloved William Hill (Bill Hill as she still liked to call him) and never actually recovering from a broken heart, there was a certain comfort in it for the sensitive, loving creature that was…his mother.

If the truth were known, heart and Irma Scroggins were never companions in the same sentence without the adjectives 'cold' or 'hard' attached, but then Henry's dear imaginary 'flutter mother' had not a jot to do with the breathing cadaver who tormented him daily.

So he had committed assault, smashed a window, resisted arrest - again, only trusting in the arresting officer's word as he had no clear, or even vague, recollection - and all this whilst drunk and disorderly, the fourth charge lumped upon his sorry soul. No, there was no way out, not even the Goddess Millicent could deliver him from this trespass. And if she could, what of his job? That was gone; twenty years of resolute dedication to the cause of Time and Motion within the Department; a lifetime of checking this, timing that, submissions, recommendations, commendations for saving the Department small fortunes, memoranda, thousands upon thousands of memoranda neatly-written and carefully-worded to minimise offence; economising by sharpening his pencils until he could no longer hold on to the stub and write legibly; tidying his desk and squaring up generations of trays and un-blotted blotters; a filing-drawer with every suspension file immaculately and chronologically tabbed; two more drawers that carried no surplus items, no doubtful literature and no coffee-stained drink coasters; his chair with the grey metal frame and bottle green PVC upholstery, polished by time like an army private's boot; and his cushion. His cushion! He'd left his cushion behind! The small round floral pad that had supported him through rain, shine, reorganisation and redistribution, through changes in décor and desking, through generations of tormenting upstarts who knew nothing of loyalty and dedication, and above all - through two decades of Peregrine Spencer.

Henry sat there sipping at his cocoa and peering at the intricate design of the rich blue Persian rug at his feet, thinking how odd that he and Spencer were the only two survivors of the famous Sixties reshuffle, the Departmental reshuffle to end all reshuffles, when Henry at the age of twenty had dared to express his humble future aspirations for the chair of the newly-arrived, arrogant, tall, handsome Department Manager, ten years his senior, a prima donna in Savile Row suits and garish red and yellow ties suppressed by gold collar studs and stuffed into tight-fitting red and yellow waistcoats; a bombastic peacock if ever there was one.

But now there were no longer colleagues in the Department. That was over, finished, gone forever. There was no possible chance of reinstatement. You didn't hit bosses and smash windows, then go to court, shake hands and carry on as if nothing had happened. He was a criminal and could never be normal again.

The words rattled around his head, confused, over-lapping, 'Oh dear Henry - Henry, Henry, Henry! Knew it would happen - one day - always different - something odd there - too reserved for his own good - doesn't mix - not like the others. His poor mother…'

Oh yes, his poor mother. Her face appeared above him as he sat and looked up at her. She was much younger, unlined but still as granite-hard as ever. Sometimes he imagined that she had only hardened with age but then images of his childhood would faithfully return to remind him, lest he ever forget, that she had always been the same; always his tormentor, always his captor.

He listened to the tyres swish by below on the wet road, to the revving-up, the tooting and shouting of a late night reveller, the gurgling of the rain in the down-pipe outside the window behind him, and he imagined her lying rigid and seething in her bed, her mouth clamped tightly shut, her jaw set hard apart from the tiny muscles that always twitched when she was angry, and her head full of revenge, plotting and scheming a punishment to fit his crime. He chuckled, a small private inward chuckle, as suddenly it occurred to him that she as yet knew nothing of his crime, his real one, not the silly one she had created for herself, but the one that he had quite personally perpetrated, with a little help, and the one that far from strengthening her tenacious grip on life, could possibly, just possibly, have a sufficiently debilitating effect to…

No! The thought was too much of a luxury but it should now be recorded that it was at this very moment that Henry had the first notion to kill her. He glanced at the dog, hunched like a lioness with an antelope carcass, engrossed in chewing and tearing its prey apart. The glove was now a saliva-sodden remnant incapable of gracing a hand ever again. Henry then stared fixedly at the dog and remains of his glove, his head now a little clearer and his heart a little lighter, for out of the muddle he had now made a decision. She had to go. She *had* to go! It was his duty, his duty not only to himself but to all those whose lives she'd blighted past and present, and nobody, but nobody, could ever deny it; or deny him.

After all said and done he was now a criminal in the true sense of the word and he couldn't erase that from his life. It had happened. Never mind the provocation and extenuating circumstances, the drink and his previous unblemished record; it all counted for nothing now. He had erred, erred badly, and in erring he had broken a forty-year tradition. It really mattered not how harmless or heinous the crime, for a crime was a crime in his book, not having any previous experience of dabbling on the wrong side of the law, and if divine retribution was a fact of life (or death) then who was to say that the Supreme Judge distinguished between taking the life of a wicked old lady and dispensing with the window of a Ladbroke's betting shop.

It was during this deep deliberation that the dog returned and dumped the soggy remains of Henry's glove onto his knee. Henry immediately made a grab at it but the animal had far more entertaining plans. It also, at the first movement of Henry's hand, lunged and sunk its teeth into the wool, causing a lightning withdrawal by the man followed by a slap on the snout for the dog's trouble, which in turn saw its eyes emerge from a reflex blink into a maniacal blaze. Another sucker had fallen for the oldest trick in a dog's book. The game was on! The wet-nosed antagonist, in a gesture of mock friendship, offered the glove once more onto Henry's knee, and Henry like a fool took up the offer and found himself back into the fray, the glaring, jerking animal now delightedly tugging back rhythmically on its haunches, emitting an 'Ergh!' with every tug, pink bow bobbing backwards and forwards to add a little more colour to the already colourful scene.

'Drop it!' hissed Henry, 'do you hear me, drop it!' And with the exertion of this command, his glasses slipped down and onto the tip of his nose.

It should be mentioned that Henry was still holding his mug aloft in the other hand, supposedly out of harm's way, but with every tug from the playful little thing at the other end of his outstretched arm, a slop of tepid cocoa was seen to leap over the edge and onto the blue velvet of the chaise longue. This sight of Henry, looking for all the world like an overgrown Boy Scout practising semaphore, a face anxious as they come, glasses now resting precariously on the bulbous tip of his nose, and muddy Tufs turned in below knees that were held tightly together, was quite one to behold, as was Millicent Carter in the reflection of her wardrobe mirror. She stood sideways on, examined the contours of her body, took one bare-footed step to her dressing-table, lifted a glass to her lips, drank, straightened a curtain, looked around, thought of the strange little man outside - and wondered what the hell she was doing.

She listened at the door and heard the tussle going on between man and beast. George could always be relied upon. His role was rather like that of a talkative receptionist with nervous applicants; for a short while he took their mind off the job and eased the nerves.

'Drop it! You little…you little…*bastard*!' snapped Henry most uncharacteristically, his teeth now clenched not unlike the dog's as he fought for possession of what was rightfully his, his mug now placed on the carpet and his two hands determinedly gripping the emaciated article that had now taken on such immense importance. He glared at the dog, worked up a degree or two more dislike for it, checked to make sure its doting owner wasn't looking, and lifting his foot gave it a meaningful thrust in the ribs with the toe of his shoe. Far from deterring the hairy end of the tug-of-war, now partially blinded by the bow that had fallen across its face, it had quite the opposite effect, raising the 'Ergh!' now angrily bursting from its larynx several decibels higher and bringing forth a deposit of white froth from its mouth and onto its whiskers. Henry's eyes widened in horror and, convinced the animal was rabid, he let go.

The dog, not aware that it was foaming, and in any case not aware of the devastating reaction that a combination of foam and dog had on the human race, was taken completely by surprise and duly catapulted, glove in mouth and bow in face, several feet backwards, climaxing in a reverse roll into the base of a small wine table that just previous to the dog's arrival had been very ably supporting a silver tray, cut glass decanter and six matching sherry glasses. If there could be any luck involved in such a calamity, it was that the decanter only contained a drain of sherry, which remained intact.

'Oh, my God,' muttered Henry watching the last glass roll to a halt and raising a hand to his open mouth, 'oh my goodness gracious…' but he got no further. The door handle to Millicent's room clicked and a sliver of light fell across the carpet in front of him. He heard her voice ask 'What in heavens' name is going on?' and then he saw her. He had been about to offer some sort of explanation when the sight that confronted him immediately cut off the bloody supply to the nerves that operated his tongue and all he could do was sit; sit and stare. And blink.

If ever there was a vision of loveliness thrust upon eyes that through habit had seen little but ugliness, then here it was in the flesh - and flesh being the operative word. Henry turned towards the window, blinked, pushed his fallen glasses back into position, returned his gaze to Millicent, made several attempts to speak, accidentally licked his lips, and swallowed loudly.

'I was…' he croaked, clearing his throat and starting again, 'I was trying to get my glove back off him and well…he started to foam at the mouth and so I let go and he, well he rolled back into the table. I'm terribly sorry, it was my fault really I suppose, so you'll have to let me pay…'

'Don't be silly,' said the vision somewhat curtly, stepping away from the light of the bedroom behind her and into Henry's full view. She was no longer a silhouette in the distance but flesh and blood wearing the briefest black underwear right under his nose. Henry saw a sudden flash of advertisements on the escalator and just as when confronted with these brazen images, he instantly averted his eyes, imagining the world was watching him.

'You bad boy George!' she shouted at the dog who until this moment was looking quite pleased with itself. The reprimand could quite easily have been 'George and Henry' for the similar flinching effect it had on both, and picking up the broken neck of the decanter the only non-guilty party sighed and said, 'What will Sir Rodney say?'

'Sir Who?' enquired Henry.

'Oh - just another client,' murmured Millicent dismissively.

Henry watched as she bent and picked up the table and contents lying scattered around on the rose pink carpet. He felt an urge to get up and help but under the circumstances that was completely out of the question. Instead he stared in disbelief at the smooth white expanses of flesh and the lace-trimmed bra and panties that were the only relief (if that is the word) from the

57

milky whiteness that stretched from head to painted toe. Millicent glanced over her shoulder at the dithering, rain-coated spectacle perched on the edge of the seat and noticed the mug close by his feet. 'And I should pick that up,' she nodded at the mug, 'otherwise that'll be next.'

Henry immediately did as he was ordered, almost jumping to attention, pleased to have a job to alleviate his embarrassment. He stepped towards the nearest flat surface which just happened to be an antique rosewood drum table, the beauty of which was completely lost on him and may as well have been a Formica picnic table for all the aesthetic pleasure it gave him.

'Not on there!' cried out the vision, sounding now to Henry slightly less of a vision than she looked. 'Put it in the kitchen - through there,' and still in a crouched position, nodded towards a door to her right from where Henry remembered her emerging some fifteen minutes before, fully-clothed with his cocoa. To reach the door he had to pass in front of her and try as he may, for he knew he shouldn't, he found his eyes being drawn into the deep cleavage that had the enviable task of separating one smooth, brimming white breast from the other. In the split second that he allowed himself to stare, he suddenly experienced feelings that had never before been a part of his life. He neither understood nor cared just at that moment about why such an exquisite creature as she, should take him home and present herself in such unabashed near-nakedness; or why, when obviously accustomed to the upper crust company of such notables as Sir Rodney Whoever, should she bother with his plebeian level. It didn't matter. She was lovely.

With this one thought totally occupying his mind he ghosted into the kitchen, placed the mug into one of the double stainless steel sinks, and looked around. It was a long, narrow kitchen with dark wood units lining the walls top and bottom on both sides, only broken to accommodate appliances. His gaze was attracted to the most prominent item overhead, a bronze, stippled extractor fan hood that stuck out like an ice-cream parlour blind over a gleaming, spotless hob below. Then he noticed a piece of white card on the wall just to the left of the hood. It had a decorative border of pink and pale blue flowers joined together in a looping, twisting chain inside of which was a heart-shape formed from the same flower pattern. He took two steps forward to focus better and read the words inside the heart, *'LOVE IS THE SHORTEST DISTANCE BETWEEN TWO HEARTS'.* Below the heart was another arrangement that bore a remarkable resemblance, albeit in the same twisted flower chain, to two naked figures entwined together. Leaning against the worktop, his eyes screwed up and lips mouthing the words, he then read *'AND SEX IS THE SHORTEST DISTANCE BETWEEN TWO PEOPLE.'* Henry regained his upright position, glanced at the card again, thought about it for a while, read it once more, gave it more thought, and then frowned and peered in the direction of the lounge.

Through the gap between the half open door and the frame he could see Millicent moving silently and stealthily about, glimpses of black and white, lace and flesh, not enough visible to make out the quite perfect shape of her body, but having that already indelibly printed on his mind, just a teasing hint for his imagination to play with; an imagination that had never before in the field of Henry's mundane existence been called upon to perform such primitive carnal duties. The canvass stretched out across his mind that had until this moment seen everything in shades of grey was suddenly tinted with the odd splash of colour, and the aura that hangs on every living being and that hung around Henry like dirty dishwater, was now glowing very, very dimly, like a dying ember caught in a sudden life-saving draught.

The revolution had begun! Oh yes, there was no doubting that - but like all good revolutions it would have to fumble its way through humble origins before any real fire could be lit. Henry, to be truthful, was not particularly aware of any revolution beating inside his breast, nor was he in any fit state to further a cause of any kind, least of all one of a sensual nature; but with one small, insignificant gesture of rebellion he had unwittingly launched himself on a roller-coaster ride that could end...who knows where? Like a child who finds a well-thumbed pornographic magazine behind a lavatory cistern, he was filled with a naïve excitement that was frightening, yet rather compelling.

From his hiding-place behind the kitchen door, where in the silence of his racing thoughts he had forgotten to breathe for a full thirty seconds, he was brought abruptly to his senses by the sound of shattered glass sliding from dustpan into tin waste-bin. Then another brief silence followed and again Henry listened with baited breath, until a yelp for attention from the dog brought a whispered reply from its mistress and a movement passed the gap in the door. A dilemma seized Henry. Did he go out and risk further embarrassment or did he wait just that bit longer to give her chance to get dressed? An answer was provided with the click of her bedroom door and a dimness that came over the room outside, no longer illuminated by the light from the room into which she had just passed. He tiptoed out into the lounge and looked around. George was sitting outside the bedroom, looking up expectantly, his bow now restored to a dignified position on top of his head. On sensing Henry he turned his head and uttered a token yap before returning to the door, expecting at any moment to be let in.

Henry, alone and confused once again, quietly walked into the centre of the room whispering 'good boy' to placate any violent thoughts that the dog may be nurturing towards him, and stared at the closed door and thin rectangle of light that was evidence of the room's occupation.

'What a strange lady,' he thought to himself, 'what a peculiar way of behaving'. From an angel of mercy whose bubbly optimism had cheered and lifted him out of his gloom for a short while, to the irritable vision who quite openly paraded before him semi-naked and equally as openly made it obvious that she no longer desired his company.

For the first time since making her acquaintance it crossed Henry's mind that he had no means of getting home. His trust in her had been absolute and in placing that trust he had unconsciously passed over all other responsibilities, which included how to get home. Millicent had promised him help, had taken him home for cocoa and advice, but now he felt she had betrayed him with this odd behaviour. What sort of solicitor was she to behave in such a manner? Why bother to go this far and

60

then shun him? There was no doubting her wealth; a flat with views across Regents Park wouldn't come cheap, and the furnishings that surrounded him as he stood looking around were further evidence that she wasn't one to stint on quality; and of course she knew Sir Rodney Whatsisname, and he wouldn't settle for cocoa and a ginger biscuit, no fear. So why offer a hand of friendship - and then pull it away?

This melancholy pondering was doing Henry no good at all and his throbbing head, which he had quite forgotten about for a while, was back with a vengeance. He was wishing with all his heart for the clock to be turned back, for the security and spartan familiarity of his dinghy little bedroom, for those few joyful moments of ecstasy by the fire with his racing guide and slippers after his mother had taken herself to bed. Oh what he wouldn't give for that right now. Just then he noticed George shuffling excitedly, his head cocked on one side in anticipation. Then as he watched the animal working itself into a minor frenzy he heard Millicent's voice and thought he recognised his name, although he wasn't sure. He stepped closer to the door, jumped as his shadow loomed up beside him on the wall, and then bent his head on an angle identical to the small creature that sat dutifully to the right of his feet, no longer an adversary but now united in a common cause, offering to anyone who happened to walk into the room at that moment, a most curious pantomime.

'Henry.'

Yes, he heard it again, quite clearly that time, and the dog, sensing that he was once again about to play second fiddle to an intruder, looked up and growled at the man towering over him. George's possessive streak, which had been heavily tested over the five years of life with Millicent, was no closer to a cure now than the day when as a newly purchased puppy he had met his first 'uncle'.

'Henry? Henry, are you there?' came the gentle voice again, drifting through the door and landing like rose petals on Henry's finely tuned eardrums. If he had ever in his life been exposed to overtures from the opposite sex or spent even a little more time watching David Attenborough's animal mating programmes on television, he may have been better prepared for the scene in which he was about to become a leading player; but Henry, inveterate celibate and doyen of the downtrodden, didn't have a clue. And thus equipped, he turned the round white doorknob and slowly entered the bedroom.

There cannot be many occasions in the average man's life when he strolls unsuspectingly into a room and is confronted with a female form devoid of clothing and so perfect in construction that it transcends description; a face with its small, fine features arranged in such a manner that pouting precociousness are the only words that fly to mind; and a pair of hands with such fine, delicate porcelain qualities travelling, caressing and moulding the body of which they were a part.

It was the reflection in the long wardrobe mirror that Henry noticed first, for this was facing him as he walked in. Millicent's eyes, on catching his, lit up like beacons and set off the faintest smile across her lips. Henry's facial features, the cause of this smile, were completely out of his control, in fact in total disarray. His epiglottis, a fairly prominent feature when not immersed in fat whilst sleeping, had now taken on the size (or so it felt to Henry) of a pumpkin, and the saliva that had returned to his mouth on leaving the police station had now deserted him in his moment of greatest need.

Millicent turned, still smiling, and ran her hands over her breasts, pushing them up and then letting them drop gently back into their rightful place. Henry, riveted to the spot, unable to talk, unable to think and most definitely unable to act, started to rock on his heels.

'Do you know,' asked Millicent, turning her back to the mirror and running her hands down her hips and around her buttocks, 'do you know, Henry, what narcissism is?'

Henry opened his mouth, realised he no longer possessed the necessary ingredients inside it to create words, swallowed once, dragged a totally dehydrated tongue over parched lips and croaked in a rather high octave, 'It's a…flower…isn't it?' - this eventually coaxed out on a third attempt. 'A sort of…a sort of daffodil I think.'

Millicent threw her head back and laughed out loud, to which Henry felt forced to join in with the weakest of smiling chuckles, grateful for a little light relief, even if the joke was lost on him. Millicent turned and took a step towards him. Henry took half a pace back.

'You are so funny,' she said, placing two cool fingers on his burning cheek, 'such a funny little man. I don't think I've ever met anyone quite like you.'

Henry could have been flattered or insulted but being Henry, he was neither; just numb.

'Narcissism,' continued Millicent, again turning to face her reflection, 'is an extreme self-love.'

'Oh really,' mumbled Henry, wishing the subject were either horse racing or departmental time and motion.

'Yes,' said Millicent, now raising her arms above her head and clenching her hands together, her breasts jutting out and her eyes all the time watching Henry's. 'Narcissus was a very beautiful young man who fell in love with his own reflection.'

'Goodness me,' said Henry with a slight nod as he examined his shoes, 'I only know the flower. I didn't know about...about the young man.'

'I'm very proud of my body. I enjoy looking at it. I enjoy touching it. Does that seem wrong to you Henry?' Millicent turned her head with artificial coyness towards him.

'No,' gasped the poor man with absolute truth, 'not at all.'

'I don't think I could do my job half so well if I didn't. Don't you agree?' asked Millicent, quite matter-of-fact and business-like.

Henry, for the life of him, could think of no earthly reason why a solicitor would need to love and touch her body in order to carry out what had always appeared to him (agreed without any firsthand experience) a fairly dignified and highly paid profession. However, at this precise moment, in the company of a naked one, all rationale had flown freely through the window and he was prepared to believe anything.

'Henry, why don't you take your coat off and relax,' said Millicent, moving in silent tip-toe grace to a wide, white dressing table the opposite side of the bed to where Henry stood.

'No, I'm fine thank you,' said Henry, his heart-rate having accelerated to the point where it could almost be measured as one continuous beat, 'quite relaxed.'

He watched her pick up a glass from amongst the perfumes and sprays and with a toss of her head that saw her hair and breasts sway in unison, she lifted the glass and drained the contents. She then picked up a bottle from the dressing table, exposing the label just long enough for Henry to read Gordon's Gin, and poured a sizeable measure onto the ice within the glass. She then slopped in some tonic from an open bottle, swilled the drink round the glass, stared poignantly into its clear depths and with a quick movement, again tossed back her head and poured the contents straight down. During this little excerpt Henry had been transfixed, almost as if the torture of his previous evening were being replayed before him like the Ghost of Christmas Past, and when Millicent's head tossed back to drink, so too did Henry's head make a slight involuntary jerk backwards and left a wince on his face that was still there when Millicent turned to offer him the glass. Henry snapped out of his reverie and declined, shaking his head and politely whispering 'Not for me thank you. I think alcohol has caused me enough trouble for the time being.'

Millicent took a deep breath and turned to face Henry full on. Her expression, at first a frown, broke gradually into a gentle smile and in the quietest voice she held out a hand and said 'Please Henry, take off your raincoat. For me, please.'

There were certain clients and certain situations that created a need within Millicent for a stiff drink before action. It was her common practice with most of her better class customers to sit first in the comfort of the lounge and relax bodies and souls before consummating transactions. It was there that she massaged the tired minds and battered egos of many a London dignitary (they having spent a hard day *at* the Bench, *on* the Bench - Front or Back - in the boardroom, office or pulpit) who took it upon themselves during the day in moments of stress, boredom, or extreme randiness, to pick up the telephone without the help of a secretary - an action almost impossible under normal circumstances - and book themselves in.

The lady, they knew, was an expert. She massaged egos and then massaged bodies; fat bodies, thin bodies, hairy and smooth bodies; bodies that heaved and flagged and expired long before their money was up, and bodies tuned by lunchtime squash and gym sessions that seemed to have interminable reserves of energy. The good, the bad and the ugly, they came in many packages for various reasons at various times of the day and night. Some, not many, she classed as friends, sad cases despite their outward gregarious natures and obvious wealth. Millicent knew she was the saviour of many marriages in the higher social echelon of the city where many a wife sat in the luxury of her home congratulating herself on a lifetime of mutual love and devotion, achieved quite easily with only the odd capitulation between the satin sheets - a minor inconvenience and meagre sacrifice to keep her in the manner to which she really had to remain accustomed.

Millicent knew these men as their wives would never know them, for the wives were not a novelty, a fantasy, a plaything who asked no questions and told no lies. They were nuisances with Harrods accounts who in their rare moments of capitulation required showers before, after and sometimes during - if it got too messy. So where did Henry Scroggins fit in? Well, like the City in a stock-market crash and Industry in an oil-crisis, all realms of business are subject to the odd depression. Millicent's was no exception. Two scandals hard on the heels of each other had sent shockwaves through the upper circles, creating, as in previous instances, 'a kind of hush' to spread throughout, as those ranging from cautious to downright terrified scurried off to the safety of their country foxholes to wait patiently for the dust to settle and for big Farmer Press to get bored and point his shotgun elsewhere.

So Millicent with her philosophic approach to life and her keen sense of fun had taken to 'the streets' once more, as in the early days, and far from being fearful of the prospect, viewed it as an exciting challenge, a return to the halcyon days of fifteen years ago when first she became drawn into her 'iniquitous' lifestyle. Besides, the streets never were her shop window. Why should she when the bars and lounges of London's best hotels offered comfort, dignity and an endless procession of iron filings for her delightful magnet. Class cannot be learnt or bought but is so, so easy to sell. It's said there is a slut in every woman and Millicent at times felt she had grown just too respectable. So in the recent hard times the hotels and clients had become a little 'down market', and accordingly the occasional arrest that went with it and the different type of person she attracted, were all part of the game. She didn't need the money, the flat was long ago paid for as were her other expensive tenanted properties dotted around St. John's Wood and Swiss Cottage, but she needed the kicks, the slight element of risk and the power of superiority over men in high places, and whilst the peculiar little man at the police station had seemed quite incapable of providing either money, kicks and certainly no apparent risk or elevated position in London society, there was something indeterminate that had attracted her, like a decorative moth to a dusty thirty watt light bulb.

Even now she knew very little about him, this oddball in a raincoat that he refused to remove. Apart, that is, that he lived with his mother in Lewisham and that his short-lived spree of mayhem was completely out of character; that much she had prised from him in the taxi home to her flat, but beyond that he was a mystery, a rather pathetic little mystery who drank cocoa, would not undress, thought Narcissus was a flower and as yet had failed to be driven crazy by her body. If only she knew.

The gin was now clouding, just slightly, her ability to remember the details of their meeting and the reason for her softening towards him. She tried to convince herself that it was purely business that had motivated her change of heart, but she knew it wasn't. There was nothing vaguely attractive about the man to induce her to take him home in the early hours of Christmas Eve; absolutely nothing. So why? Why was he there?

At that moment the subject of her ruminations, who had taken off his raincoat and folded it into a neat square, was searching for somewhere to put it. She watched with a mixture of amusement and sadness, his worried piggy eyes flash from her full frontal nudity to the window, to her breasts, to the pillow, to her pubic hair, to the floor, and finally back to his Mac gripped tightly between his podgy white hands. Millicent was quite accustomed to this with new clients, most of whom had never been confronted at close quarters with such undoubted erotic magnificence, and she enjoyed the teasing magnetism that her body had on their eyes; the poor creatures, either starved of sex altogether or starved of a woman who would let go and perform the stuff only their fantasies were made of.

'Put it on the floor,' she said, nodding at Henry's mackintosh, 'and come here beside me.'

With those words she sat on the bed and without taking her eyes from Henry's, lifted one slender leg and then the other up on to the white, glossy smoothness of the satin duvet cover. She then laid back and stretched full length, her arms touching the brass rods of the bed head behind her, which she gripped whilst peering wide-eyed at Henry, the sight of which was too much for the poor man and sent his already scrambled brain into orbit.

'Wh–why are you doing this?' stammered Henry.

'Why am I doing it?' replied Millicent who, having closed her eyes, now opened them wide and stared again at Henry who was staring beyond her body at a spot on the pale blue velvet curtains that hung behind the dressing table. 'Henry', she continued, noting the bead of perspiration sliding down over his cheekbone, 'Henry - have you ever made love?'

Henry looked down at her, started, checked himself, glanced at the enquiring expression fixed on her beautiful face, and after clearing his throat asked 'You mean…to a…woman?'

Millicent nodded. 'Preferably. Although I suppose anything would be a start.'

Henry flashed a nervous smile at her. 'Please don't do that,' he said.

Millicent raised herself on one elbow and patted the bed beside her. Henry instinctively sat down, as close to the edge on his side as he could without falling off, his crumpled shabby grey suit contrasting with the soft white luxury of the duvet.

'Do what?' asked Millicent.

'Poke fun at me.'

'I wasn't poking fun.'

'You were.'

'Henry, look at me.'

Henry knew from her tone that she meant her face and not her body, and he turned. As he turned she reached out and placed her hand on his arm. She felt the greasy dampness on her fingertips but far from being repelled, just felt sorrow. Now she understood what had brought them together, now she knew the one thing that had made her, in a moment of feminine intuition, offer her coveted company and kindness to this man. There was never a question of a financial transaction taking place. It hadn't entered her head, which was just as well because she would have been somewhat disappointed. It was now apparent to her that the reason they were locked in this bizarre scene was quite simply that Henry was a child, and she was childless.

'You're very beautiful,' said Henry, without thinking. Millicent acknowledged his compliment with a smile and the slightest inclination of the head. 'Very beautiful,' added Henry, and then suddenly overcome with the tenderness of the moment, something he'd never before had to cope with, he felt tears well up and, turning to the wall, blinked them clear. He continued.

'I know looking at me you'd think I don't have any pride but I - I sometimes do have, you know. Not now of course, but...sometimes. Or perhaps it's self-pity, I don't know. I haven't got much to be proud of but I think we all want to feel proud sometimes don't we.'

Millicent thought for some time, watching the man staring at his hands and then at the wall and back again at his hands, straightening the corners of his mackintosh as if to demonstrate the pride he had in his folding.

'They say,' she said, 'whoever *they* are, that pride comes before a fall but I've no idea what we are without pride, or vanity, or whatever it is that makes us want to make an effort to present ourselves as we want to be seen by others.'

Henry nodded and placed his hands squarely on his folded Mac, staring at his fingers and quietly said 'Yes.'

Millicent took a deep breath. 'Henry?' He quickly turned and looked her in the eyes, taking her by surprise. 'Do you mind telling me - and please don't feel ashamed or take this the wrong way -'

'Have I ever been with a woman?'

'Yes.'

'No.'

'That's fine. Nothing wrong with that,' said Millicent, so softly that if the rain hadn't suddenly stopped a moment before, the words would have been lost in the noise. Now, all was silence; silence until Henry involuntarily heaved a sigh and shivered and then sat motionless. After several seconds he removed his glasses, made out to rub his cheek with the back of his hand, replaced his glasses and sniffed.

'After all,' continued Millicent in a matter-of-fact manner, 'sex isn't everything in life.'

Henry looked at her, the tiniest whimsical grin flickering around the corners of his mouth. 'That's all very well for you to say,' he said. 'I've managed - had to - stagger through forty years without it.' And with that they both laughed, shoulders shaking in unison, quite forgetting the absurdity of the situation, a beautiful naked lady and a fully clothed middle-aged infant.

Millicent sat up straight-backed on the bed and began to say, 'Is that all you...' and stopped.

'Yes,' said Henry, 'that's all I am? Forty. A month ago. I know I haven't worn too well. It's the cocoa and high living. Takes its toll, that's a fact.'

Millicent's eyes and mouth danced for the first time into the magnetic smile that had hit Henry like a thunderbolt in the police station. She laughed silently and he watched her breasts and their deep pink tips as they quivered, wanting desperately to put his hands on them and kiss her. But life wasn't like that for Henry Scroggins. The lightness and tenderness that had pervaded the atmosphere of his world for a few brief seconds, a momentary anaesthetic, was not, for the time being, to last.

Millicent rose from the bed and taking two steps to the wardrobe, opened the door. Henry, somewhat perplexed that their conversation had terminated so suddenly, studied the bareness of her back and the line of vertebrae just above her perfectly-formed white buttocks as she searched through the garments.

Eventually she plucked from a hangar something white, silky and full-length that to Henry's untrained eyes could have passed as a nightdress, a dressing gown, or even at a push a slightly daring evening gown. Many years of co-habiting with only one haggard specimen of the female species had taught him that nightdresses were thick, cotton and buttoned up to the neck, but unfortunately not down to the floor, thereby revealing knots of varicose veins wrapped like blue spaghetti around hideous bony ankles and shins. Fortunately, dressing gowns were thick, candlewick, maroon and ground level, offering some visual respite when the wearer in question was standing.

'Will you excuse me please Henry,' asked Millicent, tying the cord around her gown and adjusting the lace edge that crossed her chest. 'I'm feeling a chill. I think I'll take a shower and warm up. Do you want one after me?'

Henry didn't take showers. He didn't take showers because he didn't have one and had never been in one and in all honesty would have been quite lost in one. So he checked his watch, the first time he'd thought to do so since his arrival at Millicent's. It showed ten past two. Ten past two and he was due to appear at Bow Street Magistrates Court at eleven. That made nine hours; less in fact; less than nine hours to sort something out. The dreadful reality of what he'd done and the more fearful prospect of the possible ramifications precluded all other thoughts. Feeling a wave of nausea roll through his stomach, which at any other time would have meant hunger and been abated with a cheese and pickle sandwich, he looked to his Guardian Angel.

'Millicent.' This was the first time he'd called her by her name and it sounded quite pleasant to her. She closed the wardrobe door and raised her eyebrows.

'Yes Henry?'

'Can we talk after you've showered please?'

'We've talked haven't we?'

70

'No, I mean about the morning. The court procedure and all that horrible business. I've got to know exactly what to do and say, and I just don't have a clue.'

He started to shake and the pained expression on his face led Millicent to believe he was about to burst into tears. But he didn't, he just looked up at her like a dog awaiting the word 'walkies'. And, as if Millicent knew she was in the middle of a dog analogy, she patted Henry on the shoulder as she walked past him towards the door and said simply, 'You'll be alright, don't worry. I'll give you a run through in the morning. I think it's best that we get some sleep. The sofa pulls out into…'

Henry was desperate, thinking Millicent was disappearing off to bed as blasé as though they were going shopping in the morning. He got up from the bed, looked down for his folded mackintosh, picked it up and took a step towards her.

'No, *now* please Millicent. I've got to sort it out with you now otherwise I won't sleep a wink and be even more useless in the morning. I never sleep when I've got a problem and this isn't just a problem, this is…well, it's awful! Please…can we talk?'

Millicent frowned and shrugged, a trifle bemused at the lofty pedestal on which Henry had placed her. 'Henry, I'm not sure I understand what you're saying. Of course I'll help you all I can, but first…'

'Yes?'

'Well, to be honest,' she said, 'there's not much I can do. It's you in the dock. You'll need a solicitor though. I know a good one you can trust.'

If she hadn't smiled when she said this, Henry would not have mistaken it for a joke. He grinned nervously, one that came and went in a flash as havoc reigned in his head, one terrible image leapfrogging another. Millicent's casual approach, which was all very well in the light of her vast experience and familiarity with the law, and which should have been serving as a comfort to the inexperienced guilty party, was not having the desired effect. But then solicitors, from what he'd seen on television, were like that; cool, composed and never needing more time than just enough. He felt a little better with this reasoning and decided there and then, as Millicent disappeared through a door in the room and the sound of a shower burst into life, that having got himself into a dreadful mess, Fortune had shone so providently upon him and sent Millicent. Any suggestion at this stage that he was entirely on his own in his predicament would have engendered drastic symptoms and even more drastic action.

Five minutes later Henry stared hard at the wall ahead of him as Millicent gathered up a few items from her dressing table in a small bag. He studied the tiny pale lemon flowers on the white wallpaper, scratched one of his chins, consciously ironed out the furrows in his brow (to appear equally unperturbed) and said:

'Okay, so what do you want me to do? You're the solicitor. I'm the client. Just give me the rap!' Henry had watched one too many American movies and the 'lingo' he'd always regarded as mildly decadent in his public service role, now seemed appropriate. 'Of course, I don't expect you to do everything,' he rambled on, 'I just want to know the procedure, that's all. It's a far cry from writing memos in the department. Do you know Millicent, of all the....'

He stopped in mid-sentence, suddenly aware that Millicent was demonstrating every indication that a ghost had made their gathering into a threesome.

'What's the matter?' asked Henry.

'Matter?' replied Millicent, her previous mellifluous tone reverting to one bordering on panic.

'Yes, you've turned awfully pale. Are you alright?'

'Yes - yes of course. It was just - just nothing really. Nothing.'

'You look dreadful.'

'Thank you.'

'No - I mean, well - not well. You know - shocked.'

'It was just something you said. Made me think...'

'Think? Think of what? What did I say?'

'Nothing. It doesn't matter. It really doesn't matter. Now, where were we?'

'Umm...'

Millicent at this point, having to her abject horror mentally retraced the vital scene at the police station, was now in dire need of a sanctuary. Somewhere to give her breathing space to think and plot her way out of this unbelievable mess; a means of getting rid of Henry before the morning and all its problems and implications. She looked at the human burden that sat fumbling in his jacket pocket for something. The stupid, stupid little man! How in God's name could anyone be so totally naïve and idiotic? He thought she was a solicitor. All the time he'd thought she was a solicitor! In her mature world of high-flyers and aristocrats, where men weren't always men but at least had a basic grounding in life, she had been handed Henry.

This very same man, who had been fervently searching, tapping and delving into his numerous overcrowded pockets, and had to his delight now discovered the object of his search, a crumpled Polaroid photograph, grinned triumphantly and thrust the trophy under the nose of his 'solicitor'.

'Evidence!' he cried, 'I've just thought of it! They forced me. They forced me to drink. I never drink, *never*, and they forced me. Isn't that provocation or something? Can't we…'

'Henry, please, I'm tired and the shower's running.'

And with that and a flashed smile she was gone through the door, leaving Henry clutching his evidence and staring vacantly from it to the void Millicent had left. Into this void, close to the floor, George appeared, with his bow no longer warranting that exact description, both the pieces of bedraggled ribbon now dangling down over one ear, possibly as a result of much fretting and attempts at self-harm during his banishment. He peered up at Henry who was still the object of a grudge for shutting the door on him, emitted a low, rumbling growl that built up into a crescendo, and with a defiant yap as a finale, turned tail and with consummate arrogance befitting a solicitor's dog, was gone.

Millicent, under the soothing influence of her shower, had in a matter of minutes resolved the whole catastrophic situation. The taxi would arrive within minutes of her call, Henry would be suitably bundled off to his mother in Lewisham, she would be curled up in her bed within half an hour, and having already negotiated a 'loss' of PC Steele's notes to prevent a tiresome appearance in court the next morning, could now look forward to the tranquillity of a Christmas with George. For two days, she was entirely his.

She rehearsed her lines and composed her face into the mould that suited the occasion. She would be firm, but kind. One thing was certain, Henry had to go. But she knew she couldn't hurt him. She would never hurt children.

## Chapter Six

# THE LETTER

The downstairs of 52 Viola Street, the house that the newlywed Irma and Henry Scroggins had bought shortly before the outbreak of World War Two, had not altered a great deal in the ensuing forty odd years. Henry, the First that is, had put every ounce of energy, pride and hard-earned cash into each lick of paint, each carefully cut and hung length of wallpaper, each nail and screw and smoothly-planed and sanded piece of wood, and as testimony to his sterling efforts - most of it was still there.

The front room, or parlour as Mrs Scroggins called it, looked directly out onto the street and into the front room, or parlour, of the Wilmot's at No.37. The Wilmot's being an extremely respectable, orderly family, kept an extremely respectable, orderly house, for Mr and Mrs Wilmot were cleaners of the highest and most diligent order. Mr Wilmot, in his capacity as verger of St. Michael's & All Angels Parish Church three streets away from Viola, had given the word fastidious a new and exalted meaning and drawn ridicule from the more cynical members of the Sunday congregation (of which he was mercifully unaware) and had therefore, over the years, adopted eccentric tendencies that kept him just this side of the lunatic asylum but at the same time safely insulated from the potentially harmful mimicry of the more humorously gifted altar boys.

Mrs Wilmot's incumbency was the house, and in particular the net curtains. These outstandingly durable items went up and down more times in a month than a fiddler's elbow, apart from occasions when disaster struck; significantly in 1977 when young Oswald Wilmot, in full Jubilee spirit and left alone one day, took it upon himself to paint one curtain (just one) red, white and blue, incurring an extended chemical cleaning for the luckless curtain and an extended period of isolation for young Wilmot in his bedroom. This household disaster meant whitewash was administered on the window with a whiteness and precision befitting the curtains they temporarily substituted.

As Mr Wilmot the verger drew ridicule with his fastidiousness in the church then so it could be said that Mrs Wilmot's own fastidiousness in the house was verging on the ridiculous, all of which would be highly irrelevant to the story but for one important fact; the movement of the curtains were directly responsible for the tea-drinking habits of Irma Scroggins and her next door neighbour and chief information service, the irrepressible Lily Bunce. Both friend and confidante but never, in spite of this, one to neglect her role as newscaster, Lily represented to Viola Street what Reuter did to the world.

And so it was that this particular afternoon of Christmas Eve, as grey skies hung ominously over rooftops, threatening another wet instead of white Christmas, the two ladies peered across at the fervent activity going on behind the Wilmot's bare windows as Mrs Wilmot and her only child put the finishing touches to decorations and re-dressed the tree for the umpteenth time. From time to time the young Oswald would appear offering a bauble or piece of tinsel to a branch only to have his hand slapped and a reprimand delivered, resulting in his disappearance for a while until, to his great credit, he returned to try again.

Lily Bunce being of short, stout stature, was having some difficulty from where she sat seeing over the arm of her friend's high-backed armchair, and with the Wilmot's lights now on (it being such a gloomy afternoon) and so much taking place, she felt the need to examine at closer range the current weather situation. So strolling casually to the small bay window and looking up with a shake of the head and a sigh, she announced that Mr Wilmot was obviously still at work or maybe busy-bodying around the church in preparation for his major event of the year - Midnight Mass.

Ah, Midnight Mass, when vergers must be especially vigilant in readiness to ward off the incursion of drunks shuffling in at the back halfway through the service, singing too loudly, smiling too festively and smelling like a brewery. Add to this the sheer excitement of the altar boys and their more static confederates, the choirboys, being encouraged to stay up late but more importantly having only hours until they opened their presents, and the occasion was a true test for the most pertinacious verger.

'He's there. I've seen him,' snapped Irma Scroggins, 'he just stuck his head in the room and said something.'

Now, in view of Lily Bunce's remark being meant merely as a primer for her main question, she just said 'Oo-er' and waited a respectable few seconds before opening her mouth to begin her conversation properly.

'I - er,' she finally ventured, 'I didn't see your 'Enry go past this morning Mrs S. Is he working today? Working today is he? Mm?' A sip of tea was taken whilst a hawk eye hovered over the cup studying her friend's face.

Irma Scroggins didn't always reply to Lily Bunce's perpetual questions that demanded comment of some kind and so Lily had come to the conclusion over the past few years, as the responses from her friend decreased, that the old woman was going deaf. This was, however, far from the truth for if ever there were senses honed to the finest degree then there they were on Irma Scroggins. But conniving, scheming old hag that she was, only she knew the extent of her faculties and with age and decrepitude as a cover, she applied it to her advantage at every opportunity. Even Henry, who thought after so many years living under her roof and dominance that he knew all her devious whims and ways, was invariably tricked by her guile - and invariably paid the penalty.

Lily Bunce, having waited her regulation ten seconds before re-addressing important questions, was about to do just that when the kettle started its low warble from the kitchen and put a temporary halt to her interrogation.

'Blinkin' kettle!' she exclaimed irritably, getting up and striding to the door, wiping her mouth on her sleeve until turning and adding over the shrill crescendo that the offending kettle was keeping up, 'It's about time your 'Enry fixed up its switcher-offer!'

At the sound of her son's name, Irma Scroggins mouth could be seen to tighten, her eyes darken and her chest under the crocheted shawl, heave a little. Lily Bunce by this time was halfway down the hall, a bundle of bustling vexation, repeating mumbled oaths alternately at the kettle and Henry. The subject of all the noise and half of her irritation was enshrouded in billows of steam and, as she groped to switch it off, still muttering to herself, her attention was arrested by a small, manila envelope. She looked around furtively, which was unnecessary as Irma Scroggins never moved from her chair once seated during tea sessions, and picked it up. She noted that it was addressed to Mr H. W. Scroggins, had already been opened and not very cleverly re-sealed. She scoffed at this amateurish attempt, her professional pride coming to the fore, and with deft fingers that would have been a credit to any safe-breaker, peeled back the flap of the envelope and, with a final swift glance over her shoulder and up the hall, took out the letter.

*Ace Credit Collection* loomed in large black print at the top of the page and at the sight of this Lily Bunce knew immediately that she had struck gold. Nervously, impatiently, her eyes travelled down, scanning the whole page until they alighted on a sum of money, a figure no less than three thousand, three hundred and seventy-nine pounds and fifty pence. Eagerly she read on, her mouth moving silently and her eyebrows rising and falling intermittently.

'Well I never,' she said to herself over and over, 'well I never, who'd have thought it. Young 'Enry in debt.' And as she shook her head and tt-tt'd, the voice of Irma Scroggins pierced the gloom of the hallway and entered the kitchen, where the open-mouthed Lily Bunce visibly leapt, returned the letter to its envelope, performed a highly dexterous re-sealing job identical to the one she'd discovered, poured water into the teapot, wiped hands on her pinafore, propped the envelope back in its original position - and all this executed in a mere blink or two of an eyelid. The lady was a credit to her breed.

'Coming Mrs S! Just waitin' for the tea to brew how you like it. Won't be a jiff!' And true to her word Lily Bunce was beside her friend, pouring tea and issuing Arrowroot biscuits to two blue china plates within a minute, or a jiff - whichever is soonest.

'Oo-er, it's gettin' dark,' she observed, peering out of the window as she handed the old lady her tea, 'spect your 'Enry'll be in soon. Won't he Mrs S? Your 'Enry? Mm?'

Mrs S. offered a quick nod and just as quickly offered her cup to her mouth followed by a bite of her biscuit to avoid any further answer. As she crunched loudly, her jaws rotating like a cement mixer and eyes fixed ahead, Lily Bunce continued.

'Dangerous on the roads this time of the day. All those drunks after their Christmas parties. Disgraceful. I just 'ope the cops catch a few. Mind you they're probably all arf' sloshed 'emselves. Not like in the old days Mrs S, is it? Mm? No. I mean the worst that could 'appen to our men was they'd fall off their bikes and get trampled under the baker's 'orses 'ooves!' She laughed raucously at the thought, choking on her tea spluttering 'Oo, do excuse me, do Mrs S,' and then adopting a serious expression to give every indication that the subject was about to be changed.

She peered sideways at the hunched figure wrapped in the shawl, still staring ahead and crunching the remnants of her biscuit. The figure looked up and peered out of the almost dark room across at the brilliantly illuminated Wilmot's parlour where the tree now glowed in dazzling splendour, and sniffed disparagingly. Lily Bunce was sitting poised for her next phase of questioning and as she glanced at the profile of Irma Scroggins, it suddenly occurred to her how she resembled Punch, with her large hooked Roman nose, wide thin lips and chin that jutted defiantly.

'Your 'Enry 'avin a little flutter over Christmas then d'you reckon Mrs S? Does 'e still like a flutter? I know 'e used to like a little flutter - just of course on the Grand National or Derby, that sort of thing. But then we all do, don't we? I mean who doesn't? It's a sorry world if you can't have a few pleasures ain't it Mrs S?'

The younger and more talkative of the two acquaintances turned from the window-gazing that had been occupying her through this oration and met the icy glare of Irma Scroggins frighteningly face on.

'Oo-er, there you are!' tittered Lily Bunce nervously, instinctively aware that she had over-stepped the boundaries of subtlety a smidgeon or two, 'can 'ardly see you in this light. Shall I put the light on Mrs S? Mm?'

'Why did you mention horse-racing?' snapped Irma Scroggins.

'Orse-racing? Did I mention 'orse-racing?' queried Lily, dragging cup to mouth for those few vital stalling seconds often required, discovering no tea and sucking convincingly on fresh air. 'There y'see, I say things and I dunno what I say 'arf the time. I swear I don't!' She chuckled dismissively and sighed, placing her cup on the tray and motioning to take the old lady's. 'Doing anything special for Christmas, Mrs S, you and your 'Enry? Mm?'

'You've read that letter haven't you.'

'I beg your pardon Mrs S?'

'The letter woman! You read it!'

'Letter Mrs S? What letter's this then?' Lily Bunce was now, in sheer desperation, engaging major defences and promptly adopted a coughing fit that saw her thrashing herself on the chest, taking deep asthmatic breaths, gasping 'Oo-er' between each one and blaming the perfectly innocent Arrowroot biscuits for her condition.

'You know exactly what I'm talking about Lily Bunce. The letter in the kitchen by the kettle. Don't lie to me!'

'I never see any letter Mrs S, God's truth I didn't! On my Wilfred's life I didn't!'

'Your Wilfred? He's been dead nine years!'

'Well on 'is soul then, an' may I join 'im in 'eaven if that's not the God's honest truth Mrs S. How could you say such a thing!'

Lily Bunce was now shaking and starting to sob whilst Irma Scroggins' wide eyes blazed and the venom that she had been spitting with her accusations, now trickled down her jaw from a corner of her mouth, bringing a bony hand up to wipe it away.

'You wicked, wicked woman! You're lying! I know it!'

The unfortunate Lily Bunce had for all of Wilfred Bunce's earthly years with her, taken his life on oath as the ultimate proof of any story she was imparting, if anyone dared to doubt its authenticity. This had worked perfectly well and verified many a story until suddenly one day, either through coincidence or maybe one oath too many, she had found Wilfred slumped in his chair in front of the television clutching an unopened Guinness bottle in one hand and his Vernon's Football Pools coupon in the other. That was how Lily remembered the exact day of the week on which he departed, for Wednesday was always his pools day. And so it was that a lifetime's habit, which had been brought into use at least a dozen times every day *before* his death, had been rather hard to shake off, such that now, in the absence of any children or close relative to back up her stories, it became necessary for Wilfred's departed soul to be gainfully employed in this vital evidential role.

It might seem strange that one endowed with such an over-abundance of wickedness as Irma Scroggins should be aiming so vindictively that very same quality at another fellow human being, but as often happens in life the bad see everyone else as far, far worse and by their own misguided sense of relativity promote themselves to Almighty status. Lily Bunce fell into many personality categories; meddlesome some might say; over-zealous in her many and varied investigations - yes that's perhaps not without a grain of truth; prone to embellishments here and there - maybe; a little loud with some of her favourite hymns at St. Michael's and during Songs of Praise on summer evenings through her open windows; but wicked? No, she wasn't wicked. And just to prove the fact (without taking an oath and further jeopardising Wilfred's spirit) - she burst into tears.

'I'm sorry Mrs S!' she sobbed, 'truly I'm sorry. I did look at it. I did an' I never ever 'ave done anything like it before in me life, God strike me dead (*her* dead!) on this very spot if I ever will again! I am wicked Mrs S, you're right, 'an if ever you speak to me 'agin I only 'ope you can forgive me. There! I can say no more. No more.'

And with that she plucked from her cardigan sleeve a miniscule handkerchief and blew her nose loudly into this square of linen hardly equipped for the job, whilst continuing to sob great jerking sobs that wracked her torso like hiccups you'd expect from a rhinoceros, and shaking her head despairingly.

Irma Scroggins sniffed impatiently. 'Alright, alright, don't go on woman,' she scoffed, 'just think yourself lucky I'm not the vindictive type, that's all. Prying into other people's private affairs. What on earth were you thinking of? You should be thoroughly ashamed of yourself and I hope you are! Do you hear?'

Lily Bunce heard alright. Lily Bunce heard and was so grateful to be let off the hook that Lily Bunce was agreeing with anything that her dear friend Irma Scroggins cared to suggest. But then - and why-oh-why we'll never know - the silly woman in a suicidal moment of recrimination, sobbed, dabbed her nose with a corner of her handkerchief, and pursued the subject.

'Mind you,' she snickered, watery-eyed and waiting for a large sob to pass, 'I think someone not a million miles away from here had a little peeky-boo too, didn't they? Eh Mrs S? Mm?'

'Peeky-boo,' and the ingratiating tone in which this was delivered was of course intended to mellow Lily's counter-attack to a level that could hardly cause offence, but, like the lemming she was, Lily Bunce had once again taken herself to the edge of the cliff - and hurled herself off.

Irma Scroggins, in the dark satanic chill of her drab lounge, stared ahead, nostrils flaring, cheekbones and the tiny muscles attached to them twitching violently, poised for terrible action. Gripping the gnarled arms of her chair she slowly turned towards the shivering woman a few feet to her right, pausing for maximum effect before delivering her damning summary.

'He is my son,' she enunciated slowly, red hollow eyes wild with rage, 'my son do you hear? I made him, I keep him, I own him, and I have a right to do what I like with him. Do you understand Lily Bunce? Do I make myself perfectly clear?'

There was no doubting the clarity of the message or the sincere manner in which it was spoken. And thus the spirit of Christmas at 52 Viola Street was clothed in a mantle of something falling short of goodwill, but then there hadn't been a Christmas at that address garnished with anything remotely resembling goodwill, or festive, for many a long year. Not a decoration, a holly-wreath on the door, a card on display, a turkey in the oven, or one word of good cheer from the lips of Irma Scroggins; not since her husband decided enough was enough, met Betty Mathieson at Waterloo Station and sat holding hands and making plans as their train sped through the night to Southampton Docks, whilst the rest of the nation celebrated the relief and glory of D-Day.

## Chapter Seven

# FATHER OF THE SON

This speck of dust in the heavens we call Home; this small star in the solar system whose very existence depends on Mother Sun not wavering one degree in her daily routine; how odd that it flushes out its inhabitants with all their frailties and imperfections at least once every hundred years only to replace them with a whole new set who, far from improving the place, seem even more intent on its destruction.

Mammon's usurping of previous old favourites like God or Zeus - whilst the blindingly obvious Mother Sun still remains largely ignored - must shoulder a fair portion of the blame, but if Mankind is responsible for enthroning Mammon as their main, if not sole, provider of happiness and *raison d'etre* then Mankind must bear the consequences of the greed creed enslaving its current population, for there truly is nothing shallower than a deep ocean of gold and those who guard it with their lives.

A bald, stumpy-built chimpanzee of a man, who from his outward appearance would seem to be one of Mammon's favourite sons, lay on a sun bed in the late afternoon on the deck of his yacht moored off a deserted island in Queensland's Whitsundays. The sun, ending another journey across a clear blue sky uninterrupted all day by a single cloud, spun dizzily over the island just a gentle half-mile swim across a coral reef and its myriad tropical fish. The island rose steeply on one side with a precipice that served as home and launch pad for a pair of sea eagles. Above this craggy face a jumble of bushes and scrub tumbled haphazardly over the top, dwarfed by hoop pines and the odd towering coconut palm. The scrub scattered down the gentle incline until the land met the warm Coral Sea where a huge ring of boulders seemed intent on holding back the palm trees from marching across the white beach into a watery grave.

The man raised himself gingerly onto an elbow and squinted up at the sun's position, shielding his eyes with his hand. His heavy gold neck-chain and bracelet, diamond-encrusted rings on all but two fingers, spoke of an ego to match his wealth. He stared deep into the landscape spread out before him and, as he had on so many occasions, prepared to speak words that were no more a reflection of what he really felt than were the gold adornments a reflection of his true personality.

'Life's been good to me Janie.'

He had lost count of the number of times he'd said this to people who didn't really matter, and Janie, with her twenty years, her slim, exquisite figure tanned to perfection, her pretty face and sun-bleached hair, and her devotion to serving his every need, was no exception. The young lady looked up from her magazine, peered over her sunglasses at the man, smiled and spoke in a sweet, soft Australian drawl.

'No Henry, you've done it all yourself. Don't praise life. Praise yourself.'

The man was quite accustomed to being patronised but to receive it from such a source, not known for any great reserves of intelligence or profundity, it came as something of a pleasant surprise. The cynic within him said that she must have read something similar in her magazine not a few minutes before, but the human in him decided to give her a little more credit. He threw a crooked grin across at her.

'Give us a kiss darling and tell me you love me.'

The voice rasped from deep inside a throat that had swallowed the smoke of a million cigarettes and a sea of alcohol. She, being only a foot away on a towel spread on the deck, rolled towards him with lips pursed, sunglasses held out in one hand and magazine in the other, eyes closed. As he leaned towards her the tinkle of ice in his glass and the rattle of his gold bracelet were musical embellishments to a scene that could only be constructed with money and power, cemented firmly together with a bottomless pit of the same.

'I love you Henry,' she murmured, which would have satisfied him if she hadn't added, 'you know that.'

He laughed out loud, throwing his head back. 'You're a liar Janie! A bloody liar! And not even a good one!'

'Henry!' protested the girl, 'that's not fair.'

'I know it's not,' spluttered Henry, sitting upright and grinning at her, 'but I'm prepared to live with it.'

He swung his bowed legs around over the edge of his sun bed and resting grey hairy forearms on hairy thighs, stared her in the face.

'Now, look me in the eyes and tell me you love me. Go on. Tell me straight that if this ugly mush, this bald head, this pot belly, this withering skin, these bandy legs and this cockney accent were poured inside the uniform of a London bus driver whose pay just covered the bare necessities - like it used to forty years ago - tell me you'd still love me. Go on, tell me the truth.'

The challenge was an unfair one and the poor girl was thrown. She sat up and stared sullenly across at the island that seemed to her the sort of place that she'd prefer to be at this moment. The man slumped back onto his bed, picked up his glass, took a long swig, wiped the back of his hand across his mouth, slotted a pair of sunglasses over his eyes and said, 'Don't take it personally darling. I don't mean it. You know me, call a spade a shovel, no harm meant. You're young, beautiful, got a lifetime ahead of you and need all the money you can lay your hands on without working too hard. Don't be ashamed. We all come into the world with different assets and the trick is to use 'em best we can. That's life.'

She shrugged sulkily and acceded. 'I suppose, if you say so.'

'Good,' said Henry, 'now we have mutual respect and understanding, the basis for every successful relationship. I'm old, batting out me innings with more dosh than I know what to do with….' He spread his hands in a flamboyant gesture, 'so what have we got?'

The girl shrugged and said with absolute truth, 'I don't know.'

'We got L-O-V-E, LOVE!' expostulated Henry, opening his arms wide to demonstrate the extent of it and in the process laughing and nearly choking. Between recovering coughs, he continued. 'Look, it's not the sort of love you're thinking of, not your Mills and Boon crap, but it's still love. You love what I got and…' With this he leaned over and tapped her ankle, '…and I

85

love what you got. Simple ain't it. I love to pay for your love and you love to take the money. For love or money or for the love of money - what's the difference?'

The Money-Lover was somewhat lost in this tangle of words.

'I don't understand what you're talking about half the time Henry. Sometimes you talk in riddles. I think I understand but often when you've finished I don't know what you've said. You're such a funny man.'

Henry chuckled and slid his hand up to squeeze the top of her thigh, letting it rest there. 'That's why I'm where I am darling.' He spoke softly and sincerely and spread his arms wide again to signify that all around them was a proliferation of what he was about to elaborate on.

'You see, you talk big, but you talk - as you say - in riddles. Sounds impressive but they haven't got a clue what you're on about. And do you know what?'

The girl knew from experience that Henry was about to launch into what amounted to no more than a soliloquy; an uninterrupted, self-indulgent luxury afforded to the rich and powerful by their subjects who knew better than to attempt to utter a word. The subjects' role was no more than to act as a buffer, requiring nothing more or less from them than a nod, shake of the head or quiet gasp of amazement to satisfy their keeper.

'Most of 'em, *all* of 'em I'd say, in fact,' continued Henry, 'are so stupid they haven't got the guts to admit it. They nod, they grin, as if to say "oh yeah Henry, we getcha," but they're too stupid and gutless to question you. Don't like to seem ignorant y'see. They gotta play the smart-arse, never show they ain't up with it.' He shook his head and sneered with contempt. 'And do you know my real secret Janie love?'

The use of her name made her feel comfortable again, so she smiled.

'No Henry.'

'I don't care. I don't give a stuff what people think. I'm from 'umble beginnings, back streets of London, no airs and graces. If I don't know what someone's on about I say "what the fuck are you talking about?" Disarms 'em, throws 'em completely. The Emperor's New Clothes, that's what it's about. The whole bloody world's nothing but a hoi polloi of sheep, nodding dogs, kow-towing bastards; apart from the few, that is, with the money and power.'

'What Emperor?' asked Janie, remembering what Henry had just said about honesty and fearing further questioning on the particular subject of Emperors. Henry looked at her in disbelief until his expression transformed into one of resignation.

'The crowd in the story; everyone in the crowd cheers at the gear the Emperor weren't even wearing just because they think they should. Then a little boy sittin' on his dad's shoulders pipes up and says "Oi, he's got sod all on! The Emperor's bleedin' starkers!" Y'see? The kid's the only one who don't know he's not allowed to say what his own eyes are telling him is the truth.' Henry peered out to sea. 'Innocence - it all goes when we grow up - becomes pretence - we're all actors. The world's nothing but a stage, and all that caper.'

The idea of a stark naked Emperor and Henry's unique cockney rendition of the story appealed to Janie's simple sense of humour and she giggled saucily, whilst the moral of the story landed safely on stony ground. Henry, suddenly reminded of her sexual presence, returned his hand to her thigh and dipped the fingertips of his other hand into his glass to dribble the cold liquid onto his perspiring forehead. The late sun seemed as if it had gathered strength, causing him to overheat. He was aware that he was again being loud and boastful, aware that he was only holding her attention because of who he was, aware that most of what he was saying was just part of the armour, the smokescreen that had forged his success. Aware, above all, that it was not him, not truly him. Betty had been the only one who could read him like a book, for she was the co-author of his life since the day they'd fled to Australia. She'd penned most of his lines until he knew them so well he'd become almost self-sufficient. Only with her was he totally honest, for anything less was to insult her. She knew his thoughts almost before he thought them. For over forty years she'd been his only true love, and his only lover.

'That's me,' he murmured vacantly.

'Beg yours?' said the girl.

'I said that's me, the little boy - seeing is believin' - total honesty - nothing less - don't take nobody's word. If you see it, it's happening. If you don't see it, then who's to know if it happened or not? Trust is as rare as hens' teeth in business and the dirtier the business, the less you trust anyone. I've got hotels, clubs, massage parlours and strip joints from Cape York to Coolangatta and not one of 'em owes me a cent. I check the books of every one every month, personally. I've got an accountant who checks my accountant and the first accountant hasn't got a clue. That's why they used to keep changing 'cos they kept trying to fiddle me. But they only do it once, then God 'elp 'em. I shop 'em to the taxman and before they know where they are, not only haven't they got a job or a business but they're in the soft and smelly up to their eyeballs. I got nuthin' to hide, nuthin! Everything declared, nuthin' fiddled, pay my taxes and share it all around. The Great Philanthropist! I love it!' He barked a hoarse laugh, coughed into his fist and thumped the frame of his sun bed, wincing in pain. 'Total honesty, that's all I ask - only way to run a business.' He coughed again, cleared his throat and staring once more out to sea, muttered almost indistinctly, 'Only way to run life.'

Janie's concentration was being tested to the limits. She hid a yawn behind her magazine and shook her head in mock amazement.

'Did you know Betty?' asked Henry suddenly.

The question took a short while to register. The girl wasn't expecting to be drawn back into a conversational role quite so quickly and with a finger marking the page in her magazine, was longing to find out what Paul Hogan's wife thought of him.

'Betty? Wasn't she your wife? Did all the bookings and arranging stuff?'

'Yep, did the bookings and arranging stuff, as you say. Wife? We never married…but yeah, as good as. Better.'

'Didn't she die or something?'

Henry stiffened and wanted to throw his drink over her for her callous, thoughtless question. '...or something.' Stupid dumb bitch, how dare she! But he paused a while and answered, 'Last Christmas Day; year tomorrow.'

Janie rubbed sunscreen into an arm, picked a tiny fly off her skin and said with equal indifference to the memory of Henry's beloved, 'Then I couldn't have known her. I didn't start stripping until Easter Sunday.'

Henry quietly forgave her and even found some humour in the religious connection between the two events. She was just another pretty schoolgirl who'd decided to take the easy life and help guarantee his dollars kept rolling in. She didn't do it to listen to old men who thought they had all the answers. But that was tough. He wanted to talk about Betty, a subject he'd avoided since her death, as had everyone surrounding him. This simple creature rubbing in cream and listening because she had to, devoid in his eyes of a sensitive or serious thought, an ounce of diplomacy or intelligence, was the perfect sponge to soak up his past year of introspection and recrimination. Yes, now was the time and his heart beat fast as his mind flipped through the pages of his life whilst his companion opened the pages of her magazine and sucked through a straw. But five minutes later the magazine was placed to one side. Henry had his audience in the palm of his hand.

He told her about the woman he had married in wartime London. He told her of the nights when he would return home happy-drunk and how his wife, Irma (how the name lodged in his throat) would verbally and physically attack him with all the spite and crockery she could muster. How he never had the inclination to retaliate but just took it - anything for a peaceful life, anything to avoid the indignity of conflict. A glimmer of light shone in his eyes when he related how Betty Mathieson had come into his life and changed him. How, amidst the D-Day celebrations, they had planned their escape to Australia and within weeks were immersed in the excitement of the train ride to Southampton, making plans for a future together far, far away down under. How Betty's husband, who was also his best friend, had been killed in an air raid right beside him one awful night; he showed the girl the long scar on the inside of his upper left arm from the shrapnel of the blast, a wound which she knew well but had never queried. Then he spoke of the overwhelming love and sense of freedom on the ship as they sailed across the world to their new life, a journey tinged with the sadness of his betrayal of Henry Junior, a five year old boy bereft of self-esteem if ever there was one, a child he'd selfishly left behind to the wicked manipulation of his evil wife - The Witch, as he and Betty called her from thereon.

There followed a long pause as Henry lay unmoving, deep in his thoughts, and the girl by his side knew it was a time to say nothing whilst he silently reflected. It was five minutes before he left his reverie and resumed. He revealed the clandestine visit he'd made to England eight years ago. How he had surveyed, undetected, the clockwork comings and goings of his own son, a pathetic figure grown no more confident with adulthood than he'd been as a child; a wreck of a human being bearing all the scars of one ground into total submission by the woman who tried so hard to do the same to him. He then told how he had followed his son to work one day from the house at 52 Viola Street, sat opposite him in the train carriage to Charing Cross wanting so much to speak to him but, swallowing back wave after wave of emotion and guilt, unable to. How he had followed him across the concourse, watched as he bought a newspaper and then an apple at the fruit and flower stall outside and heard his own son's adult voice for the first time; a voice that, as he chatted to the genial fruit vendor who sold the apple and called him Henry, didn't have his own cockney brogue but spoke soft and gentle, almost 'posh' in his bumbling, polite way. He had closed his eyes and realised it could easily be the voice of someone who had made it in life, given half a chance.

He then told of how he had followed his son's waddling gait through the rush hour crowds, left down towards Whitehall, desperate to catch up with him and touch his shoulder and tell him that everything would be alright from now on, but Henry had suddenly turned right into the grand office of a government department building and the opportunity was not only lost but the father knew he would never see his son again. The next day he was at Heathrow, bag in hand, a heart of lead, a head full of plans to change his son's life.

Janie had never seen her old lover anything but the man in charge of his life and affairs, a man respected but never crossed, a man seemingly insulated from normal human emotions. Now she watched silently as he seemed to age in front of her, his body contracting like a dead spider, his face wizened and contorted as he fought back tears, shaking with the effort of holding on to his reputation and dignity.

Finally he swallowed hard, took a deep breath and nodded several times before telling her of the vow he had made as he stood outside the building in Whitehall, searching the office windows for a glimpse of his son; a vow to recompense him for all that he had suffered by his father's desertion. How one day Henry Junior would inherit all his worldly goods and how it would make a man of him as indeed the building of his empire had done just that for him. It could be said that a self-made man would expect his son to labour before he tasted the fruits of his father's hard-earned success, but no, that wasn't how Henry saw it; for he had been given Betty without whom he would have been no better than his downtrodden son who came and went from Viola Street, just as he had thirty five years earlier.

There followed a prolonged silence, broken only by the cry of gulls and the waves slopping against the side of the yacht. Janie, the model, a study in wide-eyed astonishment and Henry, the man, shaking with the nervous excitement of his revelations. The girl was the first to speak.

'I think you need a drink Henry. You've turned a bit pale.'

Henry shook his head to clear it and wrung his hands before rubbing one roughly up and down his other arm, unaware for a moment of where he was or what he was doing.

'Thanks darling, I do feel a bit queasy. Too much sun. My back's burning.'

She responded immediately, picking up the sun cream and moving quickly to his side. His hands were shaking and his lips quivering.

'Stay where you are, I'll do it. You don't look good at all.'

She rubbed the cream gently into his reddening shoulders and stroked his neck with the other hand as a comfort when he winced with the pain. He looked up at her and placed a hand on her back, just above the waist; gently, affectionately stroking. There was now tenderness in her touch he noticed, tenderness not motivated by money. She was feminine and sensitive and the look on her flawless face and the touch of her fingertips told him she now understood him. He had chosen her as a listener because of her dumbness, and in opening his heart had brought out the woman. Baring his weaknesses to one who was not aware he had any meant she could respond as every woman wants to respond. He was, she now understood, a vulnerable man, and she wanted to say something sincere and reassuring but words didn't come easy to her.

The silk sheets that they retired between were soon marked with the grease and sweat from their skins but the moment had not provided for showering and was all the better for it.

'You look better now,' said the young girl, 'you've got some colour back in your face.'

She stroked his cheek with the back of a fingertip, her hand supporting her head as she lay on her side next to him.

'I should bloody think so,' he gasped, laughing through a cough, 'jeez, that was hot work.'

'Work?' she teased.

'Work,' he affirmed. 'When you're my age girl, it's work. The little pleasure area down below might say it feels as good as it always did but the poor old ticker says "slow down mate, I can't keep up!" If you know what I mean.'

He looked at her and grinned impishly. She flashed a sweet smile, natural and uninhibited and he thought how delightful she was. Then a pain arrived in his chest and as he drove a hairy fist into it to help quell the agony, the thought entered his head that if this was the last thing he did on earth, he had little to regret. Apart from one thing; an oversight that in the vigour of good health and the velocity of his lifestyle, he'd failed to take care of.

'Janie,' he said, 'pass me the telephone will you please love?'

Her attention had been diverted whilst the pain had seized him and he'd made sure by the time she turned back that his fist was removed and his expression normal. She rolled to her side of the bed and rolled back with the telephone. Henry took it, frowning, trying to disguise the pain that had returned, as no more than an itch. But it travelled across his left shoulder and down his arm as he positioned the phone on the bed to dial.

'What's the time in England?' Henry asked, but could have been asking the time in Tibet or on the Moon for the blank look he received. Then the blank look changed to one of concern as the hand pressing hard into his chest and the tortured expression were impossible to hide. His colour had faded again, the deep tan that had returned during his recent exertion now sallow and clammy.

'Henry! You're ill! What's the matter?' The girl bent over her crumpled old lover and held his head and desperately kissed his forehead. 'Henry! Sit up! Please!'

The man raised himself breathlessly onto his right elbow and laughed. 'Shit!' he winced, 'bloody indigestion! Now look up Bodger and Snapes in this book for me please Janie darling, and read out the number. There's two numbers. Give me the one that says *Bodger Home*. It's 001144 something.'

The pain had now passed into his jaw and he gasped with the effort of speech. Beads of sweat pumped from his forehead and down the side of his face. Janie, flashing glances from address book to Henry and back again, found the page in seconds. She read out the number and he dialled and settled back on the pillows, panting, listening to the line connecting. They stared at each other, gripped by tension, only the ISD pips and then a ringing tone and Henry's laboured breathing breaking the silence. Henry, his jaw and mouth now set rigid, stared ahead at the cabin wall and began to inhale deeply through distended nostrils, desperately trying to relax his mind and body. Slowly, he shook his head back and forth in weary, agonised frustration.

'I changed my will eight years ago after seeing my boy in London. I changed it, leaving everything to him. I sent it to my English solicitor, David Bodger, and a letter to Henry explaining everything about Betty and me, about a secret we'd kept for all those years since we left England, but...but...I never heard back from 'em, neither of 'em. Just assumed that Henry didn't want to know me, the father that abandoned him - but not hearing from my solicitor was a mystery. Betty kept on at me to chase him but I was always too damn busy. Just assumed he'd got it and didn't think there was any need to confirm. How stupid! How bloody stupid! Me, the great businessman! The great idiot!'

He turned his face, now deathly pale, slowly towards the girl. 'For all I know...everything's still in her name. The Witch!'

His face darkened, eyes blazing with self-recrimination and anger, as he lifted the phone above his head and mustering what little strength he could, hurled it across the room.

'No stuffin' answer!' he screamed.

The phone dislodged a picture on the wall which slid down and thudded on the wooden floor, the glass remaining intact. He thumped his chest repeatedly, face contorted. The girl threw her arms around his shoulders and buried her head in his neck, sobbing and repeating his name.

Gently he lifted her head and kissed her hair. 'Janie darling, can you pass the dictation machine?' He nodded to the chest of drawers. 'It's in the top drawer, under my shirts.'

Within seconds the small Philips machine was in his hand and he was fumbling with one hand, trying to press record. 'Go outside love. This is private. Please.'

'But Henry, I can't leave you in....'

'Go! Now! And shut the door behind you!' The effort of shouting left him clutching at his chest and wincing in agony. The girl slowly got up and kissed the shiny brown dome of his head, lingering for a moment before walking to the steps leading up to the deck, pausing briefly to look back.

'Thank you,' he whispered, and smiled at her, his eyes now warm and kind, barely open. She smiled back and walked up the steps and out onto the hot deck, closing the door quietly but firmly behind her.

Ten minutes later, when she tapped on the door and cautiously entered, Henry was dead. The girl moved calmly to his side, knew instantly that he had gone, gently closed his eyelids, saw the machine was still running, pressed the stop button and lay down beside him, stroking his saturated head. Then, wrapping her soft, slender arms around his body she lay there to keep him warm, until he grew cold.

Chapter Eight

## COURT OUT

The worn, stone steps of Bow Street Magistrates Court had over their distinguished career peered up at the soles of many famous personages; Casanova, Casement, Crippen, the Krays, the Pankhursts and possibly most infamous of all, Oscar Wilde, had stepped across them - some no doubt flying over jauntily, anticipating nothing but success, whilst others dragged across in dismal resignation of their fate. But never had the steps been graced with the rain-spattered Tufs of Henry Winston Scroggins, shoes that had for some years not been on speaking terms with his trousers apart from a brief hello as the latter passed by daily on their way to or from a hanger or chair-back.

The rain tippled steadily down from leaden grey skies reflecting the sombre mood of Henry as he stood blinking at the human traffic hunched against the elements on their way to wherever normal law-abiding people went in London. Up until yesterday he had been one of them and had never for a moment stopped to consider just how law-abiding everyone looked until he wasn't one of them. Now he was sure the mark of Cain was branded on his forehead and, unable to leave the spot where Millicent had told him to wait for her, he was intent on trying to look as invisible as possible, standing far enough away from the entrance to disassociate himself with any attachment to the building and whistling and squinting skywards like a mole that has inadvertently popped up in the middle of a bowling green on match day and can't reverse fast enough.

Through misty, spattered lenses the little bald hatless man read the date inscribed above the doors; eighteen-seventy-nine; and having read this several times decided to count the small pillars on the concrete balustrade immediately above. There were ten, so he counted them again as was his golden rule in the Department. It was impossible for him to count anything once. Count twice, write once, a maxim that had stood him in good stead throughout his career but oh, how he had wished many times that he'd something similarly reliable when picking horses.

Having now run out of distractions to temporarily divert the panic poised to gush past the sluice gate of his brain, the slam of a car door and sight of Millicent Carter's fur-clad back bending into the driver's window of a taxi, reminded him that he wasn't alone in the world. It had seemed an eternity since she'd left him there, not just the five minutes she told him she needed to make a brief call, this being the call to Constable Steele to receive his confirmation that the notes concerning her own arrest were in fact 'lost'.

Concerning taxis, Henry had avoided them like the Plague in his years commuting to London. The thought of actually being forced to endure a one-to-one conversation with a total stranger alone in a car was bad enough, but an even more terrifying prospect was of not having enough money to pay what he imagined would be an extortionate fare. The nightmare image he'd created of the taxi driver whistling up a policeman (who of course would inevitably be standing just feet away in readiness) had always mortified Henry beyond words and whilst the need for a taxi had rarely arisen in Henry's clockwork existence, it was a fact that he'd made a pledge to himself that sooner than risk the almost certain embarrassment of taxi-travel he would walk anywhere, even all the way home to Lewisham barefoot through a blizzard in the wee small hours, if necessary. So in more ways than one this was indeed a day of unwelcome firsts for Henry.

Amongst those 'firsts' was the night, or remaining hours until he finally awoke, spent on the sofa at the home of Millicent Carter, which would without doubt remain in his memory long after the small, round, inflamed impression of a button from the cushion that had served as a pillow, had faded from his cheek.

To elaborate on what had followed Millicent's well laid plans of packing Henry off home and spending Christmas alone with George would take another chapter, but can be briefly summarised as follows:

Millicent returned after no more than five minutes in the shower to find Henry slumped and snoring half on and half off her sofa, George in close and watchful attendance. She had then attempted three times to rouse him, including two quite rough slaps to the cheek, none of which had the slightest effect on the comatose man, or corpse as she for a while thought she had on her hands until checking his pulse. Millicent then dragged him, ably abetted by George excitedly yelping and nipping at Henry's trouser turn-ups, into a position as close to prostrate as she could manage given that the weight was dead, so to speak, and the body totally incapable of providing any assistance to itself.

After sitting and watching the potential corpse for twenty minutes, with both herself and George alert to any slight sign of consciousness, she had placed a blanket over him, shaken her head and gone to bed, setting her alarm for eight and sinking beneath her duvet with Lady Chatterley and her lover. George, taken by blissful surprise when lifted and dumped on Millicent's bed, would spend the night in utter comfort and contentment, hardly daring to move an eyelid for fear that the treat might end and he be dispatched to his basket in a corner of the lounge. Millicent had decided that having George in with her was far preferable to the potential savaging Henry might endure if he moved a muscle or made a sound in his sleep. Death by shock might have solved all Henry's problems in one sharp hit but she didn't really want the responsibility and mess that went with it. So, with her mind trying desperately to think of a solution about what to do with her human burden come daybreak, a very happy dog trying to meld into the duvet, Millicent found the place in her book where she'd been interrupted some three hours earlier and read the same paragraph three times without absorbing a single word, before sinking into the deepest of sleeps.

And so it was that Millicent's life from that moment changed beyond anything she could have imagined in her wildest dreams. Once again her determined and carefully thought out plan, which Henry had quietly accepted on waking up to the cold light of day - a plan to accompany him to court and give what advice and moral support she could before he caught a train back to Lewisham and God knows what - was about to be shot to pieces.

And as for Henry, what happened next as he stood pondering the dreaded unknown that lay beyond the doors of Bow Street Magistrates Court, was also to become a major pivotal point such as everyone experiences at some time or other; one of many seemingly minor crossroad moments that send the straight and narrow plotline of our lives spiralling elsewhere. There are some of course, through an adventurous or reckless nature, who invite more crossroads and sidetracks than others, but there could be little doubting that on Henry's Highway of Life, so few major slip roads or exit opportunities were ever encouraged or provided, that this momentous event on this memorable day could only be described as truly, dramatically - pivotal! And as usually happens with people like Henry, the decision had little or nothing whatsoever to do with him.

At the very moment Millicent finalised the transaction with the taxi driver and turned to look for Henry, it happened that the figure of a tall, distinguished-looking, silver-haired gentleman in a long, billowing navy overcoat embellished with velvet collar, rushed past her. On spotting Henry, the man stopped and confronted him, immediately pouring out a tirade of abuse and threats, violently jabbing a finger repeatedly into the untidy yellow knot of a scarf that poked from Henry's grey mackintosh until it looked as though the poor man was going to tumble backwards onto the wet pavement. People stopped and heads turned to stare at the terrible scene, so unusual a sight was it on the normally civilised streets of London in the middle of the day. Millicent, with eyes blazing and a deep inhale sucking through her distended nostrils (not dissimilar to a Grand National horse that has just finished the course, but lost) strode towards the two men - but alas, strode not quite fast enough, thus providing a foxy-faced, bespectacled individual clutching a brown leather briefcase time to grab Henry's adversary by the elbow and with a whispered word in his ear, steer him rapidly and determinedly over the stone step and through the door of the Court.

Now, if Millicent had a chance to see the man's face, which she didn't, she would have first noticed a purple eye, swollen cheekbone and what could possibly be a broken nose. She would then have recognised the features temporarily camouflaged by these injuries as belonging to one of her regular clients; a man, who like so many others across London, owed his marriage and career to her absolute discretion; discretion without which he and they would be despatched to marital and professional oblivion. (It's worth noting therefore that this made Millicent, alongside Margaret Thatcher - who according to a member of her all male cabinet (in his diary) kept all 'her men' in perfect check with the rise and fall of her bosom - potentially the most powerful woman in England and possibly therefore, the World.)

If Millicent *had* arrived five seconds earlier and if she *did* see these things, then the following half an hour in court would have been avoided. But she hadn't and she didn't, thus forcing Henry to endure the most humiliating experience of his life, even trumping his drunken foray of the previous evening. However, if Henry's humiliation was deep, it was at least short-lived, for nothing on this earth could compare to the humiliation and abject terror about to be thrust upon the afore-mentioned silver-haired, distinguished-looking gentleman seated in the same court who had only moments earlier been poking a finger into Henry's beleaguered scarf.

After Henry had quickly explained to Millicent that his angry attacker was the ex-boss he'd allegedly assaulted the previous evening (allegedly because Henry still had no clear recollection of anything), the two had entered the building and had just time for Millicent to revise with Henry the brief instructions she'd imparted in the taxi about the court procedure and protocol, before he was called and entered the dock shaking like an autumn leaf about to drop and wither. His voice could hardly be heard and his tear-stained eyes hardly focus on the scene that surrounded him as he looked around in shame and dejection. He knew he was doomed to some dreadful period of damnation but far worse to come before that everlasting sentence was the Purgatory of his mother's tongue.

And so it was that as the clouds that fuddled Henry's brain transformed into a melancholic daze of acceptance with the reading of the charges against him, followed by the arresting officer's glib statement and the high, nasal, accusing staccato of Peregrine Spencer's barrister, he was convinced that his life was now over and the judge's black cap a mere formality.

Thus anaesthetised, he floated up above the melee of benches, papers and heads into a slightly premature out of body experience, looking down at himself standing bound in an open cart pulled along Oxford Street in the fateful direction of Tyburn. He could feel the jolt of the potholes beneath him as the bent and bony head of an old nag trotted him to his swinging end. He saw a clear image of his white, podgy stripped body twirling at the end of a rope, Marks and Spencer socks and Y-fronts providing the only remnants of dignity as the baying crowd screamed and mocked until, growing bored, they slowly dispersed to let him hang over for a day as was the grizzly custom.

Hangover! He recollected from his library of useless information the origin of the word; hanged felons left to dangle overnight after being permitted one last drink on their final journey to the gallows, *one for the road*, and he thought what cruel irony it was that this fuzz still lingering in his brain, his one and only hangover, should lead directly to - his last.

So there he twirled above the rush hour traffic around Marble Arch, his mother's wagging finger below chastising him to his very last pop-eyed gasp, until...he thought he heard a woman cough. Yes, a cough it was. And then another cough, this time louder. The cough seemed to come from the area in the court where he'd seen Millicent take a seat, the court that thankfully he'd now returned to (only by his own Theory of Relativity where courtroom humiliation outshone hanging), but he couldn't be sure of the cough's precise location as the combination of tears and damp, dirty lenses were keeping his visibility down to approximately three yards beyond his nose. The next cough was then overlapped by a deep male groan directly ahead of him and Henry, removing his glasses and blinking several times, saw a blurred Peregrine Spencer and his barrister sitting opposite locked in frantic conversation.

Yes, just as in the rush of entering the building, Spencer's face had been obscured from Millicent's view, so had hers been obscured when Spencer had been somewhat taken aback to see an attractive well-dressed woman bent talking in earnest to Henry with what appeared to be more than just a professional interest. But giving it no further serious thought Spencer had taken his place in blissful ignorance as Millicent had taken her place away from his direct view and his diverted mind. That is until the lady had looked up, performed a wholly disbelieving double take at the man smugly peering at Henry through his undamaged eye whilst nodding sagely at his barrister's whisper, and realised to her utter amazement just who Henry's accuser was! She could think of nothing else to do to bring matters to an immediate halt but cough; so she coughed. But not any cough, not a single or quietly stifled cough as the court was accustomed to hearing this time of the year, but a repeated exaggerated cough that left little doubt of its purpose. Peregrine Spencer, concentrating on the message being relayed into his ear, was possibly the last person in the courtroom to notice the origin of the cough but no sooner had he gazed nonchalantly across to see what the fuss was about, did his mouth drop open and his one good eye 'pop'. A second later the little man by his side winced as his thin arm was seized in a vice-like grip and *his* ear became the receiver.

Everything then appeared to leap into fast forward through Henry's restricted vision as first a murmur crept around the courtroom followed by a bustle of moving silk, a soft gabble of voices, a clearing of a throat, a bustle of returning silk, a rapping of a hammer, and finally a loud gruff announcement of 'Case dismissed!'

Henry's head pivoted like a blind man caught in a revolving door. This was too much, one minute on the gallows and the next a free man - or so it seemed. And whilst his own private drama quietly abated, Millicent glared across at another rather more public drama gathering momentum. To the quaking, perspiring figure of Peregrine Spencer who at that precise moment was drawing a monogrammed silk handkerchief from his top pocket and mopping his glistening brow whilst chairs scraped and babblings built to a rapid crescendo as a foxy-faced barrister nervously stuffed papers into a briefcase and snapped the clasp shut with a loud *click!*

Millicent Carter's comforting smile, which beamed out from beside the figure of the recently-acquitted on whose shoulder she rested a hand, transformed into a tight-lipped glare of serious intent as she looked across at Spencer and jerked her head and thumb in vigorous unison towards the door. Peregrine Spencer knew that the owner of the jerking thumb and piercing eyes was about to issue some unequivocal instructions; instructions that he was in no doubt he was about to assent to readily and wholeheartedly. But first Millicent had to deposit Henry somewhere out of view for a short while and if Spencer had any doubts about what was going on, the sight of her turning and talking to the pathetic figure of his Department subordinate and placing a comforting arm around his shoulder whilst the subordinate stared ahead and nodded, would have made things perfectly clear. In Spencer's mind there could be only one obvious deduction; he, Peregrine Spencer, had worked twenty years with either a beloved relation or lifelong friend of a woman whose bed he had been sharing for almost as long! The very thought sent a shudder down his spine, first of disbelief, second of revulsion, but most importantly - of intense fear.

Settling Henry safely onto a bench in the corridor, Millicent returned to where she'd ordered Spencer and his irritated little barrister to wait for her. She then spent two minutes addressing the quivering man and his somewhat dazed legal eagle in a manner that could leave no doubt by their compliant listening and nodding, that the lady was in charge of matters. Several attempts to interrupt by the barrister were hastily halted by a raised hand from Spencer who of course had every reason on earth to keep his secret the domain of just two people. She concluded her lecture by plucking two business cards from her handbag, placing one firmly in the hand of each man and with a final word and fawning nod of agreement from Spencer, turned with a glorious beam of pinched-lipped victory to attend to her waiting 'client'.

As her high heels clacked along the hard corridor and turned the corner to where Henry sat on his bench like a naughty schoolboy outside the headmaster's office, she silently applauded herself. 'Millicent, my girl,' she thought, as Henry flashed her an instant smile of recognition, 'you are indeed *the* best solicitor in town!' And at that very moment, she probably was. Henry, a man of forty who had never loved or been loved in his life, let alone known the slightest degree of serious affection, felt his heart, soul and spirit leap collectively into Millicent's care as her fingertips gently rested on his shoulder and her serene, crimson-lipped comforting face beamed down into his. Already, without even a conscious thought, he didn't know how he could face a day, an hour even, without her. Not only was she a solicitor par excellence, not only had she for some inexplicable reason offered him his first awakening of a dormant libido (not currently recognised as such, or in operation), but above all, and for whatever reason he currently had no clue, she had offered him kindness and friendship on a level he never realised existed.

'Come on Henry. I think we need a stiff drink to celebrate your freedom.'

Millicent took Henry's arm and exchanged a fleeting glance with the two men who walked hurriedly past them towards the old worn stone steps. Then, as the little man rose unsteadily to his feet, she tidied his scarf and picked cotton off his lapel, stopping short of spitting on her fingers to smarten his hair - there being none to smarten. Tossing the cotton to the floor she slid her arm through his and walked beside him towards daylight and goodness knows what, but with a distinct feeling that she'd just signed adoption papers at a rescue centre.

The very last thing on this planet that Henry Scroggins needed at that moment was the very thing that had landed him where he was, a drink, but his protests were in vain. Within seconds the people strolling and striding about their business up and down Bow Street felt smiles creep upon their lips at the sight of a lady who, if she stood still for a moment and posed, could quite easily be mistaken for a mannequin in a Bond Street or Champs Elysees window, marching arm in arm across the road with a man who could quite easily be mistaken for a cross between Charlie Chaplin and Mr Pickwick.

Henry tottered along the pavement with Millicent's arm linked through his, more for protection than affection, and peered about him at a part of London that whilst so close to his place of work for twenty years, might just as well have been any city in the world, his mental A-Z extending no further than a triangle whose three points of Charing Cross Station, Whitehall office and William Hill's betting shop in Shaftesbury Avenue, were surveyed by the imposing figure of Lord Nelson perched on his column, a man whose understanding and compassion for the 'Henry Scroggins' of the world was renowned.

Suddenly, without warning, the current Henry Scroggins found himself almost dragged off his feet as Millicent Carter took a sudden left turn through a door, momentarily forgetting to inform her companion of her intentions. Henry had no time at all to see where he was being dragged before he was seated at a small round table next to the window in a public house.

'Hair of the dog Henry - it'll do you good,' said Millicent several minutes later as she sat down next to him, handbag tucked under her arm and three glasses clutched between her hands, one containing water and the others whisky and soda and gin and tonic, having ignored his pleas for just a glass of water. 'It's drowned in ginger so can't hurt you.'

'It'll do you good...' mumbled Henry, staring vacantly at the glass, 'that's what that awful woman said to me last night.' He peered down at the brown liquid like Socrates eyeing his cup of hemlock, and shook his head, which was instantly followed by a violent shudder the length of his body as the smell of whiskey swept up his nostrils.

'Ugh, no thank you Millicent. I can't. I really think I'd be sick. In fact I don't think, I *know* I'd be sick. It's vile stuff. But thank you anyway.'

Millicent frowned at the glass and looked around to where an old man in a battered brown overcoat and matching hat sat in animated conversation with himself, his three grey, stubble-covered chins wobbling up and down as he put a point to one of his selves only to have it disputed vehemently by another. The empty glass in front of him to which the conversation was directed, was obviously the subject of the dispute, possibly as to whether it deserved the honour of being refilled, or more to the point whether the tight-fisted Exchequer in his ragged pocket would permit such a thing. The dispute, before it had a chance to develop further, was quickly settled by the arrival of a full glass delivered in the delicate hand of Millicent who cheerily declared 'Happy Christmas!' with a radiant smile, and returned to her seat.

'You lucky boy, Ben,' called out the barman who had observed the scene whilst flushing a beer pump. Ben, his heated argument with himself brought to a sudden halt, stared at the glass for a moment, then sniffed and turned to shower Millicent with the broadest, beaming smile that betrayed a distinct deficiency in the incisor department.

'Blimey, m'darling, and a merry Christmas to you too!' he cried out, and picking up the glass took a small testing swig before holding it critically at arm's length, licking and smacking his lips and observing 'not too particular about American Dry but …' and with a concessionary nod at the drink, threw open his parched gullet and downed the contents in one.

'Ungrateful old devil,' muttered Millicent and turned to Henry. 'Are you sure you won't have anything else before we go? Nuts, crisps? You must be starving.'

Henry shook his head and said he was fine; really he was fine, thank you. But the words 'before we go' had sent a ripple of tiny shock waves to his stomach.

Millicent, suddenly recalling Henry's earlier remark asked, 'What did you mean by "that's what that awful woman said to me last night?" What awful woman?'

'The woman at the office party. The one in the photograph. Didn't I tell you about her?'

Millicent shook her head. 'You haven't told me anything apart from you went to your office party and got drunk for the first time. Apart from the charges read out, which I must confess I find hard to believe, I know nothing of what happened before.'

Henry fumbled in his raincoat pocket and took out the now crumpled Polaroid which he handed to Millicent.

'They took this photo and put it in my pocket, I suppose hoping my mother would find it. They know all about her I'm afraid. Twenty years in the same office makes it very difficult for even someone like me to have secrets.'

Millicent stared at the photo for a few seconds, turned it around and upside down, then frowning, decided she had it the right way up in the first place. She saw Henry's head and arms pinned back behind him by several pairs of hands, a study in abject terror staring at a bottle of whiskey held over his tightly closed mouth, and what appeared to be his spectacles just visible in someone's hand. Millicent's breathing deepened as anger welled up at the outrage. Her eyes then concentrated on the oversized breasts thrust into Henry's face, two pure white bulbous mounds overflowing the lowest of red necklines. The woman's face was mostly hidden, just a pair of swollen red lips to match the size of the breasts and colour of the dress, but turned up in a drunken leer with a hideous slug of a tongue hanging out from one side. The whole scene reminded Millicent of a public school initiation, a fresher torn from the security of his home life and within days forced into ritual humiliation for the sport of a mindless few.

'*They* did this to you?' she said.

Henry nodded. 'It was horrible. I've never been to an office party before and only went to this one to annoy my mother...and...and...it backfired.'

Millicent turned and looked at him incredulously. 'To annoy your mother? At your age? Why would you do that? Don't you get on?'

'Get on?' said Henry with a small scoffing laugh, 'if only it was just a case of not getting on. You don't 'get on' with my mother. Nobody 'gets on' with my mother. Everyone 'puts up' with my mother. The fact is I hate her. I hate her as much as anyone can hate anyone. More. She's a witch!'

Millicent thought for a moment. 'Nobody hates their mother Henry. Hates a very unpleasant word.'

'And she's a very unpleasant person. Despicable. In fact I'd go as far as to say she's truly evil.' Henry turned his sad eyes to

Millicent and swallowed. 'You know they say that some people are born evil…'

Millicent shrugged. 'I don't believe it. I think that if…'

Henry interrupted. 'No, no, Millicent, I'm afraid you're wrong and if you met my mother you'd believe it. Trust me, she's the personification of evil, I wish I could say something nice about her - of course I'd like to, she gave birth to me, somehow - but there's nothing good to say. Do you want me to list her qualifications? Even Pol Pot would have to throw up his hands and concede victory if there was a contest. Hitler, Stalin and Attila wouldn't even be in the running.'

His reporting of this colourful, damning indictment of the woman whose womb he had spent nine months inside, using despots from history to back-up his case and all so seriously and emphatically delivered, found Millicent forced to hide a smile behind her hand. Henry continued, now in full unstoppable flow.

'Five minutes in her company and you'd know what I meant. She's just a thoroughly nasty person without any redeeming qualities and quite frankly, and you'll not like to hear this I know but…' Here he stopped and glanced around before lowering his voice and saying, '…I'd kill her today if I thought I'd get away with it. I would.' He nodded in strict affirmation then looked out of the window across the street and murmured softly and sincerely, 'I dream about it.'

At this point his expression glazed and a contented smile beamed from his eyes as he conjured up one of the many fittingly terrible ends to his tormentor that were stored in his head, before blinking himself back into the bar and saying, 'But I think I've done enough damage for the time being and I can't even afford to pay you for your soliciting work just yet. But I will, I promise.'

He suddenly remembered what Millicent had actually done for him and added quickly, 'I haven't told you how grateful I am to you for everything you've done. I don't know why you helped someone like me and to be honest I don't know why you're wasting time here now. But thank you and I apologise for dragging you into my stupid, shallow little life.'

'I haven't done much at all,' said Millicent, laying a hand reassuringly on his, 'and please don't worry about paying me anything. All I did was embarrass you last night and it's me that should be apologising. I have no idea what came over me.' She wasn't a lady to lie but felt one was required in this instance, so added, 'That was so entirely out of character, so shameful of me. I think we'd both had too much to drink.'

Henry swallowed, secretly regretful that what she did was out of character and induced by alcohol, and looked down at the small white hand with its pale blue veins the colour of his blotting paper and her long red shiny nails that weren't unlike the top of his pocket stapler. He inhaled deeply, straightened his back as if ready to ask a difficult question and, exhaling, did precisely that.

'Millicent, would you mind very much if...' and then followed an arrangement of words that twenty-four hours earlier would have been an impossible permutation for his teeth, tongue and lips to synchronise, '...if...if...I...' (a short clearing of the throat)...if I kissed you? Just a very small thank you one for Christmas that is.' He looked around self-consciously before adding, 'Please.'

Without hesitation she bent her face towards his and whispered, 'You can kiss me Henry, of course you can kiss me', and pursed her lips and closed her eyes.

'Oh no, just a cheek's enough,' said Henry, 'I know I disgust women and you might be ill when you think about it later, especially if you're eating your dinner, so a cheek will be perfect thank you.' And with that he licked his lips in preparation, immediately wished he hadn't, and, keeping his errant tongue well out of view, continued. 'They look so...so lovely and soft, like peach skins, and I know it's silly but I can't stop looking at them and wanting to...well, I've never kissed anyone in my life apart from (a shudder) my mother, and that was when she paid for a day at Epsom for me five years ago and...and...her cheeks are like...' He stopped and searched through his limited glossary of dried fruit before choosing '...prunes.'

Millicent cupped Henry's chin in her hands and touched his cheek with the faintest brush of her lips before pressing harder and lingering for enough time to ensure the memory became indelible. She had no idea where this relationship was going but even if the papers for the rescue centre were invalid, Henry must be left with one moment of tenderness that he could recall for the rest of his life. She knew only too well that small gestures of affection from those who have it in their power to sprinkle them liberally can bring the greatest joy to those starved of love. How often she'd wished that the world could survive on such simplicity; she'd happily be Queen of the World.

But for now she picked up her glass, finished her drink, and then lifted the photo and examined it closely once more.

'What's your boss's name?' she asked.

'Spencer. Peregrine Spencer.'

'Was he responsible for this?'

'Oh yes, he insisted the moment I arrived at the party that I must have a drink and that he had *slap n'tickle* I think he called it, lined up for me. I told him just one but...' He nodded solemnly at the photo, '...well, need I say more?'

Millicent, now staring at the picture at arm's length enquired, 'Does he know you don't drink?'

'Yes. I've never been to a party or social function in all my years at the Department and he resents it I know, but I'm not a social person and...' Henry looked up nervously '...Millicent?'

'Yes?'

'When you coughed in court - when you coughed and suddenly everything changed and the case was dismissed - how, how did...what happened?'

There followed a prolonged silence as Millicent, taken completely by surprise, toyed with the truth or another lie. She went this time for the truth.

'I'm sorry Henry. I know Spencer. I meant to tell you.'

Henry was flabbergasted. 'You know Spencer! Peregrine Spencer - my boss - ex-boss that is. But how?'

Again Millicent was torn between the truth and a lie. Truth triumphed again. 'Just business,' she answered glibly, 'he's been a client of mine for years.'

To say Henry was impressed is a gross understatement. To say he was shocked was equal to it. To say what he said next was probably not what Millicent would have wished.

'But to have that much power over him,' he gasped in astonishment, 'you must provide a totally indispensable service!'

It was within Millicent at that precise moment to burst out laughing and indeed, took the greatest restraint on her part not to, but restrain herself she did and like all great solicitors, switched the subject as seamlessly as a points change at Clapham Junction.

'That's very clever Henry,' she said, 'Indis-spencer-ble. Was that intentional?'

'What?'

'The pun.'

'What pun?'

'Indis-*spencer*-ble.'

Henry blinked a few times whilst working his head around his apparent cleverness and once he finally fell in, he had to admit no, it wasn't (intentional) but the flicker of a smile briefly lighting up his face showed that he was pleased he'd said something (albeit unintentional) that Millicent found amusing, for his only past experience was of nobody ever finding anything he said vaguely amusing or clever and he'd therefore long ago lost confidence in attempting jokes or witticisms. He often *thought* them and even smiled to himself sometimes at how very clever they were and how people might enjoy them if only they found him interesting or he could deliver them properly - but no, they were never aired nor shared. Apart from, that is, his office 'Scroggisms.'

'Are you aware,' said Millicent, twiddling the photo around between thumb and forefinger, 'that what Spencer did to you is illegal, a gross infringement of your human rights, and if you so desired you could take him to the cleaners...and back.'

Henry stared at the photo twiddling back and forth. 'All I want is my job back,' he said, 'I'm finished without it. I'd never get another. It's all I know. And of course I'd have a criminal record as well, so who'd employ me anyway?'

Millicent looked out of the window and Henry watched her eyes narrow and her (very kissable) jaw set firm before she swiftly turned back to him, stared him straight in the eye and proclaimed adamantly, 'And so you shall have your job back Henry. So you *shall.* That much I faithfully promise you.'

And with that concluding vow she leaned across and kissed him once more on the cheek, whispering 'Happy Christmas. Trust me. Fear not.'

Chapter Nine

## A GENTLE TOUCH

On the taxi ride to Charing Cross Station, Millicent had refused to elaborate on her promise to reinstate Henry in his job but simply told him again, to trust her and that she would not let him down. The last vision he had of her was she telling him to be brave and wait for her letter after Christmas, of her sweet smile and stockinged knees in the back of the taxi, and then she was gone; just a silhouette through the back window of a taxi turning left into the gloom of the mid afternoon traffic, a gloom illuminated by the festive decorations of Trafalgar Square and Millicent's reassuring words repeating softly in his head.

His train pulled in to Lewisham Station an hour later and as he waited patiently for the carriage to jettison its human cargo of commuters and bag-laden shoppers onto the damp platform, he felt nothing but gratitude that out of the hopeless mess he'd got into through one small act of rebellion, life was actually offering a glimmer of hope and the promise of a new horizon. It all of course hinged on Millicent, his angel of mercy, and Henry couldn't help feeling that despite his atheist viewpoint of the world some form of divine intervention had arrived with a helping hand. Or wing.

He got up and followed a young mother grappling with a pushchair, shopping bags and small child in her arms, to the open carriage door. As she struggled to cope with her load Henry instinctively rushed to her assistance, clumsily offering to carry the pushchair or child. Suddenly he found a baby in his arms and the mother thanking him profusely as she opened up the pushchair on the platform.

Henry carefully stepped down with his precious load and felt a tiny arm around his neck and little fingertips touching his cheek and pulling his glasses as the baby smiled and gurgled at him. Then the mother took the child, once again thanking Henry and strapping the little girl safely into place, she still smiling and gurgling and reaching up at Henry with chubby little grasping fingers.

He stood riveted to the spot, unable to take his eyes off her and still feeling the touch of the tiny arm and fingertips until they disappeared in a bustle of bags and he stood alone on the platform with the rain drizzling on him, in disbelief that the child had instantly trusted him and was not frightened. Adjusting his glasses and biting his lip he looked up towards the exit door through misty eyes and instantly felt strong and ready to face the other end of the human spectrum awaiting him at home.

Henry's habit during his years of walking to and from the house had been to exit from the front door and arrive through the back door, via the back alley and back garden, if a crumbling shed, twenty square yards of cracked concrete and a border of dirt and unkempt shrubs did in fact warrant the description of garden. But this particular evening, for the first time ever, he made a last second decision on reaching Viola Street to take a right turn leading to the front of the house instead of a left turn to the back alley. It wasn't an easy task, for his brain and feet were programmed to only go one way and they fought quite a battle to follow their normal route until capitulating to the force of will that had in the past half hour taken over their owner.

It was this unwavering arrival and departure habit of Henry's that provided Lily Bunce with her daily clocking in and clocking out of his movements for the five working days of each week. In the morning she clocked Henry out as he walked past her window at precisely eight o'clock, checking her clock and nodding to herself each time, and in the evening she clocked him back in; not visually, unless she happened to be in her back bedroom and could witness his arrival through the back gate, but usually by the sound of the gate and his footsteps. So imagine the discomposure that ensued at 50 Viola Street when the figure of Henry walked, whistling, straight past her window at four forty-seven in the afternoon. It was not so much that he was one and a half hours earlier than normal, for it was Christmas Eve when most workers got off early - no, it was his arrival at the *front* instead of the *back* door! This, together with his non-appearance that morning - the

114

keen observation of which it must be remembered had incurred upon her head the dreadful wrath of her neighbour, from which her delicate nerves were still recovering - was an event of such monumental proportions and importance that her mind was sent into an instant frenzy as she tried to figure out how on earth she could unravel this conundrum of all conundrums.

Given that one single ferreting enquiry by Lily to Irma Scroggins would be tantamount to her being forced to fall on her sword, or bread knife in her case, this was going to take the investigative guile of a Sherlock Holmes. Add to this the fact that her steaming open of Henry's letter had revealed that he was in debt to the tune of over three thousand pounds and it would seem that the Wilmots across the road were going to have to play very much second fiddle in Lily Bunce's orchestra of reconnaissance this Christmas.

Chapter Ten

# THE CARTER CONSULTANCY

George was happy. His mistress was home alone with no sign of uncles. He'd checked after she'd arrived home by running at the front door several times, hitting it with his front paws and yapping, just to make certain all was clear before settling down in his basket and following Millicent's every move with anxious eyes.

Millicent smiled at the sofa, recently Henry's bed, and folded the blanket and plumped up the cushions. One of them, his pillow, had a slight stain on it where he'd obviously dribbled in his near death state, but whereas before he'd fallen asleep the sight of the dribble would have disgusted her, she now felt almost fond of it - but turned it over all the same.

A sherry glass on its side by the skirting board caught her eye and she bent down to pick it up and place it on a table. Then she stood for a while and thought. She'd already thought quite a lot walking George around Regents Park for half an hour but now she was impatient to put her plans into action. Suddenly a most unexpected purpose to life had emerged like a Phoenix out of the ashes. As mentioned earlier, life had become rather predictable and mundane and if she thought that going out and looking for some stimulation would change that, well then, yes, it certainly had - but not quite in the way she'd imagined. For there was nothing guaranteed to arouse the ire of the tenacious Miss Carter than bullying and injustice performed on helpless innocents, and here she stood on Christmas Eve having accidentally walked headlong into a cause encompassing both. Such is life.

She had two letters to write, one to Peregrine Spencer and then once she'd received his reply, which she expected to be immediate, one to Henry. It must all be done by letters, just in case. But there were surprises awaiting of which, had she been aware of them at that moment, would have made for a very happy Christmas indeed for her and her worthy cause. But first there was the photograph to photocopy for enclosure with her letter to

Spencer. If he had any doubts about her serious intentions plainly imparted at the court, then the copy of the photograph and one or two of her invoices spanning more than a decade would incontrovertibly erase any hopes he might be nurturing of escape.

Yes, everything had to be in writing; indisputable, corroborating print on paper, an invaluable piece of advice that her dear father had drummed into her from an early age and for which she been grateful many times over. She could hear his gruff voice stating clearly 'If there's any remote chance you might need it to your advantage in the future, get it in writing! Phone calls are useless - get it or put it in writing!'

Millicent thought of her father as she strode to her office, and wondered what he'd think if he ever discovered that her company, *The Carter Consultancy,* had in fact more intimate one-to-one meetings than his sketchy knowledge of Millicent's career led him to believe. He'd once or twice queried exactly what *Comprehensive Business Therapy* was (the sub heading on Millicent's headed paper) but soon lost interest when Millicent offered her superbly worded ambiguous definition, learnt long ago, which guaranteed to send him deeply absorbed back into his Times crossword within seconds, just nodding from behind his paper in polite distraction until she went away.

Millicent had never attempted the Times crossword but felt she 'owed it' for the numerous occasions it had diverted her father from any chance of an inquisition beyond his mock interest and polite questioning before growing bored with the answer that he didn't really want anyway. That would be *anyone's* answer to *any* question, unless it had 'Across' or 'Down' above it. That's how he was; rich, retired, owed nobody money or favours so take away the Times crossword and brandy from his coffee and he might as well be dead. His long-suffering wife's party piece was that if she ever had a heart attack in the same room as him, she prayed it would be near the end of his crossword otherwise the outcome would almost certainly be fatal.

Millicent opened the flap to her mahogany bureau and took out a pristine sheet of cream letterhead, almost parchment in thickness, and ran a fingertip lightly over the brown embossed

117

heading, *The Carter Consultancy*. It exuded class and was a perfect shop window for whatever business it was called upon to represent. Placing this on her desk she then opened the second to top drawer of her matching solid mahogany filing cabinet and plucked out a thick wedge of similar coloured documents, setting them down beside the pristine letterhead. These too were cream and headed the same but with the word' STATEMENT' in bold capitals centred below the heading.

Millicent sat down and started to sort them, making a separate pile to one side. Occasionally she would stop and study one a little closer and an eyebrow, or maybe two, would rise and a smile appear. Those on the separate pile were all addressed the same 'To: Mr Peregrine Spencer, Senior Officer, Department of_____, Whitehall, W1' and were for varying amounts from one thousand to five thousand pounds, dated the last day of the month, starting in July 1967. Millicent checked that July 1967 was indeed the earliest statement, marvelled at the length of time she'd put up with Spencer's bad breath, hairless body and sock suspenders, thought how interesting that it should have started in the so-called Summer of Love, thought 'what a joke', and changed her mind when her eyes fell on the amounts.

A few minutes tapping on her calculator produced the sum of just over £325,000 and she wondered how delighted Britain's taxpayers would be if they knew what they were getting for their hard-earned money. Add this to the rest of the names and addresses on the other pile, all of whom had enjoyed the immeasurable benefits of *The Carter Consultancy*, and one can only hazard a guess at the public esteem in which the names on the statements would be held. With this agreeable thought in mind, Millicent switched on her typewriter, inserted the pristine sheet of paper, drummed her manicured nails on the desk whilst gazing at the wall for some seconds, and then with resolute determination sent them to the keyboard where they began tapping furiously.

*24th December 1980*

*Dear Mr Spencer,*

*Further to our most recent meeting at Bow Street Magistrates Court and the assurances you gave me at the time, I would be pleased to receive written confirmation by return post that Mr Henry Scroggins is a valued employee in your department who can look forward to many more years (good health accepted) in his current position, or indeed any promotion that may ensue.*

*I am enclosing a copy of a photo of Mr Scroggins taken at a recent social function at your office which, whilst appearing to seriously infringe his human rights as a confirmed teetotaller, may I'm quite sure be easily explained by yourself and other witnesses of the event. The original of this photo which was 'kindly' presented to Mr Scroggins by your staff to mark his first (if somewhat unwelcome) experience of alcohol, is in my possession and you can be assured of my absolute discretion, as you have been for the past 13 years since our first transaction (sample copy of a statement also enclosed for your reference).*

*I look forward to your immediate reply in order that I may advise Mr Scroggins of your complete agreement.*

*Sincerely Yours, Millicent Carter.'*

Millicent read it through, changed 'valued employee in your department' to 'valued member of your department' and switching on her photocopier to duplicate the evidence, congratulating herself on being such a professional and impartial 'solicitor.' She then glanced at her watch which showed five-thirty-five and imagining Henry would by now be home, dearly wished she was a fly on the wall at 52 Viola Street; but not just any fly, a fly with the power to direct Henry's speech and actions or, failing that, a fly that could exit the house, zoom north over road, rooftop and river to report back absolute assurance that her man was steadfast and strong in the face of his adversary; a man who, whilst under the seventeen hours or so of her influence had grown in such self-confidence and determination that no mean-spirited mother or bullying boss would ever again hold sway over his gentle soul. Self-confidence and determination to do just quite what, she wasn't sure, but there was a feeling deep within her that this crushed, naïve man had the potential to rise and challenge his mother, his past, his reputation and anything that stood in the way of filling his forty-year old shell with something rich and rewarding.

As it so happens Millicent need not have worried one bit about 'her man', for Henry had in the five and a half minutes that it took him to walk from the station to his house, acquired such fire and resilience in his chubby belly that wild horses would not have dragged him away from his mission, a mission to make it perfectly clear to the woman he'd allowed to dominate his mind and body from birth that her days of domination were over. He frankly didn't care whether he had a job to go back to (although he had every confidence that Millicent would not fail him), all he cared about at that moment was the incontrovertible truth that there was not a remote chance from now on that the embodiment of a living devil lurking behind his door, yes *his* door, would ever again be permitted to control or destroy what remained of his life. After all said and done, had he now not drunk alcohol, quite severely injured his boss, caused criminal damage to a shop window (a shop that itself would have damaged or destroyed enough good lives, he could now attest), been arrested and charged and then, if that wasn't rebellion enough, spent the night at the luxurious home of a beautiful lady? A lady who wasn't just any lady - no, a lady who was a lady *solicitor!* And had he not seen her in all her glorious buff, sat talking to her whilst she remained in this state and indeed flaunted herself at him (albeit slightly drunk); then had he not appeared at the famed Bow Street Magistrates Court under her inestimable care (she clothed by now of course) and gone on to a pub afterwards with her - *his* solicitor - to discuss the miracle of his salvation by virtue of the extraordinary coincidence of Millicent knowing his accuser and having an equally extraordinary power and control over him? And had he not held a baby in his arms and felt the gentle grasp of an arm around his neck and tiny fingertips on his cheek and an innocent smile that said he was trusted and even looked like he had potential as a playmate? Didn't all this make him something better than the piece of excrement he'd become under the sole of Irma Scroggins despicable boots?

By the time Henry had walked with these thoughts in his head, the influence of Millicent on his shoulder and now (without him knowing it) the grit and guts of his father, down the back alley and clicked open the back gate which led to the kitchen door that he for so long had dreaded opening - he felt he had grown at least a foot taller and was ready for anything.

(It should be noted that his rebellious march to the front door had been thwarted on arrival by his mother having, out of habit, put the security chain in place, but in order to deny Lily Bunce any degree of satisfaction, he avoided walking past her door again by continuing down the street away from her house and up the alley from the opposite direction; something he could never in his life remember doing and thus adding yet another first to this glorious day of firsts.)

Henry placed his keys on the kitchen table, noted the envelope addressed to him propped up behind the kettle, listened for the sound of his mother, opened the cupboard door containing his secret teabags, flagrantly placed one in a mug with a dramatic flourish and devil-may-care grin, and switched on the kettle.

'Henry!' The pincers gripped him above the ears - he being unprepared - but not for long.

'Yes Mother!' he shouted, with brazen insouciance rather than his usual timid reply. 'How are you?' He cocked his head as the kettle began its rumble. 'You there Mother?'

From the darkness up the hall came a weak wail. 'Henry, Henry! Where have you been, I've been so frightened?'

Frightened? Ah, what a shame thought Henry, what a wonderful terrible shame. Henry opened the letter, noticed that it had already been opened and re-sealed (not aware, twice) read the contents, shook his head to relieve himself of the shock of the amount, shrugged and walked up the hall to the lounge where, without any light on - which he guessed was for dramatic effect - his mother sat crouched in semi-darkness in her chair, trembling. He took two steps and was by her side with a hand on her bony shoulder, the feel of it almost causing him to shudder.

'What are you doing sitting in the dark and cold?' he asked. 'You'll catch your death of cold if you're not careful and we don't want that do we?' whilst his mind continued with 'not much we don't!'

Irma Scroggins wailed once more and, faking a sob, cried out again, 'Where have you been! All night I've been alone. Alone!

Never in my life have I been alone at night. Anything could have happened!'

'Anything like *what* Mother?' enquired Henry. 'Anything like the sort of thing that happens to millions of old people who live alone and do not have a son or daughter? Or do you mean anyone like you who has someone to care for them and look after their every need night and day? How do they survive eh, those poor lonely old codgers, how do you think they survive, eh? Hmm?'

This was too much for the woman, spoken to with such insolence and disrespect. She knew not what to do and quite involuntarily found herself screaming at her son.

'Where have you been! How dare you stay out all night!'

'Oh, quite easy Mother,' Henry nonchalantly rambled on, opening the letter in his hand and ignoring her histrionics. 'Would you like me to open a window so the whole street can hear you being murdered? Would that help? Hmm?'

'You're mad!' she cried.

'I certainly am.'

'Just like your father!'

'Am I?' enquired Henry, turning to her. 'Why? Did he also dare to object when you opened his letters?'

His mother said nothing but the depth of her breathing, the iron clamping of her mouth and the rigid set of her jaw said it all. She was, literally, speechless. Henry threw the letter onto her lap.

'Did my father get into debt? Did he? Did he get into debt through drinking maybe, like I do through betting, because our lives are made so desperately miserable by one person; one person so full of hate for the world that we feel we have to find some small comfort from somewhere? Did he Mother? Hmm?'

And with that Henry announced he was hungry, was going out for fish and chips and would she like some? Receiving no reply, he walked from the back door and pulled it firmly behind him, deliberately making sure she heard him not locking it before he strode with an exaggerated whistle and a spring in his thick-soled Tufs - that seemed to have miraculously transformed into ballet shoes - the two turnings and half mile stroll to the chippie once owned by Sid Mathieson and his pretty teenage wife Betty.

And as Henry stood chatting amiably to the swarthy owner who hauled battered cod and chips from the sizzling fat into layers of greaseproof paper, popping in a free giant pickled onion "for Christmas", what joy it would have given him to know that his father had spent endless happy hours standing in the self same spot swapping jokes with his best friend and wondering how life's pack of cards had dealt him Irma instead of Sid's fair Queen of Hearts, his aching heart trying to avert his eyes from the young girl's beauty whilst asking himself the same question over and over again - whatever possessed me to marry *that* woman?

# Chapter Eleven

## RETRIBUTION

And so it was that Christmas 1980 passed as the happiest in Henry's memory. If Irma Scroggins had been part of it, it would still have been happy because Henry had snatched away her control, but the reason Irma Scroggins was not physically part of it was that she chose to lock herself in her bedroom and refuse to have any form of communication with her son for three days; three blissful days during which Henry - once he'd tried to offer food and a truce but been rebuffed through the door with a hideously growled 'You swine! Go away!' - had settled down to immerse himself in the glorious release from her perpetual presence.

Liberated as a caged bird with an open door but, like the bird, feeling tentative, excited and a little unsure quite how to behave and what to do first, he was like a pools winner without a natural ability to spend.

It had been three glorious, blissful days of living the happy bachelor life that he'd hardly ever let himself dream about, of coming and going as he pleased from room to room (apart from one) and eating what he wanted when he wanted it; being creative with meagre rations retrieved from corners of cupboards and fridge, watching what he wanted on the nine inch 1953 Bush television bought like so many at the time, for the Coronation, admittedly in black and white and restricted to the BBC but what did it matter. To sit and watch without her constant criticism of everything in which he dared to express enjoyment, including one and a half relaxing hours of racing at Wincanton on Boxing Day, caring not one iota who won or lost (although he played secret bets with himself). And without doubt the naughtiest thing of all - watching 'Jim'll Fix It' and pretending it was 'little Henry' on the couch with a list of things he'd like done to his mother! Oh the wondrous childish Christmas joy of it all!

Christmas Day being a Thursday, Millicent's letter posted on Christmas Eve to Peregrine Spencer and marked *Strictly Private & Confidential* on the envelope, did not land on his desk until the following Tuesday. Contrary to Henry's (and indeed Millicent's) Christmas, Spencer's festive period had been, sadly for him, far from peaceful and solitary. As a man of some considerable wealth and a nature that was both forceful and gregarious, Christmas normally provided him with the major opportunity of the year to flaunt these characteristics with pride and passion upon - some might say, *inflict* upon - as many friends, family and neighbours as possible.

Warming up at the office party as he did every year, this 'warmth' was then transferred to his grand mansion in Surrey which rang out all Christmas Day and Boxing Day to the sonorous chimes of the overbearing conductor's jokes and self-aggrandisement, where not a trace of modest restraint could be found infiltrating the expensively decorated inner sanctum as guests old and young alike gathered around Peregrine's imaginary proscenium arch to give him the due freedom of high-volume expression and applause that he demanded. As guests arrived and crunched, gift and bottle laden, across the wide circular, gravel drive to the house, *his* voice and *his* choice of music were the first things they heard penetrating through windows and doors, and always the last things they took with them on leaving. That was how it was every year; every year that is when his facial features were in the finest shape and not one precious aristocratic inch of flesh required any form of concealment.

However - and the *however* cannot be exaggerated enough – this was a Christmas when those same features were not quite so fine; in fact anything but fine; in fact rearranged in a manner and colour that brought unwanted attention and demanded difficult answers.

It could be said that if ever there was a Christmas when Peregrine Spencer wished he'd contracted something highly contagious or sustained injuries more grievous than those he actually carried, then this was it. But with just a swollen purple eye and cheekbone, and a nose that was now more meandering towards his mouth than its previous direct route (for it was indeed broken), the welcoming and entertaining of the usual melee of guests arriving and departing throughout the two days was not only muted, but totally predominated by his various explanations of the means by which his injuries were acquired.

Being the man he was, these were injuries that would only, could only, be attested to something that made him appear even more worthy a human being than he imagined he was already perceived to be, so they were converted to a story of daring-do whereby he, the great protector of the underdog, had fallen for the old trick of trying to help what appeared to be a young man being beaten by another, only to discover when he intervened (with no hesitation and scant regard for his own safety) that the man was nothing more than bait who had turned around and, with his 'attacker', proceeded to beat him! Peregrine! The Saviour! The Good Samaritan!

'Yes, I know! Can you believe it?' he exclaimed a hundred times to a hundred expressions of incredulity.

The astonished reaction of the listeners to Peregrine's impassioned tale, told with his renowned false self-deprecation, was the same in every instance and so much so that after he'd told it roughly ten times he was actually believing it and even adding to it and consequently starting to walk the thin line of going too far with his embellishments which - combined with that most demonic embellisher and memory betrayer of all, Alcohol - was beginning to have the embarrassing effect of fundamentally changing the story and making him forget to whom he'd told what. Only his wife, the only one privy to the truth and from whom it was impossible to hide anything, prevented him putting more than a toe over the thin line by dragging him into the kitchen and giving him a severe warning. For what became her husband's embarrassment naturally became her own.

There was though, in all this, one blessing, and it was that he only ever invited to his private festive gathering one member of staff from the office, and this member of staff happened to be the only other person who, along with Henry Scroggins, never attended the office Christmas party and was therefore not a witness to the assault. Peregrine Spencer's secretary of twenty years, Miss Phyllis Wallace, was a nervy, prim, frizzy grey-haired little creature of about fifty-five years who tottered and stomped on chunky high heels that looked forever about to collapse, and who flinched a dazed smile rapidly on and off at the world through pink-rimmed thick lenses.

She was an extremely sweet-natured, obliging and totally non-judgmental soul was Phyllis, spending her whole office life missing the point of everything and flashing those nervous smiles that came and went as quick as the point she'd just missed. Possibly because of her need for thick lenses, she was also the only one (apart from Henry) who failed to notice that her moustache had grown longer and greyer in recent years which provided her with the office nickname of Walrus - close enough to Wallace for her not to notice. The fact that she also had no knowledge of Beatles music and therefore unaware of the tune *I Am The Walrus* being hummed or sung as she stomped and tottered past desks was an enormous blessing for her. Almost as enormous a blessing as her being the lone office presence at her boss's house on Christmas Day was for Spencer, for Phyllis's unmitigated discretion came automatically with her sweet dithering forgetfulness and point-missing and was the reason her job as Spencer's secretary was unassailable. She also, in her innocence and naivety, worshipped him for everything that everyone else loathed - which helped.

So having eventually somehow survived the Christmas domestic assault course of all this unwanted interrogation, Peregrine Spencer arrived at his desk on Tuesday morning to find Millicent's letter awaiting him. In case he'd missed it, Phyllis Wallace had put it to one side from the rest of the post and helpfully pointed it out with a lingering finger, as extra security in case the words *Private and Confidential* were overlooked. Spencer thanked her and said that would be all thank you, which saw Phyllis totter and stomp out with one of her nervous smiles, closing the door behind her and throwing one more look through the glass at her boss to ensure he knew he was now under her *Private and Confidential* care.

Spencer drew a deep breath and sliced open the fat cream envelope with his letter opener. The first thing he saw was the copy of the Polaroid photo that slipped from the folded letter and landed face up. Spencer stared at it and, like Millicent when first seeing it, he had to turn it this way and that before it was evident that here before him was revealed the full and terrible extent of Henry's nightmare and the sole reason why he, Spencer, sat there nursing a battered face, now suddenly accompanied by an intense feeling of dread and the threat of impending public humiliation.

Until this moment he had given no thought, or indeed had no recollection, of a photograph being taken, but now faced with the irrefutable proof which included the unmistakeable features of June Catchpole and his clearly visible monogrammed cufflink poking from a striped jacket sleeve holding a bottle of whisky, it was all too memorable and the blinding flash and whir of the camera's action returned and penetrated his consciousness like an arrow through the eye.

The only thought swimming in the whirlpool of his drowning future was 'I am finished' and so with shaking hands he unfolded the letter, flinching at the familiar sight of *The Carter Consultancy* headed paper and placing the two photocopied statements (the very first and last transactions of his with 'the consultancy' lest there be any doubt of the time frame of his secret life and the size of his embezzlement) before shuddering uncontrollably from head to toe as he began to read.

A cold shiver coursed through his body, at the end of which the shuddering stopped, leaving him momentarily paralysed. He read without moving a muscle and then read again. Then he looked up, started shaking once more and peered out of the two sides of the half glass partition that made up his corner office, convinced the rest of the staff were at that very moment reading his mind and watching his violent physical gyrations.

It was some time before his body was able to resume any normal function and his first instinct was to get up and walk to the glass window to make sure that the office had not turned into a fiery underworld manned by leering gryphons and demons. No, there were the skeleton staff sitting drearily at their desks or standing languidly at filing cabinets and office machines, all displaying the comforting signs of post-Christmas office life.

Several, on seeing him, became rather more occupied and interested in their various tasks, reminding him that he was still Peregrine Spencer, Department Head, and a man who would always command their respect; a man who, despite the attack upon his person by a member of staff who couldn't take an innocent jest, was there at his post when he should really have been at home recovering.

If only he knew the truth; the truth about the profound and collective guilt of the staff, particularly the direct members of Henry's 'lynch party', June Catchpole having already resigned in shame, although offering 'personal reasons'; the truth about the meeting they'd had in the canteen - a place where Spencer would never be seen dead; the truth about the letter of apology and regret signed by all staff and only awaiting the signatures of those not yet returned to work, before being presented to Henry, *if* he returned; and if he didn't return by next Monday, the truth about the action they had so far all agreed to take against their bullying boss. Yes, the milk of human kindness may have deserted them under various influences in that same office space just a week before but in the cold light of day had returned to protect a thoroughly decent colleague and fellow member of the human race.

If Spencer had known all this, it would naturally have compounded his humiliation currently just resting in the form of Millicent's enclosures, but not having the slightest inkling that behind the bland faces outside his office lingered a festering insurrection, the contents of the envelope would have made the manageable, short term problem of office politics a mere drop in the ocean. He knew only too well that the envelope and everything it contained and implied, spelt - not to put too fine a point on it - Severe Lifelong Damage.

He returned to his desk and the first object on it that met his gaze was the black onyx smiling Buddha given to him as a Christmas present by a well meaning staff member, but unfortunately also the first thing that Henry had grabbed when confronting Spencer about the last four (non) pay rises that had been, as far as Henry was concerned, deliberately and vindictively overlooked - not that he was able to pronounce either of those two adverbs with any clarity at the time.

If Spencer hadn't laughed in his face and told him to 'Sod off and find another job!' then he, Spencer might not have been sitting with a face disfigured and a job in jeopardy. But as it was, Henry, bereft of all self-control, had plunged the smiling Buddha into Spencer's grinning face; not once, but twice. And there rested the simple reason why Henry's hands were unmarked and uninjured and why Spencer's face wasn't.

The physically and mentally battered man picked up the small square of paper lying beside the Buddha, a piece of paper that came enclosed with the gift, offering useful information about its benefits. He read:

*'Black onyx is said to be good for grief, gout, stress and anxiety, anaemia, poor circulation, depression and it is thought to reduce sexual desires. Black onyx takes away the fear of death and so is a good stone for terminal illness. Black onyx promotes the ability to make wise decisions and encourages self control to the wearer.'*

Spencer's waste bin clanged to the sound of a descending smiling Buddha followed by the flutter of its descriptive note. Picking up the cream letterhead he read Millicent's words once more, during which he lightly fingered his damaged nose. Then, after a very deep breath and shoulders bent under the weight of his desperate anxiety, he took out a piece of blank paper from his desk drawer, scribbled rapidly for three or four minutes, occasionally pausing and looking up for thought, scribbled some more and then after reading it through, signed it (without his usual trademark flourish), folded it, inserted it into an envelope, addressed it, and again pulling open his drawer, took out a first class stamp and stuck it firmly on the envelope.

He then got up and strode out of the office to the polite glances of the staff, down the flight of stairs to reception, ignored the deferential smile of the uniformed doorman before hesitantly walking the few yards down the road to the post box outside the pub, where he stood some seconds with the letter poised in the

130

mouth of the freshly-painted red box, before letting it drop, his hand briefly remaining poised mid-air.

Turning around he almost collided with Richard Gaines (the post room supervisor already preparing for his 1981 Christmas celebrations in the manner he'd ended 1980) who chirped a query about 'my franking machine not good enough?' and disappeared, rollup in hand and shirt flapping from under his jacket, through the door of The Carpenter's Arms.

His manager, who would normally have snapped some form of timid reprimand about drinking alcohol at tea-break time, simply watched the pub doors swing shut and returned up the single flight of stairs to his desk, where he closed the door to his office and remained deep in thought under the blackest and heaviest cloud of gloom for the rest of the day.

# Chapter Twelve

## FREEDOM!

On the Friday morning following Spencer's shock, which was the day after New Year's Day, Henry heard the mail drop through his letterbox. Normally he would allow his mother to collect it with a groaning bend, as was her practise, but this time he was there at the door, heart racing in expectation.

Irma Scroggins had made an appearance from her bedroom precisely three days from the hour and minute she took up her self-imposed solitary confinement, refusing to speak a word to Henry but obviously driven by an innate urge not to turn her confinement into a life-threatening hunger strike. This was something of a disappointment for Henry but he did get some small pleasure out of hearing her scurrying around the cupboards for food and muttering to herself about whatever it was she wanted, not being there.

The chippie had never been so busy as he had since Henry's recent discovery of his excellent fried cuisine but even he, Henry, was now getting a little sick of half inch thick batter - gloriously golden, greasy, crispy and naughty as it was - and needed supplies of something a little fresher and green, supplies of food *he* liked and which *he* alone would prepare.

His heart beat faster as he realised that the handwriting was Millicent's and this was the letter she'd promised him before the end of the week. He raised the envelope to his nose and sniffing deeply with eyes closed in heavenly expectation, smelt nothing but Basildon Bond but convinced himself there was a faint hint of her perfume and without doubt an abundance of her DNA, no doubt along with that of several sorters and postmen - a fact he chose to ignore.

His trust in her was already infinite and this now, appropriately sealed it. How he'd longed for her next contact, how he'd dreamed of seeing her again and sitting beside her, watching her lovely peachy face and discussing what happened next. If indeed there was to be a next. There must be, there couldn't possibly not be. Henry wasn't disappointed.

*Dear Henry,*

*I do hope your Christmas was as happy as possible and that everything on the domestic front is peaceful. I have today received a reply from PS, immediate as expected, and am delighted to let you know that he is looking forward to seeing you on your return to work on Monday next. And there is a surprise for you. Apparently he has inadvertently overlooked your last four years' pay increases and therefore has rectified the matter and is pleased to inform you that your salary will increase by £1000 per annum, backdated to the beginning of the financial year 1976-77. He offers his profuse apologies for the oversight and has personally contacted the Department's Pay Officer to ensure this total amount appears in your next pay packet, with a tax adjustment to reflect any loss of interest you may have incurred.*

*Do you think we should celebrate this with a meal, maybe after work one day next week? It's entirely up to you but please call me if you can spare the time. I know you haven't got a phone at home but I'm sure PS will have no objection to you calling me from the office.*

*Hoping to hear from you soon.*

*Best, Millicent*

*PS: (not him) I was also thinking you might need a hand with some shopping. PS (yes him) has accounts in various clothing establishments in Savile Row, Jermyn Street etc. and I'm sure would be delighted if you used them to ensure your appearance matches your new financial status. What do you think?*

Henry could hardly believe his eyes. Millicent had secured his job and with it riches beyond his wildest dreams. The only slight disappointment was the 'Best, Millicent' which he wished could have been 'Love, Millicent', not for one moment expecting it to mean anything but just wanting to have the word addressed to him for the first time in his life (apart from aunties long ago at Christmas), and especially from Millicent. This wishful thought was quickly replaced by a sudden *Eureka!* moment that saw his eyebrows fly skywards, followed by his body run skywards, (another first) to his bedroom to grasp from his jacket pocket the manila envelope carrying the franked name of *The Ace Credit Collection Company.* Gripping the nasty object in one hand and

Millicent's letter in the other, he flashed glances between the two before his eyes shot skywards - to the crack in the ceiling above his bed - his lips moving in rapid calculation, followed by a sudden smile that broke out across his face like the sun bursting over a clear eastern summer horizon.

This dazzling warmth and light instantly spread down his whole body creating a yelp of delight and an unconfined bounce onto his bed as he cried out 'Millicent! Millicent! I don't believe it! My debts are cleared! I'm free! My darling, I'm free!'

Never in his life had he spoken the word 'darling' and never did he ever expect to, but then never had there been a moment when all the cares that had mounted into one huge constant depression had lifted as if caught in a trawler's net and swept high above the ocean and dumped on a deck; on the deck of a ship that would sail away to Never-Again Land and bother him no more!

Temporarily recovering his composure, Henry narrowed his eyes, raised a fist towards the door and hissed 'You old witch - I'm free! Do you hear - I'm *freeee*!' and bounced again on his bed in silent, fist-clenching, tear-jerking relief.

Then he sat, sat still, and as he sat and stared at the hideous wallpaper and old, round, brown light switch, energy surged into his brain and limbs like a bushfire out of control. Suddenly the world was brighter, lighter and anything seemed possible. Anything! He had to walk. He had to burn off this energy that had arrived from nowhere and was demanding to be burnt off. His lungs needed fresh air, his legs longed to be stretched, his heart cried out to pump like...like...Stevenson's Rocket!

Whiteheath! That's where he'd go. A mile's brisk walk uphill across the common to the village where he would stroll amongst the poets and painters and people he felt so uncomfortable with, and would smile a jaunty smile at them and even wear his scarf in a rakish way and maybe go into a bar and order an orange juice without a shade of fear or embarrassment. Oh yes!

And so he did.

Chapter Thirteen

# NEW YEAR RESOLUTIONS

Henry sat at the window seat of the wine bar feeling perfectly at peace with his fellow humans, most of those he'd met on his walk having returned his jaunty smiles with mutual warmth and even a cheery 'Good morning!' or 'Happy New Year!'

By the time he reached the healthy, bracing air of the heath and its wide-open grassy spaces dotted with strollers and dog walkers, even giving himself time to appreciate how spectacular the needle thin steeple of All Saints Church looked as it pierced into the steel grey sky, he was utterly convinced of the contagion of happiness and goodwill to all men. And women! Apart from one.

He studied the racing pages of the newspaper provided free by the amiable Irish barman and enjoyed the rustle of the three plastic bags of food at his feet, just purchased from the equally friendly and round-faced lady at the delicatessen. He checked his scarf in the mirror opposite and felt that it was tied in a perfectly appropriate, slightly sloppy knot and looking all the better for his mackintosh being open at the top and not buttoned up as was his normal fashion, if fashion is the correct word.

It being the second day of January nineteen-eighty-one, he had decided to make a slightly belated resolution on his walk up the hill and there seemed no better resolution than to waste not one more penny on horses and jockeys, that turf-based fraternity who had obviously long ago conspired in a sinister cartel to prevent him winning. He didn't resent this conspiracy - far from it - in fact he was now delighted that he could at last admire their common sense and heed the sound advice that they had been trying to impart since it was apparent many years ago that Henry wasn't very good at sorting out equine wheat from chaff.

And so it was that with an uncluttered mind he now scanned the horses and courses on the page; horses and courses he knew better than anyone or anything, the familiar but ever-changing family that had always let him down and all of whom now looked like certain losers instead of certain winners.

Across the road, almost directly from where he sat sipping his orange juice and casually humming into his paper, a teleprinter was at that same moment chattering out its staccato rat-tat-rata-tat-tat in the first floor office of Messrs. Bodger and Snapes, Solicitors and Commissioners for Oaths. By sheer coincidence - this being Henry's first foray into the uncharted bohemian territory of Whiteheath Village since childhood - the teleprinter was actually tapping out his own name; tapping out a message from Australia about the sad demise of Mr Henry Scroggins of Mermaid Beach, Gold Coast, in the Sunshine State of Queensland.

Archibald Snapes slowly looked up from the legal document he was studying, lifted his eighteen stone bulk from his chair and wheezed two painful paces to the teleprinter. He peered at the message as each line printed out, his brow furrowing deeper and deeper as his curiosity grew, until his eyebrows lifted and he began to gently pull the bristles of his thin grey moustache. Waiting until he was sure the message had finished, he ripped off the sheet with a hand resembling a pack of five extra large pork sausages with some of the pig's bristle still poking through, and taking it back to his desk wheezed and dumped his bulk back onto his long-suffering, sturdy chair.

The person sending the message, one Dean Mansfield, Mr Scroggins accountant and business partner, needed to speak to Mr David Bodger urgently about a sizeable legacy of money, property and businesses owned by the deceased, in Australia. Both Henry Scroggins and his late partner, Betty Mathieson, had left no trace of a will with their Australian solicitor, just information verbally given to a young female member of staff moments before he died, and a tape recording which it was imperative the deceased's son heard. This they would send on hearing from him, David Bodger.

Across the road Henry put down the paper, worked out how much he reckoned he'd saved by not going straight to the nearest Turf Accountant, and with an immense sense of self-righteousness, got up, collected his bags together, wished the barman 'Happy New Year!' ('and to you Sor!') and stepped from the wine bar.

He stood on the pavement for a while, blinking into the light, wondering whether he dared do what his heart was craving to do and not wait until Monday to call Millicent. He just wasn't sure he could wait until Monday and after all what difference did it make and what were phone boxes for? Nobody seemed to use them these days and it always struck him as such a waste, especially not having a phone at home. And there by a stroke of luck - one that he chose to imagine was more destiny than luck - stood one on the opposite side of the road from him, its emptiness begging and beckoning him across.

Deciding it was meant to be, he checked his loose change and, with the slight encumbrance of shopping bags, finally managed to open the heavily hinged door and fight his way into the booth. A powerful smell of urine greeted him immediately on entry and made him plant his bags onto his shoes, although he really wanted to lift his shoes onto something too, but this not being possible he decided his stay would be very brief and to the point as he took out Millicent's letter from his mackintosh pocket for her phone number. Squinting at the instructions on the side of the coin box, which appeared far more complicated than last time he'd used a public phone in the Sixties, he eventually heard the dialling tone and held his breath. Within three rings Millicent's soft calming voice was greeting him as he listened frozen in grinning wonderment before remembering to ram coins in the slot. The next thing he heard was a girlish giggle as she heard him fumbling, cursing and retrieving a dropped twenty pence coin before calling out, or rather shouting:

'Hello! Millicent! Is that you?'

'Yes Henry, Happy New Year!' she laughed, 'what a lovely surprise.'

'I've got your letter. I'm so, so…thank you so much.' How can I…?'

'Are you in a phone box?'

'Yes. Smells awful. Can you smell it?'

'They all do. Drunks pee in them.'

'Oh…really?'

Henry looked down and gave his bags an extra lift up with his toes, the riddle of phone box emptiness now solved. Millicent continued.

'The filthy swine forget they were built for phone calls and not calls of nature!'

Henry looked at the damp patches on the ground with disgust, regretted picking up his twenty pence piece and decided there was no time to waste on small talk.

'Millicent, when can we meet?'

'Are you definitely going back on Monday?'

'Oh yes, you bet I am,' replied Henry with such enthusiasm and confidence that Millicent had to restrain herself from patronising him like she did George when he performed tricks for his favourite 'uncles'.

'Good. How about after work, outside your office?'

Henry panicked, visualising work colleagues seeing him meeting a beautiful woman and, not at this stage aware of how he was to be greeted on his return to the office, opted to avoid the risk of further ridicule.

'Do you think we could make it somewhere else? Somewhere close to Charing Cross perhaps?'

'Do you know Gordon's Wine Bar in Villiers Street?'

'I know Villiers Street.'

'It's at the bottom. You can't miss it. It's got a very private, intimate little cellar bar.'

'That's nice,' said Henry, not convinced he was quite ready for intimate but quite liking the private. 'What time?'

'What time do you finish work?'

'Five-thirty, so, can we say six o'clock?'

'I'll be there. Are you okay by the way? At home I mean? Your moth…'

'Everything's fine. Really - fine. And Millicent…'

'Yes Henry?'

'I've made a New Year's Resolution.'

'Oh, good. Let me guess.'

'Go on.'

'Giving up sex.'

The brief silence that ensued and the shock of this comment took a second to register with Henry but his instinct was to chuckle, which encouraged an unladylike snort from Millicent followed by an attempt to stifle her laughter until she heard Henry's chuckle develop into something he tried but failed to suppress, which in itself coming from Henry was instantly contagious and spread the infection back to Millicent who was also trying desperately hard not to let it become too big a joke for the sake of Henry's feelings, but unable to hold back, burst into hysterics until before long they were unable to talk, until with much sighing, stopping and re-igniting of laughter, they finally composed themselves.

'I've also made one.'

'Made what?' asked Henry, having forgotten the reason for their laughter and now feeling that in laughing he'd sucked in far too many urine fumes and desperately needed fresh air.

Millicent's voice, so light and sweet and feminine in Henry's insatiable ear, chorused, 'A New Year's Resolution Henry. But it's a secret. Six o'clock at Gordon's. Bye.'

And she was gone.

Henry stared into the receiver with a frozen grin and an overpowering feeling that he was now a man. He staggered out of the phone box with his bags, inhaled a giant lungful of fresh air and with the smile still riveted to his face, possibly for eternity, set off with his bags across the common and down the hill towards home, imagining that not one single person he passed could fail to realise that he was now a real man and had a real woman as his best friend. A beautiful, sophisticated lady - a lady *solicitor* no less - who found him funny and wasn't ashamed to be seen with him in a London wine bar.

Henry wanted to walk forever, he was so happy, but was now sure that if he really needed to he could also call a taxi. Just like Millicent.

So it was, with this burning *joie de vivre*, that he took his uplifted spirit home, insulated from the truth of Millicent's New Year's Resolution; a resolution she had been contemplating over

139

Christmas and had in fact already put on trial, ignoring two invitations to 'dinner'. These notable clients had left messages on her answering machine, obviously feeling they were safe to emerge from their foxholes thanks to the Press's current preoccupation with rumours of an imminent royal wedding announcement, coupled with their more basic need to treat themselves to Millicent's unencumbered company after the terrible endurance of their highly restrictive festive family duties.

Millicent had not returned their calls, her simple and accepted code for being otherwise engaged, but now it was far more than that. Her trial had ended, and her resolution - New Year, New Life, call it whatever - was cast in stone; cast the instant she replaced her receiver after Henry's call. A resolution she knew would not under any circumstances, for all the time she called Henry a friend, ever be broken.

Poor, happy Henry; how Millicent's heart ached at the thought of him ever one day finding out the truth.

And whilst Henry with his bags and smile trudged blissfully the last few yards of his journey home, breathlessly half-humming, half-singing *Seventy-Six Trombones* and adjusting his step occasionally in time with his version of the march, thinking to himself that he hadn't actually got round to telling Millicent what his life-changing resolution was, Archibald Snapes informed his secretary he was nipping across the road.

Five minutes later, placing his glass of chardonnay on the table in the window seat of the wine bar, the overweight solicitor took the folded teleprinter page from his pocket, slowly opened it and once more scanned it from top to bottom before staring up into the vacant yonder of his imagination outside the window, little knowing that the namesake and son of the recently deceased person whose name in print was feeding his hungry eyes and stirring up notions and plans in his weasel brain, had only half an hour ago vacated the seat currently supporting his fat cashmere-clad buttocks.

Chapter Fourteen

## HENRY'S RENAISSANCE - PART ONE

The scales had shifted at 52 Viola Street since Henry's night out, and both mother and son were acutely aware of it.; aware that the equilibrium had swung for the first time towards Henry, but both were tip-toeing around it and resuming their normal routines as best they could, Henry back to his morning tea duty and his mother seated back in the parlour where she kept up unusually animated commentaries on the Wilmot's hedonistic lifestyle, which had not seemed to cease or even abate since Christmas Eve, a stream of visitors coming and going each day, bringing armfuls of food, drink and presents and arriving and leaving with a lot of car door banging and excessive alacrity.

Irma Scroggins, being a 'devout but private' worshipper, as she liked to point out to the hypocrites who attended church, had placed so many curses upon the Wilmots in so short a time, mainly about them flying in the face of the sanctity of her religion, that Henry, in no doubt that his mother had more clout with God's greatest adversary than with the Deity himself, was expecting the Wilmots to all fall down or be huffed and puffed into flames at any time.

Lily Bunce had also been permitted back to resume their afternoon sessions and thereby never had the parlour known such utterances of damnation as during these current hours of neighbourly togetherness. In a strange way it had almost brought the two ladies closer, as often happens after a violent falling out. Having a common enemy to direct attacks upon is such an edifying and unifying thing and the Wilmots were fulfilling that role perfectly - which brings us back to Henry.

He was no longer Irma Scroggins' easy target and had even prepared meals from his visit to the delicatessen, food that had never graced the table of the house before but which even Irma Scroggins, after picking and poking at each plateful for a while, had grudgingly awarded a grunt or two of approval, and, on all but one occasion when she spat anchovies over the floor as if they were arsenic, had given her son the closest thing to a seal of approval he'd ever known.

As for Lily Bunce, she was positively bursting to know the reason for Henry's uncharacteristic buoyancy on the few times they met over the weekend, particularly in the light of his non-appearance on the morning of the twenty-third of December, his reappearance later the next day (but by the *front* entrance to the house), and the forever unmentionable knowledge that he was heavily in debt.

It was all very mysterious and what she wouldn't have given for a crash course in clairvoyance instead of being forced to endure the torment of guessing and waiting for further clues or something dramatic to happen. But then she was nothing if not a patient woman and knew from decades of experience that eventually human nature must take its course, inevitably revealing a conclusion to reward her patient suspense; not always a satisfactory conclusion but at least a conclusion of sorts to enable her to put a story to bed and await the next street drama, if indeed it hadn't already appeared and overlapped the first.

Henry lay in bed staring up at the crack in the ceiling just as he had done at the exact same time on the last fateful morning he'd gone to work just eleven short days ago, it being Monday morning and a day he was both dreading and excitedly anticipating. Dreading, because he had no idea how he would be received by his colleagues after the debacle of his drunken, violent outbreak; excitedly anticipating, because whatever happened at the office he could cling to the prospect of being afterwards in Millicent's divine presence. And, apart from merely bathing in her divine presence, he might also possibly discover what divine *powers* she possessed that caused courts to instantly dismiss cases, bullying bosses to submit and quaver in fear, and overdue rises to be awarded and backdated; incrementally.

But unlike two weeks ago, Henry was not going to even bother telling his mother that he was going to be late. She'd find out soon enough, and anyway he would only be an hour or so later than normal and what business was it of hers? He lay and thought of

Millicent and panicked momentarily as he struggled to construct an accurate picture of her. How could he possibly forget what she looked like in just twelve days? It was inconceivable, but try as he may the instant he saw her face smiling down on him she dissolved just as a happy dream dissolves on waking, fracturing into vague elusive pieces that refuse to reform like a broken, once cherished, kaleidoscope.

He heard movement in the room next door and checking his watch realised that he was actually fifteen minutes late getting up, yet miraculously not a word had pierced the wall behind his head. Not one syllable. Yes, those days were over he told himself, the pendulum had most definitely swung. He wondered what was going on in the twisted mind through the wall, she knowing the full extent of his debt yet having to watch him come and go with a fearlessness bordering fecklessness, a situation she not only couldn't understand but as yet had not worked out a plan to combat and defeat. He wondered, not really caring either way, whether it would herald her great Conversion, like Paul on the road to Damascus - one minute holding coats for the stone-throwing murderers of Stephen and then, after his 'vision', writing a best seller on Jesus. Would she, could she, finally see the light?

'Hen-*ry*!' The noise of her light switching on accompanied the screech. No, she hadn't seen the light.

Henry sighed and responded with the laconic weariness of one who is complying out of courtesy but no longer needs to, and shook his head wearily.

'Yes Mother?'

'It's late!'

Late, yes. Of course it was late and of course it was too good to be true, his foolish idle mental ramblings of a tyrannical woman realising the error of her ways after all these years. How can a mind like a satanic mill whose conveyor belt only ever streams negative thoughts and actions, suddenly flick a switch and start manufacturing a gleaming product line of goodness, hope and charity? When would he ever learn? Stupid boy.

'Henry! *Henry!*'

'Oh shut up woman,' he muttered to himself and walked along the short landing, past her door, to the bathroom where he proceeded to run a bath. A bath! At 52 Viola Street - possibly a first - certainly a first for Henry.

He looked at his reflection in the mirror as it began to steam up and his first thought was that it wasn't anything like the head that had stared back at him over the years, the head that since it was actually high enough to look into the mirror had grown sadder and balder and bleaker and meeker month by month, year by lonely year. The one he saw now was still undeniably boring and unattractive but all the same it was a new one, a happy one, even a slightly cocky one, one with hope instead of despair, one not as ugly and repulsive as he'd grown accustomed to, one quite nice and bright and reasonably acceptable and possibly even able to make others happy; perhaps a lady happy.

'Henry!' But not this one.

Henry took the few steps back to his mother's door and putting his lips close to it, enunciated over the noise of the gushing water.

'I'm taking a *bath* Mother - a new year's resolution.'

He felt like telling her the truth that he was meeting a lady that evening, one who had already bared her body to him and tried to entice him into a sexual liaison, but not feeling quite ready to announce such cataclysmic news - not unless there was a genuine chance of it inducing something fatal - he merely listened at the door and hearing nothing, shrugged and returned to his new early morning steam experience.

Once Henry had taken his bath and shaved as close as possible without decapitating himself, by virtue of having to shave blind due to the mirror refusing to clear of steam, he rummaged at the back of the bathroom cabinet for a bottle of aftershave that he knew was there somewhere, a red container that had been sitting gathering dust for oh, it must have been fourteen or fifteen years he calculated, just offering a rare, brief appearance when he groped for an elastoplast or indigestion tablet at the back.

'Old Spice! Ah, there you are!' he muttered in triumph.

144

Heaven above knows who bought it but obviously it came as a Christmas present from one of the last relatives to grace their house with a visit. He blew years of accumulated dust off the bottle's top and shoulders, unscrewed and sniffed. Then he stroked his smooth, soft chin that felt much like the baby's face that had brushed his when he'd carried it off the train. He stopped for a moment and wondered whether the baby had ever given him a second thought but, deciding that babies almost certainly wouldn't have such things as second thoughts, he shook the bottle and dabbed some on his skin, wincing as it found a cut beside his lip. Then he dabbed some more and sucked the aroma deep into his lungs hoping it would stay there until evening, imagining Millicent sniffing and complimenting him. He thought she'd give him at least a peck hello and be pleased that he no longer smelt of dank wet mackintosh. Should he take the bottle with him for a refresher before meeting her? He decided no, in case it fell out of his pocket.

The steam of the bathroom, the feeling of cleanliness and pungent smell of aftershave made him feel restored, revived, re-incarnated. Why had he never done this before? Why had he allowed one person to strike the fear of the devil into him since childhood and dictate his every action, even to the point of him being too terrified to contemplate a bath before work or the putting on of aftershave, in case she read into these simple actions - actions that every other man and woman took for granted - some devious intent.

Malice aforethought; the expression suddenly arrived uninvited into his head as he stared at his face, still blurry due to steam and lack of spectacles, and listened to the worthless obstacle to his complete happiness banging and crashing the noisiest items she could lay her hands on in the kitchen downstairs. Could this face, he asked himself, could this very ordinary bland soft white face hasten the departure of another human being from the world? Could it? Was it so wrong to want to humanely remove his mother somehow from his life? Confessing this desire to Millicent in the pub had been like an exorcism. It had popped out of his mouth so freely and unexpectedly yet in doing so had relieved him of the guilt he felt whenever the prospect of her early, possibly assisted, demise, entered his head. But now, supposing that Millicent was prepared to help, just supposing, then what was stopping them getting rid of her and living happily ever after? What a stupid thought, what a glorious thought. What a free, guiltless happy thought!

Henry peered once more at his face and the dreadful realisation entered his head that he looked not unlike a plump John Christie, he of 10 Rillington Place and quite a number of murdered women interred therein. He sucked his cheeks in hard as a trial but instantly relaxed them on discovering that he really *did* look far too much like a plump John Christie for comfort, and vowed not to make any attempt to lose weight until his mother was dead and fairly well decayed, being pretty sure Christie's waxwork was still in The Chamber of Horrors at Madame Tussauds and seen by a lot of people on a daily basis - all potential witnesses.

By the time Henry had dressed - selecting a colourful blue and yellow tie that he'd never before dared wear anywhere, least of all to the office - and made an appearance downstairs, his mother had somehow managed to make herself tea and deposit herself in her chair in the parlour. Henry looked in and saw her sitting clutching cup and saucer as she stared out of the window and slowly bit a chunk off her Arrowroot biscuit, pausing a moment as something caught her eye, before her bony jaws started slowly turning, grinding into action.

'Nobody,' thought Henry, 'could do something as innocent as bite a piece off a biscuit with such a degree of sinister intent. Even Bette Davis in *Whatever Happened to Baby Jane* couldn't do it.' But then Irma Scroggins, as we've already witnessed on more than one occasion, was nothing if not a consummate actress when duty called and could have given the formidable Miss Davis a run for her money any day.

'Where have you put my tea Mother?' enquired Henry mischievously.

He expected no reply and received none. Just the jaws grinding, the teeth nibbling and the nose sniffing irritably like a rabbit discovering a piece of peppered lettuce; cold watery eyes staring unblinking out at the dawn breaking over the grey slate rooftops opposite.

His mischievousness suddenly turned to fury as the full extent of her selfishness and nastiness compacted into the sight of her hunched and greedy figure, sitting slurping tea and biting a biscuit without a thought in her head of ever making a cup of tea for him. In that moment, all the hatred that she had instilled in Henry through her wicked ways and years of oppression burst out of him like a lanced boil and if he'd had a brick in his hand he could happily have brought it crashing down on her miserable parsimonious cranium. As it was he stared at her nibbling profile, took a deep breath, thought of the other woman who had brought such a brief but blissful period of companionship and joy into his life, wondered yet again how both women could possibly come under the same gender umbrella of 'female', and decided that not only was it not wrong to get rid of her - it was his positive duty and right. So, putting down his mental brick and picking up his battered brown leather briefcase in the hall he left the house with head erect, teeth gritted in seething determination, and Lily Bunce's laser eyes penetrating his skull as he passed by her window.

By the time he returned that evening on the 7.05 train from Charing Cross, Henry was without doubt a changed man. The trepidation about what awaited him at the Department was not only dispelled the instant he set a nervous foot through the office door but transformed into a veritable launch pad to Nirvana.

Henry Winston Scroggins, tortured and ridiculed into drunken submission just two short weeks earlier, was greeted by those very same perpetrators (with two notable exceptions) as a returning hero. Immediately on his entry, Peters and Lee's song *Welcome Home* leapt into a deafening, unsteady start from a tape machine somewhere on a desk before being turned down, then up again. Cheers erupted, balloons left over from the Christmas party burst out loud, and streamers fizzed and flew all about him as his colleagues gathered, smiling and cheering and gently easing off his mackintosh and scarf, to lead him triumphantly to his desk where a huge envelope stood propped against his nest of well-squared, empty in-trays.

John Deighton was the senior member of the welcoming party and the only other person apart from Henry and Phyllis to have endured twenty years of Peregrine Spencer's bullying, blustering dictatorial management. He was an inoffensive decent family man, small-boned and pleasant-looking with delicate features and a moustache and mousey fringe that although both a little too regimental in design were more than compensated by a gentle soft voice, eyes that sparkled when he spoke, and a heart that had bled for his long-standing colleague as he had stood back in shame during Henry's humiliation. Oh, how this man had since lost sleep with regret at being powerless to stop the pack of wolves that, once scenting blood, had torn their prey mercilessly apart, led from the front by the head of the hunt and ground into the soil by his common, red-lipped co-assassin. Both these unpleasant characters, as Henry was about to find out, were not part of the crowd who now formed a half moon gaggle of bodies in front of his desk eagerly awaiting the opening of the envelope and John Deighton's speech.

They watched as the dazed portly little man sat and slowly picked up the envelope, looking up and around at them all, blinking a smile with lips that formed several times to speak but gave up as the noisy chatter and good wishes gradually abated to a hum of expectation. Henry slid out the card, examined and admired the front picture of a clear mountain stream crossing boulders and then opened it up to reveal a mass of signatures, apologies and best wishes. He could find no words, such was the intensity of the shock he was once more suffering at his desk, a desk that had for years prided itself on maintaining a tranquil state and utmost dignity whatever the circumstances that surrounded it, but had now been subjected to more drama in two weeks than any tranquil, dignified desk deserves in a desk lifetime.

Being Henry, tears came too readily and fight them as he may and swallow hard as he tried, one or two found their way down his cheeks and dripped onto his blotter. The emotion soon spread, as is prone to do in such situations, and it was a while before throats finished clearing, noses finished sniffing and tissues finished stuffing back into trouser pockets or cardigan sleeves.

'I, I don't know what to....' began Henry before John Deighton stepped forward and, placing a hand gently on Henry's shoulder, looked up at the gathering, cleared his throat to avoid a potentially embarrassing croak, and began to speak.

'Henry, two weeks ago in this office, you may remember...' He looked down at Henry and patted his shoulder, '...well, the first bit anyway.' Everyone waited for Henry's reaction which was to offer the tiniest good-humoured shake of the head, before they could join in the joke with him. John Deighton continued. 'What happened Henry - there's no point in beating around the bush - was utterly shameful and we, your colleagues who stand here ashamed and full of the deepest and humblest regret, can only do what any decent human beings would do - and I hope you can still see us as decent human beings - (Henry with a slight nod and mouthing 'of course') and that is ask you to forgive us.'

There followed a general hum of agreement and a few here-here's. 'There is no excuse,' continued the orator, 'no excuse whatsoever for drunkenness and high spirits to turn to bullying. There is no excuse for being egged on by someone who we all acknowledge should be setting an example instead of encouraging cruel and infantile behaviour. I repeat, there *is* no excuse.' He looked around him. 'You might not have noticed yet but there are two absentees today, one of whom has now left the Department with, I can tell you Henry, her head hung low. June Catchpole has asked me to pass on her apologies for her part in the goings-on and I have agreed to do so. Our illustrious manager (a few boos and rhubarbs were quelled by a raised hand from John), who is not looking quite so illustrious of late (lots of laughs and whoops and a 'Well done Henry!' subdued again by the raised hand), chose not to attend. We gave him the opportunity, as we are all equally guilty - and I include myself of course - to offer his apology, but he, as I say, chose not to. Might I say, without risking my pension (more laughs), that you have our fullest respect and support for being the first person ever in twenty years of - certainly in my time here in this office - to stand up for himself against the - *over-*

*exuberant* - nature (cries of 'bullying!') that a certain person has chosen as his preferred style of management. There are those who abuse their positions of authority and enjoy trampling over common decency and those, like you Henry, who make no waves, cause no offence but when pushed too far, as we have all witnessed, decide enough…is enough', the second 'enough' subdued and almost incomplete, adding pathos to the silence that followed.

Here, he squeezed Henry's shoulder playfully and added, 'It's just a pity that it took a drop or three of unwanted alcohol to bring things to a head - and there's a few of us long sufferers here who may regard it as a pity you didn't start drinking a long time ago!' This was greeted with a loud round of applause and the beginnings of 'For he's a jolly good fellow' over John Deighton's final shouted joke, 'Then maybe *you'd* be sitting in that office!'

This really brought the house down as John jerked his thumb over his shoulder in the direction of Spencer's deserted office. Henry, beaming and flushed with self-effacement, suddenly looked up and squinted over his glasses as the rest of the staff slowly dispersed to their desks and duties, with pats of good luck and more apologies.

'Phyllis,' he said, 'Where is Phyllis? I haven't seen her.'

'Phyllis has taken the day off,' replied John, somewhat cagily, 'she rang this morning and said she wasn't feeling too well. Asked to give her apologies to you and wished you a nice day.'

Henry looked sad, as if he was responsible, and said, 'I hope it wasn't because of me John. She's very loyal to Peregrine and with her not being at the office party she may think that I've…'

'Henry, she's fine. She might look daft but she's not stupid, as we both know. How long have you, we three, known each other?'

Henry nodded. 'Twenty years.' Then he sighed and continued. 'Poor Phyllis, she has the blind devotion of a beaten child and the heart of an angel. Not a good combination in this difficult world.'

Henry had always had a soft spot for spinster Phyllis. They were affectionately seen by the Department as being rather like the back and front ends of a pantomime horse; doddery, harmless, badly-dressed, never altering one tiny bit and clumsily dependable.

Once upon a time they were quite close and would have lunch in the canteen together and talk about their common problem of overbearing mothers, but the death of Phyllis's mother six years ago and Henry's increasing problem with tardy racehorses had slackened their quaint bond to a point where they had returned to being just polite colleagues, both grown battle-weary under Spencer's regime and with each passing year ever more frightened of putting a foot wrong for fear of being thrown overboard without a life jacket. Like everyone acutely aware of their limitations, they knew they could never risk biting the hand that fed them, uncaring as it was.

John Deighton peered around at the office in general and then over to Phyllis's desk outside Spencer's office. For the first time it reminded him of a dog basket outside its master's bedroom.

'Henry, she's in a difficult position at the moment. But you're not, and I want you to know - if you don't already - that you have won untold respect from everyone here. Spencer is a broken man, trust me; broken forever, and I don't just mean his nose. Well done by the way - we all liked that - best use for that ghastly Buddha. He's had it coming to him for years and it just happens that the last person anyone suspected of giving him his come-uppance – namely you - did just that. I sent a memo to the powers-that-be explaining the whole situation, the provocation of not just the party night but everything that has built up over years of his management, and - I've been interviewed.'

'What?' Henry looked up in disbelief. 'Interviewed? By whom?'

John touched his nose and said 'Who else? The only person higher than Spencer, that's who.'

Henry stared at his desk and carefully straightened his blotter with the fingertips of both hands before speaking. 'It was all so unnecessary. I was only trying to annoy my mother.'

'Your mother? What's she got to do with Spencer?'

'That's funny you should say that John. I've never thought about it before but she has everything to do with Peregrine Spencer. They are both bullies who have now lost control over me.' He looked up at John. 'That's rather good isn't it?'

'Yes Henry,' replied John cheerily, 'that *is* rather good.'

Chapter Fifteen

## RED RED WINE

'Henry, we're just filling in time. All of us, we're all stumbling around on this planet filling in time.'

Millicent had reached across their table in the wine bar and placed a hand over Henry's clenched fist resting next to his empty plate, her face imploring him. He stared at her hand on his, felt the small, warm softness and looked up at her. She released her hand and leant back in her chair, waiting for Henry's reply, glancing at a young couple who had just sat down next to them.

After a happy start to their date and conversation buoyant and positive, Henry had fallen into a taciturn frame of mind. Millicent, who knew the minds of men better than most, calculated that the reason for this was the recent emotional turmoil Henry had been forced to endure, far exceeding any previous experience in his mundane world and suddenly all coming to a head. Things were brighter, life was full of hope for the first time, but in the midst of what should be moments of extreme happiness she knew too well that sometimes the delirium is too much and the spirit plummets for no obvious reason. Henry looked up from staring at his plate and into Millicent eyes, holding his gaze on her face for several seconds.

'Is that it then? Is that what I've been putting up with for forty years? Just filling in time as *she's* just filling in time, only *she's* filling it by making *me* as miserable as possible?' He shook his head dismissively. 'No, sorry Millicent, I can't believe that.'

'But Henry we all get through because we have no choice in the matter. None of us ask to be born do we? So we make the best of it, we try to be happy; we search for peace of mind. But it's not easy so we do whatever we can to bring peace and happiness. Some are naturally happy, some aren't; some are naturally gifted, some are naturally hopeless, most fall in between. There's no passport to happiness whatever we're given. There are blissful idiots and depressed geniuses, and vice versa. There are blissful teetotallers and happy drunks, depressed teetotallers and depressed drunks. It's life.' She leaned forward and checking either side of her, whispered in a sing-song voice, 'Life's a piece of shit, when you think of it…'

Henry frowned. 'Shit' wasn't right coming out of Millicent's pretty mouth and it was loud enough to attract flashed glances from the couple and a grin from the young man who smiled at Millicent and, dancing slightly in his chair, began to sing with his mouth stuffed full of pie, 'When you're chewing on life's gristle, don't worry, give a whistle!' to the dismay of his girlfriend who, like Henry, was oblivious of anything relating to Monty Python.

'But it's never too late for change,' continued Millicent, 'life can change in a flash. Look at you, in one week you've taken control back from racehorses, a bullying boss and a domineering mother. Isn't that an excellent reason for being alive?'

Henry thought for a while and then confidently cocked his head on one side, gave a few seconds thought, and nodded. He got up from his chair, to Millicent's surprise, and glancing at the young couple's table where they both had a glass of red wine, asked discreetly from behind his hand, 'I think I'm ready to try red wine. What does it taste like?'

'That's for you to discover Henry,' said Millicent victoriously, getting up and brushing crumbs from her navy skirt. 'Stay there, I'll get them.'

Henry placed a hand on Millicent's arm and, still in a whisper, said 'Please Millicent, allow me. '

Millicent sat down, crossed her arms, smiled up him and said, 'I'd like a large please Henry. House will do nicely.'

'House?' enquired Henry, 'house what?'

When he returned it was with pride that he carefully deposited two glasses of red wine on their table and then took his seat, eyeing his glass and wondering how he now advanced safely to the next step, that of drinking the contents without making a fool of himself.

It was enough that he actually had a glass of alcohol in front of him, especially in the light of recent history, and something as exotic as red wine; *house* red wine at that. House didn't sound terribly exotic but he had been pleasantly surprised when he'd said the word at the bar and wasn't subjected to any advanced questioning about what sort of *house* he'd prefer, beyond a simple colour choice. This was a good lesson for him as wine had been another of his prime social phobias (alongside taxis); that if ever he was placed in a situation where he had to choose wine he wouldn't have a clue what to ask for. His brief look at a wine list many years ago had reminded him of the trouble he endured in his French class at school, where a language that had seemed fairly elementary to most of the others, had remained a constant mystery to him for three years. His teacher's idea of ten minutes homework used to take him at least an hour and the only word he had carried with him into adulthood was 'Alors', it being the one that his various teachers seemed to precede every sentence with, and despite hearing it possibly a thousand times, he still to this day hadn't a clue what it meant apart from, he surmised, the French equivalent of 'Umm...' Henry didn't imagine there would be a wine called 'Alors' to make his choice easy so had always deliberately avoided the snake pit of wine selection.

'Happy birthday Millicent,' he announced, lifting his glass of red house wine, to which the young man cheekily grinned and lifted his, chorusing 'Happy birthday Millicent!'

Henry glanced at him with a degree of irritation, feeling his sacred wine moment was being hijacked

'I thought you said this was private and intimate.'

Millicent acknowledged the chirpy chappie with a raised glass, feeling for him, for it seemed he would much prefer to be sharing their evening than with his sullen partner who sulkily stabbed at her food with a fork in one hand whilst the other hand cupped her chin at the end of a supporting forearm, elbow on table.

'Sorry. How did you know, by the way?' she asked.

'Know what?'

'That it's my birthday.'

'I read it on the calendar - in your kitchen,' replied Henry, hesitantly. Millicent raised an eyebrow as she sipped, recollecting the reason why Henry was in the kitchen. 'I had to do something whilst I was waiting for you to return.'

Millicent swallowed hard and nodded. 'Waiting for me to appear almost naked you mean.'

It was unfortunate that Henry had plucked up courage to take his first ever swig of wine at this precise moment, a swig which at the mention of the word *naked* was busy swilling around his mouth and about to be dispatched to his oesophagus, but due to the overt emphasis Millicent had accidentally placed on the word *naked* and the instant snigger that erupted from the chirpy chappie beside them, it had diverted up his nasal passage and emerged as a red liquid torrent snorting from his nostrils.

There are some people, mostly light social tipplers, who spend their lives drinking without mishap. There are others, the regular to heavy drinkers who generally do the same, maybe causing themselves and others occasional embarrassment at the tail end of their sessions; and then there are people like Henry, who rarely, if ever, take a drink, but when they do, through absolutely no direct fault of their own, something happens that makes them wish they'd never bothered and likely won't ever again. Such was the case right now in the low-ceilinged intimacy of Gordon's Wine Bar on a busy Monday evening.

If it had been in a quiet corner on a quiet evening, Henry could have secreted himself away in the shadows and privately recovered, but with all tables occupied in what was to Henry no more than a candlelit cave, and a pretty small cave at that, there really was no hiding place. So he took the only course of action he could think of, by glancing around for the toilet sign, which pointed upstairs, and hastily making towards it, trying to stem the flow of wine down his nose whilst coughing and spluttering every step of the way, thus drawing even more unwanted attention to his very public plight.

By the time Henry emerged from the toilet five minutes later, breathless, eyes bloodshot and small blobs of purple on his tie and shirt collar, Millicent was standing outside with his mac, scarf and briefcase to whisk him into daylight, away from any further embarrassment. She had mopped up the wine on the table whilst apologising to the young couple, the young man expressing concern for Henry and seeming disappointed that his fun had no doubt ended for the evening.

Standing on the pavement outside Millicent helped Henry on with his mac and handed him his briefcase.

'Are you sure you're okay?'

Henry nodded, the after effects of wine-burn to his nose and throat still acute. 'Yes thank you, but maybe we'll try white next time. Or maybe I should have swallowed straight away instead of trying to show off by swilling it round my mouth at precisely the time you chose to say the word *naked*. Loudly. In public.'

Millicent placed a hand to her mouth to try and stifle laughter, without success. Henry saw the funny side and smiled.

'It was a lovely meal Millicent and I'm not going to let a choking fit spoil the memory. Just the wrong word at the wrong time to the wrong person, that's all. Maybe I should stick to Wimpey Bars instead of wine bars for safety.'

And with that he pulled back the sleeve of his mac and with the instinct of a time and motion man far too regimented as yet to react with the nonchalant souciance of a lover, observed:

'If I hurry I might just catch the 7.05.'

Millicent linked her arm into Henry's and smiled quietly to herself as they walked together up Villiers Street to the steps leading to the station concourse, she examining her navy shoes and thinking of their conversation over the meal and he glancing furtively around, imagining the whole of London was watching and mocking their strange union, more than a little concerned that one of the forty-something members of his office would be converging on the station at the very moment he walked locked in arms with Millicent.

They stood under the large round clock, Henry squinting across at the train times and noting under his breath that he had three minutes to board. As he turned back he felt Millicent's soft lips planted quickly on and off his cheek, a brushed peck, and then watched her eyes shining into his as she pushed a curl of hair from her forehead.

'And that's my thank you for a lovely hour,' she grinned. 'What are you doing on Thursday, same time?'

Henry was still savouring the soft surprise of the kiss before the sensation faded, the nerve endings of his cheek hanging on tight as he peered mesmerised at the lips that had planted it.

'Nothing,' he gulped.

'Then meet me here at 5.45. We're going shopping.'

'Shopping?'

'Yes, it's late night.'

'What for?'

'Clothes.'

'Who for?

'You.'

'Me? But…'

A whistle sounded and with a push on the arm from Millicent and a 'Quick! Run!' Henry was shuffling towards the barrier and disappearing in a flap of mackintosh and wave of briefcase that, if the guard holding the gate hadn't taken instant evasive action by bending his spine backwards forty-five degrees, would have possibly removed, or at least loosened, several of his teeth.

Millicent stood for a moment deep in thought, peering at the barrier where Henry had just bustled through and listening to doors slam and a second whistle before the train pulled out.

She thought of previous liaisons under the old round clock above her, too many of them, and knew that nothing came close to this. Then she thanked her lucky stars that Henry, who over their meal had happily told her his New Year Resolution, had not thought to ask about hers.

## Chapter Sixteen

# HENRY'S RENAISSANCE – PART TWO

The following week saw the curve on Henry's Graph of Life (first mentioned the day he decided to embark on his brave retaliatory experiment) take a dramatic swerve upward.

The ponderous machine that was the Ministry, for whom he worked equally ponderously, though efficiently, had suddenly found a new momentum and taken instant action in calling Henry in. He had been summoned on the day following the Gordon's Wine Bar experience with Millicent to an office he knew existed but had never entered, been warmly greeted by the Minister and ushered into the depths of a very large, deep red leather chair next to a wide, low coffee table and adjacent to a long window reaching down just two feet above the luxurious beige carpet enveloping his Tufs, offering one of London's most attractive vistas. But Henry's backside was effectively now so close to the carpet that any admiration of this otherwise scenic sweep of Horse Guards Parade and St. James's Park beyond was rendered impossible - only permitting him a glimpse of the tops of the tallest of the trees in the park.

So he sat, or rather slumped, like a bewildered Lilliputian whilst the Minister made small talk over tea, coffee and biscuits delivered on a silver tray by an attractive secretary who on depositing said tray on said coffee table ghosted in a small-stepped, silent glide from the office.

The Minister's chair was several inches higher than Henry's which, as anyone who has attended an important interview will attest, is the interviewer's prerogative and pleasure, but to show that he considered Henry to be someone of undoubted importance the Minister proceeded to do the table waiting and with a faint superior smile flickering upon his thin lips, poured the coffee that Henry had requested and then lifting a plate, offered him a chocolate biscuit. Yes, that's a Government Minister waiting on Henry; Henry Scroggins, office clerk with special responsibility for Time and Motion. This was how Henry entered, under this lowly title, but how he exited was something quite, quite different.

After fifteen minutes of a serious ministerial monologue where he was eventually asked, and to which he readily agreed, not to take the matter of the Christmas Party any further and not to court publicity of any kind that might cause the Ministry to be brought into disrepute and possibly damage their otherwise proud unblemished reputation, Henry left the office as Henry Scroggins, *Department Manager* - with his salary doubled.

After a short period of stunned incredulity and not hearing a coherent word the Minister was saying, Henry's first thought on recovering his senses was to enquire - genuinely concerned as only the gentle, naïve Henry could be - about what was to happen to Peregrine Spencer. He was informed that the gentleman was taking time off indefinitely and would be performing consultancy duties from home for the foreseeable future. Whether he, Mr Spencer, returned to the Department was a matter to be considered at a later date but it would not be in any direct management capacity, of that Henry could be assured.

Henry, after having had everything repeated to him to ensure he clearly understood the gravity of the situation and the gravity in which indeed the Minister personally regarded the situation, signed a prepared declaration agreeing to everything that had just been repeated to him. The Minister, watching over Henry's shoulder like a hawk, tried not to whisk the paper away too quickly and did his best to conceal an enormous sense of relief, whereas for his part, Henry, not having been groomed in the same elite political school of duplicity, did not have any means whatsoever of concealing an advanced state of dazed nervous tension. When he did finally gather himself together, his attempts at extricating himself from the leather hole he seemed to have fallen even deeper into were hampered by very chocolaty fingers, caused when the shock of the Minister's announcement had left the biscuit suspended between his finger and thumb for around a minute, after which he switched it to the other hand and in doing so compounded, by one hundred percent, an already sticky chocolate situation. Thus encumbered he attempted to prise himself from the bowels of the chair by pushing up with just his chocolate free palms and swinging rather than rising into a standing position, only to find that his attempts at concealing his chocolaty digits were entirely thwarted by the Minister thrusting out his hand for Henry to shake. Caught off guard and vainly trying to keep his forefinger and thumb curled up inside his palm, this probably left the Minister with the distinct impression that Henry was a freemason.

With a guiding hand the new Department Manager was moved towards the door through which he passed and was greeted by the smiling secretary from behind her typewriter.

'Goodbye Mr Scroggins,' she chirruped, smiling with a breezy air that said 'Mr Scroggins, one of *us*', and showed him the way out, the only way out, with an usherette's flourish of the hand. Henry, by now quite disorientated, looked this way and that until eventually locating the lift and in a fuzz of time suspension found himself moments later wandering outside for fresh air. The Minister, meanwhile, disdainfully wiped the recently transferred chocolate deposits off his palm with a serviette and then tried to do the same with a chocolate fingerprint from the document that Henry had just signed.

The sun was shining for the first time in weeks and Henry sensed almost a touch of spring as the faint warmth of the sun's rays caressed his bald head. He wandered slowly towards the park, deep in thought, until eventually he sat down on a bench by the water and watched the ducks and squirrels compete for bread and nuts offered by a lady and gentleman arm in arm. They were laughing at the animals' antics and seemed very much in love, she adoringly clutching his arm and resting her head on and off his shoulder, giggling infectiously at her lover's clowning mimicry of the ducks' vain attempts to secure pole position over the squirrels.

Henry watched for a while and smiled at them when they turned and caught his eye, which made them inhibited which he was sorry for. He wanted to say to them 'Please do carry on, I know how it feels.'

For the first time in his life he could watch happy couples in love and not feel embarrassed. He'd never felt excluded before because it never entered his head that he was missing anything. Love was for lovers not for Henrys. But now it suddenly dawned on him that he was almost a lover. Millicent had held his arm in public with no apparent shame. She had kissed him under the clock at Charing Cross with no apparent shame. She had made it obvious she valued his friendship and company. Why, he didn't for the life of him have a clue, but she seemed very sincere, so was that love? He thought about it as the couple strolled off arm in arm. He'd quite forgotten that he was now a Department Manager until the Minister's voice returned to him, echoing the words over and over again, apologies and offers and agreements; things that were no part of his normal working world, or his world full stop, until now. He stared up at the blue sky.

Henry Winston Scroggins, Department Manager, earning - he wouldn't let his brain calculate the amount. It was too greedy, too sordid, too soon and just all too surreal for him to take in. He thought of Millicent and wanted to phone her. Would she now respect him as a man and not merely as a friend? Was he only her friend because she felt sorry for him and was just reacting to his uselessness and temporary dependency? Would that change now, like the child turning into a teenager who feels duty bound to reject and scorn those who gave it life and unconditional love? The sadness of the prospect gripped Henry and the full impact and realisation of his new position hit him. Panic surged through his podgy frame; an overwhelming feeling of insecurity and fear that set his hands and legs trembling. He wanted to turn back the clock and be normal, not be a lover (if that's what he was) or a boss. He couldn't do it. It wasn't him. How had it happened? How had he let it happen? All he'd done was made a somewhat rash decision to fight his mother back to try to win a little self-esteem and control over his miserable life before it was too late - and look where it had got him.

The sun went behind a cloud and the park became a dark, gloomy forbidding place, not the happy sunny one with the laughing lovers of a few moments earlier. Again, he felt impending doom descending upon him and the power of his mother return to sit like lead upon his shoulders, pushing him firmly back down into place; his proper place where he belonged.

He squinted through the gloom that was increasing by the second as a swirling cauldron of nimbus rolled across and loomed black and menacing overhead, threatening a downpour. He stood up and walked quickly towards the building, needing shelter but terrified of returning to his office and everything it now implied. He'd left as an ordinary colleague who had been welcomed back only the week before with open arms but now was returning as their manager. How would this change his relationship with colleagues? He'd only had this brief period to wallow in the soporific relief of actually having a job to return to and not being tarnished forever with a criminal record, and now inexplicably he'd been elevated onto a pedestal higher than anything he, or more to the point *they*, could have imagined. Or *he* could manage. Would their respect for him now alter into something unnatural, something inhibited, something he'd fought all his life not to be - special? That just wouldn't do.

The most important thing was Millicent. He needed to speak to her. The vulnerability he'd felt in the early hours of his first hangover, when the terrifying prospect of a court appearance had hung over him like the Sword of Damocles, had now returned and was lodged in the pit of his stomach. He felt for the piece of paper with her phone number and remembered it was in his mackintosh pocket in the office. He had to go back. The time had clicked over into his lunch break so he felt justified in ringing her, but even that thought was now one he would have to adjust. Peregrine Spencer, indeed all senior management, adhered to no fixed hours. They pleased themselves, came and went without question - quietly despised for it by lesser mortals forced to work within the confines of a different set of rules - but answering only ever to themselves, and caring not a fig.

Already preparing himself, despite his fear and despondency, for the changes that would automatically come with the new job, he made a vow as he walked faster through the large freezing raindrops now bombing his head and shoulders that he would manage as he wished to be managed. Do unto others and all that.

He'd quietly revolutionise the department, make everyone glad to be part of it and look forward to coming to work. In fact as he tottered faster towards shelter he started breathlessly vocalising, growing increasingly excited as the idea evolved by the second.

'Yes!' he gasped to himself with the concentrated tongue-protruding smile of a child painting its first classroom masterpiece, 'that's what I'll do!' How many years had he watched how *not* to do it and now he was being handed the opportunity to show *how* to do it! Perhaps the twenty years of Spencer's bad example was an apprenticeship, one he could put to good use and thereby make everyone's life much happier. With this uplifting cascade of tiny plans leaping one over the other his confidence surged, his sense of foreboding dispersed, and the sun pierced the vanishing nimbus like a glorious, brilliant, inspiring defiant arrow!

Two floors immediately above where Henry chattered and hurried along, the Minister peered down from the long window where Henry had shortly before been drinking coffee and listening to his life change. Glum-faced, the man watched Henry's scurrying figure before turning and returning to his desk where a photocopy of a cream-coloured letter headed *The Carter Consultancy* stared ominously up at him. It was a statement for the financial year April 1978-79, very similar to the one addressed to Peregrine Spencer and clipped to a compliments slip that bore a few words in a distinctive hand.

It read simply *'My dear friend, and your employee, Henry Scroggins, begs your understanding and my discretion. Please oblige. Millie.'*

The Minister politely ordered his secretary to go to lunch which she knew from years in his employ meant a non-business conversation possibly to book a private 'assignation', so she dutifully left within moments, closing the Minister's door and walking to the lift with a heavy heart and slight shake of her head. The Minister's wife was a sweet, serene, charitable lady and had offered the secretary discreet support on more than one difficult occasion over recent years.

The Minister waited a few seconds until he heard the lift door close and then, picking up the phone, slowly dialled the number on the compliments slip, rehearsing a speech in his head and taking a deep breath. He listened to the engaged tone, with a sense of relief that the moment was delayed, and slowly let the phone click back onto the receiver, fearful that his every move and sound was detectable and suspicious.

At that precise time and approximately one mile due north, Millicent gripped her phone to her ear with a heart as light as the Minister's was heavy, curled up on her bed with George snug and safe against her belly. She listened to Henry whispering his extraordinary morning to her and she, ever the obliging actress who knew that to truly convince others one must first truly convince one's self, effused excitement and pleasure as genuine and fresh as if hearing his news for the very first time - which indeed in a way, she was.

Two evenings later Millicent stood outside a changing room in a Savile Row tailors, making polite conversation with a tall, ramrod straight gentleman wearing a dark grey tailcoat and sleepy deferent smile. He nodded sagely at everything she said as he had done on many previous occasions whilst the same lady waited for a different man to emerge than he who hopped and stumbled into and out of trousers and jackets behind the changing-room door. As they chatted amiably, human noises emitted from the confines of the cubicle whose sides were enduring a severe buffeting; noises and buffeting that were beginning to turn the tail-coated manager's smile into something decidedly watery and anxious as he endeavoured to retain a cool demeanour whilst fearing the imminent collapse of his changing-room.

To the gentleman's relief, not to underestimate Millicent's, Henry burst out looking like a manikin whose face had been accidentally painted vermillion red and whose torso had been dressed rather quickly in a whirlwind. The desperate expression on Henry's face mixed with that of slight relief at being no longer incarcerated in a small, stuffy room was too much for Millicent whilst the tail-coated manager, who by his expression would have been quite at home in a Buckingham Palace sentry box, looked Henry over with a professional eye as if Cary Grant had just emerged in a perfectly fitting suit. Millicent was unable to contain any dignity whatsoever and burst out laughing. There followed just a few seconds of freeze frame as the threesome stood in their various states, before the manager's shoulders started to move very slightly up and down and his right delicately clenched fist moved to his mouth to cover the tiniest of leaked smiles.

Henry stared at them both, imprisoned as he was in a suit mistakenly labelled several sizes larger, before bringing far more than a cubicle - namely the whole 'house' - down with the question, 'Have you got something a little bigger?'

It was an hour and nine suit changes later that Millicent gave the shop manager the account name to which payment was to be assigned whilst a proud Henry stood before a mirror in the changing-room satisfied that he'd made a good choice and feeling as though if he visited any racecourse now - not that he would - all the horses would show him the respect he deserved and cross the line in the correct order, unlike their normal sequence.

When Millicent had written the letter to Henry with the postscript suggesting a little flutter with Spencer's expense account, she could not have had not the remotest idea that Henry would very soon be the new legitimate owner of that taxpayer-funded perk, proof that life sometimes favours the frail and not always the felon.

'Thank you Madam and we will call you as soon as the navy and grey are ready,' said the manager, who nodded his sleepy smile in the direction of Henry, adding, 'I think Sir is happy.'

'I think Sir is very happy,' said Millicent, and as Henry turned and stepped from the changing-room to join them she couldn't help thinking that his head was held a little higher, his back a little straighter, his shoulders a little less droopy and his face exuding a confidence she hadn't seen before.

'Are you sure it's okay to wear it?' asked Henry.

'You've just paid for it sir, and you have every right to do what your heart desire's with it sir,' interceded the manager.

'Definitely keep it on Henry,' said Millicent, 'you look great. And besides, we have shirts and shoes to buy.'

'What? Tonight?'

Henry's shocked response was delivered in a manner that King Harold's men might have used in 1066 when told they were urgently needed back in Hastings after having just marched from that town all the way to Yorkshire to defeat Tostig; one battle too many.

'Yes tonight,' affirmed Millicent, 'strike while the iron's hot, I always say.' She then stopped and looked him directly, and at close quarters, in the face, before reaching up and carefully removing his glasses. Everything for Henry, beyond Millicent, then descended into a blur as he heard her saying, 'Henry, have you ever thought about contact lenses?'

The Jermyn Street shirt makers and Bond Street shoe shops had never before seen anything quite like Henry. Their clients in the main knew what they wanted and sailed through the selection and ordering process with consummate ease. The challenge that descended upon the shop managers this particular Thursday evening was therefore something quite different, but nevertheless they rose to the occasion and by the time the man and his beautiful companion had left with either bags in hands or order slips in pockets they felt prepared for any future eventuality and prided themselves on their ability to treat every highly-valued and individual customer with the same professional aplomb.

The Saturday following this Thursday evening shopping extravaganza, an optometrist in Hampstead village was also feeling much the same way as he waved the odd couple goodbye through his shop window, feeling as though he'd just helped a dithering blind badger survive future busy road crossings.

Chapter Seventeen

# HOW TO COMMIT 'EUTHANASIA'

Having dressed Henry, Millicent now intended to polish Henry; not intentionally change his character in any way but simply hone his many positive characteristics, qualities that exist in most decent, honest human beings but ones that rarely have the opportunity to shine, through no fault of their owner but more the tarnishing effect of day-to-day rigour.

Though many 'bright lights' force their way to great achievements from an unprivileged beginning without the luxury of infinite time and money at their disposal and the encouraging hand or driving influence of a determined parent, it cannot be denied that many of the names we know and revere both past and present would have remained anonymous but for the simple luxury of not having to bother with the tedium of kow-towing to bosses for the paying of soul-asphyxiating bills. There are the millions who have carried the dream of financial freedom throughout their life only to die with the dream sadly intact and the realisation unfulfilled, but who are sometimes the happier for it; and then in stark contrast we find the millionaires grown fat on the sweat of their workers and the writers, poets and painters grown famous on the fawning devotion of readers and buyers, dying depressed and lonely. So there are no favourites it seems, in the whole scheme of things, and happiness and misery are there in abundance, readily available for anyone to take and spread if they wish. And Death never fails us in its constant duty, always the obliging, omnipresent leveller.

So Millicent had made her mind up, was on the mission of her life. In one short month since having this unusual man inadvertently thrust upon her, her life plan had changed inconceivably. It was hard for her now to imagine, in the presence of Henry's childish innocence, that two lives so different could be thrown together like rag and silk, but now she knew that to take that next step towards happiness and fulfilment he had to join her in a conspiracy of some ruthlessness. His mother really had to be 'managed'.

Henry's two weeks as Department Manager had seen him take to the job like a duck to water, implementing with ease the plans that he'd excitedly made whilst running for shelter in Horse Guards Parade. His nervous arrival at the office on his first day in the new role - dressed in one of his new suits, shirts, ties and very shiny Italian brogues which though looking a trifle incongruous on Henry's duck-splayed feet were a necessary replacement for the highly durable but dated Tufs - was greeted with wolf whistles and high praise.

His face, now a spectacle free zone for the first time since his ears were big enough to support them, looked slimmer, and his cheekbones slightly defined, giving him the surprising appearance of a city banker or music impresario. One of the women commented that he was actually quite 'fanciable' which drew ready agreement from others and prompted one of the young male jokers to link arms with his new manager and play a little camp. The obvious discomfort this gave Henry and the sudden realisation by the young man on seeing his new manager's discomfiture, reminded first the young man and then the rest that Henry Scroggins was no longer the bumbling, amiable Henry of the annoying racing analogies and clipboard, but someone with authority who carried that authority well as if born to the job; a job vacated by someone born to it for all the wrong reasons but no more qualified than a pig, in the literal sense, is to fly.

The first thing Henry had made clear in his short but strong speech was that he wanted everyone to feel that the department was *their* department, and their own particular job was *their* own business. 'Take pride in what you do as if you'd created it from scratch, then you won't feel a grudge working for this big monster (laughs all round) we call the Ministry. Let's make our days happy days and when we wake up, think that we want to come to work because it's ours, not the Ministry's. That's how I'd like us to be. And always respect that we are different and will have our differences (here he coughed and smiled in memory of the dearly departed incumbent, which brought some here-here's) but they must never be allowed to fester and destroy our happy atmosphere.'

Yes, it was a *happy* speech all about *happiness* and it was all because Henry was indeed - *happy*. He finished, after a far bigger rapturous applause than he felt he deserved, with the declaration that he would not be using Peregrine Spencer's old office as it seemed entirely inappropriate and he would instead be taking up residence alongside Phyllis outside the office to save the poor lady the bother of having to risk life and limb on her high heels negotiating two corners and a doorway to get to the manager's desk. This way she could throw things at him without leaving her desk.

Phyllis, at this, had thrown up her hands, smiled the broadest of smiles and giggled, 'Oh Henry you are awful!' to which the whole assembly had replied in one voice 'But I like you!' in homage to Dick Emery's famous man-eating dame. This was entirely lost on Phyllis so she just imagined she'd accidentally fed them a line they'd all invented in spontaneous unison.

The poor lady, whilst happy for Henry and in a way glad for the regime change, still carried an odd torch for her boss of twenty years and in her sweet, unconditionally loving way, lamented the passing of an era that had seemed to her secure and unchanging in a world that had raced past and left her behind. Peregrine Spencer, bully, loudmouth, egotist, had represented a weird kind of stability for Phyllis and she couldn't help but privately mourn his, and its, passing.

As for her old friend Henry, with his new position in life and the confidence that came with it, inevitably came a shift in other relationships, manifested one Saturday afternoon in the second week of February at the National Gallery, where Millicent had suggested they go to look at some of the greatest works of art in the world. On asking Henry whether he had ever been there he could only reply, with some awkwardness, that he had passed it every day of his working life for twenty years but had no idea what the building actually was apart from a grand structure 'behind the lions, pigeons and Nelson's Column' of Trafalgar Square, on his right, as he headed left towards his only focus in life (apart from the betting-shop), his office in Whitehall. He had in fact harboured a vague idea that it was St. Martin's-in-the Fields church but having had to confess to Millicent that he had no clue that the National Gallery was in fact the National Gallery, he certainly wasn't going to compound his ignorance by admitting that he thought the Gallery was in fact its famous ecclesiastical next door neighbour.

'Henry?'

Henry turned from squinting at the description of Van Gogh's *Haystacks* and raised his eyebrows at Millicent.

'Why are you squinting?' asked Millicent, 'I thought the contact lenses were okay.'

'Oh, they are but I've been squinting all my life. I suppose its habit.'

'Well, best if you don't,' mildly admonished Millicent, 'it makes you look...' She suddenly wished she hadn't started.

'Dumb?' helped Henry.

'No, not dumb, not dumb at all but just...well, what's the point in them if you're still going to look like you used to?'

'I didn't mind what I used to look like, actually.'

Henry, a little miffed, went back to reading about the painting but could no longer concentrate because all his concentration was focused on doing what Millicent had said and not what came naturally. Of course he knew she was right and that he was being pedantic but already he was getting used to his new position in life of being in control. So why did women want to change him from the Henry he felt he was? First his mother and now Millicent. Why couldn't he just be himself? His new self that is. His interest in the painting, which wasn't all that much in the first place, was now lost completely. He turned to Millicent.

'I don't really think that's very fair of you,' he said crossly, 'I've only had the lenses a few days and you're talking to me like I was a child misbehaving. I've got to adjust, not just to the lenses, but everything. I'm doing my best. It's embarrassing for me Millicent talking to me like that, very embarrassing.'

'I apologise,' said Millicent and continued her stroll from painting to painting, occasionally glancing discreetly back at Henry who was reading the same line for about the tenth time. Finally she sat down on a seat in the centre of the room, crossed her legs, placed both hands on the handbag on her lap, and watched him. He had chosen his navy suit for the gallery visit and had spent time on his choice, parading in her flat, amusing her as he appeared first in one suit and open-necked shirt, then another and another until all combinations had been tried and both were agreed that the navy suit and pale blue shirt, top button undone, hit the right note.

Eventually Henry turned around several times looking for Millicent, located her impatient, cross-legged stance and walked over to her.

'Was that a tiff we just had?' he enquired.

'I believe it was,' replied Millicent, glancing sideways, 'our first. There has to be a first.'

'Then perhaps I'd better buy you a cup of tea from my fabulous earnings.'

'That you haven't got yet.'

'True.'

He smiled at her and pretended to raise his glasses to see her better. She grinned, shook her head and got to her feet.

'And a Banbury cake.'

'Please.'

'Please.'

Having obeyed Henry, Millicent thrust her hand through his arm and led him away, but not before they'd swivelled several times on the spot until Millicent pointed to a sign saying 'Cafeteria' which they marched towards with great zest.

They carried their trays to a vacant seat, Millicent still smiling at the thought of her funny little man's renaissance evolving before her eyes.

'Millicent, I'm very sorry for being short with you about the lenses. You are completely right and I'm extremely ungrateful.'

'And you Henry my man look a million dollars. I was sitting watching you and imagined I was seeing you for the first time and…'

'Pounds,' interposed Henry.

'Pardon?'

'Pounds. You said dollars. We live in England.'

'It's a figure of speech.'

'I know.'

'And you are being pedantic.'

'I know, but I have a thing about Americans. The only ones I really like are cowboys, the goodies that is, and President Kennedy.'

'So, a bunch of unwashed cattlemen and a deceased serial womaniser. What about Native Americans? Do they count?'

'You mean Red Indians?'

'If you wish.'

Henry looked around and leaned towards Millicent who leaned towards him until their heads almost met in the centre of the table.

'Don't tell anyone...' said Henry. Millicent shook her head to confirm her binding to secrecy. 'But when I was a boy I always thought they were women.'

'Red Indians?'

Henry leant back in his chair and nodded.

'Why?'

Henry shrugged and thought before replying, 'I don't really know but I was totally convinced they were women. I didn't even think about it to be honest. You don't when you are young do you? And there was nobody there to ask even if I did think about it. And I certainly wasn't going to discuss it with my mother as she actually reminded me of the older ones.'

'Older what?' enquired Millicent.

'Indians.' Henry pointed at his lack of hair and said, 'The long black hair.' Then he moved his finger to his nose and said, 'The nose. Hooked, just like hers. And they were pretty ferocious you know. I used to lay in bed the night after I'd watched a cowboy film on our little black and white television and all I could see was my mother riding a bareback horse with a hatchet in her hand swiping the scalp off a soldier. Or me.'

'Henry, that's a horrible vision.'

172

'I know,' replied Henry, 'and you try having it when you're eight years old trying to get to sleep with the Red Indian in the room next to you.'

Millicent was about to laugh but Henry's face had grown suddenly troubled. Millicent placed a hand on his.

'What's the matter? Has it brought back bad memories?'

Henry stared at her hand for some time before replying.

'Well, yes, but how did I know they were *Red* Indians when we only had a black and white television?'

There was no answer to that apart from the fact that everyone called them Red Indians and from his first cowboy film they had always been *Red* Indians. Henry surmised eventually that it was probably the same as black people who weren't black but various shades of brown, and yellow people who mostly ranged from light tan to dark tan but were hardly yellow. And what about white people? You were only white when you were dead and even then more grey than white. So Red Indians were probably just a redder hue than Indian Indians who were brown and it was just to draw a comparison to avoid confusion. In the end he decided that it hardly mattered at the time because they were all in black and white anyway and it's only through the advent of colour films and television that anyone now bothers to discuss it. Life was so much easier when it was all in black and white.

Emerging from his glazed Cowboy and Indian reverie and blinking several times at Millicent, Henry smiled.

'You must think I'm mad.'

Millicent pursed her lips and gave the slightest tilt of her head. 'Unusual,' she said.

'Is that better than boring?'

'I'm sitting here aren't I, listening to your interesting theories without getting up and leaving. And besides you've just touched on a subject that we need to discuss. Your mother.'

Henry plopped a couple of sugar cubes into his teacup and began stirring.

'So how do we get rid of the old witch?' This asked without any hesitation and far too loudly, bringing a look of horror to Millicent's face and a finger to her lips. 'I thought of poison,' continued Henry, unabated, 'you know, few drops of arsenic or strychnine in her tea, that sort of thing, so she slowly goes downhill and everyone will think she's just died of old age. But then I read about the effects that can have and I don't think I could cope with it, to be truthful.'

'What effects? Abdominal pain? Nausea?'

'Worse,' said Henry screwing up his face.

'Worse?'

Henry glanced around and whispered from behind his hand.

'Diarrhoea.'

Millicent looked around the café, twitched her nose as if detecting a whiff of something undesirable, and took a sip of tea.

Meanwhile, the human subject of the conversation taking place at that precise moment in the National Gallery cafeteria was holding court with her lady-in-waiting from next door. Lily Bunce was by now comfortably reinstated back in the inner sanctum of the Scroggins parlour and whilst far from being forgiven for her terrible indiscretion in opening the letter addressed to Henry - which she should have known was only a mother's prerogative - she was at least totally convinced that she was forgiven. But the mind of one such as Irma Scroggins does not forgive so easily, nor forget so lightly, and thus Lily Bunce trod a deadly minefield of which she was dangerously unaware.

'I never could have kids of course,' she threw in from nowhere. 'Wilfred's sperm count - too low.'

She had plucked this fact out of the air laced with such deep regret followed by a gulp of tea with such meaningful resonance at exactly the time Henry was mentioning the word 'diarrhoea' some distance away, that the whole moment - if encapsulated in some artistic form and put on display - could only ever have been entitled 'Bodily Functions'. Regardless, she continued.

'I'm not saying 'ee wasn't a man, my Wilfred. Oh no, Wilfred could point his pecker with the best of 'em when he wanted. And wave it longer and larger than most, but...' And here she sighed and lingered with cup held close to lips and eyes staring somewhere into history through the window '...his bullets just didn't fire.' Another smaller sigh then, 'just didn't fire.' She repeated this softly to ensure that there should be no shadow of doubt cast upon her own fertility and that whilst the absent Wilfred was all man, it was purely his lack of firepower that resulted in her being forever rendered barren and denied the privilege and good fortune bestowed upon Irma Scroggins and other mothers of the world.

Irma Scroggins redirected her stare from the window to her neighbour's face in one ominous slow movement before uttering, 'Just think yourself very lucky Lily Bunce. Think yourself very lucky. Henry might be my son but his stubbornness and cruelty come straight from his father. I gave them both everything I had and how did they repay me?' And here she let the answer hang in the air, leaving Lily Bunce's open mouth, raised expectant eyebrows and poised cup all at once suspended whilst awaiting her friend's reason. But it was too long in coming.

'How Mrs S? How?'

'Abandonment! That's how.'

'But Henry's not abandoned you like wot his father did.'

'He's got a woman.'

'A woman!' Lily Bunce wanted to laugh but kept it inside, claiming one of her more diplomatic moments. Irma Scroggins nodded, still staring straight at Lily Bunce, daring her to laugh or put a foot or word wrong.

'Don't tell me you haven't noticed he's suddenly changed, getting all spruced up with new clothes and them contact lenses instead of glasses. He even had the nerve to show me them the other day, poking 'isself in the eye and popping one out. Disgusting I call it. Only a woman could do that, force a man to change his habits of a lifetime and then go and get contact lenses. Forty years he's not changed and then suddenly…this!'

'Never trust a man I say - apart from my Wilfred that is. I must say though I did notice your Henry was looking a bit posh of late, I did notice that, yes. Has he got promotion or something maybe? Maybe it's that Mrs S, just a bit of promotion. Mm? Do you think? Promotion? Maybe?'

Irma Scroggins shook her head dismissively.

'He tells me nothing. I'm just his mother! But he's taking forever in the bathroom and when he comes out he stinks like a whore's boudoir, and…' She suddenly stopped and her jaws began their deadly demon grind. 'What's today?'

'Um, Saturday Mrs S. Today's Saturday all day. Why?'

'He's gone to London. He never works on a Saturday.'

'Mm,' muttered Lily Bunce, resignedly staring at the skirt hem she was straightening whilst placing her cup and saucer on the table, 'certainly does sound like a woman, I grant you that.'

At last able to believe and capture the full impact of what she was hearing, that Henry undeniably had a woman, Lily was at her humble, compassionate best. The evidence was certainly all there, no denying that, and how her heart bled for the caring mother beside her, despite never having had that opportunity of motherhood herself. Yes, nothing changes a man like a woman and she, Lily Bunce, knew that better than anyone, for hadn't she changed young Wilfred Bunce (pecker aside) from being a happy-go-lucky, jack-the-lad to a reserved, devoted husband, almost overnight?

Irma Scroggins jaws were now in full powerful rotating grind and only stopped momentarily to declare, 'It's a woman alright and if he or she thinks they're ever getting a penny of my money - they can damn well think again!'

Henry and Millicent were at this moment leaving the art world and walking down the steps into Trafalgar Square, Millicent looking the picture of chic in fur coat, cream skirt and patent brown heels and Henry not looking quite so out of place on her arm as he did the last time they were in the vicinity. He sported a very fashionable mid-calf navy overcoat and an expensive yellow linen scarf, tied also in a fashionable knot, he not quite ready to give up the yellow but allowing it to be chosen, and tied, by Millicent, to ensure it looked the part.

As they strolled amongst the tourists and pigeons, feeling the breeze blow the chilly spray from the fountains onto their cheeks, they had one thing on their mind. Not murder; not anything cruel, criminal or sinister, but simply the act of wishing to reduce further suffering (mainly Henry's) as with an animal in pain that can no longer give or receive the affection it once could and just needs to be at peace; in a word, euthanasia.

There was however one striking difference between the subject of their plans and the majority of animals put to sleep in that Irma Scroggins had never given affection or permitted herself to receive it. She had also never enjoyed runs and romps in the countryside or the simple pleasure of a cosy fireside or the warm glow of human kindness. Henry, however, wasn't absolutely sure he didn't nurture genuine sinister tendencies.

'I've always been fascinated by mass murderers Millicent. Not wanting to copy them but simply, sort of, you know, understand them.'

'I'm not sure they need understanding Henry,' said Millicent after first sh'shing Henry to avoid a mass evacuation of Trafalgar Square.

'I've got a book at home about a chap in America, Charles Whitman. He killed fifteen people in 1966 and do you know who he killed first?'

'Obviously not himself. His mother?'

Henry looked at her in shock. 'You've heard of him?'

'No, but it's fairly obvious isn't it when you've got the same thing on your mind. Not killing of course...removing...isn't that your word? Your mother.'

'Removing a worthless obstacle,' corrected Henry.

'Worthless obstacle - that was it.'

'So if I can't poison her...' continued Henry, stroking his chin with his leather gloved hand, '...and I certainly can't do anything that requires shedding blood like shooting or stabbing...'

'Henry.'

'What?'

'Stop it. Please. I'm feeling like Bonnie and Clyde, especially in this fur coat.'

'Ah, now there was a pair!' said Henry, beaming with admiration, 'I've read all about them too. Do you know that he was....'

'Henry, I've seen the film. Thank you.'

They strolled on, picking their way amongst the people and pigeons, Millicent in turn staring disparagingly at children chasing birds and at Henry's brow furrowed as he tried to think of a plan. He'd always thought poison was the way but having lately researched it and read a couple of Agatha Christie's it was apparent that all the tasteless poisons like arsenic and ricin, even given in tiny doses would have such unpleasant consequences (for him) and were far too quick, that they couldn't help but arouse suspicion, never mind be easily detected by a coroner. No, there had to be a better, a simpler, non-detectable way - but what was it?

Suddenly the bath water of his mind overflowed like a tsunami and with a suppressed screech of 'Eureka!' and a hand gripping Millicent's fur clad forearm, he whispered in her ear 'Millicent, I've got it! I've got it! I've got it!' and dragged her over to a bench away from the crowd.

There, perched on the edge of the bench and turned towards her like a child appealing for ice cream money, he couldn't contain his excitement.

'Her own medication!'

'You're going to kill her with her own medication. How?'

'By not giving it to her! Why didn't I think of it before? The old witch had a stroke last year, and kidney failure, and I actually found myself praying for the first time since I was a child - but if ever there was proof there isn't a god, she not only recovered but came back stronger and even more hateful, if that's possible. But now she's on heavy medication every day for her blood pressure and kidneys and heaven knows what else - hopefully all life-threatening - without which, the medication that is, with any luck, well, I'm pretty sure she'll slowly….'

He stared ahead at the paving stones and licked his lips overly cat-like, so much so that Millicent started to feel just a little uncomfortable in the company of this gentle friend who confessed to a fascination for cold-blooded murderers and had no apparent problem dispensing with his own mother, awful as she was. It was indeed fortunate that Millicent wasn't aware of

Henry's close resemblance (when his former self) to a certain John Christie of 10 Rillington Place.

Whilst listening intently to Henry's 'Eureka!' revelation Millicent had to admit the idea was quite inspired, a sort of subtle snipping of the life support system without actually cutting a pipe. But it seemed to her that there was one large and obvious loophole in his plan.

'But how on earth do you stop her taking the tablets?'

Henry smiled triumphantly. 'Ah, that's easy. I give them to her every evening crushed in a jam sandwich. So all I have to do is replace them with aspirins or something similar, just so she sees white powder in case she opens up the sandwich for inspection, which she does sometimes to make sure I put enough jam inside, greedy bitch.'

'Henry!'

'Well she is.'

'But why do you have to crush the tablets?' asked Millicent.

'She's got a phobia - can't swallow them, chokes on them so she says - it's got a name; 'pharma' something or other.'

'Pharmacophobia - one of my clients has it.'

Here she stopped, feeling the blood rush up the back of her neck and dash round to where it instantly filled her cheeks like the terrible traitor that blushing can be. The fact that only she knew what sort of clients they were and that dear Henry sat beside her still in blissful ignorance of her profession - or ex-profession - was neither here nor there. For the first time in her adult life she felt shock and guilt at ever being found out. Until then she cared nothing for what anyone thought, apart from her parents who lived in their own Berkshire bubble and hardly mattered to her anyway, but here and now the truth of who she really was had landed firmly at her feet and the moment that she knew would have to come sooner than later - when she revealed it to Henry - made her feel instantly, physically sick.

'Are you feeling okay Millicent?' asked Henry, meaning well but compounding the lady's embarrassment by stroking the throbbing heat of her cheek gently with the back of his forefinger. 'You look very hot.'

'I am, yes,' said Millicent, and laughed. 'Why is that, I wonder? A hot flush - yes, that's probably it. We women get them at certain times. They take us by surprise. Hormonal stuff, I'm sure you know about it.'

Henry didn't of course, hadn't a clue, but nodded all the same and the word 'menopause' crept into his head from conversations he'd overheard and happily ignored at work. Millicent shook her head clear and brushed her fingers through her fringe, which she tossed backwards, blowing upwards to cool her face. She raised her shoulders and let them drop with a heavy sigh, turning to Henry with an apologetic smile.

'Well, there you go. Where were we?'

'Pharma-something...' muttered Henry, not convinced that Millicent was well enough to continue the important subject of killing his mother.

'Yes, pharmacophobia. A fear of taking tablets, that's it.'

Henry watched her protectively and felt for the first time that she was vulnerable, like him. She was still the goddess that he imagined but now she'd come down off the mountain and was in human form with frailties. He couldn't help but want to cuddle her, like the baby in the train, and for her to see him as someone who could look after her if she needed it. He felt useful and mature.

'Shall we stretch our legs?' he said. 'Don't let's talk about it - her - anymore. There's plenty of time for that.'

'Henry?' said Millicent, turning her face to him amongst the fluttering pigeons. He raised his eyebrows enquiringly. 'Henry, can we please have a day in the country tomorrow? A train ride - Brighton perhaps. We've only known each other in London. Can we see if we like each other at the seaside?'

This seemed rather an odd request to Henry but he liked the romantic sound of it and he'd never been to Brighton.

The two, without even consulting, found themselves strolling slowly in the direction of The Mall and once there their gloved hands accidentally touched as they walked in silence and then locked together, fingers finding each other. By the time they'd reached the Victoria Memorial Millicent had twice rested her head momentarily on his shoulder and Henry had felt a surge of ecstasy and happiness he had no idea existed. He felt a man, a real man, no longer self-conscious as people passed by.

Millicent's mind was racing whilst Henry strolled oblivious by her side, smiling contentedly through the railings surrounding Buckingham Palace. She needed to be somewhere else when she told him the truth about her past, not in London where they'd worked for many years unaware of each other. She would pick her moment when they were in Brighton - but make sure it wasn't on the pier.

Meanwhile, an office door in Whiteheath was being firmly closed and locked by its proprietor who had decided he needed a glass of chardonnay, or maybe even a bottle, in the wine bar opposite, to further ruminate on how best he could capitalise on the last will and testament of Henry Arthur Scroggins, late of Australia.

## Chapter Eighteen

# A STROKE OF LUCK

As is the character of Fate in altering for better or worse the well laid plans of mice and men, events were to conspire later that day to rob Henry and Millicent of their planned trip to Brighton but also, in doing so, seeming to accelerate their plans for his mother's speedy trip to Eternity.

Around seven o'clock that evening, long after Lily Bunce had left Irma Scroggins to stew in her own vitriolic juices, that latter lady sat multiplying her already devious, devilish 'wild imaginings' and formulating such wicked revenge to perpetrate on her son and his 'woman!' Such was the state of frenzied hate and frustration that she worked herself into, that even her seemingly impenetrable armour lost its imperviousness - and she collapsed; collapsed like a half empty sack of potatoes suspended by a tie-string from the back of the chair, her bony, white head slumped onto her chest and her hands motionless in her lap, one claw still gripping the edge of her shawl that for a frenzied few seconds just before her collapse had served as a worthy substitute for her son's throat.

There she lay, still breathing, her eyes closed and a trail of dribble running down her cheek onto the collar of her faded purple cardigan buttoned so tight round her grizzled neck that the epiglottis popped up over it and then disappeared with each laboured, gurgling breath.

Who knows whether she would have lasted long if Henry hadn't politely refused Millicent's offer of staying the night and everything that it seemed to imply after their romantic afternoon together. He'd had to make an instant decision and may have been persuaded to stay quite easily if he'd met any resistance, but Millicent wasn't a lady to insist upon anything and simply shrugged her shoulders and kissed Henry once more goodbye under the clock at Charing Cross after making arrangements for the next morning's trip to Brighton.

Henry entered the house by the back door into the kitchen and on giving out his now habitual cheery, intentionally annoying greeting of 'Hello Mother', and receiving no reply, cocked his head on one side and held his breath momentarily, listening for signs of life. There was always some sign; a cough, clearing of the throat, a moan of discomfort, shuffle of feet or rattle of a teacup, but not a sound reached his ears. She was asleep, he surmised, and before going into the parlour he took out some cheese from the fridge and cut off several slices which he placed rather carefully and geometrically onto a Jacobs Cream Cracker, ensuring that no piece of cheese overlapped the biscuit before it entered his mouth and became instantly masticated. So enjoyable was the biscuit and in such high spirits was Henry, with his mind flooded by images of the afternoon and the now very real prospect of his permanent escape from the presence of the woman whose prolonged silence he was now getting slightly inquisitive about, that he found himself cutting more cheese and placing it carefully and geometrically on a second biscuit, smiling at the pleasures that life was at last bestowing upon him.

With this in his mind he took a few jaunty paces up the hall, consciously noting for the first time the threadbare carpet runner and chipped dark brown paintwork, wondering quite unconcernedly what to say when questioned about where he had been. He half relished and half disliked these moments now, for whilst there was the perceived freedom of no longer being in her financial clutches, there was still her unpleasant presence and his undeniable duty to her, whilst alive. She remained, however badly she had treated him, still a daily responsibility standing in the path of his total freedom. Quite simply she had nobody else, apart from Lily Bunce, and even in his darkest, murderous moods Henry knew that all the time she breathed, she still had him emotionally trapped.

By the time he reached the parlour door, Henry had slowed and softened his last few steps and chewed the remains of his biscuit silently, listening for a snore or snuffle. He peered round the door and with eyes wide and transfixed on the slumped figure, instantly recognised that this was no normal sleeping posture.

'My God, she's dead! Mother! Mother!' he cried through a mouthful of mashed cheddar and biscuit, unsure whether to panic or punch the air. As he gently lifted her jaw, grimacing at the touch of the sagging, soft layers of skin that hung from chin to chest bone, she felt cold and he tried to quell feelings of excitement. He gently tapped her cheek with his fingertips and as she groaned and moved slightly, he jumped, one foot completely off the ground leaving the other suspended for a split second on just a big toe.

'Mother? Are you dead? I mean, can you hear me?' asked Henry befuddled, sensing instinctively that this was a situation he was not equipped to cope with unassisted. He stood up straight with hands by his sides looking down at her, then out of the window, then back at her, before sinking his teeth into his bottom lip just short of drawing blood, and dashing next door to Lily Bunce.

Lily, who was at that moment watching television from her dining table chair whilst mopping up the remains of a rabbit stew with a lump of bread, got up with dripping bread in hand as she heard Henry's loud rapping and calling at her front door.

In less than half a minute the two stood side by side, peering in useless unison at the form moaning incoherently before them.

'Oo-er,' said Lily, bending closer but not touching for fear that the woman might suddenly leap up and tear at her face. 'Henry, I think you'd better call Dr. Johnston. You can use my phone and better tell him it's an emergency.'

Henry nodded, not needing to have the obvious stated to him - that it was an emergency - but grateful he didn't have to grapple with the vapours and vagaries of a phone box again, after his previous experience.

'Don't you think we should dial 999?' asked Henry.

'Oh no, not all them wailing sirens outside in the street. We'd never live it down. There's a lot of people round here with noses like periscopes and minds that make mountins' out of mole'ills.'

'But suppose we have to wait for the doctor and she…dies?'

Lily Bunce seemed transfixed by the sight of her friend and could only manage to say 'Oo-er, she don't look the ticket do she?' before Henry, growing impatient with the silly woman, declared:

'Right, I'll phone the doctor. Now where will I find his number? Not having a phone, we don't have a phone book.'

Lily managed to transfer her transfixation from mother to son and stared up at Henry in a sort of trance. 'Ee's my doctor too so he's under 'D' in the book next to the phone. I'll show you.' And after returning her ghostly gaze back to what was looking like a potential ex-friend if they debated about sirens or doctor for much longer, she eventually turned and left the room with Henry following close behind.

As he followed the waddling little figure out of the back door and round via the alley into her back garden, Henry was also feeling secretly relieved that they would be spared the wailing sirens of what he imagined would be an emptied fire station, ambulance station and police station all descending upon Viola Street at once for want of anything more interesting to do. Add to this the plain fact that there was more chance of his mother being saved by lots of them than by a single, busy doctor with other patients to attend to and it just seemed too much like looking a gift horse in the mouth.

The all important thing was that he'd rather cleverly, if inadvertently, secured for himself an alibi in that he'd tried to insist on a 999 call but had been overruled by Lily. Should he be questioned later he could simply plead being so traumatised that he'd allowed his mother's best friend to make the decision. After all, he deduced, financially disinterested old ladies can get away with 'murder' much easier than middle-aged sons.

Dr. Sam Johnston, who had fortunately been closing his surgery early for a rare social evening, arrived half an hour later with his black bag and permanent tan and smile. He had been named by his eminent orthopaedic surgeon father, Dr. Samuel Johnson, after the famous writer (as was he by his own father) but as often happens in the naming of children, completion of the birth certificate is often in the hands of someone who is far removed from the parental ecstasy of the birth and not that interested in paying attention to the dotting of the 'i's' and the crossing of the 't's', the 't' being the problem in this particular case, leaving the proud father cursing on discovering that his first child had already spent two weeks of its life as a 'Johnston' and would remain so, as far as the Registrar of Births, Deaths & Marriages was concerned, forever after. Dr. Johnson went on to have two daughters but resisted the temptation to call either of them Amy.

Dr. Johnston was a tall, handsome, smooth, cultured man to the point of being described by some as debonair. His square jaw and slightly stooped square shoulders, aquiline features, smooth baritone voice and already mentioned permanent smile and tan meant that he was always going to struggle to retain his professional integrity when confronted with attractive, flirtatious female patients, and so with two marriages, two divorces and three children already to his credit, or debit, at the age of forty-two (although he only looked thirty-five) he had a much deserved reputation of being a lady's man. He didn't promote this or flaunt it in any way for the simple reason he didn't have to. He was one of those charmed and charming creatures for whom much of life had been a series of open doors through which he had sailed with golden locks flowing and winning smile smiling, from Eton to medical school, where he studied little and revised even less but came out with flying colours and a practice in Central London. Whether nepotism had anything to do with this is not clear but all that remains to be known to complete this history of him is that whatever got him there, counted for little on his way down the slippery slope to a back street surgery in Lewisham. The marriages and divorces were his private affair but the affairs with patients were not. There were those ready to knock him down at the first opportunity and, resilient, cheerful and charming as he was, even he had to finally succumb to the bad publicity and be grateful that he had any sort of practice at all and not been struck off.

When we find him now in the parlour of Irma Scroggins, diagnosing within seconds of entry that she had indeed had another stroke, his reputation had been squeaky clean for three years, despite the best endeavours of Irma Scroggins, Lily Bunce and other fine moral vanguards of the community, to blacken his name. And these best endeavours had only been possible thanks to the compulsive decorating nature of the Wilmots across the road, in the days when all three parties were speaking to each other. Oh no, the dastardly doctor's deeds would never have emerged! Emerged that is from under the Wilmot's kitchen lino where they had lain in perfectly preserved newsprint for several years, if Mr Wilmot had not decided that their kitchen needed modernising.

Now, as avid decorators will readily contest, newspapers present far greater fascination when discovered unexpectedly after a passage of time than ever they did on the day the news was fresh. Journalistic gems of the day that would have been passed over with just a cursory glance suddenly become hypnotic, holding up decorating progress, creating serious redness of knees, stiffness of backs and wasting of productive time whilst every word on every page, even the advertisements and decades old horoscopes, are devoured and then shared with often disinterested family members.

So, what a golden news nugget Mrs Wilmot had spotted over her husband's shoulder as he knelt engrossed in some article or other from July 13th 1976 - his untrained eyes unaware that on the same page was a picture of a smirking Dr Johnston leaving the offices of the General Medical Council with his reputation besmirched but career, at that stage, tenuously intact. How that page was picked up and caressed with kid gloves by Mother Wilmot until she had digested every sacrosanct word ready for selective distribution. In short - the confines of planet Earth.

The doctor in question, now four and a half years older and one would hope much wiser, stood up straight from examining Irma Scroggins, stretched his back, shook his head slightly and with a comforting hand placed upon Henry's shoulder broke what he thought was bad news.

'I'm afraid Mr Scroggins, your mother has had another stroke. (He was in attendance at the last one). A pretty bad one too. You're lucky she's still alive to be perfectly honest.'

To be perfectly honest Henry wasn't feeling at all lucky that his mother was still alive but his face and general demeanour gave nothing away as Lily Bunce began a Middle Eastern style wailing beside him. Almost shouting above the wailing Dr Johnston said he was calling an ambulance, and on discovering that he was in possibly the only house in the district without a phone, was soon following Henry around to Lily Bunce's after she pointing frantically at the door for them to use her phone, unable to talk through the very distressful noise and mucus she was making whilst signalling through several further pointings that she'd stay with her friend whilst they made the call.

Irma Scroggins wasn't going too far too soon so Lily's guarding of her was purely a platonic, not practical, role. However, the level of her true distress could be measured by the fact that she had forgotten to request 'no wailing sirens' from the ambulance, possibly because she was at that precise moment doing more than enough wailing for ten ambulances.

Later that evening, around ten o'clock, when Henry returned from the hospital where his mother lay wired up and still unconscious, he sat by the fireside and tried hard not to enjoy the solitude. His mild spasm of guilt was brief. It was bliss. Heaven. He poked the small mountain of coal piled high in the grate which was beginning to burn and spit and smoke with all the gusto that Henry felt inside and, unable to wipe off a smile that comes with utter peace and contentment after a long period of stress, he calculated the last time he had ever felt free in the house. There was the time a few months ago when his mother had imposed three days solitary confinement upon herself during her great Christmas sulk, but she'd still been there, lurking upstairs in her bedroom, her silent menace percolating the walls and ceilings. No, it must, he reckoned, have been in the summer of 1967 when she'd visited her ailing sister in Dorset for two whole long days and nights, returning with tales of sisterly ungratefulness. All her relationships seemed to end the same way, with the pot calling the kettle black. Nothing was ever her fault, her responsibility - it was always the others; the world, life, luck, the devil - but most of all, two men called Henry.

Nearly fourteen years since his last domestic seclusion and all was quiet, all was peaceful, all was how he imagined it could be forever; and his thoughts turned to Millicent. She'd never been far from his mind since he'd discovered his mother slumped in the chair, but being a little too preoccupied to do anything about it he'd concentrated on the job in hand, that of being *seen to do the right thing*.

But there in the midst of his silent fireside reverie Millicent's face and voice came to him whilst his hand automatically, from years of programming, dropped down the side of the chair to feel for the racing guide. Quickly he withdrew his groping fingers with a feeling of shame, imagining Millicent was watching and that he'd betrayed her. Then suddenly, he thought of the plans they'd made to go to Brighton together the next day. Her idea, her wish, to be alone with him somewhere else apart from London. How romantic. He sat up suddenly, heart thumping. Brighton! They were meeting at London Bridge at ten o'clock!

'Oh, good grief! Millicent! What am I going to do?' Henry muttered to himself, mind whirring trying to think how to contact her. Why didn't they have a damn phone? How had he let his mother dictate whether or not they had a phone for all these years? Because he'd never had the money to afford one that's why, he consoled himself, and felt slightly less cross with her. It was going to be his first job at work on Monday, order a phone for home. If his mother did ever return it was highly unlikely she'd have the strength to impede him having a phone. It would be in his bedroom and she could do nothing about it. What did he care anyway? He pleased himself now. Her days of despotic rule were over. But it didn't solve the problem of contacting Millicent. He resolved that there was nothing he could do that evening and he would set his alarm for seven o'clock to make sure he was up and in the phone box by eight.

With this sorted out, he sat back, relaxed and watched the fire, now blazing brightly with flames and smoke leaping up the chimney as if they too felt liberated without the old skinflint rationing the grate to one or two lumps at a time. Flames of freedom!

If he'd known that his 'love' - for that's how he now felt and privately called her in the poetic recesses of his mind - was sitting at a candlelit table in a bistro off the Marylebone Road opposite a man dressed expensively and stylishly and smiling as he refilled their glasses with a carefully chosen Bordeaux, Henry's state of euphoria would have been cruelly interrupted. But as Millicent smiled back at the man and laughed lightly at his latest witty remark, Henry sat dozing in blissful ignorance.

## Chapter Nineteen

# THERE IS A GOD! MAYBE

Two weeks passed during which Henry became something of a legend at the office as he implemented his desire to make the department what he'd promised in his speech. If any had doubts about his ability to move seamlessly from being the back end of a pantomime horse to a manager exuding dignity and commanding friendly respect, these doubts were dispelled completely. And the one time front end of the same pantomime horse, Phyllis, positively bloomed under Henry's gentle management. She had become so accustomed to Peregrine Spencer's abrasiveness and so deferent under his macho dominance that she'd grown to believe that this was the only way; this is what it took to be a good manager and control staff properly. The iron fist, the fear of reprisal or the sack for non-compliance was always there throughout his reign, threatening and controlling. What looked strong was in fact weak and what was done with joviality and backslapping was done with an edge, a sharpened blade ready to slice at any moment for the vital retention of power.

Henry had requested from the Minister that a spare room off the main department be used for tea-making facilities to avoid the trek to the canteen two floors up and back again, which cut the break time by about five minutes and had always been a muttered bone of contention. Not only had his request been readily accepted, but also great surprise and cheers erupted when a fridge arrived the day after his request, albeit a second hand one no longer required by the Minister - who coincidentally had been badly in need of a new, much larger one for some time. But this small early victory for Henry was seen as a mark of the man and his management style. The qualities that had either been benignly smiled at or caused mild irritation in his previous role, now served him well; his meticulous attention to detail; his quiet, unassuming coaxing and ready praise; his non-judgemental, non-threatening, calm manner. It all spoke volumes and made the office as he had so badly wanted it, a place the staff felt was their own and where they wanted to be, not had to be. Work was done with pride and therefore, ironically, no longer was there any need for a Time and Motion man. Henry had made himself redundant.

His role as a son had also not been neglected. Irma Scroggins had been showing signs of progress when Henry visited each evening from off the train and, disappointing as this progress was, he would dutifully arrive in the ward clutching a small gift; some flowers, some fruit, a magazine, the usual hospital visit necessities, all of which were much appreciated by the nurses who realised that these token gestures were never going to be used or even slightly appreciated by the unpleasant old woman they had to be nice to.

She had been placed in the same ward as on her first visit the previous year and her reputation had lingered over it like a malignant cloud ever since. Nurses, porters, doctors, even the secretarial staff, all of whom met with a variety of disagreeable patients as part of their everyday work, were singing from the same hymn sheet when remembering the awful woman with the intolerable demands - demands that multiplied as her faculties improved until finally and regrettably the use of her mouth returned and with it an inability to ever utter a 'please', 'thank you', or offer a flicker of a smile.

Frail and helpless as she was, dependent upon the careful attention of the staff she may have been - which they were duty bound to provide as professionally as to any other patient - there wasn't a member of the staff or one patient in the ward who privately wouldn't have gladly tipped her, bed and all, out of the window. A fall of five floors should have done the trick but like the hydra she closely resembled, it was always on the cards that two of her would have climbed back up.

The main saving grace for Henry - there were two, one slightly trumping the other - was that her speech had not yet returned and was showing no signs of returning; and secondly, which from Henry's point of view was only marginally more important (the joy of not hearing 'that voice' only narrowly nudged into second), the doctor had made it clear that what was absolutely critical for her survival - 'tough old bird' as she was - was the strong medication he was prescribing; medication that had to be taken daily without fail; medication that whilst not to be exceeded because of the high strength of the dose, must certainly not be missed one single day.

To all of this Henry had nodded soberly in full understanding of the gravity of the situation until, immediately on turning out of the ward and dancing sideways like his hero Gene Kelly down the stone stairs, sang out under his breath on every step 'Oh, thank you, thank you, *thank you* God!' but, unlike when we first met Henry in his dingy bedroom months earlier, he really meant it and might even have started to believe.

It was all too good to be true. Just too good, and with the bonus of only having partial use of one arm, her right - 'the tea-drinking arm' as Henry mirthfully pointed out to the doctor - it combined to make as good a prognosis as he could wish for, short of her permanently running out of breath.

Jumping the last two steps, instinctively putting a finger up to hold his spectacles which were no longer there, he then strolled merrily through the swing doors into the early dusk descending over the hospital car park, taking a deep breath which he then expelled with a gasping, grateful 'Yes!'

For he now had two, not one, excellent means of passing her over into purgatory, where if there really was a heaven and hell, they certainly wouldn't need her for more than a few seconds to decide which way she was going.

Two glorious options. Two! *Not* giving her the medication – or giving her *too much*! Oh joy! Life was so good.

Then he faltered for a moment and stopped in his tracks. It couldn't be that easy surely. There had to be a hitch. For about a minute he stared at the tarmac and thought it through before beaming and continuing his walk with another joyful outburst of 'Oh yes it can!'

He could see no possible obstacle to his plans apart from a coroner's report showing too much or too little medication. But then he'd just plead innocence or forgetfulness, especially if she couldn't talk or take it herself. Things were moving ahead now, his sketchy plans given a boost beyond his wildest dreams.

Not wishing to waste the good fortune or lose the momentum just handed him on a plate he marched straight into Boots the Chemist across the road where he had to carefully hide his disappointment in only being permitted two packets of Aspirins. Not to be thwarted he called into a mini supermarket on his way to the bus stop where he purchased a further two packets, ensuring before he went in that the other packets weren't obvious through his jacket pocket. Ah yes, this was going to bring out the best in him, his meticulous nature at the office now being put to the best possible use in his life so far. He felt confident, proud, invincible, and his desire to share the news with Millicent was overwhelming.

But things had altered. During his mother's confinement Millicent had been keeping a low profile which was quietly troubling Henry, although he didn't feel it his place to bother her when she was making it obvious she didn't want to be bothered.

He'd noticed a distinct change in her since the day in Trafalgar Square, and when he had phoned her on the Sunday morning after his mother's collapse she had shown no real disappointment in missing the trip to Brighton and no obvious excitement at his mother's stroke. In fact she didn't have much to say at all and eventually confessed she was nursing a hangover and probably wouldn't have been the best company anyway.

Henry had stood in the phone box for several minutes after saying goodbye to her and slowly, reflectively, replaced the receiver remaining deep in thought with one hand motionless on the door, ready to exit. How had she got a hangover? Where had she been the night before, after she left him, to get one of those? She hadn't made any mention of going anywhere, in fact hadn't she asked him to go back home with her, inferring he should stay the night? Various reasons entered and left his mind before he settled on the one he preferred to accept, that she'd simply gone home, opened a bottle of gin, curled up in front of the television with George - and drunk too much.

But in his heart he knew he might be fooling himself. He feared that what he'd at first believed in the first glow of meeting his guardian angel, was correct - it was all simply too good to be true. In moments of honest reflection there seemed no earthly reason why a lady like Millicent would feel the need to prolong a relationship with a nobody when there were all the important people she'd spent her life working and socialising with. She'd let slip a few names and professions during their conversations, people who worked geographically almost alongside him in the corridor of power down Whitehall to Westminster, but with whom he had no more in common than did Millicent to Lily Bunce, or his mother; just lives that were poles apart, sometimes a novelty for a time when thrown together at an event or meeting, but nothing sustainable.

People always find their level, he mused, and although finding temporary stimulation in muddier or cleaner waters, will eventually drift back into the waters where they feel safe and where comforting, familiar rocks exist to cling to when the ebb and flow of life takes control and storms erupt to threaten and wreck. He knew this better than anyone.

A first week of messages left on Millicent's frustratingly ever-present answering machine - and these only returned after a second more imploring one - had left Henry feeling that this was his fate. He'd naively hoped for, even expected, Heaven, when Lewisham it seemed was really his allocated Nirvana.

By the second week and with just a few curt, difficult telephone conversations and one brief meeting in a Strand coffee bar, where Millicent only had a moment before dashing off to an important appointment, Henry was feeling crushed.

Crushed maybe, but not broken, for the effect this had on him was to pour his full attention and affection into his work and shower those who it seemed were the true friends, uncomplicated friends at the office without the emotional maelstrom that love - 'whatever in love means', as Prince Charles had just that week remarked - brought with it. He knew that the qualities he possessed were making lives better. Surely, he decided, it was far less selfish and vastly more fulfilling to make a whole department of people happy than just one person? Surely.

He decided eventually that he was better off without the heartache that he was experiencing, heartache that he'd never in forty years been exposed to - until Millicent. Better not to be the man he once was but to be content simply with the new man he'd created; a man with pride, position and independence. But then he remembered that it wasn't him who was the creator - he was merely a protégée of an infinitely superior being than himself and he had no right to wallow in self-glorification. There was hardly any credit he could take for what had miraculously evolved in such a short space of time. However he looked at it, all routes led back to Millicent. She had saved him. In every way she'd saved him, lifted him from his gloom and a seemingly unbreakable enslavement to his mother; polished him and pulled strings (he still didn't know how), until here he was. So what should he do? Accept the miracle and just gratefully and gracefully back off?

After consideration, the new Henry decided to take a leaf out of the old Henry's book - and do nothing.

## Chapter Twenty

## ARCHIBALD SNAPES HATCHES A PLAN

Archibald Snapes faced something of a dilemma. Having sat for a month on the letter and small Phillips tape that had arrived two weeks after the teleprinter message from Dean Mansfield in Australia, he had finally decided to track down the widow; not with any intention of meeting her but simply to ascertain whether she was in fact still alive and residing at the address given in the will. With no trace of her in the phone book he had driven the mile or so to 52 Viola Street and leaving his Jaguar parked several streets away strolled to the house where he stood outside peering at a slip of paper to check the number, when a postman arrived on his bike.

Snapes smiled at the postman as he dismounted and propped his bike against the wall. The man was about to go next door to Lily Bunce's house when Snapes called out to him.

'Excuse me, does Mrs Scroggins live here?'

'She does. Not sure livin's the word but she's there alright.'

'Thank you.'

'Pleasure.'

The postman turned to walk next door when Snapes called him again.

'I'm sorry to trouble you again but - does she live alone?'

'Nope,' replied the postman in an offhand fashion, peering suspiciously at the slip of paper in Snapes' hand, 'she's got a son. She's just had a bad stroke though, so poor blighter's got his hands proper full. Why? Is there a problem?'

'No, not at all. Just a business matter and I couldn't find her in the phone book.'

'That might be because she ain't got a phone,' stated the postman emphatically. 'I know that for a fact.'

He didn't say how he knew it for a fact and Snapes wasn't interested. All he needed to know he had just found out and so thanking the postman and glancing through the small bay window to check that he wasn't being watched from behind the soiled net curtains, he went on his way up the street.

At that moment Henry was on the train to work having administered sips of tea to his mother in bed and leaving her slumped against her pillow and staring ahead like a ventriloquist's dummy waiting for a hand up its back to propel it into life. Lily Bunce had volunteered to be her daytime carer whilst Henry was at work, for which Henry was exceedingly grateful, but Lily's duties could only begin after the postman's arrival, which was usually very soon after Henry's leaving for work.

So the ever vigilant Lily was peering through her window waiting for the postman, and she would have had a clear view of the discussion that had taken place between the two trades of solicitor and postman but for an alder bush that Henry senior had planted in the small front garden during the few enthusiastic weeks after his wedding; a bush that had not been pruned since. For three decades the bush, or tree of triffid-like proportions and design that it had matured into, had prevented her from seeing not only what went on outside the Scroggins house but also shielded her view into the Wilmots, who were opposite at thirty-three degrees to the left as opposed to an unimpeded view straight ahead from Irma Scroggins' window, the elder bush being to the right of the small front garden, forming a dense mass of foliage more on the Bunce side than the Scroggins side. This had proved a source of intense annoyance and frustration for poor Lily over many years, easily equal to the pleasure it gave Irma Scroggins in refusing to remove it or trim it. They had once, about ten years ago, had a serious argument about it and even Henry had dared at the time to mention to his mother that their neighbour did have a point and it really should go, but Irma stood firm. And so did the tree.

But thank goodness for postmen. As the solicitor disappeared up the street, Lily Bunce was informed at her door that a 'posh fat, nosey geezer has just been asking about the Scroggins,' which saw Lily snatch the letters from his hand and make her front gate like an Olympian, just in time to take a mental snapshot of a flapping black jacket, huge head, wide girth and long, lumbering, knock-kneed strides; a veritable walking bear.

Once back in his office, the bear unlocked his filing cabinet by the window overlooking the wine bar, took out a scuffed beige folder that by the look of it was scuffed merely through age and not activity, and after ordering an extra strong coffee via his intercom, settled at his desk, stretched his huge back and neck, pushed out his chest and sniffing, peered slyly at the two files gripped between his pork sausage fingers. Both were marked *Will - Strictly Private*, one for Mr H. A. Scroggins and the other labelled Mrs I. L. Scroggins, the 'L' being for Lucretia – just one letter away from a Borgia.

At that stage Archie Snapes only had a rough plan of how to proceed but with the help of a heavy dose of caffeine, an hour of uninterrupted silence and a spiv's instinct for the main chance, he had no doubt that the opportunity he'd been waiting for since his partner David Bodger had somewhat mysteriously passed on to the great bar in the sky eight years ago, had finally arrived.

The initial problem that he could foresee was precisely what use a chain of hotels, clubs, massage parlours, strip joints and nights clubs, plus a luxury yacht and cabin cruiser, several blocks of holiday units and a five bedroom house, all in the Sunshine State of Queensland, Australia, could possibly be to an old lady in Lewisham. Or even more bizarre, to the Battersea Dogs Home, her sole beneficiary. The fifteen million dollars in the bank wasn't a problem. He could handle that all right.

For a brief moment he permitted his hardened conscience a lapse of sensible judgment in feeling sorrow for the son, but the lapse was only brief for no sooner had that train of thought commenced than it led directly to a possible solution, already partially formulated on his way back from Viola Street.

As the small, slight, gaunt, bespectacled secretary entered with his mug of strong coffee, she saw on Archibald Snapes' face an expression that she'd not seen since her beloved husband David had killed himself by carbon monoxide poisoning in the company garage beneath the office. The same wide eyes, the throbbing veins on the forehead, the beads of sweat appearing around those veins, the manic stare into nowhere. He really had taken his partner's death badly.

'Are you okay Archie?' she enquired, only momentarily taking her eyes off his face to tentatively place his mug centrally on his leather drinks coaster.

He broke his stare and smiled softly up at her.

'Yes thank you Dorothy. Never felt better.'

Dorothy Bodger felt a slight shiver course through her spine and with a wan smile, made her exit, quietly closing the door behind her and resuming her seat, deep in thought.

Chapter Twenty One

## MILLICENT BOOKS A ROOM

Like Archibald Snapes, Millicent Carter was also facing a dilemma. Having paced the floor of her lounge for half an hour with George glued to her heels - he wondering why this walk was confined to home and not spreading to the grass and fresh 'messages' left by the neighbouring bitches of Regents Park right outside the window - Millicent picked up the phone. Then she replaced it and walked to a window box where hyacinths were showing their heads and demanding attention. Her face was set in a severe preoccupied stare as she poured water into the box and wiped a bird's deposit off the white metal railing with a tissue. This was not the Millicent that Henry knew; not the calm, sweet creature he now couldn't help loving more because of her recent cool indifference.

Finally she returned to the phone and dialled. Henry, who'd made a rule that private phone calls were now permitted in the office, but only if kept short and during lunch breaks, had asked Millicent to respect this rule in order that he maintain his new regime of total equality throughout the department. This had indeed not been a problem for the past two weeks as she hadn't called him once, so it was fortunate that he was actually sitting in Peregrine Spencer's old office when her first call came through. The fact that he had Richard Gaines opposite him in a serious discussion was good enough reason to tell her that he was busy and would phone her straight back.

Henry was engaged in his first difficult situation since taking over. Richard Gaines, unlike every other member of the department who had fallen in with Henry's enlightened ideas, refused to budge from his old ways and still continued to blaze a trail to and from The Carpenter's Arms as and when he pleased. Henry had tried a quiet word or two with him but as is the way of the ignorant and arrogant, Gaines chose to carry on in the manner to which he had always been accustomed, until Henry decided the time had come to exercise his right to take action with staff who were not prepared to follow the rules.

So the reason for the silly man's glum, shocked expression was that he'd pushed and abused Henry's good nature and patience a jot too far and had just received the news that he was of that moment no longer Post Room Supervisor. His pleas of a second chance were useless as Henry reminded him that he'd already had several second chances and had frankly given him no option.

With this Gaines stood up, took a deep breath, deliberately lit a half-smoked roll-up in front of Henry and with a 'Fuck off you jumped up little bastard!' turned and left the office, slamming the door so hard that the whole flimsy partition looked as if it were about to collapse around Henry's ears. As Phyllis clapped her hands to her face in shock and the entire staff turned towards Gaines, Henry simply studied the position of his blotter before straightening it, carefully opening his door, walking calmly out of the office and announcing, as the man stormed from the office shouting 'Fuck the lot of yer!' with a double handed V-sign, that 'Mr Gaines is leaving us.'

Whether the ex-Post Room Supervisor heard the tumultuous spontaneous applause that broke out as he stomped petulantly down the stairs, we'll never know, but there was no doubting that this hugely unpopular man would be missed about as much as Peregrine Spencer. Richard Gaines' aggressive manner had always been too much for Spencer to handle and accordingly the aggressor had got away with behaviour not extended to anyone else. But that of course is the way of bullies the world over; a yellow layer of cowardice never lurking far from the surface.

Whilst the chatter of excitement started to abate and staff returned to their work, Henry made an apology - as only Henry would feel he had to - that he had an urgent private call to make and would they mind if he closed the door of the office again for a few minutes. They, all suspecting that Henry had to report back his dismissal of Gaines to the Minister, smiled, shook their heads amiably and felt what a thoroughly decent, democratic chap their manager truly was.

Henry quietly closed the door behind him, took his seat, and prepared for what he imagined was news he had been expecting but didn't really want to hear, and dialled Millicent's number.

'Henry?' Millicent sounded light and friendly, her old self. Henry's spirits rose and he had to force himself not to smile in case his happiness was misinterpreted through the glass as smugness in sacking someone. Despite that someone being Richard Gaines, in the fickle world of office politics there was no point in risking a smile that could swing opinion.

'How are you Millicent?'

'I'm fine, feeling much better than I have for a while. I've had a lot on my mind, stuff to sort out, which I've now sorted.'

'Nothing serious?'

'Just making a few changes here and there. I've sold one of my flats. At least, I think I have.'

'You own *flats*?'

'I told you I did.'

'Did you? Yes, maybe you did. Property tycoon eh?'

'A little hobby.' Millicent laughed self-consciously keen to change the subject. 'How's your mother?'

'Ah, mother. What can I say? She's recovering but lost all speech and the use of her left arm. She's been home now for three days and Lily from next door is, thankfully, in her glory. She's a terrible gossip but a natural carer who's been without anything to look after for so long that my undeserving mother is getting service fit for a queen.'

'Is she going to live?'

'Not if I can help it. The doctor told me that her medication was vital for her survival and that too much or too little could kill her, so…' He hesitated as one of the male staff appeared at the door of the office with a file in his hand. Henry raised five fingers to denote he'd be out soon. The man went away and Henry heard Millicent say:

'So?'

'So I had to decide what to do. And I decided too little was probably the easiest option, in case I had to answer questions. Almost impossible to detect I'd imagine and I can always plead stupidity or forgetfulness, or something, I don't know. But too much might look a bit suspicious. People might jump to the wrong conclusion.'

'Or the right one.'

'Quite.'

They both chuckled and the distance that had spread between them over the past two weeks seemed to close in an instant.

'You're going through with it then.'

'Oh yes. No question. I nearly weakened when she did something vaguely pleasant yesterday - no, not pleasant, that's impossible. Normal. But all I had to do was think of the thoroughly miserable life she's given me and it quickly wipes away any shadow of doubt. I want a life Millicent, you know that, I deserve a life and now things have improved and I'm feeling independent - thanks to you - she's like a…what's that bird that hangs round the neck?'

'Albatross.'

'That's it. She's like a bloody albatross.'

'I've never hear you swear before.'

'Haven't you? No, I don't do I? Not out loud but I do quite a bit in my head. Anyway darling…'

He stopped short. There was a long silence before Millicent broke it.

'Something else you say in your head Henry - dear?'

Henry was mortified. 'Millicent, I'm so terribly sorry, I have no idea where that came from.'

'Don't be sorry. It was nice. Quaint. Thank you.'

Quaint? That didn't help the poor chap one tiny bit. He'd never called anybody darling in his life and it sounded quite ridiculous coming unchecked from his own mouth. A solitary bead of sweat pumped from his forehead and began a slow trickle down his cheek. He wiped it quickly away.

'Look, someone wants to speak to me urgently. They're hovering outside my office. Can we meet?'

'That's what I phoned for. Are you owed holiday?'

'Holiday? I never take holidays. I just work and have the pay in lieu. Spend it mostly at the Costa Bookmaker.'

'Book two days, we're going to Brighton.'

The words 'two days' sent a shiver down Henry's spine. Two days meant a night, and a night meant…suddenly a kaleidoscope of Millicent's naked form in various positions appeared tauntingly over the filing cabinet facing him. He blinked it away thinking his vision could be shared by most visible staff members through the glass. His heart leapt into loud, thumping overdrive and the saliva in his mouth evaporated, leaving his tongue searching for assisted lubrication before he could speak.

'Tonight, six 'o'clock at Lyons Corner House in The Strand for tea. Or would you prefer wine at Gordons?' said Millicent with the hint of a chuckle.

'Tea, I think, Millicent,' croaked Henry.

'Tea it is. See you in Lyons. Bye.'

The phone clicked and Henry sat with the receiver in his hand watching the hovering young man outside with the file and trying desperately to compose himself and at least return some moisture to his mouth before he signalled him in. He put the phone down, wiped away another errant bead of sweat and got up from the desk, feeling that being outside the office confines would return him and his bodily functions to normality and avoid any suspicion being aroused. He needn't have worried, poor man, for any nervousness would only have been interpreted as their kind, sensitive manager just having completed what for him was an unpleasant task in dismissing Richard Gaines. If only they knew.

Having answered the man's query, Henry then had one more important job to do. He returned to the desk in the office, flipped through the telephone directory and once satisfied he'd found the right number, dialled. After thirty seconds of drumming on the table and trying hard to replace Millicent's naked body with a bowl of fruit - the standby he'd been using since Christmas to distract him in these dire revealing moments - a voice asked him if it could help.

'Oh yes. I'd like a telephone line installed at my house please. No, never had one before.'

The meeting with Millicent that evening was brief due to Henry now having to be home promptly to relieve Lily Bunce of her nursing duties. Henry would have liked to have stayed longer, stayed with her forever in fact and never have gone home, for she truly had never looked more beautiful. Instead of her usual impeccable clothes and make-up she was wearing a matching denim skirt and jacket with a skin tight pink crew neck sweater beneath which, when the jacket fell back, revealed perfectly the roundness of her breasts and the faint outline of her bra. Her make-up was also less, minimal in fact, and for the first time he could see her natural beauty, the soft down on her cheeks and neck. She had also forsaken her high heels and instead wore what were almost flats, pink to match her jumper, so that she appeared smaller, petite and altogether more fresh and girlish; a classy mature art student. He could hardly concentrate on what she was saying; such was the distraction of her new, youthful look. The old one was distracting enough but now the erotic tangents his mind were flying to were making cohesive thoughts and responses nigh on impossible.

He listened as she begged him to take two days holiday as soon as possible and suddenly all thoughts of whether it was the right thing to do by the Department fled like the Israelites from Herod. He cared not a jot for what the Department thought. When love arrives in its full powerful force, sudden and unshakeable, there is not a mundane human duty on this earth that can stand in its way. It has changed history, turned battles, reduced men to mice and transformed the rock of burning ambition and vanity into pathetic deferent ashes at the flash of a smile and the promise of unfettered carnal delight.

Forty years of monotonous celibacy, taken for granted so his body was conditioned for nothing else, and here, here at last, not far from Nelson's gloriously erect column, Henry Winston Scroggins finally felt ready. He could, and he would. He was now manager of a government department on a fat salary that was all his and not the bookmaker's; he looked the part, walked the part and talked the part in his own mild-mannered way, and now felt ready to play the part, his part, in enjoying what seemed the most natural progression in this new life with the most wonderful woman in the world. How lucky was he.

206

'I'll book the hotel room in the morning. The best room in the best hotel,' said Millicent. And oh, if only Henry could have read the rest of what was running in her head - 'You'll like it. I've used it a few times before'. But he couldn't, and so left her outside Lyons Corner Shop with a heart so light and happy, turning every few seconds as he blundered his way towards the station, to capture last fleeting glimpses of her standing there, a sweet pink and denim dream; smiling, waving, not making any attempt to leave, letting him enjoy the sight of her until he vanished into the people and traffic.

# Chapter Twenty Two

## LILY THE LEMMING

When Henry turned the knob on the back door to his kitchen he didn't see Lily Bunce until she jumped the other side of the glass panels, as if caught out. The poor woman quickly made a play at wiping crumbs from the orange formica surface and then, wiping her hands on her apron, looked up and gave Henry a wave and a sad smile of imminent bad news.

'How is she today?' asked Henry, placing his briefcase on the floor and loosening his tie.

'Not so good I'm afraid 'Enry. No, not so good I'm afraid today. Seems to be worse than when she came out of 'orspital to be truthful.'

'Oh, really?'

Henry tried to disguise his satisfaction that the reduction in medication had kicked in already.

'In what way?' he asked.

Lily heaved a huge sigh, shook her head and lifted her arms in a helpless gesture as if to say that if her sterling nursing qualities weren't working then *nothing on this earth* could save Irma Scroggins. She was - effectively - doomed.

'Just more droopy and not with it at all, that's all I can say really,' was Lily's expert diagnosis.

'Oh dear, that's not so good,' replied Henry, noticing an envelope propped up in Lily Bunce's usual letter propping place beside the kettle. He picked it up to read the name on the franking stamp - 'Messrs Bodger and Snapes, Solicitors and Commissioners for Oaths.'

'Oh yes, that came just after you left this morning, so I put it there ready for you 'Enry,' chipped in Lily.

'But it's addressed to Mrs Irma Scroggins,' said Henry, turning just his face to her.

'I know,' she replied timidly, almost apologetically, 'but I thought, like, you might want to give it 'er. Seeing as she can't open it or read it 'erself.'

'Yes of course. Thank you Lily, quite right.'

Henry stared back at the envelope and turned it over, not making any attempt to open it, whilst standing next to him with eyes fixated on his hands, Lily's heart beat a little louder than she'd have preferred; she who had been almost beside herself since the moment of its arrival, desperate to be privy to its contents.

In fact so badly had this desperate need continued unabated, that by early afternoon it had grown into burning desire, which very quickly transformed into uncontrollable compulsion, until at three o'clock, as the kettle boiled for the umpteenth time that day, the lady's insatiable curiosity forced her hands to unbelievably, suicidally, but *oh so carefully* - waft the envelope back and forth over the steam until the flap began to ease apart and offer up to the breathless Lily the news of Henry senior's sad demise in Australia and, more shockingly, his incredible wealth. Lily the Lemming had leapt again but this time risked all - and won the jackpot.

A gambler deserves the long wait for success and her day had finally arrived. How many times that day had the wretched lady walked in and out of the kitchen, unhindered by the time restriction of a fully-functioning Irma Scroggins, seeing before her probably the greatest temptation of her life lying there begging to be opened; a harmless quick steaming and resealing the easiest thing for her deft, experienced fingers to perform, and the prize always threatening to remain a secret, a mystery to her, for the rest of her days.

But if she'd expected an ordinary prize then her reward was so, *so* much greater; a veritable bonanza of Klondike proportions beyond even Lily's wildest dreams.

Nonchalantly tossing the envelope onto the kitchen top and smiling pleasantly at Lily, Henry enquired, 'Does she know it's here?'

Lily shook her head, peering at the envelope and trying hard to cover any traceable intimacy that might be detectable between her and it.

'No, I picked it up off the mat and brought it straight here. Then completely forgot about it,' she added with a chuckle. 'Me all over. Things wot don't concern me I just put right out of me 'ead is if they'd never 'appened. It'll be the death of me one day.'

And she finished with another chuckle of reprimand at being such a silly, forgetful old thing, not ever imagining at that precise moment that it might just 'be the death of her one day.'

'I'll open it in a moment,' said Henry, acutely aware that he was ruining the moment for Lily just as he was acutely unaware that the only thing he was ruining was her seeing his reaction to the contents, not her own. That was history. He glanced up at the kitchen clock that had once been white but like many things in the house that had started life as white or cream, now co-ordinated with its peers in varying shades of brown and grime.

'Time you were going isn't it Lily,' quipped Henry, before deciding to feed her a titbit of news for her trouble.

'Oh by the way, I've ordered a telephone to be installed so we won't need to bother you for yours should there be further emergencies.'

Lily, on behalf of her friend Irma Scroggins, was visibly shocked. 'A phone? Here? Whatever for?'

'Well I thought it would be useful for sending and receiving calls you know Lily. Isn't that what they're meant for?' replied Henry, bending down to see what the fridge offered for supper. 'In my new position at work (another cruel titbit thrown in) I'll probably need to be in touch with the office at all hours and, well, it doesn't concern you anyway - apart, that is, from the fact that I won't need to bother you again.'

Oh, if he knew how it did matter to her, how the 'not bothering her' was as bothering as it could possibly get. Henry, crouched, spoke from behind the fridge door.

'It'll go in my bedroom so that it doesn't annoy Mother but is always there to safeguard her. That's my main concern.'

He stood up with a small gasp, examining the date on a packet of mince, and smiled at the open-mouthed lady before suddenly brandishing the hand holding the mince towards the door that he then stepped towards to open for her exit. Lily, frozen to the spot, still riveted in her 'new phone' moment, stirred suddenly to life and proceeded to gather up handbag, magazine and knitting piled on the kitchen top in readiness for Henry's arrival home.

'I've given 'er 'er medication so you won't have to worry about that,' said Lily as she bustled carefully past Henry out of the door.

'You've what!' cried Henry, straight into her ear.

'I've given 'er 'er medication,' replied Lily, her head recoiling from his voice as if she'd been dealt a physical, not verbal, blow.

'That's none of your business! How dare you! That is for me to administer and nobody else. The doctor made it quite clear that she's to have precisely the right dose and that's my responsibility if you don't mind. Please Lily, for once, do not interfere.'

Poor Lily looked up at him aghast. 'But it's got the dose on the packet an' she looked so peeky that I was worried she was going to cark it if I didn't do sumfin' quick. I was only trying to do the right thing, that's all. That's all I ever do 'Enry.'

This potentially heartbreaking plea for clemency on the doorstep was too much for Henry. Lily was distraught at the accusation, rightly so for once, and was about to burst into tears when Henry realised his spontaneous outburst of anger was a serious error of judgement - or lack of any sort of judgement - and placing an arm around her shoulder, soothed his tone into one of sincere, grudging apology.

'Lily, Lily, Lily, I am so sorry. You just took me by surprise and frightened me. I'd never forgive myself if anything happened to Mother because I'd neglected my responsibilities and, well, it was a bit of a shock what with the correct dose being critical.'

Lily nodded in sad, humble acceptance and with a throat gurgling and rattling like a blocked drain said, 'That's alright 'Enry, I was just doing me best for her. And for you. You know that's all I've ever tried to do in me life.'

'I know Lily and I cannot apologise enough. We are deeply indebted to you, both Mother and I. I have no idea how we'd manage without you. Well, to be honest, quite simply, we wouldn't - couldn't. People like you are gold dust Lily and that was extremely ungrateful and uncalled for. Just, well, as I say, a bit of a shock, took me by surprise - that's all.'

Lily laid a comforting hand on Henry's forearm, nodded forgivingly in the vague direction of the dustbin against the fence outside, sniffed and swallowed, tapped his forearm, stepped down the one step from the kitchen with a heaviness that can only come with the burden of a grave injustice suffered, and departed up the path like the wounded martyr she was.

Henry watched her disappear through the back gate and heaved a huge sigh of relief, leaning back against the kitchen top and placing the palm of his hand firmly on his forehead.

'You idiot! You damned idiot Henry Scroggins. Think, think, think!'

And with that reprimand, twined with extreme annoyance at his plan being subverted by the interference of the silly woman, he turned to the envelope and with a glance up at the ceiling as if expecting those red, watery eyes above to pierce the plaster like some demonic laser, he proceeded to gently slide a finger inside the flap, not noticing in his advanced state of curiosity, just how easily it sprang open.

Chapter Twenty Three

# THE POWER OF LOVE AND HATE

Henry stared out of the window at the countryside rushing past as his train sped southwards to Brighton. His mind was awash with confused thoughts as he tried to grapple with the notion of having a multi-millionaire father, one he knew nothing else about but who had obviously spent a life so far removed from his own that it was hardly conceivable. And now his father was gone and with it, extinguished forever, any remote chance Henry might have nurtured of them one day being reunited.

The excitement of spending a night with Millicent had been almost nullified by the letter resting in his jacket pocket. He took out the envelope for the third time during the journey and possibly the tenth time since he'd opened it the previous evening and unfolding the letter read the words he already knew almost by heart.

*Dear Mrs Scroggins,*

*I regret to inform you that your husband, Henry Arthur Scroggins, passed away in the state of Queensland, Australia, on December 24th 1980. I have been advised this by his Australian business partner who confirms that his estate, left entirely to you in his Will (in our possession) dated October 1943, consisting of money and various properties in his adopted country, is considerable – at first estimate in excess of ten million pounds. It is therefore my recommendation that we arrange a meeting at your earliest convenience to discuss this in more detail.*

*As your own Will, made out at the same time, still names your late husband as executor, but no longer a beneficiary – The Battersea Dogs Home being your sole beneficiary - our company will be pleased to offer any advice to ensure that the settlement of your late husband's estate, which by virtue of its size and complex nature is anticipated will require a great deal of time and work, is expedited as speedily and smoothly as possible.*

*If you are happy to proceed on this basis we will need your agreement as soon as possible to avoid any unnecessary delay and inconvenience for you.*

*Please accept our sincere condolences and I look forward to hearing from you. When contacting our office it is <u>imperative</u> that you do not speak to anyone about this matter other than myself.*

*Yours faithfully,*

*Archibald Snapes*

Henry smiled painfully, shaking his head as he muttered 'Battersea Dogs Home' before folding the letter and returning it to his jacket pocket. Then his gaze fell again to the fields and trees flashing past the window in a blur of shapes and shades of green, grey and brown, the odd row of back gardens arriving and disappearing before any discernible detail could be absorbed - his mind empty for a while until returning to the mother and father who obviously never wanted him.

He'd once read somewhere that reincarnationists believe an unborn child chooses its parents, ones that will help it grow in preparation for its next life. He mulled this weird theory over in the blur of countryside.

'What's the point of the next life which I won't even know about?' he thought. 'What sort of an idiot unborn child must I have been to choose two people who hated each other and didn't want me? Stupid enough to deserve them I suppose.'

He snorted aloud in his empty carriage at the laughable idea of choosing a wicked witch and a selfish father to help him grow. 'What utter baloney!' he cried out loud, then sank into a well of sadness at the thought of his forty miserable wasted years.

How unwanted he felt at that moment; how lonely and unwanted. Both his parents estranged for so long and yet neither bothered to spare him, their only child, a thought - even less a penny. But that was unfair, his mother did spare him a thought - a hateful thought backed up by a vindictive gesture. A woman that could drown a puppy in front of her young son's eyes and then leave all her money to a dog's home.

What a sick joke - what a sick, sick mind. How he hated her. How he wanted to wring her scrawny neck right there and then.

And neither of them, not even his father, making any mention whatsoever of him in their wills as if he had never existed, never crossed their minds, never mattered. He tried to rationalise it; he would have been nearly three years old, a toddler; it was wartime, the future unpredictable. He imagined how they would have felt at the time of making their wills and concluded they were probably resigned to being together forever, gripped tight in a trap of low income and mutual dependency like so many others thrown together by the shock of war, unable to think much beyond its uncertainty and living day by day. They probably just assumed that Henry would inherit whatever little they'd accumulated through the years, possibly just the house and nothing more. No, this was pathetic, this was clutching at straws, this was giving credit where it wasn't due - certainly not where his mother was concerned.

His father, even then, might have had secret aspirations for a better life, of escaping one day to try and make his fortune, but it would have been just that, an almost impossible dream whilst reality meant a lifetime with a woman he already couldn't abide.

Despite this Henry still could not come to terms with the fact that his father, once he'd become wealthy and successful, had not given him - the son he named after himself so therefore must have felt some sense of pride in having him - a second thought. That's what really, deeply hurt; the uncaring, the total abandonment.

But then there was Millicent. His heart lightened as her name streamed into his gloomy thoughts; brightness and lightness and smiles and laughter replacing the depression. She was truly his salvation and maybe, just maybe the reincarnationists had a point. His self-pity turned in a flash to self-chastisement.

'You selfish fool Henry!' he whispered at the window, his breath clouding the already blurred view. He drew a heart in the cloud and wrote 'Henry loves Millicent' and struck an arrow through the centre, quickly rubbing it out in case anyone entered the carriage and caught him out, caught him being a silly schoolboy lover. Forty years of penance for the loveliest of rewards. Who cares about parents? Blood's not thicker than water - anyone who believes that is a misguided fool. How is it possible to compare a good friend with a bad relative apart from to prove that blood means nothing?

It was all bunkum, baloney, and he knew it. Not only had Fortune smiled so kindly upon him to provide him with the most adorable female he believed had ever walked this planet, but also with the perfect advocate, his own personal solicitor, there to advise and guide him in this complicated matter. It was almost too good to be true. It *was* too good to be true. No it wasn't. He deserved it; he was a good man; that much he knew.

He smiled to himself at the thought of telling Millicent the news when they met within the hour. It was almost as heart stopping as the prospect of spending a night in a hotel room with her. He had no idea how he was going to cope but his faith in her was intransigent and he knew all would be well. He'd chosen to change his life and had come so far in a few short months that he was now letting Millicent and fate take control. He was no longer driving the bus, just a happy passenger.

The couple had first planned to meet at London Bridge and travel down to Brighton together but Henry wanted to savour the adrenalin rush of expectation by travelling separately, a sweet gesture which Millicent did nothing to dispel. He had therefore travelled by way of taxi and Gipsy Hill and East Croydon railway stations - a feat of planning that would have until recently been practically impossible - just to enjoy a romantic platform scene with his own delectable film star.

Henry was not disappointed. As the train pulled in, the film star was waiting for him on the platform, smiling and waving so prettily under a black beret with a grey pencil-thin skirt clinging tightly to hips and thighs, its whole length revealed by a short matching grey jacket, pulled tight into the waist that had a bit of the bellboy about it. And back were the high heels, black patent and very high with matching handbag gripped between her two white gloved hands held against her abdomen; in fact so extraordinarily provocative did she look that it flashed through Henry's mind that to a stranger she could even pass as a high-class prostitute, possibly a French one. The second this appalling thought entered his head he had to call upon his mental broom to instantly sweep it away and replace it with the angel he knew she was.

As he descended from the carriage and his eyes automatically widened at the sight of her, she couldn't help returning a cheeky grin from under her fringe and shaking her head at his comical expression. Taking a step towards him as he reached her, she placed a hand on his arm and a kiss on his cheek.

'Good journey?' asked Millicent.

'Yes...thank you,' replied Henry hesitantly, 'you look wonderful Millicent. Stunning.'

'Thank you. Not so bad yourself. I like the rose.' She bent and sniffed at the red rose in Henry's lapel that he'd bought at East Croydon station. Henry looked down and began to unpin it from his navy blazer.

'It's for you,' he said. 'I bought it for you. I was going to buy a bunch but decided just one was better. Isn't that what they do, in films? One red rose for...' He hesitated until encouraged by an enquiring smile and raised eyebrow from Millicent, '...given with love, is far better than a bouquet presented out of duty. I'm sure I remember that from a film...or...something.'

'Probably not a book,' said Millicent, with a meaningful grin.

'No, not a book,' agreed Henry, aware of his reputation in her eyes. 'Perhaps you can introduce me to your books Millicent. I'd like to be able to share your authors with you, perhaps, one day. They seem such a happy part of your life.'

He took the rose from his lapel and gave it to her. Millicent took the fragrant bloom and inhaled deeply with eyes closed, then gently kissed him on the cheek again and whispered softly in his ear.

'The sweetest rose and the sweetest surprise I have ever received in my life. Thank you so much.'

'And you've had a few I'll bet,' chuckled Henry, wishing she hadn't had any.

'I've had many and enjoyed them all but what I have just said is the truth. *This*...is the best.'

Henry smiled self-consciously, suddenly aware that they were standing blocking the exit, forcing people to squeeze past.

'Blimey, you lovers!' said one middle-aged man with good-humoured impatience, as he eased past in his battered brown leather jacket quipping, 'wish I was young again.'

Millicent raised her eyebrows at Henry as they followed the man and the crowd.

'Young,' mouthed Millicent so the man in front couldn't hear and make further comment.

'He meant you,' whispered back Henry.

'Us. You look at least five years younger than when we met.'

'Same age as you then?'

She shrugged, calculating, and said 'Close enough', then locked her arm in his as they walked with their overnight bags and he felt the softness of her bosom press into his side.

Millicent had decided, after much heart-searching, against revealing her past life to Henry, not for any reasons of guilt but simply to avoid hurting him. After weighing up the pros and cons during their recent quiet period, it seemed so pointless to risk wrecking the first relationship that had ever made her contemplate giving up her 'job' before she was ready. It was a secret she had decided she could keep to herself without any feeling of betraying Henry. After all, she determined, if she'd been a 'normal' single woman it would have been inconceivable that with her attractiveness she was still, at the age of thirty-five, a virgin saving herself for Mr Right. In fact most would have considered it a crime to lock away such charms, hoarding them for a day that may never come.

So the fact that she'd made a decision fifteen years ago to turn her obvious asset into a profession and only be with men she chose to be with, men with whom she would have been happy to have a relationship under any circumstances but who were also able and happy to afford her company both inside and outside the bedroom, seemed morally far less reprehensible than a wife who stayed and slept with a husband she loathed.

Anyway, who cared about morals? Who made the rules? She made her own. Her relationships, whilst not blessed at an altar or in a registry office, were completely under her control. She had jurisdiction over of whom, when and where, and if the slightest

218

whiff of repugnance surfaced then wild horses laden with all the riches in the world would not entice her to share a bed, or even a dinner table, with a man. She simply enjoyed being with men she was comfortable with and more than anything she enjoyed men enjoying the fact that she enjoyed having sex with them; even Peregrine Spencer who, whilst a picture has been painted of someone undeniably repulsive in many respects, was not an altogether unattractive man and came with the dual aphrodisiacal components of power and money. Millicent was living proof that these qualities were not solely an aphrodisiac for the more shallow of her gender. It was a plain fact that money and power were undoubtedly an initial attraction to her, and also as plain a fact that this alone would never take her from a temporary to a permanent relationship. With not one of the men she'd known ever coming close to fulfilling the high, seemingly impossible, spiritual standards she had set herself, it was perfectly understandable to her that the man for whom she had given up all others - not to mention a lucrative profession - was the antithesis of the rich and powerful model. In the absence of a path of motherhood, which she had chosen not to follow, an accidental roadblock called Henry had arrived out of the blue and created a most unexpected diversion.

Henry was just so very different to any living being she'd ever encountered. He was not insipid, pathetic or weak as she'd first suspected. He was quite simply without any pretensions at all; in fact she didn't think he was actually capable of deliberately calculating anything, rather like an animal. But whereas even an animal has an instinctive cunning to survive, Henry was even devoid of that natural protection, which is why he was in the sorry state she'd found him, in a police station at Christmas.

His thoughts and actions were honest and spontaneous and quite without malice, apart from towards the one person who could have so easily have given him love and support but chose to do the opposite. But now - and here was the strength she admired in him - having made the decision to change all this, nothing was going to hinder his natural route of direct action. Having made up his mind and gone thus far, he was not in the least hesitant or frightened about what to do. It was just how to do it that he had to get right. Therefore the more Millicent thought about Henry and the more time she spent with him, the more he appeared as the strongest of men. What he lacked in social skills and etiquette, having never needed them up to now, was more than compensated by a will that neither tried to impress nor fool anyone. If only he could have known the parent from whom these qualities were inherited; a man who also just needed the right woman by his side to be able to be himself. Compare this to the poor wife who in good faith vows she will always love with the love she feels in the full flush of matrimony but then later finds herself sinking into a morass of physical disgust, making a sad mockery of those vows so honestly taken.

Millicent's god was a practical one who demanded no worshipping or falling down on bended knee from her. So all her decisions were made, as are the best and truest, by the simple rule of doing unto others as she would have done to herself. Nothing biblical, no pronouncement from an old man up a mountain, just a matter of conscience and human decency. Therefore, in her eyes, two people together causing each other desperate misery was both a crime and an avoidable punishment.

So it was with this solidly reasoned confidence and clarity of conscience that she walked into the reception of The Grand Hotel just ahead of Henry who, having never walked into any hotel lobby in his life, felt he should start off on the right foot with that right foot being at least a pace or two behind both feet of someone who knew what they were doing. Then the embarrassment began.

It being a quiet drab weekday morning for the hotel, the concierge stood with clipboard in hand on the guests' side of the counter ready to pounce and pander, whilst three under-employed staff stood fiddling behind the counter with anything they could find to keep them looking occupied. The concierge, delighted to see fresh human life appear through the doors, stepped forward with his concierge smile and began asking questions; questions addressed in particular to Henry; questions that only a concierge could ask because a concierge has no conception of anyone having spent less than half their life in anywhere but a hotel room.

This threw things awry for Henry who, with his aforesaid social skills still very much in the embryonic or training stage, had been prepared to stand back and let Millicent take control in a zone where she was unmistakably comfortable; after all, *she'd* booked the room. So, taken completely unawares, he was forced to flash panic-stricken glances at his glamorous partner, *Mrs Scroggins*, she who had booked in the name of Henry for some old-fashioned reason best known to herself, not envisaging for one moment that it would backfire onto *Mr Scroggins* wilting under interrogation at the counter beside her.

One of the main benefits of being with men who have money and power is that dealing with hotel staff in very public lobby settings is *de rigueur*. They know what to do and say, they've done it a thousand times before. And even if they don't, their air is never one of fluster but more an arrogant attitude of tedium, of 'frankly can't be bothered'. Enter Henry looking every inch the part in his *haute couture* clothes, with Louis Vitton overnight bag, newly defined cheekbones and the epitome of feminine class by his side - but as far removed from playing the part for which he'd never in his life auditioned as Tommy Cooper was for Othello.

It took Millicent about ten heart-stopping seconds to smoothly intervene and take action that would cause minimum embarrassment for Henry and be plausible enough to satisfy the possible sadistic tendencies of the concierge on discovering he had a novice on his hands.

So the story went that Henry had been under considerable stress for some time (forty years wasn't mentioned) and this was an opportunity they were taking for him to recuperate with the help of some restorative sea air. The concierge nodded and bowed and smiled with all the understanding in the world, imagining but not saying 'nervous breakdown - slave to a city boardroom' and peering at Henry with eyebrows and all ten fingers and thumbs knotted in the deepest sympathy.

'In that case sir,' he concluded, 'you could not have chosen a better place to lay the first building blocks of your recovery. Please allow myself and my staff to act as more than willing bricklayers.'

Millicent winced at this gratuitous, theatrical sycophancy and, thanking the concierge, took the key from him - a key that had somehow miraculously managed to transfer into his hand during their conversation without him moving from the spot - and picking up both bags whisked Henry towards the lift. Henry, who if he had entered the hotel lobby feeling moderately relaxed, had now grown quickly into the role just created for him; a man most definitely under work-related pressure.

'Bad start,' muttered Millicent after a deep breath of exasperation. 'Sorry, my stupid fault.'

As the lift doors closed and they stood with bags at feet staring up at the floor numbers ticking by, Millicent noticed from the corner of her eye Henry's shoulders start to jerk very slightly.

'Under considerable stress?' he chuckled. 'Spending a night with a beautiful lady for the first time and haven't got a clue what to do. Oh dearie me.'

'Me neither,' said Millicent.

Henry shot a glance at Millicent who shrugged and smiled at Henry in the reflection of the door. It was the first time they had seen each other together as a couple and there they were side by side, Millicent's red rose and lipstick the dominant features in an otherwise grey metallic portrait.

'And all my dear mother's got for the night is Lily Bunce,' concluded Henry, not meaning to be funny but by the time the lift arrived at the top floor, causing them to dissolve into a state of childish eye-watering mirth.

'I meant to ask what was happening with her,' asked Millicent as they wandered along the corridor examining room numbers.

'Well, I had no choice really and Lily is the only person the old bag trusts. Under the circumstances.'

'But what about the…'

'Medication?'

'Yes.'

'Well, the silly interfering woman had already panicked and given it to her on Monday, thinking Mother was going to cark it, so that set things back a bit. And like a fool I lost my temper with her, just in the heat of the moment, so had to do some serious consoling to calm her down. I've got to be very careful how I tread because if ever there is a bloodhound in human form it's Lily Bunce. If the War Office had known about her during the war they could have dropped her behind enemy lines and saved a lot of lives. No German secrets would have been safe with her around.'

Henry smiled at the thought as they located their room and Millicent, after turning the large key several times this way and that, unlocked the door.

Once inside the room and presented with such opulence that, whilst familiar to Millicent, was to Henry's eyes like a film set, the humour and banter diminished. Henry took several measured paces around, gazing at the numerous items of splendid, gleaming furniture, in particular the huge four-poster bed confronting him like some menacing ogre. It was at this moment that heavy reality descended upon the scene and Henry, dipping his fingers into the gold silk duvet with all the expertise of a first time car buyer checking tyres, swallowed hard before offering, 'Spongy.'

Millicent threw off her jacket onto a chair, kicked off her shoes across the carpet, flopped onto the bed and throwing her arms behind her head on the pillow, smiled at her friend who gazed at her and thought how wonderfully radiant and at home she looked. Millicent patted the bed beside her. Henry likewise slipped off his shoes and jacket, which he placed neatly at the end of the bed, and cautiously climbed up beside her, feeling the cool luxury wrap around him and Millicent's hand take his.

'Shall we order breakfast in bed for the morning?' asked Millicent nonchalantly, examining a spot on the ceiling.

Henry's attention had been diverted by the envelope containing the solicitor's letter poking out of his inside jacket pocket and he wanted very much to crawl forward and conceal it but that wasn't possible with his hand being held, so he examined a similar spot possibly not far away from Millicent's, and replied quietly.

'Pardon?'

Millicent turned her head to him on the pillow. 'Room service. Shall we order breakfast for tomorrow? Save rushing down to the restaurant. I hate rushing in the mornings.'

'The morning?' said Henry. 'The morning?' he repeated. 'I've got to get through the night first Millicent.'

To which, within seconds, the bed was shaking once again but this time it was only from Millicent's body as it rocked in silent suppression, unable to sweep from her mind the numerous times she had occupied rooms in hotels, but never before with the feeling that she was in the middle of a sitcom. Some of the men tried humour, knowing it was purported to be top of the list of things women found attractive, and dismally failed; some were naturally witty and charming but not particularly funny; some only there for one thing and seeking in humour the means of breaking the ice before the action; but never before had one man made absolutely no attempt to gain her favour with humour, yet caused the muscles of her stomach to ache. What was it about this funny little man that played havoc with parts of her body that were not normally disturbed in the slightest; namely heart and stomach?

Henry was too preoccupied with the envelope to join in Millicent's light-hearted moment. He had already decided that, much as he needed to share the news with Millicent, it was news of such life-changing consequences, that the next morning was the time to show her the letter and ask her advice. To raise it before would without doubt divert their entire thoughts and emotions from the reason for spending this momentous evening together. A few more hours would make no difference and whilst he was now beginning to feel extremely nervous, faced with sharing a bed with a woman for the first time in his life - a night with no clothes on next to another person with no clothes on - it was not a time to let anything else steal what he hoped would be the magic of the moment.

He had rehearsed his part so many times in preparation for this night, stimulating his imagination (whenever it lost momentum) with the memory of that first night in Millicent's flat when the divine sight of her flesh had identified a libido far from extinct and nothing more than a perfectly healthy Phoenix taking a forty-year nap.

He need not have worried about the letter. It could have been a gas bill for all Millicent was concerned - if she'd seen it - which she hadn't. Suddenly she sat up and swinging her legs round, leapt off the bed with all the vigour and vivacity of a school hockey captain rousing her team into action on a cold and frosty morning.

'Right! Let's go and get some of this sea air Henry and be damned with your mother for two days! No more talk of her until we get home. Agreed?'

Henry nodded, knowing that once she had read the contents of the letter, all thoughts of postponing mother-related discussions would be cancelled. So off they went out into the chill, damp air and were soon to be seen strolling along the promenade under a leaden sky, then skipping hand in hand down stone steps to the beach and crunching along the water's edge, Millicent having changed into trainers in anticipation of the pebbly walk she'd done many times before.

Henry had not been on a beach since childhood and soon discovered a forgotten delight in skimming stones. Millicent, after a few bad throws of her own, stopped to act as Henry's hunter and gatherer, scanning and bending and excitedly bringing him new smooth, flat ammunition, to which his eyes would light up and with extraordinary dexterity send the stones flying on their way just beyond the breaking waves, watching and counting with Millicent until the stone ran out of velocity and disappeared to cries of disappointment or victory, dependant on whether the last total was beaten or not.

When Henry's throwing arm began to feel as if all his body's blood had drained into that single limb (such is the dreadful addiction of pebble skimming) they crunched back up the beach and ran up the stone steps to the promenade, invigorated to such a pitch of red-cheeked, hot-breathed excitement, that any inhibitions separating them before, were dispersed, seemingly forever.

As all lovers know, these moments in a love affair are precious beyond compare. They are held, suspended, always with a fear they cannot last, until recalled in later years bringing smiles to wrinkled features and solace to lonely hearts. And so, arm in arm the unusual couple strolled in their own silent heaven towards the pier and then down its length, feeling just as millions before them had felt in the same place, that nothing else in the world mattered more than the moment they were in, and that their moment surpassed all others who had gone before and who 'thought' they felt the same.

The smell of the salt air, the cry of the gulls, the swell of the brown, churning depths beneath them, the seated fishermen staring at tips of rods for a telltale twitch, the aroma of coffee and fried food, was intoxicating. A breeze flicked Millicent's hair back and forth onto Henry's cheek as she gripped his arm with both hands, pressing herself close to him for comfort, occasionally dipping and nestling her head on his shoulder then looking up to take in the scene and a deep breath before returning her head, the smell of her perfume drifting into his mind mingling with the salt air, coffee and chips. The strands of hair tickled his skin to the point of him wanting to tear at his flesh for relief but he refused to lift even a discreet finger, frightened that she might apologise and tuck the strands beneath her beret and take away the thrill.

As he resisted this urge to scratch, a fleeting wave of despair suddenly swept over him, making him want to cry. His happiness, so intense, so extreme - the feeling of never wanting it to end, that it couldn't last like this - turned to despair. His life, until so recently devoid of love and affection, was being turned upside down and whatever he tried to do as they strolled along in this happiest of moments, he could not control a feeling of impending doom. He felt that in this moment of extreme ecstasy, all life now presented to him must be an anti-climax. He could not be happier, so what then followed? If this was what everyone in life aspired to, the absolute pinnacle of happiness, where was there to go afterwards? He never wanted it to end.

In panic, he scratched his cheek, feeling the enormous relief and hearing Millicent saying 'Sorry Henry, is my hair annoying you?' as she pulled her head from his shoulder and stood upright, loosening her grip on him to tuck her hair into her beret.

The moment was gone. It was true; it couldn't last forever. It would never return like it had just been. Everything now could only be just a repeat or, worse still, something to be lost. The agony and the ecstasy; Henry had experienced the astonishing, indescribable power of love - on Brighton Pier.

Chapter Twenty Four

## HENRY'S COMING OF AGE

That evening Millicent and Henry had decided to dine at the hotel restaurant. After toying with the idea of an intimate backstreet bistro in the town centre, the thought of being able to drift quietly upstairs to their room was rather more appealing and with heavy rain forecast it seemed an altogether cosier option.

Henry's depression had quickly passed that afternoon. It had gone undetected by Millicent who simply attributed Henry's quiet thoughtfulness to nervous tension as the day drew towards the night. Just as with a timid best man making his first wedding speech, she imagined he was feeling the weight of expectation upon him; expectation she would no more dream of coaxing unless he was whole-heartedly ready, willing, and possibly more to the point, able.

If she could have read his mind as they strolled up and down the hilly streets and alleyways, in and out of the shops, commenting on this and that of interest, pleased at finding they liked similar things, she would have seen a mind preoccupied with the contents of a letter that she knew nothing about.

For some reason, Henry's sudden mood of despondency on the pier had been instantly replaced by the reality of his father's death and the ramifications of the fortune he'd somehow amassed and left to a wife he'd long ago abandoned. So tense had he been about the prospect of Brighton and then organising Lily Bunce to look after his mother, that the full impact of what the letter represented had almost failed to touch him, until now. But now he was there, in Brighton, and the weekend was underway with his all-consuming trepidation usurped by a problem infinitely more earthly and potentially intricate.

The King's Restaurant was sumptuous Renaissance splendour personified and the high ceilings and fabulous drapes adorning the windows, the glimmering chandeliers and the tables laid to millimetre precision, were something so far beyond Henry's sphere of experience that Millicent had to suggest he stop staring upwards, down and around like Michelangelo licking his pencil as he sized up the Sistine Chapel.

Such was the low number of diners occupying the huge room that Henry's rapid training in table etiquette was able to take place with minimum attention focused upon them by the over-abundance of redundant waiters buzzing about or flanking the walls poised for action. Determined not to look a fool and more importantly not to make the shimmering Millicent look a fool by his dull reflection, he had quickly coped with the intricacies of what to use and when. His methodical, mensurate brain had little trouble working out the protocol of a restaurant dining-table and Millicent, delighted with her high society protégée, saw this as a sign that Henry would take no time at all in being completely at his ease in any company.

As for his dress, for some reason he had decided to include a navy bow tie in his packing, and a very posh bow tie it was too, one bought for a department function many years ago that he failed to attend and which had rested in its cellophane wrapper at the bottom of a drawer ever since. This he was sporting with his pale blue shirt, navy blazer and cream flannel trousers which together with a slimmer physique than he'd had for many a year, meant he certainly presented no disgrace at all to the gorgeous vision in a simple black dress and pearl necklace facing him across the table. But to Henry's smitten eyes the dress could have been a bin liner.

The meal was a success. Henry had chosen and tasted the wine - a lighter red they decided after his previous experience, so went for a Beaujolais to compliment the lamb they'd both selected - had read the menu with a more than passable French accent instead of taking the easy English option, and was soon, in his own self-deprecating way, charming the waiters almost as much as Millicent, who didn't have to do much else but sit there and smile at Henry's quiet charm. In fact, so on form and relaxed was Henry after his second glass of Beaujolais, for which he expressed a slightly morish propensity, that he found an articulation and wit that Millicent, and indeed Henry, had no idea existed. It was all going just too well when late in the proceedings as they were enjoying coffee, the arrival of a man at their table changed the whole mood.

Sean Swadely had been observing the couple all evening from a table in a nearby corner. The position of his table, away from the direct glare of a chandelier, and with his male silver-haired dining companion placed conveniently between him and Henry and Millicent's table, afforded him the opportunity to remain hidden from their view yet able by moving slightly to one side when required, to spy on them. Around ten-fifteen he stood up and with a word in his companion's ear, walked across to the subject of his reconnaissance, placing one hand on the back of Millicent's chair, whilst asking for Henry's permission to interrupt.

'Good grief, Sean!' said Millicent swivelling round, visibly shocked at the unmistakable Yorkshire accent delivered through what sounded like swollen adenoids. She instantly looked across at the astounded Henry with a swift glance of apology whilst regaining her composure with the help of a serviette applied to the corners of her mouth.

'Henry, this is a friend of mine, a business friend. Sean Swadely, Henry - Henry Scroggins, my…'

'Pleased to meet you Henry,' said Sean, leaning across and offering his outstretched hand whilst making no attempt to leave Millicent's chair. His interruption had prevented Millicent from stating her relationship with Henry, and his rudely pulling up a chair from a neighbouring table without asking if he could join them, threw them both to the point of complete distraction.

'What brings you here? To Brighton?' enquired Millicent, all the time glancing at Henry to make sure he wasn't excluded.

'I'm interviewing Sir Jack Crowe.' He nodded towards the elderly gentleman at his table who had found the menu suddenly fascinating. 'One of England's greatest cricketers, mainly between the wars. Wonderful man, you'd like him Millie. He's loaded and at eighty-two years old still as fit as a flea and a perfect charmer.' With a wink and the slightest sly smile at an increasingly uncomfortable Henry, he added, 'Loves the ladies, the old devil. Second thoughts, maybe I won't introduce you.'

This was followed by a dirty laugh and Millicent, sensing danger, brought Henry into the conversation.

'Henry, Sean is the person who has bought my flat in Swiss Cottage. He's a cricketer…is that right?' She looked up at Sean.

Sean nodded and smiled across at Henry. 'Gave up playing a few years ago - you've probably heard of me.'

Henry shook his head.

'No?' continued Sean with a chuckle, 'Oh well, there you go, not as famous as I thought.'

'Don't be offended,' said Henry, 'you could be the most famous cricketer in the world and it's possible I still wouldn't know your name.'

'Not a cricketing man then,' said Sean, and like the expert wicket keeper he'd been, not one to let much past him.

'I know it's a fascinating game,' said Henry, 'but so far I…'

'I commentate now,' interrupted Sean, 'on the radio and TV quite a bit, so I need to be near Lords, which as you know is the home of cricket.'

Henry thought he'd better nod, so did, and hoped the subject of cricket would be dropped quickly. Sean continued in his nasal whine.

'So Millie's flat being close to the Lords ground - as you no doubt know - I've been renting it for a year or so and when it came on the market, I decided to go for it. Made sense I thought.'

Henry thought so too and nodded once again, wishing the man would go away and leave him and Millicent to end their evening properly. He was starting to get irritated, extremely irritated, and just a touch jealous. But mostly he hated the man calling her Millie. Her name was Millicent - and she was his.

Millicent detected Henry's irritation and embarrassment and decided enough was enough. She was sitting directly facing the table where the ageing cricketer seemed to be ageing even more rapidly, turning the menu over quite a number of times and looking around him trying not to make it obvious he was feeling bored and neglected.

'Sean, I think your friend knows the menu off by heart. Don't you think you should get back to him? Completion on the flat should be next week I hear.'

'Yes, I think our solicitors have managed to drag it out enough to line their greedy little pockets as much as they can, yours in particular - fussy bugger - anyone would think I'd a criminal record, the checks he's done! If he's done 'em at all that is!' The Yorkshireman's full-blooded indignation then moderated as he concluded, 'But a pleasure to do business with you Millie m' love,' adding with a joint wink for her and Henry, 'as always.'

The unwanted man glanced over his shoulder and met his cricketing companion's wave and wan smile, standing up straight to indicate he was about to return, whilst Millicent, stunned by what he had just said and seeing Henry frown at his coffee cup at the mention of her needing a solicitor - as if the cup had the answer - was momentarily frozen with panic.

'Okay, I'll leave you two…lovers…to it then,' said Sean, 'Nice to meet you Henry. Enjoy the *rest* of your evening.'

The word *rest* was emphasised as only a complete tactless nudge-nudge, wink-wink music hall bore could, and with this he reached across once more to shake Henry's hand, but Henry was somewhere else and only after a few seconds of seeing the hand hovering before him did he suddenly snap out of his reverie, get up from his chair, and nervously thrust out his own.

The chair behind him rocked, suspended for a moment, before crashing to the floor in the path of a speeding waiter passing with a tray of empty glasses balanced precariously aloft on one palm. Fortunately the waiter's nifty footwork enabled him to skip around the obstacle and even lift it back into position behind Henry with his spare hand and a flashing smile; all performed without breaking his stride, or a single glass. Such is the dexterity and multifarious talents of a good waiter.

'That was unfortunate,' said Millicent, 'the last person I expected to see here.'

Henry resumed his seat and took a sip of coffee. Millicent chewed the inside of her cheek and, darting a glance at Swadely who was clicking his raised fingers impatiently at the same dexterous waiter, quickly sifted through a few options of what best to say to Henry.

'He's been one of my…clients…for some time. I had dinner with him a few weeks ago to sort out the flat sale. In fact it was the evening after we went to the National Gallery, when we planned to come here to Brighton the next day, remember? He'd left a message about buying me dinner that night to celebrate the sale, so as I had the evening free. Well…that's what happened. '

'And my mother had her stroke.'

'Yes. So she did.'

Henry turned and looked across at where Swadely appeared to be complaining to the waiter about something, his abrasive tongue piercing the atmosphere.

'A fairly obnoxious character,' observed Henry.

'He can actually be quite pleasant when sober.'

Henry unable, or rather, unwilling, to look Millicent in the eye replied 'Yes, I'm sure he can. Alcohol has such a lot to answer for doesn't it? I mean I wouldn't be sitting here opposite a beautiful lady if it wasn't for alcohol. I probably wouldn't have been promoted at work if it wasn't for alcohol. I wouldn't have given up the horses if it wasn't for alcohol. And…' He glanced upwards as if, in his mind, his mother had already been despatched into the ether, 'I wouldn't be dispensing with the woman who gave birth to me - if it wasn't for alcohol. I've a lot to thank it for you know.'

Millicent frowned. 'I thought you'd made a decision about your mother before you…'

'Met you?'

'Well, yes, but before you got drunk at the office party.'

Henry raised his eyebrows. 'I beg your pardon? I didn't *get* drunk, I was *got* drunk! Big difference.'

'True, but I was just making the point that you'd already made your mind up to try and free yourself from her, somehow or other. You can't really credit alcohol for that idea.'

'No, but on the other hand I wouldn't have met you unless I'd been arrested that night and to be honest I'm not sure I would have had the courage to see it through without…'

He stopped to gather his thoughts before deciding how much to reveal at that precise moment. He decided on revealing nothing about the letter until the morning, as was his original plan. He also didn't want to query why she was using a solicitor when she was one herself; there was obviously a perfectly sound reason for that, he was certain, so he opted for the old maxim of 'if you've nothing good to say then say nothing at all' - and said nothing.

He really didn't want to let one boorish character ruin what had been such a perfect day and evening, an evening he knew he would remember for the rest of his life. He softened his expression and, reaching out, touched Millicent's hand resting by the side of her empty wine glass. She sighed with sudden relief and leaning forward, gave Henry's hand an affectionate squeeze before running her fingertip around his palm.

'Incy wincy spider...' said Henry, smiling at her boyishly before glancing furtively round and whispering, 'don't posh people have port at the end of a meal? Isn't that what you do?'

'I don't know about posh people,' whispered Millicent back, 'but yes, port does usually get the blame for the hangover the next morning.'

'By virtue, or otherwise, of being the last drink?'

'Correct.'

'Poor old port. Let's prove its innocence then, shall we?'

They both turned at the same time to look for a waiter, when Millicent, without thinking suddenly said, 'It was poor old port I blamed when I had dinner with *him* that evening.' She nodded towards Swadely, 'I had a shocking hangover the next morning.'

'Yes, I remember it well; you were slurring your words and couldn't get off the phone quick enough. I must admit I guessed it was drink and did wonder how you'd got drunk when I assumed you were on your own. So that explains that.'

'Has it been bothering you? Did you think you'd got a lone alcoholic on your hands?'

'No. I actually imagined what exactly happened; that you'd decided you wanted a social evening and when I decided to go home you just found someone else. It could have been female of course but that would have been far too simple for someone like me, so all I could see was a dashingly tall, dark handsome man. And I was right.'

He looked over his shoulder in the direction of Swadely and in doing so a mild tension returned. The truth of the matter was that Swadely had left a message for Millicent which was there waiting on her return after leaving Henry. It was obvious that his motive wasn't primarily to discuss the flat; that was already well in the hands of their solicitors, leaving nothing for them to do apart from wait for completion. No, as a client of Millicent's for some years (as she'd rightly informed Henry earlier) he'd only one thing on his mind and had asked her out for dinner with the sole intent of spending the night with her. He was in fact one of 'Millicent's men' whom she had always, despite his often unfortunate manner, found physically attractive. As a sportsman, and an inordinately vain one at that, he kept himself in peak condition and being just a few years older than Millicent, his body displayed no signs of excessive high living or inactivity. On the contrary, he was trim, taught and tanned all over. She rarely had anything better to do when Sean phoned.

But that particular evening, when Henry's mother was having her stroke, she did, for she had given up Sean and every other man. She was by then Henry's and had made that clear to her ex-client, who scoffed loudly and asked her to dinner anyway, 'for old time's sake', having every confidence in the delectable Millicent's resolve weakening under the influence of drink and his irresistible company, but more so the indubitable facts of his redoubtable prowess and unblemished track record between the bed sheets. Few women could ever easily pass up an opportunity of a Sean invitation and he was therefore, as usual, expecting to go unchallenged. But disappointment awaited him and Millicent even insisted on paying the bill to make it plain that this was her way of saying thank you and goodbye. If, on walking into the restaurant that evening, he had complete confidence of her eventual submission, then he certainly left with that confidence severely battered and the prospect of a rare night home alone or a hasty late ring around to find a replacement to satisfy his sexual urges. The normally all-conquering Sean was left with a very strong impression of the man who had finally won the heart of one of the most powerful women in London - if not the world.

If only Millicent could have told Henry all this to prove her singular devotion to him. If only. She knew this was the time to do it and had prepared herself for it. But it was not to be. The waiter arrived, the port was ordered and Henry decided he liked it enough to require another. And another. After the third, a double, when his eyelids began to turn a little leaden and he'd shaken his head twice to check the clarity of his contact lenses, Millicent suggested they go to their room to which Henry promptly agreed and moved from a safe sitting position to a slightly unsteady standing one.

The stimulation of strong spirits and a journey in the lift brought a lift to Henry's spirits and with it a resumption of their banter and laughter by the time they'd fumbled with the key and fallen like a pair of silly wedding guests into the room. Henry instantly took off his jacket and ripping off his bow tie, proceeded to sing 'Smoke Gets In Your Eyes' (the last song played by the restaurant pianist) whilst simulating his afternoon stone skimming by sending the bow tie bouncing superbly off the writing desk and, to his complete wide-eyed and wide-mouthed surprise, into a metal waste bin with a clang.

This feat of part luck and part skill left them staring at each other, both now wide-eyed and wide-mouthed, until Millicent ran in stockinged feet to her skimming hero, clapping her hands together before thrusting his arm into the air with a cry of, 'Bravo! And the gold medal for bow-tie skimming goes to...Henry Scroggins of...Lewisham!'

Henry frowned. 'Lewisham? Please Millicent...England!'

A further thrust of the arm that nearly had it out of its socket, quite lifting Henry off the ground, and a new cry from Millicent.

'Cry God for Henry, England and Saint George!'

She lowered his arm gently on hearing Henry's own cry, one of pain, and added apologetically, 'Shakespeare, Henry the Fourth I think. Maybe Fifth. Sorry about that. Not dislocated?'

Henry gave his shoulder a rub and shook his head, smiling.

'You're very literary aren't you?'

'Not really. I just enjoy reading old stuff.'

'Old *stuff*? Shakespeare? *Stuff*? And...what's his name? The other chap you like.'

'I don't know. Who? I like a lot.'

'The book you were reading when we met in the police station the last time I got a little tipsy. I kept interrupting you and you were getting cross with me.'

'Oh, Lady Chatterley's Lover. D.H. Lawrence, yes.'

'That's the man.'

'And you thought he was T.E.'

'T.E.?'

'Lawrence.'

'Who's he?

'Another writer, Lawrence of Arabia.'

'Did he write as well?'

'Oh Henry, does it matter?

No, it didn't, but this literary exchange had cleared the fog and Henry was by now wide-awake, buoyed by his new talent for bow-tie skimming. He retrieved the tie from the bin and made several more attempts, but was disappointingly unable to repeat his early success. During Henry's efforts Millicent had retreated to the bed where she lay watching his childish antics and tongue-tip-protruding concentration, thinking how very different he was to the quivering bespectacled mess in a raincoat she'd taken home to her flat at Christmas. She was trying to put the two together and meld them into roughly the same human being when, as if to completely thwart her imaginary attempt, Henry abandoned his bow-tie skimming and started unbuttoning his shirt, parading around humming 'The Stripper' and doing a very passable impression of a comb and paper.

'Henry!'

'What?' he enquired over a shoulder at that moment being bared seductively.

'It's not you!' Millicent was sitting up on the bed with a look of utter astonishment.

'What's me then? Tell me - who am I?' And he continued his routine to even louder comb and paper humming and more demonstrative gyrations. 'What's the real me then, eh?'

Millicent shook her head in disbelief. 'I, I don't know but...'

'It must be the port!' declared Henry removing his shirt, then vest, and starting to unbutton his trousers, 'I blame the naughty *naughty*, hic, port! It's not innocent at all, it's....'

Henry was struggling with his trousers that were refusing to go over his shoes which he'd forgotten to remove first, and so all speech was halted whilst he removed trousers, shoes and one sock with a gasp, before standing erect and triumphant to complete his port accusation with '...guilty!'

Millicent had not seen Henry's body before. Only glimpses as he'd changed at her flat or staggered in and out of the changing room in Savile Row trying on suits. She knew he'd lost weight, in fact after not seeing him for those two weeks, she'd been quite concerned about the amount he actually had lost, but what she didn't know was that Henry hadn't actually lost, but had toned, his weight, after unearthing a Charles Atlas Dynamic Tension body building manual that he'd once sent off for as a teenager in the fifties when Charles Atlas was all the rage.

In the dire hope of improving his poor shape and even poorer self image he had for two months at the age of eighteen in his bedroom in front of the oval mirror, strained, tensed, flipped pages, got into new positions, nigh on burst every blood vessel in his head and arms - and all this performed and posed in complete silence lest the evil presence through the wall might hear - before sinking breathless into bed convinced he'd turned his flabby white flesh into rock hard muscle. But some things are not meant to be and for every night that he went to bed with hope in his heart and an excess of blood in his pink swollen biceps, this was cruelly counteracted by a morning where that same mirror betrayed him overnight and returned the pink rock to white flab and the hope in his heart to forlorn disappointment. Undaunted, he'd persevered for two months until he heard a skinny young cockney lad on the television puffing on a cigarette and claiming that it was a con and you had to have muscle 't'start orf wiv'.

This had a resounding effect on Henry who instead of refusing to accept the young lad's criticism, found himself rather glad that he had a good reason for giving up, and somewhat contentedly concluded that there were those who were born square-jawed and potentially muscular and those that were, well, like him. But never had he thrown the book away, one of the four books in the house, maybe with the subconscious thought that he had to be a certain age, or a certain stage of physical development, before his flab could respond and be reawakened for conversion into something worth taking his shirt off for.

And thus, the time had arrived. Since the revelation of his shopping expedition with Millicent, followed by the day of the contact lenses, when a spark of pride and a feeling of real hope began to beat in his flabby breast, he had gone to his wardrobe drawer and taken out Charles Atlas, he who stood there posing on the front cover, grinning above his ridiculous muscles, mockingly encouraging even the Henrys of the world to try. Henry had looked at the man, decided he was probably forty himself at the time, so was either seriously withered or in his grave by now, and had decided anything was possible!

So the physique Millicent now gazed upon, whilst still white and not shown in its best light - what with a pair of basic M&S underpants (she hadn't got round to that part of his wardrobe yet) and one sock left on - was much leaner and toned than she'd imagined. The hair on his chest tapering down in a neat triangle past his naval was just enough covering to pleasantly enhance the recently acquired abdominal and pectoral muscles and a sight she found rather agreeable to her inquisitive eye.

Henry noticed the one sock and with a final flamboyant gesture bent down, removed it and flung it over his shoulder, smiling at Millicent and slightly losing his balance. Millicent, in response, swung her legs round so they dangled from the edge of the bed and, with eyes fixed on Henry's, reached behind and undid the zip of her dress. Leaning forward, she brought her arms together to allow the dress to drop from her shoulders, deliberately but discreetly holding out her elbows to arrest its journey and not reveal too much, too soon.

'Millicent?'

'Yes Henry?'

'Do you remember the chap you were telling me about when we first… well, that night in your bedroom, when…'

Millicent looked up alarmed.

'Which chap?' she asked, rather sharply.

'The one who liked to look at himself and, you know, etc. etc. etc.'

Relief shone from Millicent's eyes. 'Ah, you mean Narcissus etc. etc, etc.'

'Narcissus, that's him.'

'The *chap*…' She laughed, 'Oh you are funny Henry. Narcissus, the *chap*…' she repeated in a sudden fit of giggles.

'Can you remind me about him please? I think I was rather too drunk at the time to remember the details.'

Millicent, with the slightest of shrugs let her dress fall to her waist and watched Henry's eyes helplessly drop into her cleavage.

'I think you need to come a little closer first, don't you?'

Henry obediently stepped towards her and Millicent, pulling her dress up to mid thigh, spread her bare knees to make space for him. She then placed her hands on his hips, and looked up.

'Well, Narcissus was a *chap*…a chap who fell in love with his own reflection.'

If sound were the only medium available, Millicent could easily have been a teacher reading to a classroom of attentive children but with the aid of vision the scene was in an altogether different class. She stroked his stomach and let her fingers slowly and delicately trace the hair up and around his chest before moving downwards, never taking her eyes off his for a moment apart from to glance at her travelling fingertips as they brushed his flesh.

'You look good Henry. Your body, I never…'

'Yes,' gulped Henry, 'I've been…exercising. Press-ups, knees bends, what have you. Even walking faster from the station to and from wo-o-o-rk.'

Millicent had gone a little further and faster than Henry was expecting and, being in mid-explanation, it took him rather by surprise. He looked to the ceiling as Millicent's fingertips hooked into the elastic of his underpants.

'Amazing what a little bit of self-respect does,' he continued unabated, 'and so I thought if this…if this…if…this sort of thing ever…ever…ever happened…(deep inhale)…I wouldn't feel too ashamed and you wouldn't be too disgust…ohh! Heavens! Heavens above Millicent! Ohhhhh!'

Chapter Twenty Five

# THE WITCH AWAKENS!

Lily Bunce looked up from her knitting beside the bed of Irma Scroggins and was not surprised to see the time was just past eleven thirty. She had been sitting there for the best part of five hours with nothing but the clicking of her needles, the tick of the clock and the laboured breathing of her patient as companions. Occasionally dozing and looking at the clock, Lily also had the self-imposed 'Neighbourhood Watch' task of checking through the window for the sound of any car engine she didn't immediately recognise, knowing every engine in the street better than their owners or mechanics.

Many thoughts had traversed her mind during this period of quiet repose, with no Coronation Street or other television programme to divert her attention. But the thought vying for most attention was the matter of the letter from the solicitors, just slightly edging ahead of her concern for the welfare of her friend, the sleeping form a few feet away who had shown no sign of communication since Lily had arrived to administer the medication Henry had left in a very neat sandwich, all crusts removed - and ample jam!

Henry had insisted that the sandwich had to be on time, at precisely five o'clock, and had even made two sandwiches, leaving one in a Tupperware container, in case he wasn't home in time the day after; which he doubted. He couldn't stress enough to Lily the importance of his mother eating all of the tablets crushed inside the sandwich, and Lily, unaware that the medication was nothing stronger than Aspirin, had sworn that it would be given not a minute before or after the hour of five. The sandwiches were cut into small squares, as everything had to be now that Irma Scroggins couldn't easily manage anything bigger without it dropping from her mouth and giving Henry the unenviable task of picking it up, should it be out of reach of her good arm.

But it was the letter that was Lily's priority and on arrival by the back door into the kitchen shortly before five, her eyes knew they had one particular job to do and that was to check the whereabouts of the envelope bearing the name Bodger and Snapes.

Blighted in her first frenetic search, which would have put a sniffer dog to shame as she foraged through kitchen, parlour and dining room - the kettle providing excellent cover whilst rising to its steaming crescendo - she could only deduce that either Henry had given it to his mother, in which case it should be somewhere obvious in her bedroom, or he had not shown it to her and therefore had an ulterior motive.

So now, as the night approached the appropriately named Witching Hour when Irma Scroggins was in the deepest of sleeps, snoring so loudly that should it stop it offered the perfect alarm, Lily tip-toed into Henry's room and with a stealth that would not only have shamed a sniffer dog but the most feline and furtive of cat burglars, she slid out every drawer, lifted and replaced every item of clothing without a trace of disturbance, and rummaged through the few jackets in his wardrobe; all sadly to no avail.

It wasn't that she needed to know the *contents* of the letter, for that she already knew and had memorised; no, it was simply the whereabouts of the letter that mattered, for if it was in Henry's room then the chances were that he had no intention of his mother ever knowing anything about it. Lily naturally had no idea of what Irma Scroggins intended doing with whatever wealth it was that she now possessed but she strongly suspected that Henry wouldn't be seeing any of it.

Suddenly, on hearing a halt in the snoring and a manic grunt from the bedroom, the crafty woman moved noiselessly across the landing to the bathroom where she flushed the toilet, a back-up plan already tucked up her bulky green cardigan sleeve. She'd even had the forethought to silently switch on the bathroom light in advance of her search, to not only provide better vision for the job in hand but also to avoid arousing suspicion in case of a surprise awakening. In a thrice the bathroom tap was running, Lily was humming her favourite tune in times of necessity (Lily of

Laguna), and just seconds later was gliding like a chubby green swan into the bedroom, wiping her hands on her dress and smiling benignly at her friend who stared up with the paralysed side of her mouth set rigid and her good arm waving in the air; slightly regal.

'Toilet Mrs S?'

The old woman shook her head and arm and shouted something unintelligible, sending globules of spit into the air and making an attempt to wipe her mouth with her moveable royal arm.

'Enry?' enquired Lily Bunce with mischievous innocence, 'something to do with your 'Enry, Mrs S? Mm?'

Irma Scroggins nodded frantically, her eyes fixed on Lily, angrily muttering and waving towards the window.

'Where is 'ee? Is that it Mrs S?'

More frantic nodding and shouting followed by dribble wiped away by the flailing, not so royal, arm.

'I told you Mrs S, 'ee's not coming 'ome tonight. 'Ee's gone somewhere for two days. Brighton I think 'ee said. Yes, Brighton. Be 'ome tomorrer he will. Tomorrer. I'm looking after yer. It's okay. You're okay.'

The gasping woman lapsed back onto her pillow looking as if at death's door, her breathing loud, laboured and rattling; pacified not out of any will of her own but simply defeated by the monumental effort of her uncontrollable frustration and anger.

Lily decided it was time for a diversion and what better diversion than to broach the subject of the letter.

'Di um…did, um…your 'Enry give you that letter?' she enquired with the same spirited innocence as before, picking up her knitting whilst making herself comfortable in her chair as if butter wouldn't melt in her mouth. She looked up casually and repeated, 'Did 'ee Mrs S? The letter? Mm?'

We sometimes hear of instances when desperate times not only require desperate measures but indeed create normally impossible acts where mind overwhelmingly conquers matter, thus enabling such incredible feats as a frail woman lifting a car off her trapped child or a man forming his body into a human

244

bridge to lead others to safety. Such was the case with Irma Scroggins, who bereft of coherent speech for two weeks, suddenly exploded with the unmistakeable words of 'Letter! Letter! What letter!'

What these words lacked in pronunciation was certainly compensated for by rabid, foaming *denunciation*. Even her left arm, the paralysed one, jerked slightly in sympathetic defiance with the rest of her tortured frame and Lily Bunce, her mouth so wide that her tonsils had a perfect first glimpse of Irma Scroggins, expected her friend to rise from the bed like Lazarus - if not exactly walk off with it, as suggested by Jesus.

The poor neighbourly carer, petrified possibly to the same high degree as Lazarus had been thrilled to bits, rose to try and calm her friend, placing one arm around her shoulders whilst desperately trying to stop her flailing about in case she did herself serious damage.

'Oh Mrs S, it was a letter from a solicitor, Bodger and Snapes!' cried the poor panic-stricken woman. 'It came the other day - Monday - yes, Monday because I made sure your 'Enry saw it as soon as 'ee came in from work so 'ee could give it yer 'isself. I'd 'ave give it yer meself but I didn't think it was me place Mrs S, truthfully I didn't, 'Enry being yer son an' all. Oh dear o' lor Mrs S, please calm y'self down, otherwise you might….'

Lily got no further. Irma Scroggins took one almighty deep breath and with eyes wide and ghostly, collapsed in a heap on her pillow, her head hanging limply to one side and her tongue dangling from her mouth as if finally meeting her maker.

But dead she wasn't. Lily, almost too frightened to move, watched her friend for a moment and then, seeing the old woman's eyes were now closed, lowered her head near the concave cage of ribs beneath the blue and maroon shawl and unable to detect any rise and fall, put a hand in front of the mouth parted slightly in ugly deformity. She felt the trace of a breath, coming and going. Then she noticed the shawl start to move, the breathing strengthen to a steady rhythm and the tongue slowly retract inside the mouth. Next, to Lily's horror, it suddenly reappeared, like a purple white-coated slug, to moisten the cracked lips before it slid back to resume residence behind the teeth; closing the door behind it.

In the immediate aftermath of this awful drama, Lily sat quietly down and calmly picked up her knitting, never once taking her eyes off Irma Scroggins as she sat with needles poised, weighing up the situation. Her razor sharp strategic mind, trained through years of urban guerrilla surveillance to instantly assess the pros and cons of any given situation, rapidly gauged the obvious advantages presented at that moment. Irma Scroggins wasn't dead, that was clear. She'd almost certainly just fainted with the exertion and shock, was Lily's diagnosis. In fact far from being dead Lily deduced that going by the animation of her tongue moistening her lips and then seemingly safely disappearing, and the clarity of her brief but highly vitriolic outburst, it seemed that the shock of hearing about the letter had quite possibly stimulated her brain into returning her power of speech. She was sure she'd read about this in one of her women's magazines, in fact she very quickly convinced herself she had and that it was therefore now an absolute fact.

This, combined with the other intractable fact that Irma also now knew of the existence of the letter and that Henry was concealing it from her was not altogether what Lily Bunce would call an unsuccessful night's work.

## Chapter Twenty Six

## THE MORNING AFTER THE NIGHT BEFORE – HENRY REVEALS HIS FATHER'S FORTUNE

Henry woke to the sound of a shower running; another first. Forty years without this experience meant that those first few seconds of suspension between dream world and real world held even more trepidation for him than for most. He could have been trapped under a waterfall.

By the time full consciousness had arrived, along with a thumping sensation and dull ache inside his head, he'd collected his thoughts just enough to know where he was and who was in the shower. Beyond that, he couldn't quite yet project to the moment of going to bed and what happened after.

Then the shower stopped, the bathroom door opened, and Millicent's wet head peeped out and smiled at him. He blinked as she moved into full view, wrapped in a towel that looked big enough and soft enough to have once performed a similar job for a polar bear, the bear likely to have been rather more attached to it than its present occupier.

'Good morning,' chirped the remarkably fresh Millicent.

A croaky clearing of the throat preceded Henry's reply.

'Good morning Millicent. What time is it?'

Millicent stepped to her side of the bed, holding her towel in place, and checked her watch.

'Nine-thirty-five. I've phoned room service and delayed our breakfast. You were in such a deep sleep.'

She sat on the bed and smiled softly.

'Thank you Henry.'

Henry removed the knuckle he'd been driving into his painful forehead and looked at her in surprise.

'What for?'

'Last night.'

'My pleasure. Yes, that lamb was delicious.'

(Henry had insisted on paying the bill.)

Millicent stood up and, turning to face him, dropped her towel. 'I'm not talking about your lamb Henry.'

Henry, in the cold light of day, felt he was seeing Millicent naked for the first time, which in fact he was, (in the cold light of day) and wasn't sure how to react. Her body was truly a magnificent sight; her perfectly shaped hips and bosom accentuated by the trimmest of waists and most unblemished of skins. So Henry didn't avert his eyes because the truth was, he couldn't. They wouldn't. So utterly transfixed was he by Millicent's brazenness that he felt it an insult to look at anything else in the room but her body, or even to try. Such brazenness in his presence banished all Henry's sober bashfulness as she teasingly placed her hands over her breasts.

'Remember Mr Narcissus etc, etc?'

'Oh heavens, him, yes - yes I do,' said Henry, shaking his head slightly and returning her smile, heaving a small sigh of appreciation as the whole film started to rerun, flooding his brain with frame after frame of what had happened to him; he, Henry, with her, Millicent, this divine creation before him; all this beauty, body and brains dazzlingly available; his, or so it unequivocally seemed, to have and to hold from this day forward. Millicent lay down on the bed beside him.

'Well,' she said, 'after your striptease, I thought I had to follow it with something special.'

Henry had quite forgotten about his performance and looked around for his clothes which Millicent had collected and either hung up or folded neatly.

'Thank you,' he said, spotting them, 'for picking up my clothes. I think I got a bit carried away.'

A wave of particularly heavy hammering broke out inside his skull and he placed a hand on his forehead whilst emitting a small groan. Anything louder would have only added to the pain.

'The port?' enquired Millicent.

'Oh no, the port is innocent,' replied Henry softly but emphatically.

'The *port* is innocent?'

'Beyond any shadow of doubt. Only twice have I woken with a hangover, if that's what I've now got, and both times you've been in the room. Only once has the port been involved, so I think all the evidence points to...'

Millicent was nodding in guilty acceptance. Henry turned his head towards her on the pillow, wincing with the sudden movement.

'I'm afraid everything points that way. It's you Millicent.'

'How do you feel? Not your head but...well, you know.'

'How do I feel?' muttered Henry, shielding his eyes from the light as he looked to the ceiling for inspiration. 'I feel...I *think* I feel...and I know this is going to sound terribly predictable but...I feel like I think every boy has felt with his first girlfriend. What a freak, forty years old and...' He stopped and turned to her. 'What about you Millicent, were you...was I...?'

'Don't you remember me telling you?'

Henry frowned, trying to recollect.

'No I don't think so.'

'I said I had never felt happier. And strange as it may seem, I also felt like a girl with her first boyfriend. I hadn't thought of it that way but now you've said it...' She stroked the back of his hand with her fingertips, '...that's not a bad description. Lucky aren't we.'

'Well, *I* am.' He turned to look at her again. 'I don't fool myself Millicent, you must have had many male friends, experienced men, and suddenly you've got...well, me, and...'

Millicent's expression darkened. The 'many experienced men' appeared before her like a visual roll call and she turned to the wall to hide her face lest the mug shots of London's elite should be visible to Henry through her eyes. Her heart leapt and her pulse raced as a timely knock at the door gave her good reason to pick up her towel and, wrapping it around her, tip-toe to answer it.

The sight of the waiter who had picked up Henry's chair the previous evening, breezing in with a tray full of breakfast with such nonchalant panache, even whistling jauntily, was too much for Henry who pulled the duvet up past his nipples and looked at Millicent to make sure she was decent.

'Morning Madam! Morning Sir!' sung out the waiter, 'Trust you had a good night's sleep.'

Henry darted a look at him for any sign of the Sean Swadely nudge-nudge, wink-wink irony but the waiter was busily placing the tray on the table and arranging things without the remotest glimmer of anything but serious interest in their welfare. Millicent, who was standing far too close to the waiter for Henry's comfort, considering the towel could accidentally drop at any time, took a piece of toast and started munching, by which time the waiter was on his way to the door backing out with a cheery smile and a 'If you're having lunch here, we have…'

'We won't be lunching in the restaurant,' said Millicent quickly, 'but thank you anyway.'

She smiled at him sweetly and with a wink he was gone, behind a discreet click of the door.

The reason for her adamant, quick response to the waiter's helpful attempted lunch suggestion was pure reflex damage limitation. The chance of Sean Swadely's presence still looming large in the hotel and the risk of any more of his mindless dangerous innuendo was to be avoided like the plague. Evacuating the hotel that morning was therefore a priority and even in the instant of her exchange with the waiter, Millicent was suddenly, acutely, aware that her deception was becoming increasingly difficult. Like any lie, whether white or downright malicious, the telling of it is so often the opener of a proverbial can of worms; a can that swells under the strain of multiplying, fatter worms until the can eventually and inevitably bursts to spew out such a chaotic landscape of uncoverable, slithery tracks when one simple truth, however hard to reveal, cuts straight to the chase and provides for an instant resolution; a resolution for better or worse, but at least a resolution.

As if in response to her thoughts, she picked up an envelope on the writing desk.

'Oh Henry, this must have fallen out of your jacket when you were entertaining me last night. I found it on the floor.'

Henry had quite forgotten about the letter in the non-stop melee of the evening meal and bedroom aftermath and, having planned to leave the subject until this morning, here it was being immediately thrust upon him with the throbbing head upon his shoulders in no way prepared for serious debate.

'I need your help with that Millicent,' said Henry, staring at the envelope in her hand with either a glazed or thoughtful expression - it was difficult under the circumstances to work out which.

'Help?' enquired Millicent.

'Yes, it's no ordinary letter. It arrived for my mother on Monday and I...er...' He momentarily lost the track of his conversation before it clicked back in. '...opened it.'

'What? Without her knowing?'

Henry nodded.

'What's it about?'

'My father.'

'Your *father?*'

'Yes, he's dead, died at Christmas in Australia. He was a multi millionaire. Fancy that.'

He was now staring ahead at his toes wiggling under the duvet, like a child confessing to a school misdemeanour and unable to look his parent in the eye. Then he looked up at Millicent.

'My own father, a millionaire. And he's left every penny to *her*. The woman he hated and abandoned.' He looked back at his toes and knotted his fingers together. 'Can you believe it?'

'Can I read it - the letter?' asked Millicent.

'Oh yes, you've got to read it, and thoroughly. I need all your professional expertise for this one. Thank god you're a solicitor.'

He got out of bed and walked towards the bathroom, his nakedness under the cloud of their serious discussion causing a slight tinge of embarrassment to them both.

'I'll shower whilst you're reading it and then maybe we can discuss it over breakfast. If you don't mind that is.'

Millicent peered down at the envelope as Henry disappeared into the bathroom, closing the door behind him. She slid out the letter with a terrible sense of misgiving as the shower burst into life and Henry ejected a muted scream. The first shower of his life and it was either a jet of very cold or very hot water that had caused the shock; but nothing like the shock Millicent was at that moment considering, one she knew in her heart was going to have to come sooner or later for Henry.

By the time he emerged in his white towel dressing gown, crimson-faced and wiping the sweat from his forehead and neck with a hand towel, Millicent had decided that now was not the time to make any shock announcements. There was nothing in the letter she couldn't handle from a 'professional' point of view. It didn't need a solicitor to work out the next step and any questions that may be asked of her were those any person with a modicum of legal experience from everyday life could quite easily hazard a guess at and offer as much common sense advice as a legal expert. Bluff and confidence is so much part of business life anyway, and Henry being so totally inept in this department until recently, would by necessity permit just about anyone to take the lead. Especially one as trusted as Millicent.

'Well my dear learned one,' asked Henry, seeing the letter lying beside the dressing table where Millicent was peering into the mirror applying mascara. 'What is your considered opinion?'

Millicent turned to him with mascara brush held aloft and nonchalantly replied:

'Bribe him.'

'Bribe him? A solicitor? My *mother's* solicitor?'

'Worth a try. They are so easily corruptible.'

Millicent returned to the mirror and her make-up.

'You've got to be joking Millicent.'

She held the brush still for a moment, looking at his reflection in the mirror with the tip of her tongue protruding before continuing like an artist putting the final black line touches to a still life.

'Solicitors have two characteristics that make them easily corruptible; three actually. First and foremost they are motivated by money; not necessarily greed but certainly an addiction to earning lots of money. Secondly, they are usually highly intelligent; and last but not least, they are devious because the profession by its nature demands it. Devious without intelligence is fairly useless and doomed to failure, but devious *with* intelligence and within the law - a rather broad canvass - means the till will never stop ringing. Like young political activists, law students start off with high ideals and precious morals but soon succumb under the mighty matching boots of vanity and avarice. It's not their fault, poor weak things, it's do or die - or lose golden opportunities that are going begging at every corner of the world they inhabit. They can't help themselves.'

Henry was still occasionally dabbing his head with the towel, a head that refused to stop pumping sweat, such had been the temperature, length and eventually, pleasure, of his novel shower experience. He thought for a while about what Millicent had said before replying, and she in turn let him. It was clear to him that Millicent was talking from experience without using the first person and yet he found it difficult to believe that she was tarred with this same greedy brush, for whatever she said, he couldn't see the lust for money as anything else but pure greed. In light of this, his considered response was brief.

'You must know so many of these people,' he said, and continued to pace the room as if the walking would eventually clear his head.

Millicent looked at his reflection in the mirror to make sure he couldn't see her face.

'Quite a few,' she replied, truthfully.

Henry, alternately dabbing his forehead and digging water from his ears, finally arrived at the dressing table and picked up the letter, reading it through again, his lips moving as he squinted and rapidly scanned the page.

'This last line is interesting,' he observed with the sort of knowing surmise that Dr. Watson might have offered before being put down by the superior Holmes intimating that the observation was far too obvious and elementary to be graced with any previous mention by his esteemed self.

Millicent nodded. 'That's what I thought. He clearly doesn't want anyone else to know, which is most unusual. In my experience, legal partners will always consult, especially on a matter like this - a will involving a huge sum of money.'

She glanced at the letter Henry had replaced beside her.

'So he's Snapes - I wonder if Bodger exists? If not, then why would it be so important for nobody else in the business to know? And if Bodger does exist, then the same goes - why keep it from him?'

'True,' said Henry, nodding sagely and much impressed with Millicent's rationale. 'You solicitors see everything so clearly, so…black and white.'

Millicent paused for a second or two before replying.

'So much of it is just common sense; common sense wrapped up in legal jargon. Most of a solicitor's advice isn't plucked from their head or from experience, it's in a dirty great dusty book on a creaking shelf. They, *we*, have to get it down and check the detail of the law before looking mighty clever to Joe and Mrs Soap.'

'Sounds perfectly Dickensian,' said Henry.

'A lot of it is,' replied Millicent, 'many of the laws haven't changed since the days of Jarndyce versus Jarndyce.'

'Who?' enquired Henry.

'A famous case in Bleak House, Dickens' great legal novel; mandatory reading for young solicitors, or should be. A classic example, possibly the greatest example in literature, of the depth of legal corruption. A family kept waiting for decades, generations, whilst the lawyers deliberately procrastinate and find numerous inventive means of delaying a conclusion.'

'To guarantee an incessant income,' finished off Henry, and then with relish, 'the bastards!'

'They certainly are.'

'They? Isn't that *you*?'

'Me?'

Millicent was caught off guard for a moment whilst off on one her favourite tangents and abiding passions; that of great literary works.

'Oh yes, of course me - but I'm different,' she said, whilst flashing through her head came, 'I'm not even a bloody *solicitor!*'

'You're honest,' said Henry looking at her with admiration and respect, content in his belief that she was the good, sweet, shiny apple in a bowl of rotten fruit.

And bang went another nail into the coffin of her deception! Bang! Bang! Bang! Every day with Henry from hereon, every conversation, now that this tumultuous event of a death twelve thousand miles away had arrived out of the blue like a giant tsunami whose waves had taken three months to arrive on England's shores. Now, here it was lapping around her ears, challenging her legal 'validity', and it was going to be hammering harder and louder until something cracked. Whether, when the crack came, it would be like the one in Henry's ceiling, lasting a lifetime, was a matter that only time would reveal.

If only Millicent could have known at that moment how easy it was going to be for her; how the responsibility of confessing all to Henry was to be plucked from her hands, very soon, by another; a man she knew better than his own wife knew him.

'Let's get dressed and discuss it somewhere in town,' she said, 'Maybe that little Italian restaurant we nearly chose yesterday.'

'Good idea,' said Henry, determined to be brave and extend his Italian cuisine beyond spaghetti Bolognese. 'But just quickly, what do you suggest I do - with the solicitor?'

'Phone him. Offer to take him for a drink, away from his office. That way you'll have an idea of whether he has anything to hide. And then if he has, take it from there. You'll know what to do Henry - I know you will.'

## Chapter Twenty Seven

# THE PLOT AGAINST HENRY

A man with nothing to lose is often thought to be a dangerous creature. One such man ambled along Whitehall from Trafalgar Square, squinting up at the buildings, every so often almost stumbling into the road as the effort of looking up into a clear bright sky sent him off balance.

On his feet was a pair of very white trainers looking as if they were on their maiden outing, nowhere near soiled enough to mingle into anonymity between pavement and leg. Their brilliant whiteness was both accentuated on the one hand and partly concealed on the other by a plentiful covering of concertinaed black suit trouser bottoms looking as if at any time they would wrap around his feet (on one of his more prolonged looking up moments) and hurl him headlong onto the ground. The black suit trousers had a thin white pin stripe and were held up by stained red braces without whose support the whole of his trousers would have entirely covered the trainers, there being almost enough room for at least half another waist of the same size inside the waistband. With minor adjustment the braces would have enabled the trousers to sit neatly upon the trainers but as it were they hung low and dragged threadbare upon the ground behind his heels. His jacket, which matched the trousers, flapped open in the light breeze of the warm early spring day, displaying a white shirt open at the neck but not as white as it might have been if fresh from the ironing board, and further betrayed by a vest beneath which showed through a touch yellow in places where the sweat glands are always at their busiest. His grey hair was thin on top and what there was, was combed over from left to right in greasy strands that always make one wonder why the owners don't just cut if off and make do with something that isn't pretending to be something it isn't; like a hair covering.

The overall appearance of this man would have been described by Victorian novelists as *shabby genteel*, the clothes obviously once adorning the same figure when it walked the same pavement with pride and position; as was the case with this gentleman not so long before.

On reaching the door of The Carpenters Arms, he stopped and stared at the building as if deciding whether it deserved his patronage. He then checked his pockets and soon stood with loose change in his palm, which he counted, poking the coins with his finger in the hope of maybe uncovering a hidden fifty pence piece. By the look of resignation on his face, the heaviness of his sigh and the slight accepting shrug, it was obvious that no surprise coin was found. Nevertheless, he lifted his head high, sucked the city's air deep into his nostrils and marched inside with hesitant aplomb.

Seated on a bar stool, one elbow on the bar and tongue licking the gum of a newly rolled cigarette, was a man who turned and raised a hand in recognition of the pinstriped gentleman's entry. But no sooner had their eyes met than the cigarette production momentarily froze as the smoker gained a full impression of the new arrival.

'Peregrine, old bean! Blimey, what the fuck has happened to you? You look like you've been dragged through an 'edge backwards.'

The speaker took a lighter from the bar and lit his cigarette, pushing the dregs of his glass towards the other man who was checking the change in his hand, still hoping for a lost fifty pence piece to appear, whilst looking up for service.

'Don't mind if I do. Pint of best please, Peregrine.'

Peregrine Spencer looked disdainfully at the man and with casual superciliousness remarked, 'I'm afraid I'm a broken man Richard, broken in spirit and pocket. You'll have to buy your own.'

Richard Gaines, late of the post room in Peregrine's late department, swigged the dregs from his glass and called to the barmaid at the top of his voice.

'Deirdre! Pint when you've finished gasbagging love! And better get one for old Peregrine tight-arse here!'

Spencer winced and cast his eyes around the bar with minimum movement of the head.

'I don't drink beer as you know, and I'll buy my own thank you,' he said quietly.

Richard Gaines laughed mockingly and shook his head.

'What a state you look. Where *did* you get those fuckin' trainers? You could dazzle a blind man with them.'

Peregrine looked down and made an attempt to tuck his feet as close to the bar as possible, as already their conversation, or more to the point Gaines' part of it, was attracting attention from the few customers dotted about the spacious bar, the same bar whose high ceilings and splendid acoustics once rang to the sound of Spencer's own bellowing, grandiloquent tones but now seemed as if specifically designed for his public humiliation.

'Can you please lower your voice?' requested Spencer, 'I may have fallen as far as man can fall in a short space of time but I'm still trying to hang on to a morsel of pride, if you'll permit me.'

Gaines looked down at the white glare around Spencer's feet that seemed to be grower whiter with every spiteful remark.

'Not in those fuckin' shoes you're not,' said Gaines, to emphasis the point. 'Pride comes before a fall some say and if you don't hitch them trousers up that's exactly what it'll be.'

So impressed was Gaines with his joke that he caught the eye of a couple of his drinking cronies watching them from across the bar and called out, 'Don't look over 'ere without sunglasses lads!'

The two men ignored him and quickly engaged in conversation, well acquainted it seemed with Richard Gaines' unpleasant character and no doubt feeling for the man he was currently humiliating, perhaps more so when they were witnessing such an obvious and monumental decline.

Spencer, whilst not a regular in the pub, had over twenty years made his mark there in various ways and was therefore no stranger to the regulars and in particular the barmaids, who had been frequent targets of his amorous intent.

Deirdre arrived, wiping her hands on a tea towel and only then recognising Spencer. Hardly able to disguise her shock at his dishevelled appearance and weight loss, she took the usual bar staff diplomatic course.

'Haven't seen you in here for a long time, Peregrine. You been all right? Your usual?'

She pointed at the Bell's Whisky bottle and he nodded.

'Double?' she asked.

'No, no - thank you,' replied Spencer hesitantly, torn between the money in his pocket and the small amount of pride he'd involuntarily mustered. 'Single will do fine thank you Deidre. And thank you for asking but as you'll see I'm not as *all right* as I once was. Life has a funny way of biting you back sometimes. How much do I owe you?'

The barmaid glanced at Gaines, who had just left for the toilet, and placing Spencer's drink beside his hand, gave a small shake of her head. She then cast another glance around and turning to the bottle, picked up his glass and added another shot.

'You've bought me enough in the past, Peregrine,' she said on her return. 'Fortunes change, I know that, had enough of my own that's for sure. I heard all about things at the office and…'

Spencer nodded quickly, making it abundantly clear that he didn't want to discuss his departmental demise.

'I understand,' she said and placed a hand on his, leaning towards him and whispering, 'but what brings you back here of all places, for Christ's sake?'

Peregrine looked towards the toilet before answering.

'He left a message to meet him here. We've both suffered the same fate it seems - dismissal - so no doubt he wants to gloat over mine and share some mutual hatred of a certain person. That's all I know.'

Deidre looked at him enquiringly as Gaines appeared at the toilet door, choosing to complete his ablutions publicly by finishing doing up his zip before wiping his hands on his trousers. He planted himself back on his bar stool, sniffed and examined his roll-up in the ashtray to decide whether there was enough to relight, decided there was and flicking on his lighter, sucked deeply on the half inch of dog end.

Peregrine looked around and picked up his glass.

'Do you mind if we go over there. I'd prefer somewhere a little more private if you don't mind.'

Gaines shrugged and gripping his pint, slid off the stool without comment, his mouth it would seem subdued by the emptying of his bladder. They settled themselves in a dark corner under a staircase leading to the open mezzanine floor of the dining area. Two battered brown leather armchairs bordered a low table, where they placed their glasses and sat down, at right angles to each other.

The next fifteen minutes took the form of a confessional. Some people choose a friend to confide in, on the basis of a problem shared being a problem halved - invariably not the case - whereas others are happier pouring out their troubles on a soul for whom they have no bond or feeling and no great desire to see again, almost as if the dispersing of the heavy weight is better off dumped on unknown wasteland than on pleasant familiar pastures. It's the getting it out, the exorcism, which matters, with no advice required or given by the listener, possibly just the odd empathetic comment to suffice.

So in a matter of just fifteen or so minutes Spencer told his renegade ex-employee, the only staff member who normally took not a blind bit of notice of anything he ever said, the story of how June Catchpole's husband, a burly security guard, had arrived on his doorstep at home with two rather hungry looking mastiffs, complete with studded collars and straining at their leashes. How the heavily tattooed husband had tied the dogs up outside and barged his way into the hall as Marjory Spencer arrived from cooking the evening meal, wondering what was going on.

How the intruder had then exposed Spencer's brief but torrid affair with his wife, she who had been punished in the man's own inimitable fashion and was at the time in the tender care of the local NHS hospital staff but refusing to press charges against her loving husband. How then, content with Marjory Spencer's horrified, tempestuous and unrestrained reaction against her husband, he had got up and left them to it, reasonably assured that she could wreak far more permanent damage on the man than anything he, George Catchpole, could provide.

Not totally satisfied that he could leave it entirely in her hands, he had departed through the front door with a finger-pointing threat, just to spread a bit of extra icing on Spencer's troubled cake; a threat that if Peregrine ever went near his wife again, to expect a return visit from him accompanied by the bit-champing Rusty and Busty, at that moment desperate to get inside the house to demonstrate how they could 'smell an adulterous shagger a mile off', as the scorned husband had so succinctly put it. He made it as clear as he could that these canine sexual predators would be let loose inside the house with strict orders to search for and destroy any living creature that didn't smell of the hand that fed them, making it clear to Marjory Spencer that she would suffer as much as her husband, not just physically but publicly.

Oh yes, he'd been 'inside' before, had the delightful George Catchpole, and wouldn't hesitate at going back in to see a few 'muckers' and languish in expenses paid luxury at Her Majesty's pleasure where he would share with said muckers the newspaper reports of Spencer's 'shagging of my wife' whilst reflecting on how best to invest the nice fat News of The World cheque nestling in his bank account. Oh yes, no worries there at all!

It was this last threat that had the most effect on Marjory Spencer. Toughened by an upbringing of military parents and grandparents, she was as ruthless and unconditional with those who committed injustice as she was kind and considerate of persons in need. Having long suspected her husband of philandering, without proof and with he always vehemently claiming total fidelity, she'd had no real choice but to accept what she knew were his lies. Her family were one of the most respected and long-standing in the parish, of which she was an active church member, and it was *her* family's money that gave them the house, the prestige and the grandiose lifestyle they enjoyed. Spencer, already a womaniser at the time of their engagement, had married her for nothing more than the wealth and status and her father's contacts in high places. Twenty years ago it was this nepotism that had shoehorned him from a lowly clerical job in a minor government office to manager of the Department from whence he had recently been removed.

And so it was that the threat of a very public exposure of her husband's affair with June Catchpole, when Marjory Spencer was still struggling to prevent the whole parish from discovering the real reason for her husband's injuries and long spells at home, that found him beaten down the hall and out of the door with his own black umbrella and told never to darken her very loudly slammed door ever again. This was rapidly followed up by all further modes of entry to the house being locked and bolted just before he reached them.

Peregrine Spencer had been forced to stand on the gravel in his suit (having just arrived home from a Rotary meeting) and socks, helplessly looking up at their bedroom as the light flicked on (far more violently it seemed than usual) as his wife of nearly twenty-five years moved rapidly around the room, driven to whatever she was doing by intense white hot anger.

First through the opened window arrived the keys to the third car, a twelve-year-old Metro kept purely for Marjory's charity attendances. Then, after him pleading for something to put on his freezing feet, a pair of brand new white trainers spun dizzily down, fresh out of their box and bouncing very close to where Peregrine stood looking pathetic. Closely following this was the cherished overcoat with velvet lapels (very thoughtful) and finally after a gap of a few minutes, his wallet, which burst open on a rhododendron bush, sending coins flying in various directions under and around.

On picking up the wallet, he immediately saw that it contained, apart from a few pounds in coins, a ten and a twenty-pound note, not a single plastic card. All forms of access to money had been quickly and ruthlessly removed; such are the vagaries of joint accounts and a wronged wife who thinks all the money is rightly hers.

As with people who make their life's bed for mainly their own selfish comfort, the laying in it when the time comes tends to be a little solitary too. And so it was when Peregrine went to seek refuge at several friends' houses.

There were no children blessed to the Spencer marriage so it was to friends and neighbours that he was forced to appeal, but to his dismay he actually found that they were far more Marjory's friends than his. Forced to explain what had happened on various nearby doorsteps - it was of course no more than a complete and temporary misunderstanding leading to a heated dispute, as far as their ears were concerned - it became apparent that the so-called friendship he'd thought was mutual had been nothing more than perfunctory, their tolerance of his boorish, boastful ways stretched to the limits simply 'for long-suffering Marjory's sake.'

So the three-month journey that followed, from Department Manager to vagrant, was a dreadful lesson of which the words humiliation and degradation are hardly worthy. The details of his suffering and humiliation in car parks and on park benches need no embellishment here, suffice to explain the reason why the crushed man in white trainers now sat silent and bowed, staring at the table in the bar as Richard Gaines rolled a cigarette and tried to take in what he had just heard.

Not once had the man, usually possessed of so many ready and virulent words, interrupted, apart from putting Peregrine on 'pause' whilst he got up to replenish their glasses, perform another toilet stop and return with the drinks and a 'Go on' to set his ex-boss on 'play' again. Such patent suffering was not to be ruined by unnecessary questions. His first question was, however, quite a sensible one.

'So how come the trainers stayed so white?'

Peregrine peered down at his feet.

'I went back to the house every Friday morning to collect any messages or post - Marjory had agreed that much, silent tight-lipped meetings that they were - and she'd given me a bag of warm clothing and my most comfortable shoes. But they were in holes by last week so it was back to these.' He lifted a foot. 'I'd put them in the coal bunker for safe keeping.'

'Fucking silly place to put white trainers ain't it?' suggested Gaines, again rather sensibly.

Peregrine suddenly laughed, appreciating the funny side of it. 'Yes, you're right, very silly on the face of it.'

'Coal face?' interspersed the joker with a wink.

Again Spencer laughed and said how good it was to laugh again, especially at his own expense, a new talent he'd formed.

'So that's how I got your note that you wanted to meet me here,' said Peregrine. 'At first I thought 'not so likely' but then I just shrugged and thought what the hell, face the demons on your doorstep or whatever they say, and imagined it might even be good for me. Instead of hiding and dreading exposure, be brazen and come clean. As I say, I now have nothing to hide and nothing left to lose in this world. It's actually quite cleansing in an odd sort of way.'

'Bit like poofters,' added Gaines philosophically, spitting out a piece of errant tobacco and staring at an inspiring spot on the wall. Spencer raised his eyebrows enquiringly.

'Coming out, all that stuff,' clarified Gaines helpfully, 'that's what they call it, innit? Poofters - coming out. More like coming in! Stand by chaps - here I come - woo-hoo!'

He chuckled, pleased as always with his jokes, and then his face turned serious.

'You know the little bastard sacked me.'

'What little bastard?' asked Spencer.

'Scroggins. He's got your job you know.'

'Yes, I know. Life's strange isn't it.'

'I've hardly slept since it 'appened. Planning my revenge. Dunno what yet, but got a few ideas. I thought you might want to help, seeing as what he did to you.'

'What did he do to me?' asked Spencer, perfectly innocently.

Richard Gaines reached out and tweaked Spencer's badly bent nose. The man recoiled in pain at this thoughtless moronic gesture.

'Look at your fucking nose. He did that didn't he?'

'Under extreme provocation.'

Spencer rubbed the bridge of his nose gently with two grubby fingertips.

'It's still very painful thank you very much Richard.'

Gaines ignored him and continued his drift.

'Provocation my arse, he's been dying to do that for years, ever since you got the job he thought was his.'

'Is that a fact? You mean Henry Scroggins was in line for Department Manager all that time ago?'

'Oh yes, I'll say he was. I'd just started as a junior in the post room and it was no secret that he was up for it.'

Peregrine Spencer chewed the inside of his rubbery lower lip and the faintest of smiles slowly spread across his face as he stared across the bar, recollecting the nature of how he gained the promotion and imagining Henry's disappointment and possible resentment - when in fact there was none; just quiet acceptance and resignation, even relief.

'I had no idea,' he said, 'no idea at all. All those years…'

'Oh yes, all those years of festering resentment came out in one belt on yer 'ooter with a black Buddha!' exclaimed Gaines, watching Spencer's reaction, relishing turning the screw on the innocent man he blamed for his dismissal.

Not blaming himself of course, not blaming his constant flouting of the rules and foul-mouthed behaviour; not for one single moment. For the world and his wife could all be held accountable for Richard Gaines' bad luck long before any personal responsibility could be remotely considered.

Peregrine Spencer snapped out of his reverie with a new glint in his eye, one that had the plotter and schemer about it; one that spoke volumes about a man with nothing whatsoever in life to lose. Nothing that is, but his life.

'Henry…' he hesitated before deciding to sink to the Gaines vernacular, 'Henry's shagging an old friend of mine, you know.'

'What! Scroggins? Shagging? He hasn't got a shag in 'im, pathetic little creep!'

Spencer tilted his head on one side, looked Gaines right in the eye and raised an eyebrow. 'You'd be surprised. She's a beauty. A high class prostitute.'

'A prossy! Oh come off the grass Peregrine, pull the other one mate. Not Henry Scroggins.' He guffawed out loud at the impossible thought.

'The only thing is,' continued Spencer, 'I'm pretty sure he doesn't actually know she's a prostitute. Maybe she's not now, I don't know - but she certainly was up until Christmas.'

'How do you know?' asked Gaines with a wry grin.

Spencer tapped, lightly, his broken nose and simply said, 'Trust me.'

'I thought as much! The bloody expense account, Peregrine. Getting yer end away on taxpayers' money! You git! We all suspected it, you disappearing off at all times and coming back - if you ever fuckin' did come back - looking like the cat that'd got the fuckin' cream. You dirty, conniving...*lucky* bastard!'

'Lucky. Oh yes. Look where it's got me,' said Peregrine.

'Your wife don't know about the prossy too, does she?'

'No, she doesn't, but it hardly makes any difference now.' He shrugged and took a sip of whisky. 'Sheep as a lamb.'

Gaines looked at him, eyes widening as the glorious solution to his bitterness and sleepless nights began to loom large in his thoroughly unpleasant brain.

'You say Scroggins don't know she's a prossy?' asked Gaines, grinning.

'Can you imagine Henry Scroggins having anything to do with a prostitute, even a high class one?' scoffed Spencer. 'And my God she was - *is* - one superb class act.'

Richard Gaines slowly got up with the slyest of twinkles in his black-ringed eyes and picked up both glasses.

'Well p'raps we'd better find out how much our 'Enry *does* know about his dear prossy then Peregrine my son. Reckon?'

Spencer looked up at Gaines, pausing for several seconds before grunting agreement.

'I think we need to drink to that my dear friend,' said Gaines, this could be highly amusing; highly fuckin' amusing and highly fuckin' satisfying. Oh yes indeedy.'

And with that he walked to the bar with an exaggerated swagger, leaning there and looking back at Spencer, narrowing his eyes and nodding to confirm the plan was not just an idea but was being devised at that very moment for maximum impact.

Peregrine Spencer, meanwhile, traced his finger round the blue border of a drinks coaster and sunk deep into thought and instant remorse. He knew Henry Scroggins was one of the most decent human beings he'd ever known.

## Chapter Twenty Eight

## SNAPES IN THE GRASS

Archibald Snapes heard the phone ring in the next office, followed seconds later by his intercom crackling into life.

'A Mr Henry Scroggins on the phone for you, Archie.'

Snapes frowned. He had no idea of the son's name and with the only Henry Scroggins he knew being a dead one, it took him aback.

'What? Who?'

'Henry Scroggins. He says it's quite urgent and he can only speak to you.'

Snapes frowned into space through the window to the street, trying to work out the puzzle until it dawned on him that the son the postman had mentioned outside 52 Viola Street during his secret visit after Irma Scroggins' stroke, was also called Henry. He scratched his cheek slowly and took a deep breath.

'Alright, put him through.'

Before he had time to properly compose his thoughts, Henry was in his ear.

'Hello? Mr Snapes?'

'Yes, Snapes here. Mr Scroggins, I don't think we know each other.'

'You sent a letter to my mother.'

'Ah yes, I did, that's right. How can I help you?'

'I'm her son.'

'Ye-e-es, I gathered that much.'

Straightaway Henry felt stupid but having never spoken to a solicitor before (apart from Millicent) he was just a little nervous and nerves often enable the brain to create the most ridiculous and instantly regrettable responses.

'Sorry, silly of me. She's had a stroke, a bad stroke, Mother that is. So I opened the letter on her behalf.'

Snapes sat up and took a deep breath. His legal mind, without him really knowing why, began instinctively whirring, almost dangerously loud. But a good sign. It usually meant high profit of some kind was imminent, the prospect of unexpected rich pickings. Golden egg and gullible goose; a winning combination. He'd had a good feeling about this one from the beginning but couldn't put his finger on any sort of plan until he'd heard back from the deceased's wife. Now, here presented on a plate, was a very positive scenario; naive non-beneficiary son, incapacitated mother - and a dogs' home as sole beneficiary. Snapes licked his lips like a jackal circling its wounded prey.

'I'm sorry to hear that Mr Scroggins, really sorry. Thank goodness she has a good son to look after her.'

He emitted a small chuckle in general appreciation of good sons everywhere, with whom it was obvious he'd had sufficient dealings to be an expert on the subject.

'Yes,' replied Henry, a flow of genuine guilt rising up in him as if the legal brain the other end was intuitive enough to read his mind.

'Has your…' Snapes thought for a while before changing 'Has your mother seen the letter yet?' to 'Is your mother able to read and understand the contents of the letter Mr Scroggins? Your father's estate is a huge one as you'll see.'

'Yes,' said Henry.

'Yes what?' enquired Snapes. 'She *has* read the letter?'

'No - no she hasn't. Not yet. I thought I'd speak to you first. I've been away - in Brighton - otherwise I'd have called earlier. What I meant was, yes, the estate is considerable.'

Henry was getting in a muddle already and wished Millicent was there to take the phone and talk legal jargon directly on this man's level. It would have been so simple for her. But Archibald Snapes knew what to do.

'Look Mr Scroggins, would it be easier if we met? Do you know where my office is? Whiteheath village, do you know it?'

At last! Something recognisable that Henry knew and could impress with. Of course he knew where Whiteheath Village was - he lived just down the road in Lewisham for heaven's sake! What a silly question.

'Yes!' he replied, instantly regretting his enthusiasm.

'Do you know the wine bar near the station?'

'Yes, I know the wine bar. The one with the red canopy outside,' said Henry, his recent dabbling with the wine list at The Grand Hotel, Brighton, aiding his confidence no end.

'That's the one,' came the reply, 'they tried the canopy inside but it didn't work.'

Henry's newly acquired confidence took an instant dive on receiving this sarcasm. This was snakes and ladders, poker, chess, Monopoly, played against a sharp brain and he wasn't sure he was equipped. So he laughed, rather too loudly.

'Very good Mr Snapes. When shall we meet then?'

'Well I'm fine for this evening. How about you? Where do you work?'

'In London, Whitehall.'

'Whitehall? Downing Street perchance?'

'Not far away. I manage a government department.'

Henry was not one to brag under any circumstances but he'd not yet had the opportunity to tell anyone he was now a manager and found it had popped out without thinking. Besides, this would let the cunning Snapes know he wasn't messing with an amateur; even if he was.

'I can get the train straight to Whiteheath from Charing Cross,' offered Henry. 'It'll probably be about six-thirty if that's not too late.'

'No that suits me fine Henry. It's okay to call you Henry, I take it?'

'Why not? It's my name, same as my father's,' said Henry, a sudden surge of pride and attachment welling up inside him at the first association of him as the son of his father, outside of his intimate conversations with Millicent.

Snapes laughed. 'Yes, might as well use it then. And I'm Archie. See you in the wine bar around six-thirty. You can't miss me, I fill up the bar as soon as I walk in.' This was followed by a wheezing chuckle which turned into a short coughing fit.

Henry mistook the remark to mean that it was his charisma that filled the bar and that the whimsical Archibald Snapes was being self-deprecating - when in fact he was just fat.

269

'Oh!' said Snapes as they were about to say goodbye, 'what about your mother? Won't she be expecting you home?'

'I have a very helpful next-door neighbour,' replied Henry, somewhat surprised at the solicitor's concern, 'who looks after her when I'm not there. I'll give her a call.'

'Oh that's good. Not my business of course but when you spend your life dealing with and caring about people it comes as automatic to consider the little things that are otherwise sometimes overlooked by the, shall we say, less *scrupulous* members of our profession. It'll never make me a millionaire Henry, but at least I can sleep at night and that's what matters to me most. A clear conscience is worth more than a pot of any man's gold I always say.'

Snapes, unaware that the 'very helpful neighbour' knew him already through her window spying, without him knowing her, simply concluded his compassionate speech with, 'See you later then Henry,' in a tone that, if spread on toast, would have satisfied the taste buds of the sweetest tooth. The smile that accompanied it as the head followed the receiver halfway to its rest could also have helped launched a thousand ships, so thick was the grease.

'Yes, goodbye,' he heard Henry say, just before the click.

With eyes narrowed and tongue licking across his lower lip, the large solicitor leaned back in his high-backed black leather chair and picked up a Bic biro, rocking gently to and fro chewing the already well-chewed cap, giant head nodding with the motion of the rocking; nod, chew, nod, chew, mind on red alert. The stakes were immense and the risks, if he was very, very careful - with a trusting soul like the father's son - minimal.

Suddenly possessed of an idea, he stopped chewing, leaned forward and pressed a button on his intercom.

'No more calls this afternoon please Dorothy.'

'Yes Archie,' came the meek reply.

He dragged his huge form to its feet and strode with purpose and several rattling wheezes to the filing cabinet where he took out the two files for Henry and Irma Scroggins, files that now looked decidedly more interesting, in fact mouth-wateringly appetising. He needed the utmost uninterrupted concentration for the job ahead, steadfast in the belief that what he was going to tentatively, diplomatically suggest to his new, if somewhat naïve, 'client' Mr Henry Scroggins, was effectively a done deal. It was really only the figures needed agreement.

Imperative to his plans, however, was the blissful ignorance of his deceased partner's widow, Dorothy Bodger, sitting in her own quiet contemplation in the outer office, the wife who felt it her duty to carry on as secretary and receptionist when it would have been very easy to become a sleeping partner in the business after the death of her husband, or as Archibald Snapes had suggested, to accept his offer of buying her out. He'd managed for so many years, eight to be precise, to conceal certain 'facts' from her, facts about fundamental disagreements between the two partners - one partner as straight as a dye, the other as bent as the Grim Reaper's scythe - and it was only at the precise moment when David Bodger was diagnosed with incurable cancer and had let it slip to Snapes that he would take no secrets to the grave, especially no single business secret that might put Dorothy, his children or the reputation of the business in jeopardy, that the desperate Archie had to act fast, be ruthless in his decision-making - as if his natural instincts had ever been to the contrary - and make haste with a plan to secure wealth way beyond that constantly thwarted by David Bodger's frustrating integrity.

That very same night, just hours after David Bodger's fateful divulgence to his partner of his intentions - and yet even more fateful divulgence that he was to add these intentions next day to his will, lest his widow's word not be believed after his death - the wine bar across the street had never seen so much money pass over the counter as Snapes introduced his good friend to the simple joys of Tequila and 'lip, sip and suck.'

It was difficult to imagine that the slim, mild-mannered David Bodger was a sick man until the illusory effect of the tequila meant that Archie had no option but to take him to his car in the open garage space beneath the office, where the semi-conscious solicitor sadly fell asleep with the engine running and exhaust pipe connected to the inside.

And so it was that the toughest job of Archibald Snapes' life came when he had to tell his partner's wife that the news of her brave, selfless husband's cancer had been too much for him to burden upon the three people in the world he loved most dearly; how he'd told Archie he wished to spare his family the pain and suffering of watching him deteriorate. How he had asked, *begged*, Archie, as his closest friend and trusted confidante, not to say a word to anyone until that time came when he would spare them.

The real tragedy for the distraught Archie was discovering that his beloved partner would not wait until such time, but take his own life that very night. Why, he had asked himself a thousand times, why had he not seen the signs the day he returned from the hospital with the terrible news of his incurable illness? Why, oh why? Could he ever forgive himself?

Yes, it was the toughest job of Archie's life indeed, for he was just not a naturally convincing actor and it took all his powers to turn in an Oscar-winning performance in front of the widow, her children, the coroner and assembled family and friends at the funeral a week later. The fact that the coroner's report clearly proved that David Bodger had indeed been that very day diagnosed as Snapes had revealed, made it impossible to imagine that his death was anything other than a terrible tragedy; a sacrifice by a brave man.

## Chapter Twenty Nine

# HENRY'S RENDEZVOUS WITH SNAPES

Henry entered the wine bar feeling like a regular, a local. His only previous exploit there had been two months and two weeks previously, on the second of January, the day he would always consider his Day of Liberation, but for one totally unaccustomed to frequenting any bar of any sort, anywhere, two visits in such a short space of time, in his mind, made him a regular and he felt quite proud and breezily familiar. So breezily familiar in fact, that it was something of a stinging disappointment, to say the least, when the Irish barman who had served him previously and whom Henry instantly recognised as a dear old friend and drinking partner, was obviously struggling to do the same with him.

'Good evening sor, haven't seen you in here before.'

Henry stared at him for a moment with a vague smile of disbelief before looking around and nodding towards the window seat where he'd sat before, a seat now occupied by a very large man in a suit who was engrossed in reading something, a bottle of red wine on the table before him.

'I was sitting over there, where that gentleman is,' said Henry, knowing this would instantly jog the man's memory.

The barman laughed and apologised. 'I'm sorry sor, usually good with faces but...when was this? Last week?'

Henry looked up from the money he'd just taken from his wallet, trying to work out whether the barman was joking or serious.

'No, at Christmas. Just after, in fact.'

Certain this would at last have the barman slapping his thigh in apologetic remembrance, Henry was saved from further disappointment by a voice calling from the window seat, where the very large man had screwed his very large head around towards them.

'Henry? Henry Scroggins?'

273

'Yes,' replied Henry, turning on hearing his name and, now feeling rightfully restored to the status of 'local', flashing a glance at the barman to let him know he wasn't doing his job properly.

'Archie I presume?' continued Henry, walking to the man and placing his briefcase on the ground.

Snapes rose with his usual wheezing difficulty and the accompanying scrape of furniture, all such items seeming to be deliberately placed to make his life one long obstacle course. Two chairs meshed instantly into one to fully illustrate the point as his bulk displaced their limited allocated area.

'I've got a bottle on the go. You okay with a house red?'

Henry froze at the mention of 'house red', his choking fit at Gordon's Wine Bar flashing up before him. But reassured by several glasses of perfectly safe red since, he replied 'Yes, fine thank you' and even screwed up his eyes to make out he was examining the label before confirming.

'Nothing like a nice drop of red after a hard day's work,' he chirped knowingly, unlocking one of the chairs from the others of the neighbouring table and managing to squeeze between it and their table whilst Snapes wheezed himself back into position and promptly filled the empty glass awaiting Henry's arrival. He then topped up his own - a little higher Henry noticed. He also noticed by the small amount left in the bottle that Snapes' glass had done a bit of topping up already. What Henry didn't know was that this was the second bottle.

'So,' began Snapes with a smile, tapping a manila folder on the table, 'your father was a very successful, and a very wealthy, *extremely wealthy*, businessman.'

'I understand he was, yes,' said Henry, adding quickly, 'I never knew him. Well, that's not entirely true, I vaguely remember him being around during the war, when I was a toddler, but then he...'

Henry hesitated to gather his thoughts. Snapes was listening intently, already calculating what sort of character he had on his hands and how far he could go. He raised his eyebrows in expectation, encouraging Henry to continue.

'He left my mother, us, and that was the last we heard of him. There were always rumours he'd gone to Australia, and yes, the rumours were also that he'd made quite a lot of money, but they were just rumours and we all know what they can do don't we.'

He looked at Snapes for the first time since he'd started talking, having fixed his gaze constantly on his glass which he turned in his fingers during his recollection.

'True,' said Snapes. 'Who was it who said 'the rumours about my death have been greatly exaggerated'?'

'No idea,' said Henry, 'but obviously someone who was still alive, unlike my father. Exactly how much money are we talking about?'

Snapes opened the folder and turned it around, pushing it towards Henry who started reading things that his eyes had never seen and his mind had not for one moment contemplated. Snapes, who knew the document's contents off by heart, began to precis the inconceivable information and figures that Henry was attempting to digest; long numbers with dollar signs before them that were so incredible they beggared belief, and the exotic names and nature of businesses that were not even closely within his realms of comprehension.

The words 'Surfers', 'Surfers Paradise' and 'Gold Coast' recurred again and again against so many of the business names and addresses. He saw 'striptease', 'lingerie parties', 'massage parlour', 'hotel', 'restaurant', 'club', attached to various exotic sounding titles as *Pink Lady, Sun Sensations, Hanging Out, Palm Beach Pleasures, Paradise Island;* another world, a world so far removed from the limited sphere of his mundane suburban existence, where his recent and daring escapades into Brighton and Whiteheath were what Monte Carlo and Mayfair were to others.

He heard Snapes turning these names and numbers into hard facts, even the dollar to pound exchange rate that Snapes easily calculated as if he did this sort of thing every day; *really* hard facts, too hard in fact to be facts for Henry's brain to comprehend as something to do with, something created by, the man who had given him his name, his blood, his life; the man with his own name - Henry Scroggins.

'Over ten million dollars in cash and probably about twice, maybe three times, that amount in property and business value,'

Snapes continued in strictly hard fact fashion. 'Your father's business manager in Brisbane is still trying to calculate accurately the whole extent and value of the businesses. The cash and properties are reasonably straightforward but it appears he was a very astute man and kept a lot of the accounts close to his chest. Trusted nobody apparently, apart from a lady, Betty Mathieson, who it appears was his partner - business and otherwise, until her death last year. I've never heard of anyone having an accountant to check his accountant but that's how he worked. The most honest man in the world according to the business manager; paid all his taxes in full and on time, looked after his staff and their families like a doting father but was ruthless with anyone who cheated him; utterly ruthless from what I gather. Basically he didn't really trust a soul apart from, as I say, the lady called Betty Mathieson.'

Snapes stopped and thought about his own trustworthiness for a moment, keen to present an image to Henry of a man as close to his father's principles and memory as possible.

'And he's left everything to her, my mother,' said Henry calmly.

'Certainly has.'

Henry nodded.

'Every penny, or cent I should say,' added Snapes, 'unless someone pops up out of the woodwork with another will, but that seems highly unlikely.'

'Nothing to Betty,' said Henry, almost under his breath.

Snapes looked up quickly. 'What? You knew her?'

Henry shook his head. 'I know of her, that's all. Our street was a nest of gossiping vipers when I was small. All this stuff about good neighbours back in the days after the war, looking out for each other - more like looking out for any gossip that they could gather and spread about. We've got the queen of them next door, looking after my mother at this very moment.'

He peered out of the window into his childhood, his lips slightly apart as he recollected, then turned back and faced the solicitor, stroking the stem of his glass.

'You couldn't avoid the gossip. They think when you're little and your father's gone off with another woman that you're deaf. I heard it all, all about my father taking Betty Mathieson, his best friend's widow, off to Australia. But they weren't stupid, the neighbours. They knew what he'd put up with. Even then everyone hated her, my mother, I could tell. Apart from Lily Bunce next door who she always seemed to have under some sort of spell. Still has. He, my father, and Betty got more sympathy from all the decent ones than she, the old witch, ever did.'

He looked again outside into the street and took a deep breath. 'And she's left everything to the Battersea Dogs Home?'

Henry couldn't resist the flicker of a smile.

'She has indeed.'

'Lucky dogs.'

'Very lucky dogs. They certainly won't want to be adopted once they hear about this.'

Henry saw the humour in the remark and couldn't help a chuckle rumbling up from his stomach, one that stopped, refuelled and returned several times. He took a sip of wine, still staring straight ahead out of the window and across the street, thinking about the old hag lying in bed with not the slightest interest in life or him or anyone, apart from her own grim determination to ensure he continued to suffer as he'd suffered throughout his life.

'Shall I tell you something?' said Henry, looking Snapes directly in the eye. 'She is evil, pure unadulterated evil. She has made my life hell from the moment I was born and treated everyone else the same. She has so much hate in her heart it's hard to describe. Isn't that dreadful talking about a mother, about anyone, like that?'

'She must love animals, dogs at least,' ventured Snapes.

Henry exploded.' What! Love dogs! She....'

He stopped as his mind flicked through the horrible, cruel scenario he was about to reveal. Snapes waited for him to continue, excited not by any compassion for Henry (or dogs) but for a new twist that was doing nothing at all to damage his stratagem. It was perfectly true that at that moment he felt more at one with Irma Scroggins than with her son.

'When I was little, I found a puppy,' said Henry, 'a stray puppy in the park. I walked around for hours asking people if they knew whose it was; knocked at every door in every street nearby but nobody knew the poor little thing. I don't know what it was, probably a mongrel, but it was the sweetest thing and cuddled up inside my jacket and kept licking my hand.'

Henry's chest rose and fell with the memory of the dog's lick. He stared ahead with teeth gritted and breath rising fast and deep, the anger and hatred welling up ready to flood through his bulging red eyes. It was a while before he felt ready to continue during which time Snapes had filled Henry's glass with the remains of the wine, a gesture that didn't go unnoticed by Henry who made a mental note not to put a foot wrong and to follow Millicent's strict instructions of letting Snapes reveal his hand first. They had decided that if Snapes was willing to meet Henry then his thought process might well be aligned to theirs and he should be given just enough information to be aware of the ease with which he could proceed to his personal benefit. Millicent had briefed Henry carefully, suggesting that he reveal only the depth of his dislike for his mother and the extent of her illness but without the slightest indication that his intention was 'terminal'. In the event of any implications in the aftermath of her death, the legality must be completely on his side with Snapes unable to prove a single motive for Henry wanting to do away with her. In fact Millicent thought it a good idea to throw in a mention of how he, Henry, had never been motivated by money and also how he diligently ensured his mother had her medication every day, even emphasising that to sink to her level of wickedness flew in the face of his Christian beliefs. They even quietly comforted themselves that God, should he exist, might have even approved of such a little white lie, under the circumstances of the suffering she caused others.

Henry continued.

'Eventually when it started to get dark, I took her home - it was a she, the puppy - and showed my mother. She told me to get rid of it but I shouted at her that she was wicked and told her the dog loved me more than she ever had. She hit me, round the head - it was always round the head, above my ear, her favourite place - and then she took the dog outside locking the back door from the outside so I couldn't get out. I heard her running water in a bucket and I knew what she was going to do so I ran to the front door but couldn't reach the latch. So I got a chair and stood on it and undid the door and ran and ran, down the street and round the corner until I got to our back alley.'

Henry's shoulders started to move up and down and tears streamed suddenly down his cheeks. A couple on a nearby table behind Henry made gestures of concerned enquiry to Snapes but a reassuring shake of the head and comforting smile from him allayed their worries. The barman too, had read the body language of the two men and was discreetly watching as he cleaned glasses behind the bar. Henry swallowed, wiped away his tears on the back of his hand and continued.

'By the time I'd run down our garden and got to her, she'd half drowned the little thing. Held her under with a brick, pushing me away as I tried to bite and kick her. The water was freezing and I saw her, the puppy, struggling under the brick, looking up at me through the water, her little paws…then… she stopped struggling and was…. '

Henry got up, strode to the door which he pulled firmly open, and walked outside into the fresh air, his rapid exit followed by the door's slow pneumatic closing as those inside watched him stride past the window, staring down at the pavement. It was five minutes before he returned, during which time Snapes was one glass into a new bottle and Henry's glass had been replenished. When he did finally walk in, calm and collected if somewhat red-eyed and snuffly, he glanced at the few people and took his seat.

'No,' he said simply, 'she's not what you'd call a dog lover.'

Snapes, with almost two bottles of wine already in his system, knew the time had come to play his hand, as Millicent had told Henry he would. The story of the puppy had as little effect on him as would the news of his worst enemy's death. His was a Faustian soul, sold long ago to the devil, and dead puppies were no competition for the irresistible scent of dollars and trips to Australia, their pungency rising far too strongly for his own good, so strong that he fell straight into Henry's trap like a blind bear in a dense forest on a moonless night.

Henry had shown emotion, got upset, but never for a moment lost the composure or forgotten the advice of his own personal, loving solicitor.

'How ill is she?' asked Snapes.

'Ill? She had a stroke last year,' replied Henry, 'but recovered. Then had another a few weeks ago; this time she lost the use of her right arm and, more importantly -' He glanced from the bottle to Snapes, '- more importantly, she lost her speech.'

Snapes' eyes opened wide, instantly sensing an excellent additional loophole. They were quickly narrowed.

'When I say *more importantly*,' continued Henry, 'I mean only that her voice has tormented me so much all my life that the sheer relief of it not being part of my day is heaven. If you heard the voice you'd understand. She hates me with an abiding, unquenchable passion - always has. I don't know why, maybe I remind her of my father. I can't imagine, from what you've just told me, that I bear the slightest resemblance to him in character, but perhaps I look like him. Maybe I'm just the whipping boy for his abandoning her. I don't know, I've never worked it out, but I do know hatred and evil when I see it. She has so much of it to share around - and she never stints.' Henry smiled at Snapes. 'So there you have it. My mother; an angel really. Sweet lady.'

Snapes moved to refill Henry's glass but Henry placed his hand over the top and shook his head.

'Enough for me thank you. I'm not a proper drinker. Never touched a drop in my life until last Christmas, but that's another story.'

Snapes sat up straight and closed the folder. The wine was fuelling his bravado into action.

'See this,' he said, 'it can be all yours if you wish.'

Henry noticed that Snapes was slurring his words slightly and looking flushed and increasingly breathless.

'Oh yes?' said Henry, without blinking an eyelid, 'and how, pray tell, is that?'

'She doesn't know the letter exists, right?' Snapes leant back in his chair and took a deep wheezing breath, shaking his head at the folder, 'and neither need she know. Are you married Henry?'

Henry paused for a while before answering.

'I have a wonderful lady and…and, I have no idea to be honest what life holds in store. Marriage?' He shrugged. 'Anything's possible. Why?'

'Just that…um…I was thinking that you and your lady could make better use of your father's legacy than your mother. I'm absolutely certain that he never intended leaving anything to her, he's just like so many busy people preoccupied with life and thinking they are invincible, as I'm sure he did. He always meant to get round to changing it, but never did.'

Henry said nothing. Millicent was 'sitting' very firmly on his shoulder, watching his every move and listening intently to his every word, whilst Snapes was busy stepping onto a scaffold, tying a noose around his neck and placing a sack over his head.

'Here's what I propose. I have a file in my office with your mother's will in it. Nobody on this earth knows of its existence but me. And you.'

Henry nodded and said, 'Go on,' mentally knotting Snapes' wrists together behind him and placing his hand on a lever.

'For ten per cent of the total inheritance, as *my fee*, the rest is all yours.'

Henry pulled the lever with a hard jerk and peered down the trapdoor.

'But my mother isn't dead,' he said, 'how can it be mine until she's dead?'

Snapes, fingers of both hands locked together round his glass, shrugged and his eyelids involuntarily fell sleepily down, the wine's soporific effect taking its toll with the added intoxication of prospective immense wealth. He shrugged again and grinned at Henry.

'You're not suggesting for one minute that…' said Henry.

'I'm sujesting nothin' Henry,' slurred the blurry-eyed solicitor, 'nothin' *whossoever.* Just think aboudit. Lemme know.'

And with that he nodded emphatically and lurched suddenly to his feet, losing his balance and sending several chairs flying. There he stood, like the great ugly bear he was, 'swaying in the breeze', exhaling a huge gasp of air as if to clear his head before making room for a deep lungful of fresh reviving oxygen.

Rapid drinking combined with intense conversation, as many will testify from experience, can quite easily double the effect of alcohol, causing it to creep up and hit the consciousness, turning tipsiness into severe drunkenness within seconds of blinking around and remembering there is life outside the bubble. From feeling fairly much in control of speech and movement one minute, a switch in the brain can close down these faculties as if it's had enough and is off to bed. One flick and it turns out the light, leaving the body behind as a dead lump of useless matter until such time as the old dependable kidneys and liver have toiled away over many hours, never giving up on their host, to revive it slowly to its former self; a thankless task, mostly not appreciated in the slightest by the carrier.

And so the corrupt lump of matter that had just arisen, somehow managed to career through the melee of tables and chairs, make two irritated attempts to push the door instead of pull and finally half fall down the one step and stagger into the road and across it, waving a hand at tooting cars swerving to avoid him and disappearing into a door opposite, after much fumbling with a key.

Henry suddenly thought about the partner Bodger; he'd forgotten to ask about him and why he wasn't involved in such an important matter but deduced he'd find out soon enough and so promptly stood up, asked the barman if there was any money owed, was reassured that it would be put on the solicitor's tab and, thanking him, departed, as if he'd just popped in for a quiet orange juice.

It was probable, after the hour that had just past, that the barman's 'forgetfulness' in not remembering Henry as a regular customer, would from hereon be cured.

Chapter Thirty

## MILLICENT'S SECRET REVEALED

Henry walked home with his head full of the conversation that had just taken place, trying to take it all in. It had terminated rather abruptly with Snapes' drunken state and so he was left without any real conclusion beyond knowing that this obviously corrupt man was looking for a substantial cut of his father's inheritance on the death of his mother.

So they both had one common interest, her death, but for different reasons. Or were they different? He had wanted her dead long before the prospect of any vast riches had been strewn at his feet and therefore his reason was, in his eyes at least, honourable and justifiable. The money made not a bit of difference. He'd never wanted money for money's sake, just enough for the freedom it would provide; freedom from her. But he'd now obtained that freedom with promotion at work and by curing his 'fluttering' addiction; cured because he'd found an infinitely better addiction called Millicent. The only hold his mother now had over him was the fact that she was still alive, just, and that he felt an inexplicable filial responsibility all the time she breathed, one thoroughly undeserved but nevertheless implanted and immoveable within him.

Plodding along, engrossed in the therapeutic quality of paving stones, the description of his father's character turned over and over in his mind. Now he felt he knew the man, a father of whom he could be truly proud; a man of principle and honour in life and business; a man who had gone from a bus driver in the streets where Henry now walked, to a powerful millionaire the other side of the world. Someone who had remained faithful, so it seemed, to the one woman he'd abandoned his wife and child for. He thought of his father and the pretty young Betty Mathieson conducting their clandestine love affair in these same streets, maybe with a stolen kiss down one of the many alleyways - maybe down his own alleyway.

He wondered what she'd looked like, whether she was like Millicent. He hoped she was. Pretty had always been the word used by the doorstep gossips about Betty and an adjective which had undoubtedly pierced Irma Scroggins alert ears like a dagger every time she'd heard it. As Henry walked and smiled at this pleasant thought of his now heroic father alongside a lady as beautiful as Millicent, he realised that he was in the street where the Mathiesons once owned the fish and chip shop and where Henry had recently acquired a taste for crispy golden battered cod.

He looked up and saw the welcoming sign fifty yards ahead of him and strode purposefully towards it, his gastric juices churning into action at the thought of a delicious and unexpected treat in store for them within minutes.

The shop now had a fresh attraction. Henry looked at the black and white tiles on the floor and the pastel green painted walls with cartoon fish motifs and saw his father's feet standing where his were and felt his father's eyes gazing at the same wall, probably a different colour then but that didn't matter. He wondered whether his father was the same height as him and saw everything at the same level he was now seeing. The new gleaming metal fish fryer brim full of its variety of golden temptations was bound to be in the same place as the one his father peered into - that's if he was able to take his eyes away from the pretty Betty whilst chatting to her and her husband. Henry had never given a thought to a shop being a romantic venue, least of all a fish and chip shop, but now that he saw romance in just about everything, even the golden array of battered, crumbed and greasy fish and chip delights and saucy saveloys spoke of lovers' secret glances and suppressed passion; suppressed that is, until poor Siddie lost his life and passed the role of worship for the young woman he and Henry Scroggins both loved, to his dearest and most trusted friend.

More than anything it was his father's honesty that had left the most lingering impression, which, in comparison with the underhand scheming of the man he had just spent an hour with, discussing together like the 'forty thieves' how best to cheat his mother for personal gain, left in Henry's mouth a bitter taste; a sense of something fundamentally, appallingly wrong and against everything his father appeared to have fought so steadfastly against.

Honesty; the word wouldn't go away and with just a vague memory of his father's voice, Henry heard him warning him against letting avarice rule his judgement. If his father could succeed without resorting to the devious, crooked or covert in the rocky climb to the top, then there had to be a better way for him, the son of the man; a real man.

Henry kept reminding himself that he wasn't ridding himself of his mother for any financial gain, it was simply for peace, for freedom and because she was evil and spread misery like the malicious, malignant cancerous growth she had become - or maybe always was. It seemed perfectly reasonable to think that his father had deliberately intended, through reasons of guilt or something known to only him, to recompense the wife and son he abandoned. If he was as good a man as Henry thought him to be, then perhaps he had lived with the guilt and could only meet death in the way he'd lived his life, by being truthful. If this was the case then Henry felt sure that Betty would have known, and of course agreed.

Henry couldn't wait to speak to Millicent as he hurried home, his meal growing hotter in his hand by the minute and smelling more tantalising with every step. He hadn't used his new phone since it had been installed the previous week and so now, once he had seen Lily out of the house and paid his duty call on his mother - who he hoped had conveniently died to make his day complete - the phone would be graced, christened, glorified with the most beautiful voice on earth!

But why is it Life never permits more than fleeting scenes of happiness in a lifelong drama of pain? Why can it not linger long enough to become superficial and boring, so the pain is almost invited like a welcome contrast? As endless sunshine can, for some, bring monotony in tropical climes when the mind and body craves four seasons and the stimulation of Nature's unpredictability, so the sensitive soul needs change.

So there stood, like the consummate messenger of doom that every tragedy requires, Lily Bunce, peering through the window of the kitchen door as Henry entered by the back gate and strode down the path within sight and taste of his hot bagful of food. Even to him, her face staring from the dim glow of the kitchen into the gloom of the yard looked somehow comforting, even more so when he was close enough to see a face of anxiety, a face that had 'Ides of March' written all over it and which he hoped was about to brighten his day considerably with 'bad' news of his mother - or offer something less welcome. Either way, the chance of his fish and chips as a hot, imminent meal was looking in serious jeopardy.

'How is she today?' asked Henry, thinking he should dive straight into his food before the soothsayer had chance to ruin it.

'Not moved all day,' spake the soothsayer, 'not opened an eye, twitched a muscle or nuffin'. And with the saddest of sighs and a look to the side of her as if looking Henry in the eyes would be too much sadness for any man to take, the lament continued. 'And 'er breathin's bin spasmelodic, comin'n'goin' an' stoppin'n'startin' and all over the place. I was that worried when she wouldn't wake for her medification, I rang you at your office - but you'd left early they said.'

There was a small hint of recrimination thrown into the last remark as if Henry had deliberately and uncaringly foiled her.

'Yes, I had a meeting in Whiteheath which I told you about,' was Henry's somewhat curt response.

'Oh yes I know, I know you told me, you did that Henry, but I panicked. I shouldn't panic but I do, my Wilfred always used to say that. Her medification, I tried to give it 'er at five o'clock, on the dot, as you told me I must, but I couldn't wake 'er. I gave 'er a shake too, just a gentle one like this. In fact I give 'er several shakes through the day.'

She took Henry's arm to demonstrate and gave it a small but firm shake, then several more to illustrate roughly the number, which reminded him he was still holding his bag of fish and chips, the heat having subsided enough for him to forget. He put it down on the kitchen top and looked upwards.

'I think you should call the doctor 'Enry, I really do,' said Lily with a tremor in her voice, as only soothsayers can tremor.

'Yes, I think you're right. I'd better go and see her first.'

He strode down the hall and turned up the stairs with Lily in hot, scurrying pursuit, all the time muttering to herself.

Henry stood at the open bedroom door and looked at his mother lying in exactly the same position he'd left her that morning with just her head exposed, propped up by several pillows so her chin rested on her chest bone revealing the full extent of her monk's bald circle where matted strands of white hair trailed down over her ears and pale, haggard face; the face now no more than protruding cheekbones supporting dry parched skin which occasionally sucked in and out like a pair of old leaking bellows, the only visible reminder that she was still of this world. A starved cow's withered carcass in its death throes could not have looked more hideous and hopeless of recovery. Yet Henry knew that all the time she was there and those cheeks sucked in and out, there was a chance that, like last year, she could summon the strength for a fresh vendetta.

Lily crept silently past Henry and went to the bedside where she turned to him with an expression of such despair that Henry started to feel desperately sorry for her. She was a genuine good friend to his mother despite receiving never a tender word or any faint gesture of thanks. Put aside for a moment the interfering, wittering and letter-opening and she was basically a good person. Henry stepped forward and softly placed a hand on Lily's shoulder, feeling it shudder with emotion from his touch.

'What do you think Henry?' she asked looking up at him pathetically as if the loss of Irma Scroggins would be on a par with losing her beloved Wilfred.

'Doesn't look good does it,' said the son, examining the untouched jam sandwich on the bedside table, the bread starting to curl at the corners. 'I'll phone the doctor. Don't you worry about staying Lily. You've done more than enough. My mother, *we*, could ask for no more.'

She turned to gather her things and so Henry lightly placed both his hands on both her shoulders as a gentle indication that it was time for her to leave and let him take charge. The poor woman nodded and cuffing her dripping nose on her cardigan sleeve, made steps to exit. But suddenly the word 'phone' spurred her memory and she sprang instantly from soothsayer to secretary.

'Oo, by the way Henry, you had a phone call today. Frightened the life out of me it did when it went orf! What with no phone ever being in this 'ouse and me forgettin' you'd 'ad it put in yer bedroom.' She managed a brief laugh through her snuffles and went on. 'I hope you didn't mind me answering it but I can't stand phones ringing and not being answered and anyways I thought it might fret Mrs S and 'ave 'er wonderin' what was going on. It was a man called Richard something…Gaines I think it was. Anyway, I wrote it down I did - yes, Richard Gaines, that was it. Just remembered, seeing my writin' on the paper, in me 'ead like. He said 'ee used to work with you. Wants you to call him back. I left 'is name and number by the phone. Sorry I 'ad to go in your bedroom 'Enry but….'

'No, no Lily, that's quite all right. You did the right thing to answer it - and take the number. Thank you. Very much.'

Henry was dumbfounded. All the way through the end of Lily's bumbling monologue his mind had been racing with why on earth Gaines would want to call him when their last parting had been under far from pleasant circumstances. Henry's heart beat fast. He loathed confrontation and felt he'd had too much in recent times whilst changing his life, the most recent involving the man he now had to contact. How had Gaines got his number, a number only in existence for a week? But then he realised that Directory Enquiries would have him listed as a new number, presenting Gaines with little investigative work.

Henry led Lily downstairs and within minutes she was out of the house, requesting that Henry pop in 'just for a mo' to let her know what the doctor said after he'd been. He closed the door slowly and looked at the greaseproof wrapper containing his meal, suddenly having no appetite. Swallowing hard, he thought for a moment before returning up the stairs and into his bedroom where he very quietly closed the door and sat on the edge of his bed next to the phone, holding the slip of paper bearing the name and number.

Slowly he dialled and waited, holding his breath as the tone clicked in and started ringing. One, two, three, four, five rings…Henry took a deep breath of relief and was about to replace the receiver, when the unmistakeable grating tones of Richard Gaines came.

'Hello?'

'Richard? It's Henry, Henry Scroggins. You rang earlier.'

Henry thought he heard a chuckle at the other end and a cigarette lighter click. A deep suck of air followed.

'Henry. How are you?'

'I'm very well, thank you. And you?'

'Oh yeah, *I'm* fine thank you very much. *I'm* fine, but how about *you*?'

'You've just asked me that,' replied Henry with as pleasant a tone as possible considering someone he detested but had to remain polite with, was asking him the same question twice.

'No, no, no - you don't get me. I mean how *are* you? How does it feel to be 'aving it off with a *prostitute*? That's what I mean Henry. Very dangerous 'aving it off with a *prostitute* - I mean they fuck anyone don't they and there's a lot of nasty little things you can catch out there if you're not careful.'

Henry slammed the phone down and sat shaking on his bed, staring ahead at the linoleum, his mouth open and his breathing fast and laboured. For over three minutes he sat in this manner, uncontrollable shudders racking his body, one forefinger lying on his quivering bottom lip, eyes never leaving the spot upon which they were held transfixed, as visions of the woman he loved and the sound of the words he had just heard ran together, overwhelming and inconceivable.

The phone rang again and on the second ring Henry snatched it up, unable to speak but having no need as two words spat at him down the receiver.

'Ask her!' And the phone was slammed down, leaving him there with the receiver dropped into his lap and his body now convulsing with giant tremors. It wasn't that he believed what he was hearing, it was merely the fact that words so base and vile had been spoken about the purest, loveliest creature he knew, debasing her purity just by association. It was so horrible.

He walked calmly downstairs and unwrapping his fish and chips set about eating with the voracity of a starving animal, handful after handful rammed into his mouth, barely lukewarm fish and chips devoured within minutes, even the pieces of batter stuck to the paper scratched manically off. He then screwed up the grease-stained paper, washed his hands at the sink, dried them on a tea towel, and striding down the hall, ran up the stairs and returned to his bedroom where he took a card from his jacket pocket, a cream card with the words *The Carter Consultancy* on, and dialled the number.

'Hello,' came Millicent's soft voice.

'Millicent?'

'Henry! I've been sitting here waiting to hear from you. How did it go? The meeting.'

Silence.

'Henry? Are you there? Are you okay?'

'Millicent?'

'Yes?' Millicent's voice was now hesitant.

'Millicent, tell me something. Are you a prostitute by any chance?' Henry's voice quivered as he spoke and struggled not to cry on hearing himself ask such a disgraceful question of his beautiful angel. Several seconds of silence followed after which Millicent, hearing Henry's attempts to control his shaking body and sobs, replied.

'The answer is…*no*…but we need to talk. Please Henry.'

'Have you ever been?' asked Henry, now shaking with the suspicion of Millicent's deception.

'Henry, please…I need to explain. It was a misunderstanding in the police station. When I said I was there for soliciting, you were drunk, and mistakenly…'

Henry slammed down the phone and rocked backwards and forwards on his bed, his hands gripping the eiderdown either side until the white of his knuckles looked as if the bone would burst through the skin. He slowly pulled back the bed covers and crawled inside, holding the sheet to his mouth and drawing both knees to his chest.

In the next room an extraordinary metamorphosis was taking place. With every desperate word of Henry's that had drifted through the wafer thin wall separating mother and son, life had started to return to the stiff, dry dormant carcass of the former, like some ghastly chrysalis breaking open with the warmth of Spring, legs stretching out beneath the covers and arms emerging above, white empty skin dangling from bone. A bat's wing of a hand reached slowly up - the hand of an arm that had lain paralysed for weeks - and scratched one corner of the thin, cracked mouth where the semblance of a crooked smile flickered on and off whilst the cold, watery eyes remained fixed and penetrating; penetrating the wall where the son of the husband who'd abandoned her lay curled in a ball, heaving noiselessly, a fist of bed sheet rammed inside his mouth to stifle his unquenchable, unimaginable distress. The wan, sunken bellows flanking the giant hook of a nose showed a faint touch of pink as the dry parchment filled with blood and bile, pumping in and out, breathing the deepest, most satisfying, re-oxygenating, restorative breath the body had taken for a long, long time.

# Chapter Thirty One

## HENRY DISAPPEARS – IRMA'S VENGEANCE

The following morning Lily Bunce, on not hearing from Henry about the doctor's diagnosis and not seeing him pass her window at his usual time, walked tremulously round the back to next door and found the kitchen door closed but unlocked and no sign of Henry anywhere.

Poised with one foot slightly suspended, like a fox on hearing a twig snap, she stood in the kitchen listening for signs of life before tiptoeing cautiously down the hall and up the stairs, terrified of what she might find.

In order to warn any decomposing bodies of her imminent arrival she emitted her own particular siren, one that had sent generations of Viola Street neighbours running for cover or holding their breath until the danger passed. It was even rumoured within the street that forty years earlier Messerschmitt and Fokker pilots had aborted missions and veered off back to Germany at the sound of her 'Coo-ee! Coo-*eeeeee!*'

On sending this signal in advance up the stairs and receiving no reply, she arrived silently on the landing and quickly glanced in Henry's bedroom, the door being ajar, which revealed his wardrobe door open and clothes strewn on the floor, including a ball of material rolled up on the bed which she noticed on closer inspection was the suit he'd been wearing the previous day. With brow deeply furrowed and head shaking, she proceeded on to the bedroom of Irma Scroggins, convinced in those few steps that Henry had murdered his mother, fled and left her to find the body of her dearly beloved friend. But no.

'Oh my *good* gawd!'

The cry erupted from the terrified woman as she stood in the doorway with hands clasped to cheeks and saw not a dead body, not even a barely alive one, but one in the full bloom of life! There it sat, bolt upright in bed, drinking tea, nibbling a biscuit, using both hands, hair tied tightly back, a trace of colour tinting the folds of skin and an expression of such intense, gloating mischief that Lily was now fearing for *Henry*.

'What's 'appened Mrs S? Where's 'Enry? How come you're so better and…how did you do yer 'air and make that tea for 'eaven's sake!'

Irma Scroggins swilled tea around her mouth and chewed the biscuit already inside her mouth.

'How? *How*?' she screeched, 'I'll tell you how!'

'Do Mrs S, do!' cried Lily, overcome with dizziness and sitting down on the bedside chair before she collapsed.

'He's gone - went last night. Abandoned me like his father thirty five ago. Not even a goodbye. What was I supposed to do, lay here and die? No, Lily Bunce - I'm made of stronger stuff than that and it'll take more than a selfish dolt of a son to kill me off, I can tell you that for nothing.'

Before the stupefied Lily could gather her wits together to form thoughts into words, desperately trying to fathom how Irma Scroggins could move from death's doorstep to her current rejuvenated state, Irma Scroggins continued.

'He's got a woman! I told you so. But not just *any* woman. That phone call you took, it was an informer telling him that the woman he's seeing is a…' Here Irma Scroggins developed such a look of disgust and contempt that she felt forced to spit masticated tea and biscuit off her lip onto the sheet before she could form the word '…*prostitute*!'

'No Mrs S! Not your 'Enry! Not wiv a… *prostitute!*'

Irma Scroggins firm nod was the undeniable affirmation.

'Oh yes, Lily Bunce - a filthy, disgusting *whore!*' The last word spoken with such gravel-throated verisimilitude that even if Millicent Carter had been proven to be Mother Theresa in disguise she would still have been forced to wear the label of damnation just bestowed upon her for the rest of her life.

'Oh my good gawd,' muttered Lily for the second time in several minutes, shaking her head once again and looking towards the window for a clue as to Henry's whereabouts.

'But where's he gawn Mrs S? 'Enry, where's 'ee gawn?'

'Gone? I don't know - but he'll be back. I heard him blubbing after he'd spoken to her on the phone. How did he get a phone in here? And then I heard him shuffling about and sniffing and pulling out drawers and opening the wardrobe doors and talking to 'isself, like the pathetic creature he is.'

'But s'posin he don't come back Mrs S - what then? What you goin' to do?'

Irma Scroggins eased her body slightly to one side as if intending to get out of bed, which was exactly what she began to do, sending Lily's eyebrows skywards and mouth agape.

In less than a minute the revived demonic female had her feet on the ground and was digging around for her slippers that she found and slid on, all the time watching Lily with a sinister smile.

'That letter, Lily Bunce, the one you mentioned had arrived from the solicitors. I can't find it. Have you seen it anywhere?'

Lily shook her head and sat rigid with fear at the mention of the dreaded letter of which she knew the contents but wished - oh how she wished - that she didn't.

'He must have it,' mumbled Irma, picking up envelopes and other items from her dressing table and flinging them back down. She grumbled incoherently to herself and flashed a fearsome glance at the quaking figure in the chair, moving round the bed towards her. 'It was from the solicitors wasn't it - the letter. *My* solicitor! *My* letter!'

Lily nodded silently, her shoulders bent in humble submission, one hand clasping a screwed up ball of tissue that she kneaded like dough, instantly alerting the arch interrogator to believe she knew more than she was saying.

'Where is it!' screamed Irma Scroggins, reaching Lily and making to grab her arm but unable to reach and clutching a handful of air, 'you know where it is woman! I know you do!'

'I don't know Mrs S! How should I know! Your 'Enry…'

'*My* Henry! He's not *my* Henry! No more he's not!'

'No Mrs S. Anyways, 'ee had it an' I thought 'ee was going' to give it yer Mrs S. It was none of my business was it, so I showed it 'im in the kitchen where I left it by the kettle like I always…'

She threw a reflex look at Irma Scroggins as the 'phantom of steamed letters' hovered over her head for a brief second, but to her relief the woman was momentarily turned away giving Lily the time she needed to remove any guilty expression that may have crept up to betray her.

'…like I always do,' she finished in no more than a whisper.

Then, at that instant, the oppressed accused one, in a torrid flash of self-belief in her innocence, took umbrage. The tissue was dabbed defiantly against a nostril, the back straightened, the jaw thrust forward defensively and once more the pungent smell of burning martyr filled the air.

'This is none of my business. I bin doin' me best to look after yer and 'elp your, I mean 'elp 'Enry out, being 'ere when 'ee couldn't, and 'ere I am bein' blamed for stuff that's not my fault. It's not fair Mrs S. It's just not fair!'

The burning martyr had decided that if martyrdom was worth burning to a cinder for, then the cause was hers to take up with might and main, and so stepping from the flames she doused herself down and with a head as cool as Irma Scroggins' was hot, got up and marched towards the door where she took a stance that would have made Joan of Arc gasp in admiration - and proclaimed with head tossed back:

'I've 'ad enough! *Enough* d'you 'ear! You've bullied me for too long like you've bullied that poor son of yours all 'is life and everyone else 'oo tries t'be nice to yer. Just like 'Enry Senior too! Gawd rest 'is soul! You don't deserve any 'elp you don't. You're wicked, Irma Scroggins! Downright wicked, wicked, *wicked*!'

And with that brave declaration of independence Lily Bunce stomped along the landing and down the stairs, stomping so deliberately on every stair that whole families of woodworm below her stomping little feet were no doubt registering an earthquake and shielding their young from falling debris.

Irma Scroggins sat very slowly down on the bed and listened to the kitchen door close, the footsteps down the path, the back gate click open and shut - no, *slam* - and then silence. For several minutes she sat there motionless, unable to believe the audacity of Lily Bunce whom she had brought back under her roof, into her house, after the disgraceful woman had read her son's letter from his debtors - the letter she had herself already steamed open to read. The audacity of it indeed!

'There's no limit to the depths that woman will sink to,' muttered Irma Scroggins under her breath, 'and my God, I'll make sure she pays dearly.'

It's true that what Irma Scroggins had endured in the past month would have weakened the resolve of most ordinary people; would have made them buckle helplessly under the physical attacks her body had suffered; made them consider their unworthiness and just why it was they were left with not a soul in the world they could call a friend, nor even an acquaintance they could depend upon in a time of crisis; but such was the belief of Irma Scroggins that the whole world was wrong and she, its chosen chief victim, was right, that she could only see all this as a sacrifice she was making on the scale of a certain man on a certain cross on a certain hill called Calvary.

Just as she was feeling the crown of thorns piercing her head and the weight of the cross bearing down on her bent, broken spine, the phone rang in Henry's room. For her, this was the first time she'd consciously heard a phone ring in the house in the forty-two years she'd lived there - the call from Richard Gaines the previous evening serving only to bring her out of her coma.

But with instincts honed so finely and reflexes poised to snap back into action at a moment's notice, the phone's ringing last night had no sooner triggered her from subconscious to conscious, no sooner sent blood rushing to every dormant cell, than she was alert to what was happening and able to concentrate on every word her son was saying; working out what the caller was saying, listening to Henry's next call to his *prostitute lover*, and finally laying there savouring his utter distress as her mind and body slowly but surely recovered. It was as if she was sucking the strength and life out of her son - to send him to infinity.

Now, instantly summoning the speed and agility of an ageing but supremely fit gazelle, she was upon the phone in seconds, breath held, listening in silence.

'Hello,' wheezed a man's voice, before clearing his throat.

'What do you want?' asked the woman.

'I'm after Henry - Henry Scroggins.'

Irma Scroggins waited a while before deciding on her reply.

'He's not here. He's gone away. What do you want?'

'Who's speaking?'

Irma hesitated before replying, 'His...*mother*. Who is it? What do you want?'

The phone clicked and Irma Scroggins replaced the receiver.

In his office, Archie Snapes released his finger from the phone's disconnect button and gently replaced the receiver, taking a deep breath and staring towards the window in the direction of the wine bar of the previous evening's meeting. He removed the lid from a bottle of Paracetamols and shaking four into his palm, threw them into his mouth before picking up a cup of steaming black coffee and wincing as the liquid scalded his tongue. Swallowing the tablets and wiping his mouth with the back of his hand, he stared at the two files before him on the desk, one bearing the name of the woman he'd just spoken to.

'Lost her power of speech has she?' he wheezed, his lips twitching into a malicious grin. 'Henry my boy, I do believe you've lied to me.'

The grin was there as a mark of respect for a fellow reptilian occupant of the grass - being in the same trade as it were - and when you're a snake of the magnitude of Snapes, then there's nothing quite like trying to out-snake a fellow snake. However, all he knew for certain was that the 'wicked woman' appeared to be in remarkably fine fettle and that Henry had gone away; if indeed he had. What to do next? Archibald Snapes really hadn't a clue at that moment but he knew something would come once the fog had cleared. No doubt about that. It always did, Necessity being the Mother of Invention.

But then, as if the line were still open and the solicitor's thoughts transmittable down the wire, Lily Bunce's last defiant speech echoed in Irma Scroggins' head. 'Like 'Enry Senior too, gawd rest 'is soul!'

*Gawd rest his soul?* Irma Scroggins' eyes widened. Gawd rest 'is soul! He was dead! Her husband was dead and Lily Bunce knew it and her son knew it! So who else would the voice be at the end of the phone than her solicitor? They were partners, all three, partners in crime against her.

Her old chest heaved and her teeth ground, her breath pouring like fire from her nostrils as she stared into the cracked mirror and smiled, straightening her back and watching herself grow stronger by the second. Her mind flashed back to the last time she and Archibald Snapes met in his office eighteen years ago after Henry had dared to paper his bedroom, the very day she decided to teach her son a lesson he'd never forget by leaving all she possessed - with true poetic irony - to a home for lost and abandoned dogs.

The more she thought about that meeting, sitting opposite the young big-boned solicitor and his diminutive polite partner leaning over Snapes' shoulder, both examining her file open in front of them, she could hear his voice as clearly as if it were yesterday. Replaying the voice she'd just spoken to, there was no doubt in her mind that they were one and the same.

Transfixed, grimacing into the mirror, rocking slightly back and forth on the bed, she started to plan. How foolish they all were to think she was dead and buried. How very foolish.

## Chapter Thirty Two

## TWO WOMEN, TWO SEARCHES, TWO SPENCERS

Henry had been missing for a week. Two women were beside themselves; one racked with guilt and anxiety, the other with incandescent rage. Millicent beside herself because she had taken every action she could in trying to find Henry, fearing desperately for his safety; Irma Scroggins beside herself through not being able to find the letter from Bodger and Snapes - her armour, her sword, her revenge, her key to everything.

The old woman's anger was as unremitting as her searches, so certain was she that her conniving son had secreted the missing document somewhere in the house and in his distress omitting to take it with him. And what a search it had been. There never was a house turned upside down more frantically; rooms almost torn apart, drawers and cupboards turned over like a burglar with an exploding egg-timer strapped to his chest, pockets (Henry's) plundered until they began to fray, lino edges lifted until left with a permanent curl; every conceivable hiding-place examined not once, not twice but at least twenty times daily, all to the hissing spitefulness of a woman cursing her son, her neighbour, her solicitor, and the entire human race on whose shoulders this, along with everything else that had ever conspired against her, was heaped.

Not only was the woman teetering on the verge of insanity - if she hadn't already been teetering there since birth - but also was she one hundred percent physically fitter than on the day of Henry's departure. Driven to the point that every human reaches when the one item desperately, desperately sought, remains desperately, desperately elusive, she could only sleep each night after one final desperate search and only eat in the morning and take her medication after picking up where she left off the desperate night before.

And all this continuous active turmoil of rage and frustration either side of solid deathlike sleeps - for her day's exertions would have drained even the hardiest French Legionnaire – serving to drive away any lingering signs of a stroke. If her son or solicitor could have seen her in full venomous flight in and out of rooms and cupboards and drawers and pockets and pots and pans, all hope of her imminent demise would have been instantly, hopelessly abandoned.

It may be wondered why she failed to contact the solicitor. After all, she knew the name well enough and she now had access to a telephone for the first time in her life. All the tools were there to aid and abet her, but there was something in Irma Scroggins that would not let her pick up a phone installed by her son, not let her demean herself to use an item unsanctioned, a rule broken; and in refusing to do this she was cutting off all means of solving the torment that was obsessing her every waking moment.

During these searches there was always half an eye kept alert for any old address book or bit of correspondence tucked away forgotten in some dark or dusty corner that would contain the solicitor's details, but as an additional weight the world was thrusting upon her undeserving soul, it never surfaced, if in fact it ever existed. How bitterly unkind it was then, that her only other source of gaining communication with the man who could divulge the letter's content - one Lily Bunce - had not ventured near since the terrible bedroom scene a week earlier, when the little woman had fought back against her lifelong oppressor just as Henry had fought back four months earlier.

What sweet irony; what cruel karma. In severing contact with both sources, Irma Scroggins had deprived herself of access to something so monumentally power-giving. Riches beyond compare, and, far greater than either the power or the money, the unmitigated pleasure of keeping it all from her son, coupled now with the glorious bonus of keeping it all from his *prostitute* lover! But the son, for all his distress, had not it seemed entirely lost his sense of perspective and she was now forced to accept the prospect that he'd carried away the letter to wherever it was he'd disappeared.

So what of the son and what of the solicitor? And what of Millicent Carter and the Department office Henry had deserted without a word?

Millicent Carter's torment the night she'd last spoken to Henry was beyond words. No man had ever touched her like Henry; no human being had ever captured one tiny corner of her heart for more than a fleeting period. Losing him after only just finding him was bad enough but in being the cause of the loss and the inflictor of so much pain upon so good and innocent a soul, Millicent's guilt, regret and misery were inconsolable.

Repeating in her head that whole sleepless night was the single thought that for the first time in his unhappy life Henry Scroggins had found a person he could trust, only to discover by the cruellest of ways that his trust and love had been betrayed; betrayed not to deliberately injure or distress but because sometimes the circumstances of life are knitted together in ways that have no pattern, no plan, and which so often lead to misunderstandings and consequences too late or too hard to repair.

In reading her literary classics, where every author had skilfully entwined the hearts and actions of lovers for dramatic and often tragic effect, little had she ever imagined that she, the once impervious Millicent Carter, would be a subject for Life imitating Art. Until now, life had been so straightforward, so under her control, until a strange little man had walked into it and turned everything upside down.

At eight o'clock the next morning she stood on her narrow balcony looking out across Regent's Park at the ambling dog walkers and urgent commuters, trying to think rationally, but it was impossible. She needed to sit with Henry and explain. She knew what to say to him and now she just wanted him beside her to explain. After that he had two choices, to stay or to go, and she had no choice but to accept whatever he decided. She would make no attempt to change his mind.

Millicent turned and stepped back into the lounge, walking over to the sofa where George lay curled on a cream silk cushion, its tasselled seam combining with George's moustache to give him a slight resemblance to Fu Manchu. Touching the arm of the sofa, her fingers resting a while where Henry's head had lain when it was his bed on Christmas Eve, it was hard to imagine how desperate she was then to get the silly man in the grubby mackintosh out of her flat and out of her life as quickly as possible. She thought of the shock she'd felt on realising that he'd been so naïve as to mistake her flippantly delivered reason for being in the police station - 'soliciting' - as anything but what it was. Of course, knowing Henry as she did now, it was not difficult to imagine at all, but that was months ago and what seemed - in fact was - a different life.

She made a coffee and sat down beside George, tickling him behind the ear. He groaned and re-positioned himself in belly-up ecstasy before his mistress stopped and leant across him, taking a cigarette from a silver case. Without hesitation she lit it, the first time since it had been one of her two New Year's resolutions.

Inhaling deeply and then sipping the strong coffee, her brain momentarily clouded before clearing, determined and alert. Glancing at the clock and seeing it was eight-fifty she would ring Henry after nine at his office where he would have to listen quietly. He could of course put the phone down on her but she thought it unlikely and hoped it would give her enough time to make some attempt at restoring sanity and calm. But it was not to be. Henry wasn't there at nine, nor ten, nor at any time during the day.

John Deighton was concerned when Millicent spoke to him at midday, for in twenty years of working together he had never known Henry take a single day off and the fact that a whole morning had passed and he'd made no contact with the office was cause for genuine concern.

It was apparent he had no idea that Henry had installed a telephone at home and Millicent was not about to tell him otherwise, her hesitant explanation of who she was being as much as she wished to divulge at that stage. She'd felt obliged to mention how the previous evening had 'not been their best' which caused John to brighten a little as it represented for him a slight consolation, in so much as it was a feasible justification for Henry acting out of character. But not so for Millicent. She thanked John and left her number with him in case he heard anything. John said he wouldn't hesitate and hoped she would also reciprocate. It was all very polite, very tense.

That morning whilst formulating her plan of action before rising from bed, Millicent had anticipated that Henry may not feel able to face the office and so she then had to decide between two courses of action. Either she took the train to Lewisham and knocked on his door - not a problem in view of his mother being in a coma - or she would call Peregrine Spencer. To her it was plain that he was the source of information about her past profession. It couldn't possibly be anyone else. Nobody had the knowledge, the motive and the means.

She knew him well enough, so she thought, to believe that with his pride, dignity and pocket hurt to such a depth, he was capable of such revenge. The fact that he now had little to lose, apart from his marriage if his own revelations should ever backfire on him, was enough reason to exact his revenge especially when it was possible, in one fell swoop, to render considerable damage to both herself and Henry - Public Enemies One and Two.

Millicent took out Spencer's business card on which he had both his work and home number. 'How foolish' she thought to herself, for someone with his clandestine lifestyle, but then such was his arrogance and confidence in his infallibility that he wouldn't have given a thought to anyone daring to ever phone his home. Millicent dialled the number and waited as it rung; ten, fifteen times, before a quiet, cultured voice replied.

'Hello, Marjory Hargrave.'

Millicent was taken aback by the name.

'I'm sorry, I think I may have the wrong number. I was after Mr Peregrine Spencer.'

'He doesn't live here anymore. Why, what do you want?'

'I just wanted to speak to him. Do you know where he's gone?'

'To hell as far as I'm concerned.'

'He's not dead?'

Spencer's wife laughed loudly, sounding suddenly horsy; very dressage.

'Oh that's good, that's very good. Someone who assumes that if he's dead there's only one direction he'll go. You obviously know him well, possibly better than I do. Are you one of his floosies?'

There really was no answering that, such a direct question and not one Millicent could deny without lying, despite a natural resentment at being called a floozy.

'I'm not sure floozy is how I'd describe myself.'

'In that case you are. Goodbye.'

'Please!' interposed Millicent before the woman had chance to put the phone down. Then, hearing breathing at the other end she continued calmly, 'Please, would you have a number or address I can contact him at. I'd be very grateful. I know how you feel and I understand, but I really do need to talk to him about something very urgent.'

Marjory Spencer, for that was still her legal name although she no longer answered to it, adopted a conciliatory tone.

'He comes back - that is, I *allow* him back - every Friday to collect any messages or mail. He is staying with a man called Gaines in Stockwell from what he told me last week. That doesn't mean he's there this week. He's homeless you see. That's what happens when you cheat on a loyal wife who owns the house you live in. You end up homeless, unless somebody decides to take pity on you. I can give you the man's telephone number if you wish.'

'Please, if you don't mind.'

Millicent heard her turning the pages of a book, quietly muttering names as she flipped through before giving the full name of Richard Gaines and his number.

Millicent just had time to scribble down the number, for her mind was racing elsewhere. The name *Richard Gaines* had pierced her brain like a knife; the man Henry had been forced to sack and who'd left the office threatening revenge. Now it all made sense. There was no shadow of doubt the two men, Spencer and Gaines, had conspired.

Marjory Spencer wasn't leaving without a last shot across Millicent's bows.

'I don't know your name madam, but let me tell you right now that you have *no* idea how I feel. No idea at all. But if it's any consolation you are one of many. Goodbye and good luck.'

Millicent replaced the phone and sat staring intently at the carpet, one hand to her mouth and the other tickling George. What next? Without hesitating a moment longer, in case her nerve failed her, she started dialling the number she'd just been given. Again it rang interminably until a voice she recognised spoke.

'Hello, Mr Gaines's residence. Can I help you?'

'Peregrine?'

Millicent heard what seemed like a nervous shuffle, then a clearing of the throat.

'Who is that please?'

'It's me, Millicent.'

'Millicent! Good grief, what are you doing ringing here?'

'Your wife gave me the number. I needed to speak to you urgently, to ask you something. Are you alone?'

'Yes, for a short while, but I've nothing to tell you. I'm broken and broke as you probably know. Life bit me back Millicent.'

'I know. I'm sorry.'

'You're not. And neither should you be.'

Millicent didn't want to lie outright because half of her was genuinely sorry for him, in a way that any decent person cannot help but feel odd pangs of sympathy on witnessing the downfall and humiliation of another, however base and vile they've been; a curious, forgiving trait in the human condition. But the other half of her was furious that he'd stooped so low in his revenge on Henry. If it was her he'd taken out his hatred on, then fine, she in a way deserved it for being complicit in his downfall - in fact solely responsible once he'd given her good reason - but not to punish Henry who had done nothing but fight back like any frightened, cornered animal beaten by its master for twenty years.

'Henry and I are in love Peregrine.'

'Yes, I think you are Millicent from what I've heard. You expected me to laugh at the idea? Little innocent Henry Scroggins and the glamorous, worldy Millicent Carter?'

'I don't really care what you think but yes, it is quite amusing.'

'I see a perfect match Millicent; two basically good people reaching life's crossroads and willing to be surprised by themselves. Open to anything, anything unexpected this is, that can offer comfort and happiness for the second half of the perilous journey that is Life. Why not indeed - why not?'

Spencer took a deep breath and without a reply from Millicent, continued. 'I'm not the man you knew and never will be again. What are the expressions - 'make your bed and lie in it' - 'live by the sword, die by...''

'You're not dead yet Peregrine, so spare me the drama. I want to know one thing, did you tell Henry about me - my past life?'

'No I didn't. Gaines did.'

'But how did *he* know?'

There was a brief silence.

'I'm so sorry Millicent - so, so sorry. I told him in a moment of weakness and anger at my situation. Humiliated, homeless and dependent for a temporary roof over my head on a man whose career not so long ago I held in the palm of my hand - I just let it slip over a few drinks.'

Millicent's anguished gasp at the end of the line touched Spencer. He'd also loved Millicent in his own strange way.

'I had no idea he was planning anything. I would never wish you any harm, never Millicent. Nor Henry, poor man. He's done nothing, nothing wrong at all, just for once in his miserable life defended himself against me. That's all. What I've done is stupid and unforgivable but, compared to Gaines...oh Millicent, please forgive me.'

In the few moments of this speech Millicent had received the shock, taken the blow, cleared her head and switched into operation mode. Spencer's desperate plight was of little interest to her beyond him helping her find Henry.

'Henry has disappeared and I'm worried he might do something awful. He trusted me and I was about to tell him about...well, you know. Anyway, it's too late. Gaines and...' She stopped herself saying 'you'. 'Gaines got there first. I've got to find Henry before he does something silly.'

'Have you called the office?'

'Yes, I spoke to John Deighton.'

'Ah yes, John, a good man.'

'Henry wasn't there and had made no contact.'

'Then he's probably at home.'

'I can't go there, but I might have to if he doesn't appear by tomorrow. His mother's had a bad stroke and it would never surprise me if he hasn't...'

'Finished her off? There was no love lost between them.'

'None at all. She's evil. But that's beside the point - I've got to find him. If he's desperate he might do anything.'

Suddenly Millicent heard a door slam at Peregrine's end and the phone instantly disconnect. Gaines had returned.

Ten minutes later George was chasing pigeons and sniffing bushes in between returning, whimpering, to the feet of his mistress who sat on a bench smoking a cigarette, sniffing and dabbing her eyes with a lace handkerchief. She patted the bench beside her and the little dog leapt up, dumping two muddy paws in Millicent's lap, wagging his tail excitedly.

'Oh George,' sobbed Millicent, cuddling him close and kissing his damp head, 'what are we going to do darling?'

## Chapter Thirty Three

## THE CONCIERGE'S CONCERN

Two more days passed and neither Millicent nor John Deighton were a step forward. On the Friday morning, almost paralysed with fear, Millicent was on the verge of phoning the police to report Henry missing, in the hope the first thing they'd do was visit his house, something she knew she would have to soon enough if the police didn't. However, on returning from yet another walk with George - who was beginning to lose weight and what had until now seemed an insatiable appetite for exercise - she noticed a message flashing on her answering machine. Tripping over the squealing, scurrying terrier, she hit the play button and sat down on the edge of the telephone chair, almost too petrified to listen.

'Hello Millicent, John Deighton here. I thought I should let you know that I've just had a call from The Grand Hotel in Brighton. Apparently Henry left his card and asked them to call me exactly a day after he'd gone, to say he wasn't coming back to work. He left there yesterday morning so the concierge has only just called me. It's ten-forty now by the way. The concierge wouldn't tell me anything more but asked if his wife, Mrs Scroggins, who he was with on Monday evening would call him back, as he has something he can only tell her. Naturally we're all extremely worried here and I cannot imagine how you feel. The hotel's number if you haven't got it is--------. Please call me if you need to. No, please call me anyway if you wouldn't mind. Good luck and try not to worry. I'm sure everything will be fine.'

Millicent pressed a knuckle into her teeth, hardly able to breathe. For an hour she paced the flat walking into and out of every room, robotically, manically, clasping her hands together then wiping them down her skirt before clasping them back again, all the time staring ahead as if following a moving spot on the carpet three feet ahead. George had followed at first, thinking it was some sort of game, but soon got fed up and retired to the sofa and his cushion, head cocked every time Millicent appeared from a room only to slump disconsolately back onto the cushion when she disappeared. Her first thought had been relief that Henry was alive, or he was until yesterday at least. But the Grand Hotel? Why? What was he doing? What was he planning? Was he planning anything at all or just…?

The time came when the pacing had to stop and action taken. But how many times did she then walk to the phone only to retract her hand and walk a few rooms more until finally grasping the phone and dialling, her chest rising and falling, hands shaking, nerves shredded. By the time the phone answered Millicent's voice was cracked and tearful.

'Grand Hotel, Brighton - Concierge speaking.'

Millicent recognised the voice but only then realised he had a soft highland brogue, gentle and reassuring.

Millicent took a deep breath, cleared her throat and began.

'Oh hello, Millicent Carter here - you'll know me as Millicent Scroggins, I was there with Henry…'

'Ahh, Mrs Scroggins, thank you for calling. Yes, about your husband.'

Millicent didn't bother correcting him. He'd obviously not heard her say her real name and it was neither here nor there who she was to him.

'I got your message that he'd returned alone and…and left yesterday. Is that correct?

'Yes, it is correct. He left for Australia.'

'Australia?'

'Yes. We managed to book him a flight to Brisbane for yesterday afternoon and he took a taxi to the airport. I was under strict instructions not to advise his office until his flight had departed. Mrs Scroggins…are you still there?'

'Yes, yes…I'm here. I'm just rather dumbstruck, that's all. But at least he's alive.'

'Alive? Oh, alive and extremely well when he left but *terribly* distressed when he arrived, which is why I hope you don't mind me contacting you. My job is to provide discreet excellence Mrs Scroggins, and I emphasise the word *discreet*. As you know there are many stories played out in hotels and it is our duty to endeavour to be the three wise monkeys at all times.'

'See no evil, hear no....'

'Precisely, Mrs Scroggins. However, there are also times when I have to use discretionary *judgement* and - if you'll forgive me interfering - I felt this was one such occasion when my concierge's sixth sense was telling me to act.'

'Yes, of course...please, go on.'

'Having witnessed yourself and Mr Scroggins together and the happiness you obviously shared, the sight of him arriving here in the early hours dishevelled and deeply distressed, it was apparent something had gone terribly wrong, and so I tried to help and comfort him. He didn't want to communicate but simply requested the room you were in together.'

'The same room?'

'And the same table in the restaurant, laid for two people. He specifically requested that.'

'Oh, my poor Henry!' Millicent was unable to stop her tears and it was some minutes of sobbing before she could talk. All this time the concierge kindly and intermittently said 'I understand Mrs Scroggins, take your time, please, when you are ready.'

'I'm sorry, please go on. You said he was okay when he left.'

'Yes, and here, I believe, is the reason. We were feeling desperately sorry for him sitting alone at the table, looking so unhappy, still unshaven and his clothes crumpled and a wee bit grubby I might add, until the gentleman you were talking to the other evening, Mr Swadely, arrived and walked over to him.'

'Sean! God no!'

The concierge continued quickly, keen to impart news that would cheer Millicent. 'At first Mr Scroggins...'

'Please, will you call him Henry. And, I'm Millicent.'

'Certainly. Thank you Millicent. Well, at first Henry seemed to rebuff Mr Swadely quite rudely until Mr Swadely said something to him. You'll understand from what I am saying that I was observing them closely only as part of my concern for Henry and a wish to help.'

'Yes, of course. Thank you. So?'

'So whatever it was Mr Swadely said, had the instant effect of Henry taking notice and inviting him to sit down at his table - the same seat where you sat Millicent. Henry then ordered a bottle of port and the two of them became locked in conversation for about an hour, Mr Swadely leaning over and placing his arm around your husband's shoulder as comfort when he became upset once or twice. By the time they departed at about ten o'clock they were shaking hands and Henry was smiling, his heart a lot lighter than when he arrived, which delighted me, all of us, no end.'

'You're very kind...very kind. And you have no idea what Mr Swadely told him?'

'Oh, no. I would never listen in to a conversation, unless invited of course, but sometimes in this job there is the need, as I say, for *discretionary judgement* when I think that a small interference can bring about greater good. I hope that doesn't sound like me trying to play God but I....'

'You did the right thing and I cannot thank you enough for contacting me. I've been going insane with worry. He found something out about my past that I'd been meaning to tell him. In fact that was the reason for our night at your hotel. I was going to tell him but - but the words didn't come - I was terrified of wrecking our happiness and...'

'Millicent...' the concierge interrupted softly, '...there are no words required. I understand more than you can imagine. The reason I feel for others in love is because my heart has been badly broken. Twice. I thought beyond repair until...' Here he lost his voice for a moment. 'So I try to help.'

The good man quickly gathered his professional pride and decided he had done what he had to do and needed to get back to work. No doubt colleagues were hovering close by to add to his need to restore decorum. As a conclusion, he added:

'Do you have Mr Swadely's telephone number? If not I...'

'Thank you, I've got it. We know each other. Business.'

'Of course,' replied the discreet concierge, 'and if there's anything else I can do to help, please do not hesitate for one moment to ask. I do like happy endings.'

'Me too,' said Millicent distractedly. 'I suppose he didn't give any clue as to why he was going to Australia?'

'None at all. But possibly Mr Swadely can help. It was only after their rather animated conversation that Henry asked if I was able to book a flight for him. I couldn't do anything until the next morning but by the time he appeared for breakfast I'd managed to get a flight, via Sydney, for the following day. So he stayed one more night after taking some sea air.'

'Skimming stones,' murmured Millicent under her breath, words caught by the concierge.

'Yes, skimming stones,' repeated the concierge quietly. 'He was telling me how you skimmed stones on the beach and how he'd tried again but his arm was too sore.' Millicent let out a small tender laugh. 'And he said…he said it wasn't the same without his lovely gatherer.'

'He said that?'

'Yes, he spoke only lovingly of you. Everything will be well Millicent, I'm sure.'

A short silence followed as each struggled quietly to keep emotions in check. Eventually Millicent was able to speak.

'Thank you. I've never needed reassurance before but, well, things are…'

'Different.'

'Yes.'

It was apparent that enough had now been said, so they bid goodbye and spent a few moments in London and in Brighton privately composing themselves in true British tradition - with tea in bone china, biscuits, and slightly quivering stiff upper lips.

Chapter Thirty Four

# CONCERN OF A DIFFERENT KIND

In contrast to the good hearts concentrated on Henry's welfare, three contrasting souls were steeped in varying degrees of fermentation ranging from festering to bitter and none of them wasting any of their time or energy on stuff that wasn't wholly under the heading of Self-Interest.

Lily Bunce, who was at the lower festering end of the scale, had allowed her hurt and indignation to simmer for some days until it transmuted gradually into concern for her housebound 'friend' next door. She had of course called Irma Scroggins 'wicked - downright wicked!' during their last meeting and that would take a bit of reversing but Lily was nothing if not dogged in her belief that forgiveness comes to all those deserving of it and heaven knows in her time she'd had a bit of giving and receiving of forgiveness to do one way and another.

But this was different. This was a matter of life and death if Irma Scroggins didn't take her medication with Henry not being there (Lily had broken two glasses that week in the pursuit of checking this fact through the wall), not to mention starvation. Even in her remarkably recovered condition it was inconceivable that Irma Scroggins would be able to leave the house and get anywhere for provisions. It must be, Lily reckoned, at least three or four years since the old lady had been near a shop, apart from whizzing past in an ambulance to hospital, and their kitchen wasn't exactly well stocked at the best of times, so the chances were that she was down to her last crust.

The noise levels had also abated after a lot of banging, crashing and cursing during the days following Henry's departure, which Lily had guessed was a search for the letter. This had given Lily immense initial satisfaction but even that was soon tempered to concern for Irma Scroggins - and not a *little* concern for Lily Bunce - for a morbid silence had descended next door which even Lily's best crystal cut water tumbler couldn't penetrate. What would be the ramifications for her, the Good Samaritan, if Irma Scroggins' body lay rotting for weeks?

It was this horrible prospect that had caused Lily to tip-toe on Friday evening down the path of the Scroggins back garden, one careful foot at a time, eyes searching windows, breath held and many glances back towards the gate she'd left open for a quick escape if required. Not seeing any sign of life she'd called 'Coo-ee' softly several times when close to the house, then louder, and louder still, until she had convinced herself that a stiff body and not a living person was the other side of the back door.

So worried was the Good Samaritan that she hurried back home and scribbled a note which read 'Mrs S, if you need shopping write it darn on the back of this paper and leave it under the buckit. If you don't I'll call the police becos I'm worrid about yer. Lily.' She then crept back and poked it through the gap between the door and the frame, watching it flutter to the kitchen floor.

The next morning she crept back again and, to her great relief, found the note under the bucket with the words printed in shaky capitals 'TEA, MILK, BREAD, SPAM, CHEESE.' Not a 'please' or 'thank you' that would give the concerned lady any faint hope of reconciliation but then those words of gratitude never flew over the cracked old lips in the best of times and so were unlikely to be forthcoming in these, the very worst of times. But 'clinger to straws' that Lily was, she clung to the note as if it had been the last lifebelt on the Titanic, toddling off to the supermarket to do what she did best, tirelessly think of others. It also indicated that Irma Scroggins had probably been taking her medication, medication that her son had been careful enough to flush down the toilet every time he replaced it with a crunched up aspirin. Meticulous as ever, Henry had made sure that this vital stone was never left unturned in the event of prying eyes ever discovering the tablets. Right on time he had called for his mother's repeat prescription at the doctors - and right on time each day he flushed it lovingly away.

Inside the house Irma Scroggins was indeed, as the note would indicate, still breathing, if only through force-feeding herself decaying broccoli, asparagus tips and other disgusting remnants of Henry's new diet - until Lily's life-saving note appeared on the floor.

Mainly to conserve energy and cause Lily Bunce maximum concern, she'd remained silently in bed since giving up her search for the letter on Thursday, but had reached the point where some sort of action had to be taken. She knew there was really only one thing for it; she had to contact Archibald Snapes by hook or by crook, reveal that she knew of his conspiracy - or at least, lull him into a confessional trap - and then once discovering the depth of his complicity with her missing son and the amount of money involved, take whatever measures were required to ensure the guilty were punished.

As for what to do about Lily Bunce and whatever part she played, that was a pleasure to be saved and savoured for when the meddling woman's use had expired.

Finally, the arch-conspirator himself, Archibald Snapes; how had he chosen to spend his time since discovering - wrongly, but that's beside the point - Henry's deception? What had been going through his boulder of a skull to ensure his avaricious scheme wasn't uncovered? How could he ensure the wealth that had consumed his thoughts since first opening the letter from Australia was still his for the taking? He'd had no contact with Henry since their meeting in the wine bar and no knowledge of whether the sad little man had returned to the house since leaving, or even what had transpired between him and his mother. He was, undoubtedly, more in the dark than he'd wish but darkness was never something that had bothered this man, being as comfortable with dark thoughts and deeds as he was in finding his way out of dark corners.

It had without doubt gone slightly awry for him on learning that far from being on death's door, Irma Scroggins had not only the full power of speech but apparently the power to mutter vindictive words about her son, but if she had no idea about the letter's existence then the door was still open for fruitful negotiations with Henry.

That Henry must be found was therefore imperative and this was consuming his thoughts far too much for his sound mental state of health, so in true legal tradition he decided to sit back and let Time, that trusty conundrum solver, do its job. At least for another week.

Chapter Thirty Five

# HENRY WRITES FROM AUSTRALIA

At the Ministry, the mood in Henry's department was one of quiet resignation once the staff had got over the shock of learning that their new manager had mysteriously vanished to Australia and wasn't returning to work. That was all they knew apart from the fact that he'd done nothing illegal and a teasing, if not incredible, intimation from John Deighton that an affair of the heart lay behind his troubles.

Millicent had met John Deighton for lunch the Monday following her conversation with the concierge - exactly a week to the day she went with Henry to Brighton - and had told him everything about her past life; everything that is apart from Peregrine Spencer and the Minister being long term former clients of the exclusive *Carter Consultancy* of which there was now only one member, and he strictly non-paying.

John had been pleasantly surprised on meeting Millicent, never having knowingly been in the company of a lady of such class and refinement but whose fifteen-year profession could not immediately be associated with those qualities.

The thoughts jangling in his head as she spoke to him whilst he sipped his cappuccino and nibbled at a prawn sandwich, thoughts of what the lady seated opposite him had seen and done, had him teetering on the verge of excitement, especially being the one-woman devoted family man that he was.

For the first time in his life since childhood he felt a bit naughty, in the dirty-book-behind-the-lavatory-cistern way; the combination of Millicent's refinement and sexual exploits (and heaven knows what they entailed) exuding stirrings that he had to keep at bay, constantly reminding himself of his own matrimonial loyalty and that this was Henry's lady. But such was the magnetism of Millicent's God-given gift on which she had traded unremittingly and enjoyably since making her somewhat unorthodox post-graduate career choice, that by the time it came

317

for parting after lunch - they having gained mutual comfort in the knowledge that Henry was for the time being safe and that they'd keep in touch - John strolled back to his office with Millicent's voice singing softly in his head and her pretty face invading his work until at least the afternoon tea break; somewhat unsettling for a good family man.

The Saturday following this meeting a letter dropped through Millicent's letterbox bearing an airmail sticker. She crouched to pick it up and her heart fluttered slightly until she recognised the writing as Henry's and the fluttering turned to pounding.

Walking back into the lounge she placed the envelope on her coffee table and glided silently to the kitchen, flicking on the kettle whilst eyeing the envelope through the doorway, not unlike Henry on the 23rd December when the sight of Millicent moving through the semi-darkness in bra and pants had elicited a similar effect on his virgin body and mind. How strange that within four short months - the date was now the 26th April - he should be able to stir Millicent in the same way.

George was now reading situations well. The 'uncles' had long since stopped arriving, giving him the luxury of his mistress's almost undivided attention, barring odd visits of the one uncle with whom he'd had a late night glove tussle some time ago. So George wasn't bothering to leave the sofa or cushion quite so readily now, apart from when his collar and lead were rattled, and even that had lost its novelty.

Millicent sat on the sofa and, after drinking half her cup of strong coffee, opened the envelope and gently took out the letter, of which there were several pages.

The address was Unit 5, Tolchard Close, Orchard Boulevard, Surfer's Paradise, Queensland, Australia, dated Friday 18th April 1981. Even to her experienced eyes it all sounded very glamorous and smelling of sun-kissed beaches, tanned bodies and sidewalk cafes; which indeed it was. She read:

*My Dear Millicent,*

*Where do I start? With a very big apology I think. Firstly, I'm well and you're not to worry about me. Secondly I hope you can forgive me for what I've done, running away, and for thinking you'd betrayed me.*

*I'm sure you'll know by now from John Deighton that I returned to the hotel in Brighton. I was very upset and they were so kind to me, the concierge especially. I'd decided to end it all, drown myself off the pier or jump in front of a train at the station - something dramatic that would hurt you. Isn't that an awful thing to confess and yes it was my honest intention in my madness. But first I had to go back to <u>our</u> room and sit at <u>our</u> table, and imagine like a child who wants every day to be Christmas that all my unhappiness would disappear. I even walked along the beach and saw us skimming stones and along the pier feeling your hair on my cheek and the smell of your perfume. Oh dear, I'm sounding like a silly lovelorn boy aren't I but that's just it - I am and I always will be I'm afraid. Please excuse my silliness Millicent.*

*Something strange then happened. A miracle I think, help often coming from the most unexpected of places? Is that what you said to me once? Or did I say it to you? It doesn't matter but your friend Sean Swadely arrived in the restaurant, the last person I wanted to see after his being such a nuisance at our table. What he told me, over a bottle of port - yes I can now say the port is to blame (in the best possible way) - was only what I forced out of him, and I mean <u>forced</u>. He didn't want to betray you as I thought you'd betrayed me.*

*He told me he'd known you for a long time and that you'd had a relationship with him, as you had with others of course – <u>please Millicent</u>, before you worry, I understand completely and how dare I stand in judgement over you? What right have I who stumbled, literally, into your life, to think I own you and your past and everything else? What a stupid arrogant fool, but then, I've never been in love before and I didn't know what to expect and how to act and…oh heavens above, here I go again. Millicent I love you with all my heart. I love you and miss you so much it's making me ache just sitting here. I hope you still like me after what I've done and how I've acted and that we can still be friends.*

*Sean told me that in all the years he'd known you he'd never seen you like you've been since we met. That you had always been lovely but always 'strictly business' as he put it, no emotional attachment, and that the night you met to discuss his purchase of your flat, he'd 'tried it on' (sorry, his words) but it was evident that there was no chance. You told him you'd given up everything because you'd met the unlikeliest of men who made you feel like doing the most unlikeliest of things - that's how he put it anyway - devoting your life to someone. Someone who had won your heart against all the odds. Did I do that Millicent? Did I really? Heavens, how did it happen? Boring little old Henry*

*Scroggins. But thank you, thank you so much my darling. I've never written that before....'my darling'.*

*So why did I come to Australia? I'm sure you've guessed by now from everything I've told you about my father. I had to meet the people who knew him, who worked with him, who could tell me what he was really like and if, if he ever mentioned me. Well, I've discovered a lot Millicent, too much to put in this letter but all I can say is that there never was a son more proud of a father who, far from having forgotten all about me, has lived with guilt over abandoning and not knowing me and was obsessed about it. And - I'm sorry, I can hardly write this without crying, in fact I am crying - look at the silly tears on this page, hold on, I've got to get a tissue - back now - and that he came back to England and stood outside my house and followed me to work, even standing behind me at Charing Cross when I bought an apple, until I went into my office. And the poor man, my poor own dear father, hadn't been able to talk to me. Me. He was so ashamed of himself and couldn't talk to me. Can you believe that Millicent? Can you really believe that? Oh, I'm snivelling again, I'll get a drink and be back in a minute. (Say hello to George for me.)*

Millicent, almost blinded by tears herself, looked down at George beside her, smiled through her damp eyes as she placed the unfinished letter on the coffee table.

'Humans, George,' she said, tickling his ear, 'think yourself lucky you're not one.'

George wagged his tail, instinctively knowing that his mistress was showing signs of happiness again after what had seemed to him a lot of anxiety. Millicent went into the kitchen and poured a second coffee, imagining Henry at that moment actually getting himself a drink in Australia before returning to finish writing.

She picked up the letter and read on.

*That's better. I've discovered gin and tonic by the way, with ice and lemon. So beautifully refreshing in this climate. I could soon be an alcoholic. Well, what can I say, what a place, what an astonishingly different world. Palm trees, golden beaches that go on forever, warm sea (I've been in twice) everyone in shorts and open necked shirts even in the banks and offices, suntanned girls in little gold bikinis and gold purses who feed the parking meters so nobody gets booked! Yes it's true! This place where I'm staying, in one of Father's apartments by the way, goes by the absurd name of Surfer's Paradise. It's like a mini Manhattan stuck on the edge of the Pacific Ocean where Rolls Royces and surf buggies (I'm learning the 'lingo' already) glide along side by side down the main street and everyone seems to be happy, relaxed and smiling.*

*Father is something of a celebrity and his properties are everywhere. I've even had my first ever massage by a Pink Lady! Are you laughing? I hope so. I've had many conversations with people who knew my father well and there never was a more respected and admired man. By the honest ones that is. He also has enemies, people who tried to cheat him and paid the price. There's so much to tell you Millicent and I don't know what the future holds but whatever happens I want you to see what my father had done with his life, what he'd achieved. And all with his wonderful Betty who left him broken-hearted last year when she died. They say he never recovered his humour and love of life, that he actually died when she died. He had mentioned my mother many times too over the years, saying what an evil woman she was, and was always talking about changing his will but like most successful men, believed he was invincible and had plenty of time to do it. But that doesn't matter, the old bag is welcome to everything. All I wanted to know I have now found out. He had never forgotten me and I hope, perhaps in his own way, he loved me a little.*

*And I love you Millicent and I can't wait to come home to you if you'll have me back. But we must come here for a holiday. You must see it! Please.*

*I've got some things to sort out before I leave which I'll tell you about later but I think I should be catching a plane in about a week's time, if I don't get too used to these massages and gin and tonics. Can you believe I'm saying this - Henry Scroggins, who was so naïve he believed you were a solicitor. Oh, how stupid of me, how idiotic. What did you think, you poor thing, once we'd started to become friends and you couldn't tell me? Millicent, I can't imagine how awful it must have been for you and what a buffoon I must have seemed - but that doesn't matter now. Not to me anyway. Thank you so much for sticking by me and for everything you've done for me.*

*I'm going out to a barbecue tonight at the home of my father's business partner who lives in this magnificent canal side mansion with his own helipad would you believe! You've no idea what a celebrity I am with everyone who works for his business. Ridiculous isn't it, me a celebrity, I've been treated like the Prince in waiting and some have even said I have his mannerisms (and bald head) although I talk much posher. I truly feel like the Son of the Father, a most wonderful feeling.*

*Please call John at work and tell him I'm well and to give my best wishes and deep apologies to all the staff. I can't go back now but I just want them to know I wasn't myself at the time, and now I am. That's all.*

*It's easy saying I love you in writing but I don't think I can when we're face to face. Bit of a coward aren't I, so just in case I don't ever say it at least you know it's what's in my heart. I feel the luckiest man on earth to have found you, and now to have 'found' my father. I'll try and telephone when I know my flight date and time.*

*Thinking of you all the time.*

*Your loving Henry XXX*

Millicent smiled at what looked like King Henry the Thirtieth, got up and walked to the window overlooking the park, George padding quietly to her feet as if to let her know he was happy she was happy. She bent down and picked him up, tucking him under her arm and showing him the green expanse before them. His eyes searched here and there, nose twitching with the smells that wafted over the balcony, until letting out a bark that made Millicent jump and put him back down again.

'Come on George, let's go for a walk shall we? A happy walk.'

In recognition of the warmth effusing from every pore in his mistress's body and every note in her musical voice, his tail began to wag and he ran to his lead.

Never had Millicent embraced the park like she did that morning. Every tree, every shrub, every waking living thing that presented itself to her was like a friend she wanted to hug and thank and dance with. She really wanted to dance. She wanted to dance so much that George found himself in her arms, serenading, ears and whiskers horizontal and legs a little unsteady when his paws came to rest on the grass.

He couldn't remember Millicent ever running before but he felt it his duty to join in and chase her and run madly in circles, yelping for…he didn't quite know what.

## Chapter Thirty Six

## LILY DEFIANT AND THE WILMOT'S DARK SECRET

Irma Scroggins did something she hadn't done for over five years. She left the house by the back door and walked the short distance past the rubbish bins and weed strewn patch of grass and pavings melding into one, to the back gate, where she struggled cursing for a moment with the latch before entering the mysterious world of the back alley. She stuck her Corialanian nose out first, guiding it left and right like a rudder to see what had changed since its last foray, then turned left, walked ten or so paces, stood and stared at Lily Bunce's gate and, reaching out a bony fist, turned the circular black, metal handle which clunked briskly into action.

Unhindered by bolts, she found herself peering down the much neater, prettier domain of Bunce world. The small narrow lawn, already rich green and lush, was lined with a bed of yellow and purple crocuses between lawn and pristine path. The large shed on the right and as far from the house as it could possibly be erected, was once the chief principality of the 'bullet-free' Wilfred. It had remained untouched since his demise; neat, tidy and double-padlocked; tools in all their right receptacles; nails and screws in bottles all labelled in his very neat printing, and several feet beneath this, several generations of spider and other insect corpses lay in the still remaining dregs at the bottom of Guinness bottles hidden from view under the bench, the creatures having gone the way that many men dream about.

Irma Scroggins hobbled down the path. Hobbled because that was the natural way of her scrawny, bowed, underemployed legs but even more so now because they'd spent a lot of time recently in a levitated position and had certainly not walked this sort of distance for some while.

On arrival at the Bunce back door she looked in and upwards for signs of life, cocked her head for the same purpose and concluding that something vocal was required, shouted out 'Lily Bunce! *Lily Bunce*! Are you there?'

A curtain twitched ten feet above the bald circle on the Scroggins head now peering through the glass of the back door. Feet were soon on the stairs and hurrying into the kitchen whilst mutterings of 'Oh, my good gawd, whatever next?' accompanied them.

Strained attempts at warm grimaces were quickly exchanged through the glass as the door was unlocked, unbolted and opened - quite a lengthy procedure which did nothing for the Scroggins temper. Without being invited in, Irma Scroggins was over the dark red stone threshold and pushing her way past her shocked neighbour before breathlessly turning and speaking.

'I want to know one thing Lily Bunce, one thing only and there will be no come back, no blame.' A pause, then, 'Did you open that letter?'

'What letter Mrs S? What letter's this then?' spluttered the desperate Lily.

'You know what letter! The one from my solicitor you damn fool! Don't play your silly games again with me woman!'

Lily was suddenly incensed and terrified all at once and reacted without a thought for the consequences. She had nothing to lose, their 'friendship' apparently doomed forever and Henry presumably having left home. She didn't care one hoot about mother or son and - she was angry; *very* angry. And the more she stood and looked at the old hag who had invaded her house as if she owned it, the angrier and stronger she grew.

'Yes I did Irma Scroggins! Yes I did and I don't care! There!'

Irma Scroggins' eyes blazed and her nostrils flared. This was indignation and delight; indignation that Lily Bunce had dared to do it and delight that she would now reveal the contents.

'What was in it? What did it say? Tell me, or I'll...!'

She took a step towards Lily who backed off, one hand held behind her gripping the kitchen top and the other stretched out in front to stop any further advance of the lunatic whom she thought had murder in her eyes. Which the lunatic did, but not for anything as worthless as an interfering old woman like Lily Bunce - just for her missing son.

'It said your 'usband was dead and he'd left loads of money and propity. Millyins, to you Irma Scroggins, all to you! In Orstralia. He must have been mad! Mad! Like you! Now get out! Get out of my house!'

And with that she grabbed Irma Scroggins by the arm and with strength gathered from who knows where, propelled the woman out of the door, which she slammed, locked and bolted in a flash! Both of their bosoms heaved like pistons, one full blown and vigorous, the other a threadbare concave cardigan pumping in and out, as they stood glaring at each other through the glass pane like two cats taking a breather from a vicious scrap, teeth set in silent, seething rage-filled faces until Irma Scroggins raised a fist which she shook at Lily Bunce and then stalked off down the path at twice the speed she'd entered, through the gate she'd left open on entering, and leaving it in the exact same state.

Lily Bunce had never in her life shaken as she was shaking then. She had never physically 'attacked' anyone in her life - not even Wilfred at his most cantankerous - and although the physical expulsion of Irma Scroggins from her kitchen had been forcible and could never be considered an attack, in Lily's mind it was, and she was both shocked and proud and not a little relieved; relieved to have had the bravado to do it but more so in having the secret out in the open, whatever the consequences. It was like a cleansing, an exorcism, a lifetime's domination now finally over - and she didn't give a damn! Not a tinker's cuss!

Oh how the kettle was filled! Oh how the switch was flicked on with panache and the cup plonked with meaningful resolution onto the kitchen top! Oh how the milk was poured and the sugar spooned, some even finding its way into the cup! And oh how the jaw was set in grim determination that she, Lily Bunce, was from now on her own woman and nothing - least of all an evil bully like Irma Scroggins - was ever going to change that! What a feeling! What a victory! What a *martyr!*

Next door, meanwhile, Irma Scroggins had one thing on her mind. The incident with Lily Bunce had become ancient history the moment she walked back into her own house and stared out of her parlour window, calculating her next move. It was

Wednesday, one week since Henry had left and wherever he was and whatever he was planning, she had to get in touch with Bodger and Snapes. Of that there was not one shadow of doubt.

Where there's a will there's a way and never before in the field of human endeavour had two wills combined to stir a potential corpse into a dangerous - exceedingly dangerous - fire-breathing dragon. One was a will of seemingly endless numbers and noughts that constituted the will of Henry Arthur Scroggins, late of Australia, and the other the iron will of his wife who, if ever a will was going to find a way, then she possessed it. Add these twin powers together and you have a sum of considerable, possibly immoveable, force.

The office of Bodger and Snapes was just ten minutes away on a bus. It had been many years since Irma Scroggins had cause to use any public transport but now she'd made the brief exploit next door to Lily Bunce's and broken the housebound taboo, even John o' Groats or Land's End wouldn't have troubled her for what she had to do. But it just so happened that the mission she was about to undertake, of getting to Whiteheath Village and the office of her solicitors, was going to be made infinitely easier than she expected.

The first thing, having decided to take the bus, was to find out the bus *times*; so she'd put on her coat and hat - items of clothing that for some time had not travelled further than the back threshold where she'd been forced to venture beyond on particularly cold winter days after Henry had selfishly forgotten to fill up the coal scuttle before leaving for work. Having donned the clothes she then set forth to the nearest bus stop several streets away and was peering at the bus times when a car pulled up and a window wound down revealing the smiling face of none other than Mr Reginald Wilmot, verger of St. Michael's and All Angels and recently damned hedonist neighbour of Viola Street.

'My-my, Mrs Scroggins, how good to see you up and about after all this time. Can I give you a lift?' chortled the irritatingly cheerful man.

Irma Scroggins natural reaction to such cheerfulness was generally to scowl and rebuke but one as cunning as she did not look gift horses in mouths, especially a gift horse that could race her plan of action along the track apace, a race of which there was really not a moment to waste. She smiled a cracked smile, forcing long dormant muscles into action and, being already by nature half bent, didn't have to bend much further to see into the car.

'Mr Wilmot, how kind of you. I'm looking for the times of buses to Whiteheath. Got to go and see my solicitor about something.'

Reginald Wilmot was thrilled to hear this. 'That's very fortunate 'cos Mrs Wilmot and me's going there this afternoon. Can it wait till then 'cos we'll give you a lift if you so wish.'

Irma Scroggins' smile spread into an expression that Uriah Heep himself could not have bettered and within seconds had accepted the offer, agreed a time of two-thirty to meet outside her house and insisted on walking back home from the bus stop to 'loosen up the varicoses'.

Mr Wilmot had driven off with that edifying thought in his mind and a frown of some discomfiture, but nevertheless very pleased that he'd had his first conversation with what he considered a prodigal neighbour who had accepted his hand of friendship after such a long period of silent enmity. He felt in the centre of a biblical moment and if Irma Scroggins had risen from the pavement flapping her arms with a white feather in her mouth it would never have surprised him. He'd waited a long time for his miracle and was prepared for anything.

At two-twenty-five the rare sight of Irma Scroggins appeared outside her front gate with handbag clasped to the stomach area of her drab brown coat whilst trying to quell feelings of impatience at the Wilmots not spotting her early arrival and instantly hastening out in honour of her presence. At precisely two-thirty-one the three of them were settled inside the Wilmot's purple Ford Escort with a sulking young male Wilmot jammed so hard against the car door as to appear welded to it, all to avoid risking contact with the demonic looking old woman sharing the back seat. The journey out of Lewisham town centre weaving through traffic up the hill to Whiteheath was not a long one and time was precious for the Wilmots if they were to worm out of their neighbour all the news they required.

The conversation was stilted at first as is common with people reunited after so many years who, with so much to say often end up saying very little, but the Wilmots being polite, sociable people and unable to bear silences of more than two seconds soon had the banter in full swing enquiring after Henry and Lily Bunce's welfare and how she, Irma, was, after her illness which they'd been very worried about.

Irma Scroggins was not about to impart any intimate details so she mumbled a bare minimum of information until, on entering the village high street and being asked where she wanted to be dropped, discovered that her solicitors were in fact the Wilmot's solicitors.

'Bodger and Snapes?' exclaimed the two adult Wilmots in unison.

'More like Snakes,' added Mrs Wilmot.

'With his reputation,' improved Mr Wilmot.

'Why?' asked Irma Scroggins, 'What's he done?'

'What *hasn't* he done, more like?' said Mrs Wilmot with a peremptory nod and deep sucking of a large percentage of the air inside the car to eliminate any lingering doubts. 'Murder - that's what!'

'Doris!' scolded her husband. 'We don't know nothing and it's not for us to go spreading malicious gossip without proof. It's not Christian and I won't have it, you know that.'

As he eased the car off the road and into the car park under the offices of Bodger and Snapes, the long grey whiskers above Irma Scroggins' top lip visibly twitched as her mouth twisted in anticipation of something juicy about to fall from above.

'What do you mean…*murder*?' she enquired.

Mrs Wilmot, chastised into silence by her husband, stared ahead and shrugged as the car came to a halt and the handbrake creaked on.

'It's been common knowledge amongst our people at the church, Mrs Scroggins, that Bodger, that's Mr Bodger - a nice quiet man he was as you know - met his maker, how can I put it…*unwillingly*,' said Mr Wilmot, forced into offering some sort of tepid explanation by his more forthright, impulsive wife.

The young Wilmot was now taking interest and had prised himself off the door and was gripping the seat in front containing his silent, deep breathing mother.

'You mean 'ee killed 'im!' shrieked the boy gleefully, his round face and small eyes lighting up like a Halloween pumpkin. 'Stuck 'im in the gizzards!' he embellished, 'like this!'

And he made to run Irma Scroggins through her middle, from a safe distance across the car seat.

'Oswald!' snapped his father turning and staring fiercely at his son, 'now just you stop that before I clip y'bloomin' ear!'

The boy sank back into his door, sulking out of the window.

As they got out of the car the Wilmots waited until their son became distracted by a punctured plastic football lying in a litter-strewn corner of the car park and then rapidly proceeded to give Irma Scroggins their idea of a brief outline of what it seemed everyone except her knew and which they now felt committed to share in view of her impending meeting with someone who she obviously believed to be respectable.

The circumstances of what they had heard went as follows; all suspicions surrounding the death of David Bodger hinged on an eyewitness statement by one of the congregation of St. Michael & All Angels church who happened to be in the wine bar the night of the unfortunate man's death. The young member of the congregation, as he was at the time, was holding his stag party at a restaurant in the village but warming up with a few friends at the wine bar. Being a Friday evening the bar was packed with mainly younger people who enjoyed the Spanish atmosphere with flamenco music and a Sangria happy hour that had become popular between seven and eight.

The pair of solicitors who walked in from across the road, on nodding terms with most of the youngsters, were soon encouraged to loosen their ties and jackets and join in the fun. After all, a chap doesn't get married every day. The happy hour had turned into a happy two hours during which some of the crowd had become uneasy at the way the larger, louder of the two solicitors seemed to be trying to get his friend drunk. The slim, quiet, bespectacled man had looked very drawn and sallow when he entered and they'd at first assumed his larger partner was just trying to cheer him up but soon a few mutterings went around that the quiet man was constantly trying to resist the rapid supply of cheap Sangria and beers, followed by a reluctant introduction to Tequila by the other man, even to the point where the imminent groom had asked him to 'ease up a bit' on his friend who was very unsteady when trying to make his way to the toilet at the back of the bar, colliding with the melee of tables and chairs and sending glasses flying.

Eventually the stag party had moved from the wine bar to the restaurant, first checking on the dazed, pale solicitor as they made their exit but being reassured by the big man that he'd be taking him home soon and all would be well. However, almost two hours later when the stag party were leaving the restaurant in high spirits, their jocularity ceased on seeing the big solicitor almost dragging the thin solicitor across the road and into the car park area beneath the office building. From a distance of some fifty yards they'd watched Snapes unlock a car, a new white Cortina, and bodily lift his burden into the driving seat. The big man had then straightened up and looked around at which time the four remaining members of the stag party had ducked behind a wall and with too much alcohol inside them to concentrate on anything further than getting themselves home, disbanded.

It wasn't until the local papers were delivered the following week that the front page revealed how a forty-seven year old solicitor, David Bodger, had been found dead in his car in the early hours of Saturday morning, having died from carbon monoxide poisoning. The keys were in the ignition and a hosepipe trailed from the exhaust pipe into the boot. The coroner's verdict of suicide went unquestioned, despite the dead man's distraught wife insisting that he would never do such a thing to her and their two daughters, was not a drinker, and would certainly not dream of driving his car after one drink, let alone several. It was entirely out of character. But then came the terrible revelation that David Bodger was terminally ill with prostate cancer, a secret he had kept from his family and only divulged to his close friend and partner Archibald Snapes. This man, helped through his emotionally charged evidence by a large handkerchief and several short adjournments, told how his dear friend had not been able to break the news to his family and was hoping for a miracle but - and this is where the distraught Snapes had to take his longest break - being the man David Bodger was, he decided to sacrifice himself rather than force his family to watch his decline and then have to care for him. Archibald Snapes' distress was such that poor Mrs Bodger was the one who was left comforting the large sobbing man outside the coroner's court and telling him that he couldn't have done any more.

And it was true - he couldn't.

As for the stag party, yes they'd discussed it and had their suspicions but the more time passed and they'd not publicly voiced their thoughts, the harder it became to say a word about what they'd witnessed. Not until almost a year later when the newly-married man, in a weak moment of confessional over early signs of trouble in his marriage, had also decided the time was right to share what he'd witnessed in the wine bar the night of David Bodger's death, the only problem being that he'd chosen not the vicar to offer up his confession, but the verger - Mr Reginald Wilmot. This well-meaning man, feeling it his duty to entrust his wife with the extraordinary story, ignited a wildfire that within a week had spread way beyond the church and remained a secret many times over.

This telling of the tale by the Wilmots on the very spot where the deed had occurred eight years and three months earlier had taken rather less than ten minutes, ten valuable minutes during which young Oswald Wilmot had kept up a constant battering of the punctured football against the car park wall and for once in his life not been ordered to stop doing something which he enjoyed. By the time he slunk back to his parents after being called, they were getting back into the car and listening to reassurances from the old lady who stood outside that she'd find her own way home on the bus after getting some shopping.

Irma Scroggins stood alone as the car drove out of the parking area. She sniffed like a dog catching a scent, which indeed she had, and surveyed the area for a few quiet moments before clanking slowly up an iron staircase at the side of the building until she stood on the top grid before a black board with gold lettering that read *Bodger and Snapes, Solicitors and Commissioner for Oaths.*

It was about two minutes of motionless deep thought and flickering smiles and frowns later that the white, granite knuckles of her right hand hesitantly moved upwards before rapping firmly on the door.

## Chapter Thirty Seven

## MILLICENT AND HENRY REUNITED

The man who walked casually behind a luggage trolley through the arrivals gate at Heathrow Airport to the welcoming smile and embrace of Millicent Carter was not the man she had last seen. It wasn't just the tan and the clothes - Henry sported a pair of nicely fitting brown jeans, yellow Fred Perry shirt with a green palm tree motif and brown leather casual shoes over bare feet - it was the confident air and whimsical grin when he first noticed her and the way he responded to her touch. After all, Henry had had massages; several.

Millicent took two steps back as he posed with arms folded and one foot on his trolley, shoulders ramrod straight. She studied him as would a wealthy racehorse owner buying a new colt, finger to lips and elbow of the same arm supported by the hand of the other. She put her head critically on one side and then nodded approvingly before grinning broadly, tossing her hair back with a flick of her pretty head and once more embracing her man, pressing a lingering kiss on his cheek. She drew back, holding his arms with both her hands.

'You look wonderful Henry!'

'So do you Millicent. Even more adorable than the adorable I remember.'

Millicent smiled and, her face still being close to his, aimed a small peck on his nose. 'Oh thank you Henry. How sweet. You must be tired.'

'Not a bit,' he said, taking her breath and perfume inside his head and almost reeling with desire. 'I've travelled back First Class and slept like a log. Not sure whether it was the champagne and oysters or the soothing attention of the cabin crew; possibly both. Awfully extravagant but I'd been so spoilt by Father's people that it was hard to give it up all of a sudden.'

'So you've learnt a lot about him,' said Millicent threading her arm through his as they weaved their way through the crowds, both looking for an exit sign before Millicent pointed up at one and they steered towards it, locked like Siamese twins, Henry almost losing control of his trolley and inducing laughter from them both.

'Everything, I believe. An extraordinary man. You read my letter?'

'Yes, thank you, it was lovely. I can't tell you how desperately worried I was and the enormous relief when that dropped through my door. I thought you'd...'

Henry nodded at the ground as they walked along. 'I nearly did.' He threw a sideways glance at Millicent who was also nodding in acknowledgement.

'Yes,' she said, 'you mentioned it in your letter.'

'I just thought you'd betrayed me and I...it wasn't what you'd been...I mean your profession...that was all my stupid fault getting that wrong...but it was just that I didn't think we had any secrets and, the shock and everything, and...'

Millicent stopped and gently pulled Henry's arm. He let go of the trolley to face her.

'Henry, we wouldn't be here now, together, if you hadn't got *it* wrong.'

This statement took Henry a few jet-lagged moments to work out the meaning, before slowly nodding and turning to peer into her eyes.

'When did you realise?'

'When you were asleep on my sofa the night we met. It suddenly hit me. Nothing made sense and then...'

'The penny dropped.'

'Oh boy, did it drop.'

'What a stupid, stupid, fool I was. You poor thing stuck with a drunken idiot who'd never had sex in his life and thought you were a solicitor! The times I think of that - and every time the shame hits me and blood rushes up so that...'

'You were *very* drunk - and *very* confused.'

'Both of us.'

'God yes, I certainly was. Not drunk, but totally confused.'

People rushed past them tutting and 'excuse me'ing' as the couple stood obstructing the entrance to a set of swing doors. Suddenly aware of the mayhem they were causing, Henry manoeuvred Millicent by her elbow with one hand, dragging his trolley with the other, to a window overlooking the multi-storey car park. He looked her in the eyes again.

'Millicent, darling?'

'Yes, Henry, dear.' Her expression was of a child being gently lectured by a parent for an innocent prank, the child trying to be serious but still seeing the funny side of it.

'Oh my, you do look so gorgeous,' whispered Henry, distracted momentarily.

'Thank you. You were about to say. Millicent, darling...'

'Yes. Millicent - will you please...' Henry glanced around to check for interlopers. Millicent followed his glance before they returned to face each other. She looked slightly up at him, nodding for him to continue, wide-eyed and expectant.

'Millicent, will you please marry me?'

Millicent stared at him for a second or two until his face became blurred by tears. Blinking, she placed an arm around his neck, oblivious to onlookers or anything at that moment, and rising on tip-toe placed her lips softly to his, leaving them there for him to feel the full softness and meaning of her response. She moved them away just for a moment before pressing them back and then recoiling to look him in the eyes.

'Is that a yes?'

Millicent dabbed her eyes with the back of her hand and nodded without moving her eyes from his.

'An absolute yes, Henry, an absolute yes. I love you so much.'

A voice passing by quipped 'Lucky man' and they both turned to see a smile from an elegant, middle-aged lady with an attractive, tanned face which had turned to acknowledge their obvious happiness as she strode on.

'Excuse me,' called Henry to the lady, 'excuse me but would you mind doing something for me - please?'

The lady stopped and flashed a look of such high eye-browed inquisitiveness that you'd think Henry had dropped his trousers.

'Go on?' she said, walking back towards them clutching her brown leather valise.

'I've just asked this beautiful lady to marry me and I'd like a witness. In case she changes her mind.'

Millicent flashed a glance from Henry to the lady, and shrugged. The lady also shrugged, absorbed the delightful humour of the situation and the innocence of the nervous, excited suitor and settled into the part with instant fervour.

'How delightfully romantic,' she replied. 'Then why not? Firstly, can I establish that you know each other?' She delivered this important enquiry with her head on one side and switched towards each of them in turn. Millicent squeezed Henry's hand and put her head on his shoulder.

'Good,' said the lady, 'and do you, um....'

'Millicent,' helped Henry.

'Do you Millicent,' continued the lady, 'accept this man....'

'Henry,' said Millicent, as Henry gratefully looked at her.

'Henry's hand in marriage on this day the sixteenth of June at Heathrow Airport?' With brow knitted she scanned around. 'So very romantic - good choice of venue.'

'I do,' said Millicent, looking at Henry.

'In that case,' said the lady, 'I hereby pronounce you fiancées. Is that what you want?'

'That sounds just wonderful to me, don't you think Millicent?'

Henry turned to his fiancée to be met with a broad smile of approval.

'Thank you so much,' said Henry, first to Millicent and then to the elegant lady who was busy delving into her handbag from which she produced a business card that she thrust towards him.

'Here,' she said, 'my card. Just in case there's any dispute about the offer and the acceptance. Beyond that - the marriage etc - may I wish you all the happiness in the world. I thought I was lucky once but it wasn't to be. That's life. Whatever you do, be faithful to each other. Anything else can be overcome but not infidelity. Goodbye.' And with that her face creased into a painful smile and she turned and walked off without a glance back in their direction.

The newly engaged couple watched her go before Millicent took the card from Henry's fingertips and read, 'Marjory Spencer, The Hollies...'

Her mouth dropped open and she stared up at the departing figure.

'Spencer?' said Henry, 'What a coincidence. That's the name of...Millicent?'

He followed Millicent's stare at the woman's figure disappearing into the crowd. She was in something of a daze having lowered her eyes back to the card and then to a speck on Henry's shirt. She reached forward and flicked the speck with a corner of the card.

'It's his wife,' muttered Millicent, looking up into Henry's face that had already taken on the appearance of a recently landed cod gasping for air, 'can you believe it?'

Recovering her senses Millicent stared after the woman in amazement. 'But surely you recognised her Henry. You've worked with Spencer for twenty years.'

Henry, rooted in gaping disbelief, shook his head.

'I've never met her before. Just spoken to her on the phone, that's all. But more to the point Millicent, how do you know it's her? Spencer isn't exactly an unusual name.'

Millicent took a deep breath and was going to show him the card with the address she knew well, but stopped. 'I'll tell you the rest at my flat. Come on, let's get a taxi.'

'No,' said Henry without hesitation, 'Millicent, I've decided - on the plane that is - that I'm going straight to my mother's house - *my* house. If she's alive - and I hope to God she's not - she's going to be the first, no second, third, *fourth* - to know that you are going to be my wife. I was going to go straight there anyway, whether you agreed to marry me or not. I'd already planned to ask you as soon as we met here, you see, because I've got business to sort out with her which will not be easy whether she's recovered or still paralysed, but sorted out immediately it must be before I take another step forward. I've also got to see that solicitor, Snapes, and tell him just what I think of his deal. My father is now on my shoulder Millicent, in everything I do. I know the man he is and I think I know he's guiding me. If he's not, I don't care, I want to believe he is and act as I think he would have acted. He's with me Millicent, do you understand? He's with me now.'

Millicent nodded slowly as she perceived a face set firm and determined. Here was a new man, she thought, and she knew that from now on her role would be at the very most, as an equal. It was a seminal moment when she felt her superiority over Henry, foisted upon her by the circumstances of their two opposing life experiences, evaporate into the ether. He was almost complete. Only his mother stood in the way of his completion and it was obvious to her that Henry was as aware of this fact as Millicent herself.

'Are you sure you're prepared to meet her?' asked Henry, 'to face her and her vicious temper, if she's capable of inflicting it, that is?'

'Yes Henry, I am, and you're right. There's no time like the present. What will be, will be. Whether she's dead or alive, or somewhere in between, she and I will meet.'

'Good. It'll work out. Honesty will prevail.'

'Yes.'

As they walked outside into the warm June evening air Millicent's mind was racing with the words she needed in order to tell Henry the one thing she believed was going to be as equally devastating for him as discovering that her soliciting wasn't what he thought. She'd already told him at his Christmas court appearance that Peregrine Spencer was a client of hers but that was a long time ago when Henry's head was muddled and hung over. Had he, since knowing her past life, put two and two together and worked out just how she had managed to stop the judge in his tracks and get him off the hook? And if he had indeed worked that out and was prepared to be equally understanding about that dreadful fact as he was about her past life, would his forgiveness go so far as learning that the most senior and esteemed man in his department, the man who had ensured Henry was reinstated, promoted and whirled into a lifestyle he could never have dreamt about - promotion, job security and riches beyond anything he'd before experienced - in short, the Minister -

was also a client? She had agonised over this since the day she'd received Henry's letter, knowing that on his return all secrets would have to be revealed for better or worse if they were to clear the way for a future together. But never, never, had she reckoned with having to reveal them under such circumstances, forced by a one in a million chance meeting with Marjory Spencer.

As they stepped off the kerbside and nestled down into the back seat of the taxi, fingers instantly finding each other and locking together, her quiet smiling gaze at the passing buildings and gentle squeeze of Henry's hand concealed the turmoil inside her head as she rehearsed and endlessly rearranged her lines, wondering if she should wait for him to remember, or take the initiative and confess before being asked. Suddenly, the decision was taken from her.

'Millicent?'

'Yes Henry?' Her heart pounded and her grip loosened on his hand, lest he should feel the perspiration that seemed to have rushed to her palm at the mention of her name.

'I think I know what you're thinking my darling.'

Millicent stared silently through the window at the buildings flashing by. She had no reply ready. Henry continued.

'Peregrine Spencer - when you told me he was a client, you meant…well, let's be honest it's obvious isn't it…he *was* a client, but not how I imagined.'

Millicent nodded and felt tears well up. How understanding was this sweet man, how gentle and understanding. There were reasons they were together; men did not come in this quiet, gentle, courteous, old-fashioned mould - not any that she'd known anyway - and the tiny spark that had ignited in her breast when he'd needed her most, lost in the isolation of his misery and helplessness with not a friend in the world, was only ignited because he'd touched the one thing within her that she had savagely protected all her adult life; her vulnerability to the unconditional love, or maybe just dependency, of a child. A child she'd never wanted, so she thought, and certainly a dependency she'd never needed for what she had planned for life. So she'd somehow reluctantly taken the cuckoo child into her nest and found that there was room for both of them and he wasn't such a bad cuckoo after all. In fact the cuckoo, despite its parasitic reputation, had matured into the friendliest, funniest, kindest, most generous and attractive of birds.

The cuckoo continued. 'I don't care. I really don't care. Why should I? How dare I? I mean, everything that happened before we met is none of my business whatsoever. I've thought a lot about it Millicent, in Australia you know, and - it just does not matter. Not one bit. I love you, I adore you, it's that simple.'

Millicent's shoulders started moving up and down, with mirth not emotion, and Henry found his hand gripped rather too tightly for comfort, her ring accidentally digging into his skin and causing some considerable pain that he just had to grin and bear under the circumstances. She had not diverted her gaze away from looking through the window all the time he was talking but now swung her face towards his and breathing in deeply, pierced him with her blue, sparkling eyes, transforming his wince into a smile.

'Henry, you really are the most unusual man I've ever known in my entire life.'

'Is that good or bad?' enquired Henry, after a few seconds deliberation.

Millicent leaned towards him and laid her head on his chest, causing Henry to dart an awkward smile at the driver who was grinning in that laconic half aware manner that only taxi drivers can, into his rear view mirror. Henry looked down and smelt the delicious hair and heard words softly floating up from beneath it, by now acutely conscious of the fact that Millicent's head had disappeared suspiciously below the driver's radar.

'It's good, my love, very good indeed.'

'And,' continued Henry, gulping as quietly as possible, 'I should imagine perhaps maybe the, um, Minister was possibly…'

Millicent gently moved an arm up to place two fingers onto his lips before adjusting the two fingers into a point in the direction of the driver, whose ears suddenly appeared to have taken on 'Vulcanic' proportions. Millicent settled back down again and quietly emitted a 'Yes' from Henry's shirt.

'That's fine,' replied Henry, 'absolutely fine. No worries at all.' He then began to put this Australian expression he'd brought back with him into a tuneless ditty, quietly singing 'No worries, no *worries* at all,' over and over through the taxi window to an audience of intense, stony-faced drivers pulling up, pulling away, or getting left behind, in the jam alongside them.

There followed quite a full minute's silence as the happy couple seemed entwined in common thought, as if both aware they were simultaneously digesting their new role as joint possessors of common knowledge; possessors of the only obstacles that might have stood in their way. Quickly and simply the final barrier was now lifted, the air cleared and the relief palpable. It was almost a miracle, almost a divine moment when love's rough edges are honed and polished and two suddenly, often unexpectedly, become one. There is nothing left to hide, all cards on the table, souls bared. The stuff that poets and painters, the posh and the peasants, the eloquent and illiterate slave all their life long to capture - the expressing of that impossible ecstasy that once known, remains forever; the memory of the moment when true love arrives, a memory that lingers - sadly not always like the love - till life's last breath.

Henry lowered his lips close to Millicent's left ear.

'Do you believe in voodoo?' he whispered, glancing up at the driver for signs of nervous twitching.

'No,' whispered back Millicent, 'but I wouldn't say so in front of an African tribesman with a machete.'

Henry chuckled and continued. 'I bought a toy voodoo doll in a shop in Australia that was the image of her.'

'Image of who?'

'The witch - my mother.'

'Oh.'

'And some drawing pins, nice ones with coloured tops, you know the sort?'

'Yes.'

And that evening I stuck all the pins into it. I was really hoping by the time I got home you'd have heard she was dead.'

'Sadly, no. I've had no contact with anyone apart from John at your office; such a charming man. Oh yes, and...'

'Yes, isn't he. I'm sorry,' said Henry, realising he'd interrupted Millicent, 'you were about to say...'

'And...' Millicent hesitated, taking a deep breath, 'and Peregrine Spencer and his wife.'

'His wife?' Henry straightened up. 'You mean before today?'

Millicent nodded, also raised herself up straight, and began explaining what she had intended saving for later but was now best said before meeting his mother. How, in her desperation to find Henry, she had phoned Spencer's home and discovered from his wife that she had thrown him out and how he was a homeless destitute forced to temporarily live with Richard Gaines, and how Gaines had planned to ruin Henry after Spencer had revealed, in a weak but apparently not vindictive moment, the truth of her past profession to him.

Henry covered her hand with his on the seat between them and squeezed it gently. Then staring out at the traffic and buildings rushing past the window remarked, 'What jolly fun.'

Chapter Thirty Eight

## GOOD CHRISTIAN NEIGHBOURS

Henry paid the taxi driver and stood with Millicent on the pavement outside his house as the cab drove off. He looked up at the top floor and pointed to the window on the left where the faded drabness of his once green curtains was clearly visible, they being pulled across as far as they would go as if in celebration of the lack of permanent occupancy.

'That's my bedroom on the left. Over forty years I've slept in there. In fact I was born in there, during an air raid.'

Millicent squinted up into the brightness of the clear evening sky, the setting sun just sinking below the rooftop and throwing silhouettes of the tall chimneys across the tarmac street behind them. A plastic football landed near them followed by a screech of brakes and a blast on a horn and angry shout before a car roared off revealing a cowering, embarrassed Wilmot boy, hand to mouth but relieved his ball was in one piece. Millicent picked it up and threw it across the road to him. He grabbed it, stared at the couple as if he'd seen a ghost, and darted indoors shrieking 'Mum! Dad!' at the top of his voice.

'I think our arrival is being announced,' said Henry, smiling at Millicent and adding, 'good throw by the way.'

'Good teacher.'

'Oh yes, the skimming stones, we must do that again soon.'

'We must.'

'Ready?' Henry, took Millicent's arm and opened the gate.

'As I'll ever be.'

They walked the few steps towards the dull, blistered black paintwork of the front door, Millicent acutely conscious of her high heels clacking on the broken red and black tiled path, her heart and head pounding and aching.

Her life had mainly been conducted within a carefully guarded comfort zone and whilst life since meeting Henry could hardly be seen as comfort, this was just about as far outside as she'd strayed.

Everything was suddenly out of her control; strange territory, strange people, apart from Henry whose new persona appeared capable of tackling anything. He was undoubtedly now her rock.

'Surreal,' muttered Millicent, looking up at the overgrown ivy covering most of the dirty, grey pebble-dashed walls and filthy windows, 'very surreal. I don't ever remember feeling so nervous in my entire life.'

'She might be dead,' said Henry, feeling for his keys, 'with any luck.'

'She's not.'

'How do you know?'

Millicent motioned with her head to the window above where they stood in the doorway.

'I saw her head peer round the curtain.' Millicent shuddered. 'Very sinister.'

'Could be Lily, she's got a key. Fat or thin face?'

'Thin.'

'Damn. She's alive.'

He tried to turn the key in the lock but it wouldn't move.

'Bitch. She's jammed the lock. Or changed them, I'll bet. We'll go round the back and try. I always use the back door. Don't know why I didn't think of...'

'But surely she'd...' Millicent's voice cracked and she held Henry's arm tight.

Henry felt her shaking as if it were a winter's day and not seven-thirty on a balmy June evening. He turned and kissed the hair hanging down matted across her forehead.

'Darling, it'll soon be over. Just this hurdle, trust me, please.'

'I'm terrified. Your disappearance was one thing but...'

As Henry placed both hands on Millicent's upper arms and again kissed her gently, there came a loud whistle. Both of them turned in the direction of the sound across the road where the figure of Reginald Wilmot in white shirtsleeves and braces holding up baggy trousers around armpit level, stood at his front gate waving one arm frantically, signalling them to join him.

'Well, well, Reggie Wilmot. This'll be interesting. He used to bully me when I was little and despite growing up in the same street we've not spoken a word since he punched me in the face, smashed my glasses and cut my eye.'

'What a horrible boy - man. How old were you?'

'Twelve, maybe thirteen. He's deeply religious.'

Henry smiled resignedly at Millicent and placing a hand on her elbow, guided her back towards the gate.

'This must be very important for him to break silence after all these years. Deep breath my dear. Are you okay to go over?'

Millicent nodded emphatically, relieved they were going somewhere other than inside the house. 'My dear Henry, from now on I am completely in your hands. I hereby relinquish all responsibility for anything that happens in my life.'

'Good. Let's go then.'

It was a very strange experience for Henry shaking the hand that the last time he felt it had almost blinded him, a piece of glass from his smashed spectacles narrowly missing his eye and embedding in his eyelid, leaving a scar that had grown with Henry.

Wilmot's memory was also not dulled by the passing years and Henry could have sworn as they exchanged embarrassed pleasantries at the Wilmot gate that his childhood foe threw a glance at the eye he'd damaged and that his stumbling, mumbling words as Henry calmly introduced Millicent in the Wilmot hallway, were an indication that Reggie Wilmot had lived possibly with a certain shame and regret at his boyhood bullying of the fat little 'four-eyed' loner across the road who sang to himself as he danced in and out of the rain-soaked gutters.

They were shown into the front Wilmot parlour and soon joined by the fussing, blushing Maureen Wilmot who, once introduced to the elegant Millicent and hearing her cultured voice, couldn't stop issuing small bows every time she spoke to her, even managing half a curtsey when the diplomatic Millicent offered compliments on the room's décor and pink bone china her tea was served in. Henry's calmness and confidence had also set them off guard and so the scene was a little strained for the deferent Wilmots, apart from when young Oswald appeared in the doorway holding his ball and staring wide-eyed at Millicent's grace and beauty, that particular quality in women being strictly confined to the film and television stars the lad believed came from another planet some universes away from Planet Lewisham.

Mrs Wilmot's tone momentarily lapsed into her normal way of addressing her child as she dispatched him to the hallway and closed the door firmly before flashing a smile at Millicent, whom she was admiring more by the minute, and taking a seat next to her shirt-sleeved husband for safety and to view Millicent better.

'Henry, Millicent...' began Reginald Wilmot, after first clearing his throat, 'as you know, we keep our own counsel in the neighbourhood, and noses clean when it comes to gossip and such like. (Henry smiled within.) When you're part of the church it's even more important to be seen as um...discreet...I think the word is.'

He chuckled slightly and Henry smiled in acknowledgement of the received wisdom.

'But, and it's a very big *but*, there are times when Christian duty calls for the truth to be told and that's why I've, we've, asked you to join us here, now. Although we did think you was, that is rumour had it that you was (clearing of throat)...dead...I must admit.'

Henry, who was perched on the edge of his chair, took a sip of tea before responding whimsically:

'Very much undead as you can see,' adding before Wilmot could reply, 'it's to do with my mother of course.'

This time Mr Wilmot required a very large intake of breath followed by a certain amount of lip-licking, sniffing and leaning forward to place his cup on the coffee table and instantly retrieve it, empty, then replace it again, before he could restart.

He related the same story that he had already related to Irma Scroggins concerning the night of David Bodger's death, first informing Henry that they had only imparted their secret when offering his mother a lift to the solicitors. It had not been their intention to share the burden they'd been carrying for eight long years since the young witness had confessed what he'd seen on the night of his stag party, but somehow (and here a cautionary glance had been shot his way by the nervy Mrs Wilmot) it had come out, mainly to prepare Henry's mother against being duped by a man they personally didn't trust any further than they could throw him. 'And that's not very far,' Mrs Wilmot had added, demonstrating the girth and height of Archibald Snapes with much stretching of arms upwards and outwards and blowing up of cheeks.

Since that day they had noticed Snapes' *very expensive* car parked outside the Scroggins home on two occasions that they knew of, and possibly more that had occurred in the rare situation of them both being absent. ('Off guard, not absent' Henry thought to himself.) They had also noticed that she, Irma Scroggins, had had the locks changed, a white van with the name of a local locksmiths clearly emblazoned on the side and much tampering with the front door being clear enough evidence of this, so they believed. Henry conceded that this did seem to confirm lock-changing and he asked Reginald Wilmot if he could remember exactly when this had happened, no stretch for the mercurial Wilmot memory that unhesitatingly named the day as the one after Henry had disappeared, or rather 'rumour had it' that Henry had disappeared.

Millicent, who under the circumstances had remained silent throughout, enquired just how they knew that Henry had disappeared, but before the Wilmots could name the guilty party and to save them the awkwardness of committing such a betrayal, Henry suggested with raised eyebrows, 'Lily?'

Yes, they had to confess it certainly was Lily Bunce who had fled to their house after the terrible scene in Irma Scroggins' kitchen where poor Lily had suffered such verbal abuse and dreadful malicious accusations that she had to turn to someone, and the Wilmots being the most understanding and discreet people in the street (Lily's exact words, it was stressed), the choice of the poor woman's chosen sanctuary was automatic. There was, however, no mention of the exact nature of the malicious accusations heaped by Irma Scroggins upon Lily's character (for in Lily's mind there existed no letter-opening propensities), only that they were all baseless lies and that she'd taken enough over the years and was never going to speak another word to the wicked woman which, as far as the Wilmots knew, remained the case to date.

'Blast,' muttered Henry, staring down at the carpet, 'that means that Lily, the only person who has a spare key to the house, won't have one that works.'

'Incorrect,' said Reginald Wilmot with an over emphatic degree of smugness, 'for it so happens that the locks were changed just days before the argument and we (nodding at Mrs Wilmot who caught the nod and threw it back with interest) happened to observe that Lily had entered the house on several occasions using *her* key.

'But she only ever goes in by the back door,' said Henry frowning, 'never the front. How would you have seen?'

The Wilmots looked a little uneasy for a moment before Mrs Wilmot pointed out that she often took a short cut down their back alley when fetching Oswald from swimming practice and had noticed Lily entering and leaving by the back gate. Henry's mental juggling of the swimming pool location in relation to the Wilmot's house indicated that Mrs Wilmot's 'cut' had in fact been of the long and not short variety but it mattered not because it was all vital information; or seemed that way.

'Anyway Henry,' concluded Reginald Wilmot with a slap of both hands on his amply-trousered thighs, 'that's what we know and what we thought you should also know. Must say it was a real shock when our Oswald come running in just now screaming you weren't dead. Poor lad nearly had a fit he did!'

'I'm sorry to disappoint him,' said Henry.

'Oh no, no, *no*,' interjected the slow-witted man, 'we're very pleased to see you're not…that is…to see you alive.'

'Thank you.'

'And far from that, looking exceedingly well! I take it you've been somewhere nice and hot by the look of that tan.'

On saying this Wilmot glanced at Millicent and observing she was quite white was about to enquire whether Henry had travelled, wherever he went, alone. But he stopped himself.

'I've been to Australia,' said Henry, 'to meet my father's friends.'

The shock that instantly registered on both Wilmot faces was palpable and the jaws that dropped with the sudden shock had to be quickly reinstated before detection by their guests. Oh the cruelty of Henry Scroggins! For the mischievous man knew precisely what he was doing and as if in repayment for the scar over his eye, he got up with an urgency that signalled instant action and held out his hand to Millicent

'Come my dear, we've work to do. I think we need to pay a visit to Mr Snapes first before any discussion with Mother.'

Millicent took Henry's hand and with stockinged knees held tightly together and to one side - which Reginald couldn't help noticing, before picking a spot on the ceiling of more interest - gracefully ascended slowly onto her high heels which in that comfy suburban parlour appeared like a sparkling fountain rising from the centre of a dank pond with gnomes dotted around the bank. Not that Henry was gnome-like but with his brown bald head, yellow shirt and stature an inch or so shorter than Millicent in heels, he could have been possibly mistaken for one.

An aroma of panic swept the parlour as both Wilmots, frantic not to be excluded from the next stage of the action, fussed and muttered as Henry and Millicent moved to leave the room, until after a series of exchanged glances and mouthings between the married couple behind the backs of their departing guests, Reginald Wilmot mustered words to solve the dilemma.

'We can give you a lift if you like. We've got to go to Whiteheath, to Maureen's sisters, and the buses aren't too reg'lar and taxis cost a second mortgage so…'

Henry was by now in the hallway and turned to Reginald Wilmot, smiling genially.

'You're assuming I haven't got a car Reginald.'

'Why - yes. Never seen you drive Henry, that's all.'

I can't,' replied Henry, 'you're absolutely right. And yes, thank you very much. A lift would be very helpful under the circumstances.'

'But Henry,' said Millicent, 'it's eight o'clock in the evening. Nobody will be there.'

Henry looked at his watch. 'Hmm, how silly of me. Lost all sense of time after a day up in the air.' He was about to suggest they paid Lily a visit and return in the morning to see Snapes, but the Wilmots weren't ready to let them escape that easily.

'He often works late does Mr Snapes,' said Mrs Wilmot hastily.

'He's also the church's solicitor too you see,' intervened her husband, quickly carrying out a risk assessment on his wife's loose tongue and divining a bad outcome, 'and we've had business to attend to recently with one thing and another so have had the odd evening meeting with him either in his office or in the bar over the road which he seems to frequ'nt quite a lot. The one where he and Mr Bodger was the night of the…the night Mr Bodger…'

'Was found - in his car - dead as a dodo.' The risk assessment had been a sound one, but fruitless. Maureen had spoken.

A gloom descended over the hallway at the revival of the grim lengths to which Snapes was capable of going; the alarming notion that they might be dealing with a murderer and a desperate one at that. Henry's brief time with him in the bar the evening before he went missing was enough to convince him that they were dealing with a man completely devoid of scruples and for whom money gained by foul means or fair was a prime motivation in life.

The fact that Snapes had had frequent meetings with his mother further reinforced Henry's suspicion that, with himself supposedly out of the way for good, Snapes would probably have wasted no time in ensuring that he could still guarantee himself a slice of the considerable cake left by his father's will. If it was the common held belief that Henry was permanently out of the picture then Snapes' attempt to coerce Henry into cheating his mother out of what was rightfully hers was a secret safe within his own fat head but providing him with no means of capitalisation.

All this had gone through Henry's head a thousand times during his absence and having now shared it with Millicent in the taxi some hours before, was now streaming through his mind as he stood absorbing the words of the Wilmots at the same time. Millicent, now an extension of Henry's being, had watched him from the corner of her eye as he stood there in the hall listening, and knew exactly what he was thinking.

Maureen Wilmot broke the tense atmosphere, throwing a cautionary glance first at her husband before blurting out, without caution:

'Mrs Bodger lives in the flat over the office and, forgive me for suggesting this, but I think she knows a lot more than she says. In fact she don't say much at all but her poor face says a lot, oh yes. That poor lady's carrying stuff in her head that I'm sure she wants to get out and I for one would like to see it out and justice done for her and her kids and…'

'Maureen! Please!'

Reginald Wilmot, petrified that his wife, whose unfortunate habit of not being able to engage any sort of filtering system on her brain once her tongue set off on a race to divulge information she felt should be in the public domain, was about to blow any credibility they might still have as 'disinterested witnesses', forcing him to once more step into the breach before irreparable damage to their spotless reputation was done.

But Henry's mind was already one move ahead and far from seeing the Wilmots as the disinterested witnesses they were desperate to portray themselves as, was rapidly assimilating their usefulness as *credible* witnesses in a situation that was appearing increasingly like it might need one - the Wilmots obviously only being available as an unconjoined pair.

'Reginald,' said Henry, 'Maureen has a point you know. Does Mrs Bodger work in the office - for Snapes I mean?'

'Yes,' replied the husband, the instant jolting back of his head and raised right eyebrow denoting not only surprise, but the happy prospect of involvement and responsibility. 'It's just the two of them - she's in reception and also his secretary. Answers all calls. You can never get straight through to him although I'm sure he's often there when she says he's not; can hear him in the background whispering. She used to work part-time when the kids were small but since Mr Bodger died and the kids reached teenage years she seems to do the lot. When her husband was alive she just worked for him, while Snapes had his own secretary and assistant solicitor….'

'But he doesn't now,' interrupted Millicent.

'Doesn't what ma'am?' enquired Wilmot.

'Doesn't have any other staff.'

'Oh no. It all changed after Mr Bodger's sad demise. We just assumed that the work was less with just one partner and…'

'But it should be more, surely,' interrupted Millicent again, glancing at Henry. 'Clients don't just go away when they've been with a solicitor for years, even if one of the partners dies or leaves. They just get another partner. Solicitors don't lose business happily, no more than any other company does. I do have some experience in this area.'

She turned and offered Henry the faintest smile, he nodding to signify the irrefutable truth of her statement.

'So Millicent, are you suggesting,' said Henry, 'that Snapes might have reason for not wanting any other staff in the office apart from himself and the wife of his deceased partner?'

'Possibly,' replied Millicent.

Henry turned to his hosts.

'Reginald? Have you a telephone I could use please? I think a call to Mrs Bodger straight away might be a good idea, to arrange an urgent meeting with her when Snapes isn't around. Do you know her Christian name by any chance?'

'Dorothy,' said Wilmot who had instantly swivelled at Henry's first request - for a telephone - to reveal behind him in the hallway the very item Henry required, namely a gleaming cream telephone on a little oak unit complete with padded seat, several directories, a notepad and, curiously, a biro propped in a small white crucifix holder which served as the cross's upright but which, when removed, would seem to offer little support.

'But what if Snapes answers?' said Millicent.

Here, Mrs Wilmot returned to the fray, buoyed by Henry's compliment that she'd made a good point.

'I was thinking the very same thing Millicent. So what about if one of us, Reginald or me that is, rings, and if he answers - which I don't think he will at this time of night to be perfectly honest - we can say we need to speak to him about church matters. We do in actual fact, so can then make an appointment and he won't suspect a thing.'

'With apologies for ringing him late of course,' added Wilmot, by now a little pumped up with pride at his wife's timely interruption and what he considered a splendid idea. 'That's an excellent idea my dear, excellent if I may say so,' he said, placing a hand on her shoulder about a foot below him. Then realising he might be jumping the gun, turned to the couple and said. 'Don't you agree Henry? Millicent?'

'Absolutely marvellous idea if you really don't mind,' replied Henry.

Mind? Would the Wilmots mind? Oh Henry, blessed man that he was at that moment in the eyes of the verger and his wife, the latter who thirty seconds later stood poised with lips slightly apart waiting for the phone to answer as the other three watched in silence. Suddenly there was a nod as Maureen heard a response and her mouth rehearsed the words she was about to speak.

'Oh hello Mrs Bodger, Dorothy. Maureen Wilmot here, how are you? Good, good, yes we're fine thank you. Look I'm sorry for this late call but we have friends here who would like to speak to you.' She paused for several seconds listening before continuing. 'No, not with Mr Snapes, not at this stage anyway - just yourself. Yes, I know it's unusual but he'll explain himself if that's okay. Can I put him on please? Thank you. His name is Henry, Henry Scroggins.' She passed the phone to Henry and scurried to one side, proud to have done her duty.

'Mrs Bodger, Henry Scroggins, how do you do?' Silence. 'Hello, Mrs Bodger? Hello? Oh hello, look I know this is probably a shock for you and I know why, which is the reason I'd like to speak to you, alone please. I believe there is something I could possibly tell you of interest concerning your late husband and also a matter that I believe you might be able to help me with which I'd rather not discuss over the phone. To put it quite frankly Mrs Bodger, I suspect certain things that I need to investigate in order to ascertain once and for all their veracity, or otherwise.'

At this point the Wilmots could have been excluded from the conversation had not the meaning of the word 'veracity' been blindingly obvious taken in context. This was apparent by the blank expressions that descended momentarily on both their faces before a light flickered them back to life and into the realms of complete understanding.

There followed fresh animation from the other end of the line as Henry listened with his expression alternating rapidly from eyes wide, to frowning, to head shaking, to staring at the others horrified, to trying to speak, to finally being allowed to.

'He's at Ascot and this evening is safe,' repeated Henry, and turning to the others, 'so it's okay to come and see you now?'

With that, the Wilmots heads nearly spun off their necks in nodding assent, whilst car keys were gathered and young Oswald was given permission to stay up and watch television after his normal bedtime but not to answer the door or phone whilst they were out - a rare treat for the normally closely guarded offspring.

## Chapter Thirty Nine

# MURDER MOST FOUL
# AND A VOICE FROM THE GRAVE

Having first booked into a hotel on the heath for the night in order that the Wilmots could (albeit reluctantly) return home, Henry and Millicent took the short walk through the late evening sunshine, past diners and drinkers outside the lively, eclectic mix of bars and bistros the village comprised of at this hour, to the office of Bodger and Snapes and the home of Dorothy Bodger, where the following two hours spent in the company of the widow and her children was time the five would possibly not forget for the rest of their lives.

The petite, softly-spoken lady who invited them into her spacious, spotless but unostentatious flat above the office premises wore silver-rimmed spectacles and a neat beige twin set which together with her short straight grey hair cropped page boy fashion gave her the appearance of a rather sad librarian who in her duty as issuer, stamper and giver of advice on books, did so with the resigned regret of never having written one. A dark cloud of unhappiness hovered over her, a cloud that seemed to diminish in darkness the further it spread away from her in the room but still left shades of grey in all corners.

She had insisted that her teenage son and daughter were present for the meeting. Both children were polite, well-spoken, quiet individuals who were protective of their mother but, obviously having been briefed about who Henry was and the possible significance of his visit, alert and keen to know anything that could put their own and their mother's minds at rest.

The boy, aged about fifteen was the image of his mother but the girl, a year or so older, had features nothing like them so the visitors felt they were looking at a young version of the father, confirmed when shown a family photograph taken in the last days she could remember them being a happy family shortly before he died.

The face of David Bodger was that of a man whose eyes shone with a love of family and life, a handsome man with a full head of dark hair as was the style of the time, next to his attractive dark-haired wife who radiated such warmth and joy it was difficult to put the photograph image and the one before them together as the same person. Such is the weight of tragedy and, even worse, despair.

The conversation was long, emotional and revelatory, interspersed with tears from Mrs Bodger, comfort from the children and periods of silence whilst the lady composed herself. The boy, domesticated beyond his years, brought tea and biscuits perfectly presented whilst his sister remained beside her mother on the sofa at all times, taking her mother's hand in moments of extreme anxiety and offering fresh tissues when required.

First Henry wanted to hear what Mrs Bodger had to say before he told her what he knew, and so they sat and listened whilst for half an hour she told how she had suspected from the day of her husband's death that foul play had been involved and knew without any shadow of doubt in her own mind who was responsible. She told of arguments between the two partners which were never in front of her but which she couldn't fail to hear through the walls, in fact had often heard very clearly by leaving the intercom open between her office and theirs, first taking the phone off the hook to avoid incoming calls giving her away.

It was a simple matter of morality, how the two differed on the treatment of clients. Her husband as honest as the day was long, and Snapes - well, Snapes' morals needed no introduction to any of the five people present. It was all about money; Snapes wanting to grossly overcharge - the very least of his demands - whilst David Bodger fought constantly against his partner's greed and ruthlessness. These disputes only ever happened whilst their young assistant solicitor was out of the office, when Snapes felt he was safe from prying ears, never believing for one moment in his arrogance that Dorothy Bodger was listening. Eventually, she revealed, it started to affect their marriage, many nights ending without speaking until her husband had reached the point of a nervous breakdown, his conscience weighed down by what he knew were the criminal acts of Snapes, and by association, himself - that went far beyond subtle manipulation of the rules.

One day, after pressure from Dorothy over his worsening mental state, David Bodger threatened to report Snapes to The Law Society and police, regardless of the consequences. A furious row had erupted when Dorothy had left to go shopping, but she'd only been a minute and had heard the men's voices from the stairs. It was a Friday and that evening Dorothy had taken the children to stay at her mother's in Canterbury, to be out of the way during the weekend should matters be brought to a head.

She'd stayed overnight, not before begging her husband to come with her to get away from the office for a few hours breathing space and change of scenery, but he'd been persuaded by Snapes to go for a drink at the bar over the road to settle their 'silly disagreements' once and for all. He, Snapes, had apologised to David Bodger late that afternoon, pleading that he'd realised the error of his ways and promising his partner the turning of a new leaf, having already, so Dorothy believed, decided on his next ruthless plan of action.

The last time she had seen her husband alive was when he walked down with her and the children to the car park beneath the office and kissed them goodbye. Her Hillman Imp was always parked between her husband's Vauxhall Viva and Snapes' Jaguar XJS in the company parking bays and she remembered the difficulty in opening the doors because Snapes had parked partly in her space at an angle. When she returned in the early hours of the next morning she found her husband slumped in the driving seat, a pipe leading from the exhaust through the boot and lying on the back seat.

The death of her beloved husband was awful enough in itself but what made it worse was the verdict of suicide passed by the coroner and discovering that her husband had terminal cancer which he intended keeping to himself until his condition became too obvious to conceal. She knew in her heart that if he'd committed suicide to save them the trauma of watching him slowly die, he would never have done so without leaving a note explaining his reasons and saying goodbye to her and the children.

She knew her man too well. It was that more than anything that convinced her that he'd died at the hands of his partner, whose nauseating pretence at mourning had almost brought her to the point of murder herself. But she had the children to consider, aged six and nine at the time, and so she'd determined to do what she thought David would have advised her, to carry on with the business as the best way to stay close to Snapes and try to uncover the truth.

So far she had not a shred of concrete evidence, just a mountain of unsubstantiated suspicion and an aching injustice in her heart, but recently had been close to giving up and letting Snapes not only get away with murder but quite possibly with far more of his half share of the business. That much, thank goodness - her retaining joint control of the company - her husband had at least taken care of ensuring.

After listening to her story and more tea and biscuits courtesy of son Christopher, it was Henry's turn to tell her his background and of his trip to Australia to find out what sort of man his father really was, from the people who knew him best.

He then told Dorothy of Snapes' plan to alter his father's will in his, Henry's, favour on the understanding that he had a substantial cut; a deal that he'd tried to broker in the very bar across the road - a convenient setting it seemed for his crimes and connivance - a meeting which Henry had walked away from in disgust, although this probably hadn't been apparent to Snapes who was too drunk at the time and, for all Henry knew, still to this day believed was a done deal until the rumours of his, Henry's, death, followed by the visit by his mother to their office.

Dorothy interrupted Henry here to mention that after his mother's visit, of which Snapes had gone to pains to ensure Dorothy was not privy to a single word, he was a changed man; a very frightened man. Whatever Irma Scroggins had divulged had put the fear of God into him because from that day on he was a bundle of nerves, impatiently snapping back at her over the most trivial matter until she knew that the old lady had effectively somehow placed her scrawny hands around his ample neck.

It was here that Henry, convinced she had no idea of the secret that the Wilmots had imparted inadvertently to Irma and then intentionally to himself, decided to tell her.

'Dorothy,' he began hesitantly, 'I know the reason for this. There were witnesses the night of your husband's death, one in particular, a young man who has not been able to come forward until recently but has now revealed everything he saw.'

Here, Dorothy Bodger gasped and seemed about to faint until her children's attention restored her equanimity.

'Please go on,' she whispered in a voice barely audible.

Henry took a deep breath to try and compose his words to minimise the shock he believed might be too much for her.

'He was a young man who had been in the bar with friends, celebrating his - the young man's - stag night. Apparently he was getting married the next day.'

'Married the day of David's...' murmured Dorothy with a tiny, pathetic laugh at the cruel irony.

'He and his friends were worried,' continued Henry, 'at the way Snapes - and there's no doubting it was him - was trying very hard to get his friend, who I'm afraid there's no doubting was indeed David, drunk. He said the friend tried to protest but the big man kept forcing him to have another drink until he could hardly walk.'

'But David never drank! Only one or two small glasses at Christmas! I've never seen him drunk in my life, never! That's what hurt so much at the inquest and in the newspapers, the suggestion that he'd had to get drunk to commit suicide. I knew that wasn't true but what could I do? Archie knew it wasn't possible but kept saying that David had insisted he try tequila, and when I heard they'd found some in his blood, I...oh, my poor, poor David!'

Henry quietly continued when he felt she was ready.

'As the young man was saying goodbye to his friends after leaving a restaurant where they'd gone after leaving the bar, he noticed the big man half dragging the other man to a car in the car park under this building. It was a blue Vauxhall Viva. He opened the driver's door, looking around as if to make sure nobody could see him, and then placed the man on the seat and closed the door. The young man was hiding behind one of the car park pillars and was very concerned - having seen what he'd seen earlier in the bar - that the big man was expecting the other to drive. That was his main thought, which I suppose is natural, that he was expecting his friend to drive. However, it was only when he read in the paper the week following of the suspected suicide of David Bodger, a Whiteheath solicitor, that he knew that something was wrong. He knew that your husband was in no condition to have been able to place a hosepipe to the exhaust and take his own life, in fact during his confession, which he made in church I might add, and only to one man - Mr Reginald Wilmot, whom you know - he also told of the last thing he'd seen before he left to go home.'

Here, Henry paused to exchange looks with the two children and Millicent, Dorothy Bodger having had her head bowed and face buried in a tissue through most of Henry's speech, occasionally lifting it to nod or blow her nose. Her face was covered by her hands so Henry's expression was one of checking to ensure he should go on with what he knew was going to be conclusive evidence that Archibald Snapes had murdered the husband and father of the family sitting before him.

The children nodded as one and Millicent reached out a hand to the boy who was close to her, which he gladly took in both his, as Henry continued.

'The young man stated that he had watched Snapes go to his car, a Jaguar XJS, and take out a length of hosepipe from the boot which he then attached to the exhaust pipe of the Vauxhall and slid inside and over onto the back seat.'

It goes without saying that at this point mother and children could hold back their tears no longer and were united in what was inevitably fresh grief, tempered by an enormous sense of relief; a burden lifted from their shoulders that would provide them with hope of release from the agony of the wrongly tarnished character of the husband and father they loved and the real possibility they could finally move on and start life anew.

Christopher looked up with jaw set, nose and eyes streaming.

'I want to kill him!' he exclaimed.

'Christopher, I think it's time for another cup of tea,' said his mother, looking up with her red eyes no longer sad and desperate but instead sparkling with gratitude and relief. The weight was lifted, her mind at peace, her heart full of love for her children and the good people who sat with them. There was lightness in her voice and gentle self-mocking laughter as she snuffled noisily into her tissue and gently squeezed her son's hand. 'Would you mind darling? Much better than killing people don't you think?'

The atmosphere was transformed instantly by this brave woman, as happens so often when the example of one opens doors of hope and happiness for others. She walked over to Henry who had stood up, and clasped him tight, wrapping him in an embrace as though she had her husband back in her arms. She then went to Millicent and did the same, Millicent struggling to hold back her own tears of relief for another woman who had been through hell and was showing them all that anything is possible to overcome.

The daughter also hugged her mother, then with a snuffle and a soft smile at all three adults, said simply 'Tea' and dashed off to join her brother whose presence in the kitchen was already signalled by a whistling kettle.

'And I've got something for you Henry,' said Dorothy. 'Tell me, can you remember your father's voice?'

Henry slowly turned to face her.

'N-not, not since I was a child when he...'

'I have a tape he recorded the day he died six months ago. It is evident they are in fact your father's dying words and, if you can bear it, I think it's best you hear them now before you confront Snapes and your mother.'

All the time Henry had been listening to Dorothy's words, Millicent's eyes had been concentrated on his face, watching it grow from wide-eyed astonishment to disbelief, to shock, until his expression darkened and she was able to move just in time to support him as he appeared about to pass out. But it was nothing compared to what Dorothy was about to reveal once Henry had been eased down onto his chair and handed an A4 white envelope which she had brought from the office with the tape.

Henry stared at the words *'For The Personal Attention of David Bodger Esquire, Strictly Private & Confidential'*, screwed his eyes up to read the Brisbane postmark dated nearly nine years ago and slowly pulled out the contents. He quickly scanned the document, turned the cover page and began to read out loud.

'This is the Last Will and Testament of Henry Arthur Scroggins, superceding all other wills....'

He raised his eyes to Millicent and Dorothy, his head moving slowly from side to side in disbelief as he read silently on, just his lips moving. Dorothy took a deep breath before speaking.

'I found it hidden in a drawer Snapes always keeps locked. It was with the tape sent earlier this year, both addressed to David. He never saw the will; he couldn't have done. Snapes saw his chance for riches and David was in the way. I don't know what plan Snapes had in mind but he certainly couldn't do it all the time David was alive. How very convenient for him that David was diagnosed with cancer at the same time. The perfect alibi.'

'You mean,' said Millicent, 'this came shortly before...'

Dorothy pointed at the postmark.

'Posted from Australia two weeks before...David died.'

The poor lady was once more overcome with grief at this reminder, if she ever needed one, of the awful truth. Quickly composing herself, she sat bolt upright and reached across to Henry with a small Phillips mini recorder that had rested in her lap with the envelope.

'It's all set up if you feel ready to hear it. Just press Play.'

Henry glanced at the side of the machine and placed his finger on the button, glancing up at Millicent as if to check he should go ahead. Millicent's response was to place her hand over his, which gesture saw Henry's finger depress the button, grimace, and hold his breath. Millicent removed her hand.

At first all they heard was hard, rasping breathing and the rustle of material and what sounded like a pen scribbling on paper;

then a rattling, wheezing cough followed instantly, and shockingly, by the gravel voice of Henry Arthur Scroggins.

"David - *David!* I think I'm dying mate - can you believe it? I'm on my boat with my secretary and have had a bad turn. Tried ringing you - no reply, so - my will I sent eight years ago - you never replied - I never chased. Mad, bloody fool I am! I wrote to my son - same time - he never replied - bet that witch got it first. You told me about that crooked bastard Snapes and I'm worried. What's happened? What a fool, what a *fool!* Tell my boy I always loved him, always meant to come for him, *we* always meant to come for him, and...I'm so, *so* sorry. Tell him that please David for me. Anyway, he's the skipper now; he's in charge and...."

With that there was a short gasp and a cry of pain, the sound of metal hitting a hard floor, and silence, save the soft purring of the tape running on.

Henry stopped the tape and stared at the machine in his hand, rocking backwards and forwards on the edge of his seat, as if in a trance. There was nothing to be said.

# Chapter Forty

# THE FINAL CONFRONTATION

It was another beautiful morning with the sun already burning through the early haze as Millicent and Henry stood outside their hotel on the edge of the heath at one end of the village. They watched a middle-aged couple playing tennis on the court adjacent to the hotel and Millicent remarked on their excellent stamina considering they were knocking back cocktails in the hotel bar until gone midnight when Henry and Millicent had retired to their room.

''Isn't it Wimbledon this week?' enquired Henry.

'Yes, big year. Borg's going for his sixth consecutive title.'

'Is he now? Do you like tennis?'

'I love Wimbledon. Have you ever been?'

'Never. And you?'

Millicent mentally ran through the times she'd been and the men she'd been there with and how she'd never once paid but always enjoyed the very best of seats on Centre Court.

'I've seen all Borg's wins. But I fear that obnoxious brat McEnroe might spoil things this year. God, I hope not.'

Henry saw a taxi appear the other side of the heath about a quarter of a mile away and pointed towards it.

'I hope that's our taxi - all this waiting around.' He returned to the tennis theme to keep their minds off the mission they were about to engage upon. 'So how do you manage to get to the finals every year? It must be difficult to get tickets and...'

Suddenly he was aware that Millicent was studying her shoes and one glance at her face told him precisely how she'd managed to see the finals. He felt foolish and was pleased to see the taxi arrive and a cheery round face lean out and say his name.

The journey down the hill and through the cacophony of traffic noise to the quiet back streets where Viola Street nestled peacefully, seemed much faster than they expected, their conversation stilted by nerves that jangled in anticipation of what could happen when Henry and his mother were back under the same roof, but this time with the additional presence of Millicent.

Henry, both of them, knew what Irma Scroggins was capable of but there was no predicting the outcome once confronted with the information Henry held in the blue folder which he clutched in one hand on his lap, his other hand holding Millicent's, each of them offering frequent squeezes of reassurance.

They had timed their arrival for half an hour before Snapes was due to visit Irma Scroggins, Dorothy Bodger having eavesdropped on their telephone conversation two days earlier and then going down to the office to check Snapes' diary whilst Henry and Millicent were with her, to confirm the time of his appointment at 52 Viola Street as ten o 'clock.

The irony had not been lost on Henry of how his act of defiance in installing a telephone had enabled the old witch to communicate with the outside world and plot against him. It had also occurred to them that she might in fact cancel Snapes' visit after the shock of seeing Henry and Millicent at her front door, but Dorothy Bodger had promised absolute vigilance on that score and to contact them or the Wilmots in the event of her hearing a change of plans.

Not that it mattered to Henry - he was there at his house, had always intended to be there on arriving back from Australia, and the delay in confronting his mother had only been caused by the Wilmots' unexpected but timely intervention. Besides, it was well within his mother's capability to actually want Snapes there, to 'legally' rub salt into Henry's wound and revel in his public misery before an audience of her solicitor and Henry's woman, little knowing what her son knew about both her solicitor and the will he was taking to her that morning.

Henry's first job was to pay Lily Bunce a quick visit for the sole purpose of gaining entrance to his house. This had to be done without his mother knowing, which meant disembarking from the taxi one street away from Viola in order to walk down the back alley to Lily's back door unnoticed.

His last task on leaving the hotel had been to call the Wilmots, as arranged, to ensure that both women, Lily Bunce and his mother, had not left their houses, a job of surveillance that could not have been better entrusted to the cream of MI5.

As both women were only known to ever arrive and leave by their front doors it would take a very unfortunate circumstance for them both not to be home and Henry's plan to be foiled.

The reborn man felt a fleeting sense of foreboding as he turned the handle of Lily's back gate and stepped inside to the tidy garden where the path leading to the back door was now bordered either side by blue lobelia and pansies and Wilfred's shed stood as a monument to his memory and happy hours of peaceful tinkering and listening to the Home Service on his transistor radio. But then a new image arose in his mind, of his father and Wilfred chatting amiably outside the kitchen door, smoking and laughing whilst little Henry stood and listened quietly by his father's side or played with a toy on the concrete at their feet.

During the many times he'd been in that garden for various reasons during his life, this image had never before presented itself, but now, since the revelation at Dorothy Bodger's flat, he could see his father and hear his voice clearly, the rough south London accent made rougher by the roll up cigarettes he smoked and the pints of mild and bitter he'd drink with Wilfred, Siddie Mathieson and other friends who fought the war on the doorstep instead of in foreign fields.

Instantly all fear was washed away. A sudden surge of adrenalin once more reminded him he had nothing to lose and that life from here on was under his complete control, come what may. And then, most importantly, he had Millicent.

'Henry, I'll stay here if you don't mind,' she said.

Henry's reverie closed and the reality of the moment resumed at the sound of Millicent's voice.

'Good idea. The shock of seeing me will be more than enough for the poor woman without you beside me.'

'Don't you imagine she's already seen me? It's pretty unlikely she didn't miss us yesterday what with all the noise going on.'

'Noise?'

'The car screeching and hooting, the man shouting at the boy, then Mr Wilmot whistling from across the road.'

'That's true. Wasn't exactly subtle was he. Okay, here I go. Leave the gate open, just in case.'

'Of what?'

'I don't know. So I can see you. Don't want you out of my sight now you've agreed to be my wife. I'm frightened I might...'

'Lose me?'

Henry nodded as he looked into Millicent's face smiling sweetly up at him. 'Never, my darling, never,' she said.

He stroked her arm gratefully and then pointed to the gate ten or so yards away.

'Do you realise that gate is the same one my father walked through a thousand times or more. He always used the back gate, which is why I do. I've always liked to walk in his footsteps and try to imagine what he was thinking. He would have gone through there with a heart full of love for Betty Mathieson after meeting her, and then...having to face...'

He shuddered as if a ghost had passed through his body, then looked up and strode down the path to Lily's back door, not hesitating to stop and survey her windows for signs of life but going straight to the kitchen door and tapping on one of the four small panes of glass. Moments later Millicent heard a bolt slide, a short murmured conversation, and in less than a minute Henry was back by her side dangling the key from a piece of string.

'You're right. Lily saw us yesterday and wanted to come out and give us a key but was terrified of being seen by you know who. But once she saw us go into the Wilmot's she guessed they'd tell me about the lock changing.'

'She misses nothing does she.'

'Not a thing. She's been counting me out and counting me back in every day of my life, and thinks I have no idea.'

'Did she say anything else?'

'Just that she's wicked. My mother that is. Funny, that's the first time I've ever heard Lily say a bad word against her. Strange how beaten dogs never bite their masters isn't it, and that poor woman's been savaged as much as me over the years.'

'And now you're biting back. Not a moment too soon.'

'And so has Lily. I suppose there comes a time when all bullies meet their match. I'd lost faith in that idea but not now. Shall we go and face the music my dear? Would you like to remove my muzzle?'

Henry looked at the upstairs windows of his house just visible over the alley fence, then took Millicent's arm and walked back down the alley away from his own gate, turning left at the end into the street and then left again into Viola until reaching his front gate.

Once more he stood before his front door and for the first time in his life placed two fingers lightly on the brass knocker, dulled through years of neglect, pondering for a moment before gently tapping twice to give his mother chance to prepare herself. No reply. The two looked at each other listening for signs of life. None came. So he knocked harder which brought movement above their heads as the window flew open and his mother's head peered down with a look of hate directed first at Henry, then switched in a flash to Millicent.

'What do you want?' she snapped, 'Don't think you're bringing that tart in my house!'

Henry's hand drew the key from his pocket and plunged it into the lock, turning first right then left. The door opened a few inches revealing a chain across the gap so without more ado he lifted a foot and gave the door a hefty boot as close to the chain as he could reach. The door gave way instantly, leaving the chain swinging limply with a screw hanging from one end.

'I put that on,' said Henry, 'thank goodness.'

He stepped over the threshold and took Millicent's hand to join him. She shook her head.

'I can't Henry. Now I'm here, I just can't. I thought I could but suddenly I'm...I'm so sorry. How weak of me, Millicent Carter, solicitor...pathetic isn't it.'

Her hand was shaking, her cheeks drained of blood, her palm damp and cold. Just then Maureen Wilmot appeared at the gate.

'Excuse me, sorry to trouble you but I couldn't help...would you like to come and have a cup of tea Millicent my dear?'

Millicent's eyes shot from the woman in her pinafore peering compassionately over the gate, to Henry, who turned to Mrs Wilmot.

'Maureen, that's extremely kind of you. Millicent, I'll be over as soon as I've finished here. '

'Be careful Henry, please, I'm certain she's insane.'

'Oh she's most definitely mad, I've never doubted that. But now so am I Millicent. Ohh, *so am I!*'

Millicent touched his forearm and strode to the gate, turning to see him disappear inside and close the door behind him.

'Mother!' No reply. Henry looked up the staircase. 'Mother!'

'Get out of my house! *My* house! Do you hear? I thought you were dead!'

'You mean *wished.* And the house is what we must discuss, so either you come down here and we talk sensibly or I'll come up.'

'Stay where you are you swine!'

There followed a thumping and rustling as if searching for suitable battle gear until her bent form and hard, twisted features appeared at the top of the stairs, walking stick in hand, lips moving in manic chatter. Step by step she painfully descended, gasping, chattering, first one foot on a stair followed by the other to free the first to venture lower; feet that only weeks ago during her search for the missing letter (sent from the man who was at that moment just a few streets away) were flying with such nimble dexterity up and down those same stairs and from room to room.

As Irma Scroggins arrived at the bottom Henry moved aside to let her pass and watched her shuffle down the hall into the kitchen muttering oaths of hatred mainly directed at his 'tart' or 'prostitute'.

Henry was going to do the decent thing and break his news gently but her references to the woman he loved and was soon to be his wife gave him no choice than to attack her with both barrels. Besides, a quick glance at his watch told him that Snapes would be arriving any moment.

'Mother, did you know that your solicitor Archibald Snapes tried to do a deal with me the evening that I left home? Did he tell you that? Did he tell you how, if you could be got rid of, he would adjust Father's will in my favour if I shared it with him?'

Henry had made this damning introductory speech whilst following his mother to the kitchen and now stood in the doorway between kitchen and hall, watching her back as she stood with one hand on the kitchen top, shaking with rage. He watched the hand shudder even harder and the knuckles turn white as they gripped the edge.

'What!'

'I also know that he's tried to do the same with you since then, obviously believing that I wouldn't be coming back and fearful that he'd not get a penny. Nice chap isn't he?'

Just then, there was the sound of a car door slamming, followed by steps up the path and a light knock on the door.

'Talk of the devil,' continued Henry, smiling at his mother who had swivelled towards him, her concave chest heaving up and down and her eyes blazing with hatred. 'We'd better let him in don't you think, so he can explain to us what he's doing and which deal he thinks is best - a deal with Mother or deal with Son.' Henry used his hands as scales, lifting them up and down indecisively. 'It's a tricky one, so best we let him decide.'

And with that he walked unhesitatingly to the door and swung it open, where the massive bulk of Archibald Snapes stood blocking out the daylight, clutching a briefcase and looking for all the world as if he'd seen a spectre, which indeed he thought he had. In fact due to the man being rendered speechless, Henry by way of proving he was in fact flesh and not spirit, reached forward and pulled him in by his lapel, slamming the door behind him.

'Mr Snapes, what a pleasure to see you on this beautiful day. How was Ascot yesterday? Did you win? Lose? Cheat maybe? Hmm? We do a bit of cheating on the side don't we Archibald?

'What are you doing here?' demanded Snapes with extraordinary audacity as if he owned the house.

'I live here Archibald. Have done for over forty years. And you? May I ask what you are doing here? I don't believe you live here unless my dear mother has let my room out in my absence.

Have you Mother?' Irma Scroggins was incapable of speech. 'Mother apparently says no.'

'How did you know I was at Ascot yesterday?' asked the terrified hulk, already guessing the answer as the words left his mouth. 'Only one person knew I was there.'

'I didn't know that. All I knew was what Dorothy Bodgertold me, that was all. Lovely lady isn't she. Invaluable to the honest running of the business I'd say.'

'You've seen *her*?' snapped Snapes.

'Oh yes. Last night.'

'Where?'

'At her flat above your office Archibald, whilst you were no doubt celebrating your good fortune at Ascot. Or otherwise. Gambling can be a terrible thing.' He turned to his mother. 'Can't it Mother? It can ruin your life and make you captive not only to the addiction it causes but also to anyone on whom you depend upon for a roof over your head. And if that person decides to capitalise on that power and make your life a misery then, heavens above, it can be hell. Isn't that right Mother?'

'Snapes!' screeched Irma Scroggins, at last finding her voice which she directed with every ounce of venomous ire and damnation she could muster towards her solicitor. 'Show him the will! Show him what he's *not* going to get, and why that common tart of his will never see a penny of *my* money!' Here she let out a demonic cackle and slapped the kitchen top hard with wrathful delight.

'You mean Millicent I assume, Mother. No, she's not a tart, she's the most wonderful person I've ever known in my life and you can call her the devil incarnate if you really feel there's room for two of you in this world and it won't make a scrap of difference. She's going to be my wife. What about that? Isn't it fantastic news? Did you ever think I'd get married Mother and escape your evil web? No, of course you didn't.'

He turned to Snapes.

'Mr Snapes - Archibald - yes, the will, my mother's asked you to show me my father's will. Can we see it please?'

371

Snapes, mortified beyond movement or speech, stared open-mouthed at Irma as if awaiting instructions.

'Show him man, show him!' shouted his partner in crime. 'Show him he gets nothing!'

Snapes bent down and slowly unclipped his briefcase, taking out a manila folder with the name 'Scroggins H' in black felt tip in a top corner. Henry glanced at the folder then looked enquiringly into Snapes' face, just a foot away from him.

'Well, well, it's got my name on it. What's your commission on this one Snapes? You were offering me, if I remember rightly, ten percent of the total but I'd like to know if Mother did better, being the old skinflint she is. Sorry, astute businesswoman.' He turned and smiled at his mother. 'Oh but not tight when it comes to buying the racing paper for me, eh Mother? Never a wasted penny spent there. No falling down on our maternal duty on that important score, eh? So good to me you always were.'

Irma Scroggins mind was currently semi-paralysed, coping with the dilemma of not knowing who to hate and fear most.

'Is this true Snapes?' she screeched from the kitchen.

'What?' gasped the beleaguered, terrified solicitor.

Henry stood back against the hall wall to allow the two conspirators a full view of each other, his head looking from one to the other, eyebrows raised, before resting on Snapes' almost white complexion, growing whiter and damper by the minute.

'Would you like to give my mother an answer?' he said with deliberate blandness, as if announcing a train delay, 'she's rather an impatient lady as you may have discovered.'

'I think you'll find...' said Snapes with a watery smile, 'that your son, Mrs Scroggins, is deceiving you. We have had no meeting that I can recall and may I suggest that it is the same disturbed state of mind that no doubt caused him to disappear for so long that is now playing tricks again on him. Imagination is a powerful thing you know, when you want it to be.'

'Oh how right you are Mr Snapes, how right you are! So let's for a moment *imagine* that both Mother and I are in possession of a common piece of information about you that you believed nobody on this planet had any idea about? Let's *imagine* that for a moment shall we? Hmm?'

'What information? What are you talking about Scroggins?'

'Well, it happens to also have another commonality now I think about it. Ha! Fancy that eh? The bar in Whiteheath village, the one directly opposite your office and home of your late partner David Bodger and his family.'

'What about it?'

'Isn't it the same place where you and I met? The place where you proffered your obscene proposal and the place where you also got David Bodger drunk the night he mysteriously died?'

'No mystery about it, you fool! He committed suicide!'

'Not according to a young man who witnessed you late that evening dragging him into the front seat of his car before attaching a piece of hosepipe from his exhaust to the back seat - a young man who could no longer live with the dark cloud of what he'd witnessed eight years ago hanging over him, and who has now confessed, in church, to another person with whom we both share some common ground - a Mr Reginald Wilmot.'

Snapes' pallor had now turned ashen and his lips even paler as the blood drained from those two venomous fat orbs quivering uncontrollably between chin and nose.

There came a sound of tumbling crockery from the kitchen and a cup flew past Henry, just missing his head and landing at the feet of Snapes, bouncing and rolling undamaged to a halt near the front door.

'Liar! Cheat!' screeched Irma Scroggins, 'You murdering double-crossing swine!'

Henry turned to his mother. 'Yes Mother, if indeed he is guilty of murder and double-crossing both of us, then how much further down the scale of despicable acts is blackmail? Blackmailing this honourable gentleman with the information you'd already been given concerning the death of David Bodger. Information that you've threatened our solicitor Mr Snapes with if he didn't alter Father's will in your favour.'

'What are you talking about?' hissed the seething woman.

'Have you not threatened Mr Snapes with taking this information about David Bodger's death to the police if he didn't comply with your wishes to ensure my father's will, my father's *unsigned will* that is, was duly signed by his two best friends at the time - something of a miracle due to the two men not being able to speak for themselves, or even *sign* for themselves, for the very same reason that my father cannot sign for himself? In fact let's have a look at the will shall we and see how it compares with the copy I have in my bag, the *original* will that is, the one *without* any long dead men's *recent* signatures, which can, as you are well aware, easily be tested as to their age.' He turned to Snapes. 'Did you wonder where it had gone Archie? Must have been a shock when you went looking for it this morning. Well, let's thank Dorothy for her vigilance and foresight shall we?'

Snapes clutched his briefcase tight to his chest and turned towards the door. At that very moment it opened like Aladdin's Cave before him and there barring his way stood Reginald Wilmot with his wife and Millicent either side of him. Snapes tried to push past them but Henry was on him like a shot, grabbing his jacket by collar and tail whilst Reginald Wilmot, sensing his assistance was required, aimed a thudding punch into the solar plexus area of the gargantuan solicitor, reducing him instantly to a gasping heap hanging limply from the jacket still in Henry's two fists.

'Help me bring him into the front room please would you Reginald,' said Henry, cool as a cucumber.

'My pleasure,' rejoined the good neighbour, thrusting one of Snapes' arms into a half nelson and half directing, half dragging the stumbling, wretching figure into the chair usually occupied until her banishment by Lily Bunce, that esteemed lady who was at that very moment putting down the glass she'd had pressed so hard against her hall wall in order not to miss a single word of the last ten minutes, that she was lucky it hadn't broken and severed her trusty listening ear.

So busy had Henry been in preventing Snapes from escaping and then making sure he was detained in the front room under the able supervision of Reginald Wilmot that he'd not had time to speak to Millicent who'd picked up Snapes' briefcase, dropped in the halting of his escape, and was offering it to Henry.

'Millicent darling, I'm so sorry about all this. Are you alright?'

Henry took the briefcase from her and felt a wave of pride sweep through him that his future wife was in his house, beside him, during his long-awaited moment of justice and retribution.

'Yes I'm fine, but I was so worried once I knew he'd arrived...' She nodded at the dishevelled figure of Snapes slumped in the chair, legs apart, hands on stomach, head back, eyes closed and mouth open, emitting a dreadful moaning, '...and time was ticking by, so we decided to check you were okay.'

'Very thoughtful. Like the Fifth Cavalry. Wonderful.'

No sooner had Henry said this than the figure of Irma Scroggins appeared in the doorway pointing a crooked finger at Millicent.

'Get that *whore* out of my house!' she growled with enough menace to send a conscientious objector headlong into battle.

Henry could have retaliated angrily but by preparing himself and Millicent, who in turn had prepared the Wilmots, for a barrage of insults along the lines of the one Irma Scroggins had just uttered, ensured that any effect she wished it to have, was completely nullified. So instead, Henry seized upon his mother's introduction of his beloved as an opportunity to expound.

'Ah Mother, may I introduce Millicent, proof that it's never too late for a good woman to change a poor man's life. Millicent Carter to be precise as she is at present but soon to do me the honour of changing her name to Scroggins. Shame really, Carter has a much nicer ring to it, but there you go. Millicent, Mother - Mother, Millicent. Good, I knew you'd be delighted for us.'

There was now nowhere for Irma Scroggins to go with her vile tirade and so she staggered to her chair by the window and lowered herself gingerly into it as if every bone in her body was about to snap. And here she sat nibbling furiously at her lower lip, wheezing like an asthmatic, more out of anger than shortage of breath, whilst staring at the still groaning figure of Snapes, who opened his eyes only to quickly close them on seeing Irma penetrating his very soul. And then, suddenly seized with panic, opened them wide again and sat bolt upright, as if thinking of making another desperate attempt at escape, before the arresting hand of Reginald Wilmot descended firmly on his shoulder.

Henry opened his blue folder marked, took out a document which he quickly examined, and then nodded, saying:

'I am glad we are all by strange misfortune gathered here, because I have something to say that I would prefer to be heard by not only the people involved but also by witnesses - if you don't mind performing that role Maureen and Reginald?'

Oh no, they didn't mind one bit but kept their consent to a dignified nod in keeping with the seriousness of the occasion. Henry continued, raising the will for all to see.

'Here is the will of my father who died a very rich man in Australia last Christmas Eve.' He turned to his mother. 'Mother, I don't know why you always hated me - unless perhaps I reminded you too much of Father - but hated me you always did and made my life as much a misery as was in your power to do so. So be it; that is now in the past. May I say here and now that when I heard of the death of my father, the last thing on my mind was money. All I ever wanted was to know him and, failing that, to find out whether he ever perhaps thought about me and wondered how I was. That is the simple fact of the matter. The first I knew about a will was when this *solicitor* sitting here before us, offered to take advantage of my mother's state of incapacitation, her most recent stroke, to make an offer whereby I benefited entirely from the will. But there was a catch. He wanted ten per cent of the total. I left him the evening of his offer, disgusted and sickened that he had attempted to soil my father's memory by such a gross suggestion, but before I had time to tell him this, circumstances overtook me and I found myself on a plane to Australia, desperate to find out what had happened to Father and what sort of man he really was. I returned a new man only yesterday and by chance met Mr and Mrs Wilmot with whom I have sadly not spoken since a child, despite living so close. They told me certain things and then introduced me to Dorothy Bodger, last evening, widow of Archibald Snapes' former partner David.'

At this point Henry looked around at the gathering and raised his eyebrows with the faintest of wry smiles before continuing.

'All of us gathered here quite unintentionally but nevertheless conveniently, have knowledge of a witness statement regarding the nature of Mr Bodger's death late one Friday evening in the car park beneath the offices of Bodger and Snapes in Whiteheath village, but it is not for me to make any further comment upon this as it will be handled through the due process of law once I have presented the information to the police very shortly. But what only Millicent and I, and Mr Snapes know - oh, and Mrs Bodger and her two children - is that David Bodger's father who started the firm of Bodger and Bodger at the start of the war, had passed to his son David a number of wills that for whatever reason had remained unsigned. These were rare cases where the documents had been prepared awaiting signature and witnessing, but due to the Blitz and the sad general loss of life throughout the war, plus other more everyday reasons, remained unclaimed. He had made every effort to contact the dependants but still a small number sat year after year in the files, just in case anyone should ever appear out of the blue with a justified claim. This will I have here is a copy of the original of my father's will, *unsigned and unwitnessed* Mr Snapes, *unsigned and unwitnessed* Mother!'

Henry then plucked out the document from the folder brought by Snapes, much to the quivering man's horror who shot a glance in the direction of Irma Scroggins, she who sat staring at the wall before her, lips pursed tight and one hand gripping the wooden arm of her chair, the other gripping the seat beneath her. 'And this one,' continued Henry, now in full revelationary flight, 'is a rather good copy of the original which had remained *unsigned and unwitnessed* but miraculously now has the signatures of Sidney Mathieson and Wilfred Bunce, two of my father's close friends - the former who died in 1940 and the latter, husband of Lily next door, who died nine years ago. It also has my father's signature upon it which when compared to his signature on various pieces of correspondence between him and James Bodger, David's father, bears no similarity whatsoever. In fact it bears a much closer similarity to the writing of Mr Archibald Snapes whose signature is here for all to see.' He took out several letters from the manila folder and held them up. 'No doubt a handwriting expert will be able to verify what is authentic and what isn't without too much difficulty.'

At this moment Henry was on the verge of producing his *coup de grace* - the only legitimate last will and testament sent to David Bodger by his father and discovered hidden in Snapes' drawer - when suddenly a violent rapping on the front door erupted, followed by Lily calling out Henry's name in the most plaintive of her fine repertoire of plaintive soothsayer voices.

Henry stepped to the doorway between the room they were in and the hallway, just feet from the front door which remained slightly ajar.

'Come in Lily,' he said quietly, 'do please come in.'

Lily Bunce entered, shaking like a leaf and clutching an envelope which she pushed into Henry's hand. Henry took it, stared at it, then with one hand guided Lily gently into the room.

'Please Lily, I'd like you to join us as this concerns you.'

Whilst Henry undid the envelope and slid out a small document, the poor woman sheepishly found a position pinioned against the wall as far from Irma Scroggins as was possible, darting a look at her former friend, now deadly foe, who refused to grace her arrival with the slightest acknowledgement. Lily then in turn peered around at the assembled company, eyes widening when her gaze came to rest on Millicent, standing closest to her and partly hidden by the door. Lily, at once mesmerised by the woman who she surmised to be 'Henry's woman', nodded and pushed her mouth into a nervous smile which instantly faded into her previous expression of terror. Then suddenly:

'Oh my God!'

All eyes turned to Henry whose colour was rapidly draining from his cheeks as he clutched at his forehead.

'My birth certificate!'

He stared at his mother whose eyes had still not moved from their position on the wall but were now dilated into bulging orbs, her knuckles transparent, revealing purple, arthritic joints and shaking with increasing rapidity up and down on the arms of the chair like a sewing machine needle in full flight, until her whole body moved as one shuddering mass.

Lily stepped away from the wall towards Irma Scroggins and pointed at her, jabbing her finger out on each word.

'She's not your muvver 'Enry! Never was, never 'as been!'

Henry slowly looked up from the document, and then at Millicent, before closing his eyes in disbelief.

'Betty...Betty Mathieson,' he murmured.

'Yes!' cried out Lily, 'yes 'Enry! Betty Mathieson's your muvver! Not 'er! That's why she's always 'ated you!'

A gasp went around the room, even from the badly winded solicitor, relieved to have the mantle of Satan's chief apprentice momentarily lifted from his shoulders. Henry looked at the figure of Irma Scroggins, watched her hand move slowly towards the walking stick that rested against the chair, then back to Lily.

'Lily, how long have you known this?' asked Henry, his breath laboured by the shock of the paper gripped in both hands.

'Not long,' replied the lady, stepping back a pace as she saw Irma Scroggins' grip tighten around the neck of the stick and her breathing expel in short, staggered breaths. 'It was when she 'ad her stroke and we didn't think she would live and I was looking after 'er and trying to do me best, as I always do 'Enry as you know, or *did* rather - and I was looking in 'er bedroom drawers for somefink, can't remember what now, and I came across this envelope and, and - other stuff, letters etsetera - and I know I shouldn't 'Enry, I know it's wrong but - I looked. Yes I looked and I saw. And I saw it was y'berf sustifikit and when I looked and read and read again, me eyes nearly popped out of me' ead they did - clean out of me' ead!'

As she spoke these last words Irma Scroggins thrust herself up out of the chair and swung the stick at her neighbour's head like an enraged bull summoning the last ounce of strength and anger from its pierced, blood-soaked body. Lily, in a reflex attempt to shield herself from the blow, half caught the stick as Irma Scroggins pulled back for another swipe. But Lily held on and tried to tug it from the old woman's vice-like grip, pulling her off balance and towards the marble chimney piece. Henry and

Reginald Wilmot stepped forward, both lunging to try and break her fall - but they were too late.

The forehead of Irma Scroggins cracked brutally into the sharp corner of the mantelpiece, jolting her head backwards and throwing her body, like a sack of potatoes, to the floor. Not a sound came from the crumpled heap of clothes, arms outstretched either side. One small shudder, a second more violent, then still.

A short whimper from Lily was all that broke the deathly silence as Henry knelt and gently turned the woman onto her back, laying her arms carefully beside her. And there she lay; motionless, no breath, eyes wide and staring still in manic defiance, at the ceiling.

Henry turned and looked up at Millicent and the Wilmots standing side by side, they dumbstruck at the lifeless form resting against his knees, a look of helplessness and despair in his eyes.

'She's dead. We'd better call a doctor.'

A loud wail erupted from the now peaceful scene as Millicent placed an arm around the shoulder of the hunched, sobbing Lily who clutched out and held onto Millicent like a drowning man to a rock, burying her head before peering up petrified into the young woman's eyes.

'Oh my gawd, what 'ave I done my dear? What 'ave I gawn 'an *done?*'

Millicent stroked the top of Lily's head and whispered.

'Don't worry Lily. It's not your fault. It's alright.'

Henry cradled the dead woman's head in one hand and stroked away wisps of wet hair that lie across the lump that had started to appear on her forehead, but would grow no larger.

'Oh Mother,' he murmured, 'oh Mother, it didn't have to be like this. It really didn't.'

They say that hearing is the last sense that leaves a dying body. The single teardrop that rolled from the left eye of Irma Scroggins and down her sunken cheek, perhaps, at that moment, spoke more than she'd ever been able to say in her whole life.

Four of them gathered in the room watched the back of Henry's head as it bent towards the corpse, his shoulders moving very slightly. It was the moment Henry had dreamt about most of his life; a moment that suddenly felt like one of his saddest.

And as he knelt watched by the four, one other rose slowly, gathering papers and briefcase and creeping unnoticed, like a snake in the dark, from the room. Only the revving of a car and screeching of tyres eventually turned heads towards the window.

## Chapter Forty One

# A FATHER'S CONFESSION TO A SON - WHERE THERE'S A WILL

Henry Winston Scroggins lay on his back in bed staring up at the crack in his ceiling thinking 'I must get that repaired.' He peered around the room at the hideous wallpaper and cracked peeling, paintwork of the window frame, door and skirting boards, untouched in forty years (apart from his wallpapering exploit in 1962) and thought 'I must get that decorated.'

He thought this and other similar practical thoughts - like a new soft carpet to replace the brown lino - in a beam of sunlight that pierced the gap in his curtains and spread diagonally across his body that lay resplendent in crimson silk boxer shorts on top of the bed covers. It was a body tanned by the Australian sun and toned from being in love and feeling proud. The fingers that six months ago were white and podgy and clasped across his chest like the effigy of a once portly bishop were now slimmer, brown and more 'knight' than 'bishop' but still clasped together across his chest because some old habits die a little harder than others. He also had all these thoughts because now, for the first time in his life, he could.

He then ran through the events of the previous evening, thought of Millicent, and smiled. As he did, the phone rang. He slid off the bed - easy in shiny boxer shorts - skipped more than stepped the two paces to the telephone on his chest of drawers and let the smile of anticipation that appeared at the first ring, broaden from ear to ear until it almost divided his head in two.

'Darling, how lovely to hear your sweet voice. Poetic? Oh, you've heard nothing yet. I was just thinking of you and your splendid idea of getting married the day of the Royal Wedding. In a little village church far from the madding crowd as you put it. Who? Thomas Hardy? Oh, right. And he borrowed it from Grey's Elegy in a Churchyard. Oh did he now? I see. You're losing me Millicent, far too literary. Don't forget my confusion at the police station over the book you were reading and which of the literary Lawrence's wrote what. My goodness, what a long time ago that seems and here we are, the drunken fool singing Jingle Bells in his raincoat and the beautiful lady 'solicitor' - about to get married! What a glorious story in itself! Someone should turn it into a book. Yes, I'm feeling wonderful thank you, all things considered. Somehow slept like a log. And you?'

He sat on the end of his bed, where the telephone cord just reached with a horizontal stretch, and listened to Millicent telling him all about the fuss George had made after being abandoned in the care of a neighbour whilst Millicent was away the one night with Henry. George now seemed to Henry more like a stepson than the arch enemy who stole his glove and tormented him the first night he met Millicent, and he was therefore able to listen to tales of George's antics with fondness and humour, knowing they were soon to be a happy family of three.

Henry then brought Millicent up to date about the arrest of Snapes at his office where he'd fled after sneaking away following Irma Scroggins's death; how the police had arrived to find him a sweating, frantic mess tearing the office apart in search of his passport which was all the time just above his fat head in the safe keeping of Dorothy Bodger who, anticipating all eventualities, had taken it from his desk and hidden it in a much safer place under her bed, along with other incriminating documents which all put together constituted enough rope with which to metaphorically hang the murderer of her husband. He wouldn't have got far anyway, as, following a phone call from Henry immediately after Snapes had slithered from the house, Dorothy had quietly locked him in during his search and the only means of escape was through the window to the street below.

Death by Pavement, they agreed, would have been a fitting, ironic end to the desperate man, just yards away from where he perpetrated his heinous crime eight years earlier. But then the chances of that happening - he leaving by the window - would have undoubtedly been hindered, if not entirely prevented, by the simple geometry of his bulk versus the size of the frame.

Henry then explained how he and Dorothy were meeting at the police station that morning to give full statements and then he on to the mortuary to sort out the necessaries of the dead woman he'd called Mother, a coroner not being required thanks to the auspices of Dr. Johnston who'd many times quietly wished the woman dead. But first he had to call John Deighton at the office to assure him he was alive and well and arrange to call in within the next few days. What the future held in The Department or in Australia, he had no clue at that moment but time would tell and all would be well.

Millicent also had things to do; she had a message from Sean Swadely to call him back about tickets to the Wimbledon final and the first Ashes Test Match against Australia at Lords - and of course the small matter of a wedding to arrange, which Henry was glad to place completely in her hands.

Did Henry want to watch tennis or cricket, Sean wanted to know? 'Tennis, no thank you, not if that horrible McEnroe's playing', but he'd always fancied the idea of a day at Lord's wearing a boater and blazer, despite not having a clue about the game. And did he have any preference as to where they should be married? No, he hadn't, but as far away from St. Paul's Cathedral as possible, he knew that much. His knowledge of the countryside south of Lewisham had been largely restricted to a vague remembrance of standing in a crowd holding his grandfather's hand at the gates of Chartwell, home of his namesake Winston Churchill near Westerham in Kent, as the grim face of the then Prime Minister whisked out and passed them in seconds in the back of a black limousine. This, and Brighton with Millicent, but beyond these rural sorties spanning over three decades Henry's geographical knowledge of the British Isles was fairly limited.

Millicent suggested a registry office would be appropriate in view of Henry's commitment to atheism but with her faith in a divine presence remaining constant throughout her life - and even stronger now she had found true happiness - she asked if Henry was averse to their union afterwards being blessed in a church, if they could find one to take an atheist. Henry had no objections whatsoever; whatever made his lovely lady happy made him happy and besides, he'd always had a fascination with graveyards and reading gravestones since a child, so perhaps that was worth a mention to a prospective vicar.

As far as he was concerned, to do whatever was possible for the 29th July that his mercurial Millicent's heart desired and her organisational skills could arrange; for her to look as beautiful as ever, to promise to stay beside him till death did them part and allow him to revel for a day in being the happiest, luckiest man on Planet Earth! That was more than enough for Henry.

Having imparted their news to each other and for the first time feeling a relaxed couple with hearts full of hope and a road ahead to hoe side by side, they agreed to speak again that evening and said their goodbyes. Replacing their respective receivers and basking in the warmth of their love, the relief of events once dreaded but now past and the hope of what the future held, embraced them both with a shared sparkling aura.

Henry stood listening to the silence. Even at eight o'clock on a Saturday morning it seemed so beautifully peaceful outside, just the occasional car passing slowly down the street and sparrows chirruping happily outside his window. He'd never noticed that before, never heard birdsong. Had they always been there trying to cheer him up but unable to distract him from the gloom that hung around him like an impenetrable fog? He had no idea.

Sunshine, warmth beneath his bare feet, birds singing, Millicent's voice ringing still in his ears, and - freedom. Freedom! True everlasting freedom! No more sinister presence in the next room, no demands for tea at the right temperature, no criticism of everything he did and said, no more control. From now on his life was his own and the woman who had tormented him and controlled his every move, was no more. The woman he'd called Mother for forty years and wondered oh so many times how someone so bitter and full of hate could be his own flesh and blood - was not only *not* his mother, but she was dead and no longer able to hurt him. What a waste, what a terrible worthless waste of a life; no giving and sharing of happiness and kindness; no light, frivolous moments; no singing along to music and smiling at passages in books together; not even a television programme to share and enjoy, even to enjoy criticising. No friends calling by, no love, no joy; just one long needless campaign of darkness when light and laughter were everywhere screaming to be let in for free.

His mind returned to the moment last evening when he held her in his arms for the first time in his life and watched the only tear he'd ever seen her shed slide down her dead face and soak into the collar of her blouse. It was such a human thing to do for someone who had tried to be so inhuman. Yes, *tried*, for it must take effort to maintain evil as consistently as she had. There must have been mornings - some mornings surely, he reasoned - when she'd woken with just a remote feeling of joy in her heart, a feeling that could have been seized upon and rolled along like a snowball by other small events, gathering happiness on its way and forcing her to break down, betray herself and show some smidgeon of exultation and then, just maybe, a glimmer of gladness for being alive and a chance of releasing herself from the constant darkness she dwelt within.

But no, not to be; never to be; such a waste. That's why he'd cried when he held her. Forty years and it could have been, should have been, so different. Then, in the blink of an eye, the hate and wickedness gone, extinguished, as if it and the misery she caused to him and others never existed at all. Like the strutting, smirking, cruel dictator felled by an assassin's bullet; suddenly lifeless, powerless, harmless - nothing more than a lump of cold, undignified matter.

And now, with her body removed from the house to the mortuary after Doctor Johnston had called within fifteen minutes of her death, all was different. All was peace, serenity, sunshine. It was as if his father felt able to walk back in and start afresh with Betty, his real mother, after the death of Siddie early in the war; to rewind the clock and change Henry's life from the one he'd known.

Poor Siddie. Henry thought about him, what sort of man he was, wondered if his father had been 'carrying on' with Betty before his best friend's death. He couldn't imagine so, from what he knew of his father and his loyalty to friends, but then love is a powerful force, more powerful than any other, as he himself had discovered. The strongest of men have been brought to their knees and ultimate ruin by the winsome smile and twinkling eye of a femme fatale, driving them to the verge of insanity with an insatiable desire to possess. But then others, like he, with nothing to lose, had made the opposite journey, restored to life by a woman's love and tender care.

He sat down slowly on his bed, hands on bare knees, and stared into space. It dawned on him that he was born out of wedlock, no disgrace in this modern age but in 1940 carrying a stigma that would have set tongues wagging in such a tight knit community as theirs.

'I am the son of my father and the woman he loved. I am the son of my father and the woman he loved.' Henry rose and walked to the window to boldly thrust back the curtains as far as they would go, reciting these words over and over. With an effort and a bit of banging with the palm of one hand on the frame, he unprised the window, jammed from years of inaction, and wrenched it from its clammed moorings upwards with a bang. Warm, fresh air poured in and Henry was sure he heard the room gasp with delirious relief as it sucked the life-giving force into every stagnant corner. He looked out and up and down the street, then down at the alder tree in the front garden where several sparrows sat together as if in shock at seeing a head poking out for the first time, their lively chattering chorus now reduced to a solo token chirrup and embarrassed shuffle on the branch.

Then suddenly the thought entered his mind that he could do what he liked in the house; go where he liked, open any cupboard, drawer; forage and find - even something as basic as sit on the toilet with the bathroom door open. Now *that* was true luxury, true liberty!

He dashed to the only other bedroom and, caught up in the frenzied excitement of his idea and newfound freedom, started opening everything that opened. Some impulse made him go to the bottom of her wardrobe where, groping through the bottoms of long forgotten dresses and coats, his fingers alighted on a tin box. He felt for the handle on top and dragged the square black receptacle out and onto the floor.

Locked! His mind raced. Her keys? Where did she keep her keys? Like a child on an Easter egg hunt he raced to the kitchen and whisked a bunch of keys from a hook by the electric meter and was soon back beside the box and fumbling through, trying any key small enough to fit, until finally the lid of the box sprung open and Henry, like Fagan drooling over a fresh bag of stolen gems, gazed inside and began to lift the letters and other relics of the past. One envelope caught his eye, for it was addressed to him. The handwriting was familiar, he'd seen it on so many documents in Australia, documents signed by his father shown to him by Dean Mansfield as proof of the immensity and value of his father's empire and an indication that everyone there knew they were already talking to their new boss.

He looked at the date, 3rd January 1972, at the airmail sticker and Gold Coast postmark, back at the handwriting, running his fingers over the attractive, flamboyant hand with its long loops and heavy commas. He withdrew the letter, opened it and began to read; read words straight from his own father's hand and heart, of how he visited England to see the son he'd betrayed; how he'd followed him to work, desperate to talk to him but unable to do so through a too overpowering feeling of shame; how he'd returned to Australia, one of the wealthiest and saddest men in that country, and how he was now writing to try in some way to right his wrong by leaving everything he owned, on the death of himself and Betty, 'your real mother', to his only son.

How Betty had wanted to contact her son but lived too much under the heavy burden of betraying the memory of her husband Siddie who was still alive and well when she fell pregnant with what she knew was Henry's baby; one small but distressing consolation being that Siddie had died in ignorance, perishing beneath falling rubble during an air raid just weeks after Betty discovered she was expecting. Sadly she'd never loved him as a woman should love a husband; it had always been Henry for her but Irma had made sure she got him to the altar before anyone else, an act of weakness and stupidity he'd performed in a rush of blood and bellyful of beer in the vain hope that she'd change for the better once married. But it wasn't to be; the miserable woman grew more embittered with every passing day and agreed to take the baby from the widow of her husband's best friend safe in the knowledge that this secret gave her total control over her husband. One false move, one word out of place, one smile in the direction of Betty Mathieson and their disgrace would be made public. She had nothing to lose, everything to gain, the spurned wife who had taken in her husband's lovechild out of the kindness of her heart; they condemned by all as heartless adulterers. It had been easy to hide; Betty sent to her aunt's in the country as soon as she started to show and Irma Scroggins already the hermit who hardly left her home and therefore no real surprise to anyone when a baby suddenly appeared at 52 Viola Street and Betty returned to carry on the fish and chip shop alone, which her parents had taken care of during her confinement.

This, his father wrote in detail, wanting his son to know the whole truth, leaving nothing of 'convenience' out of the story. He then told of the terrible life he and Betty were forced to live just streets away from each other, deeply in love, and yet ever under the despotic, evil eye of Irma Scroggins, she looking for the slightest excuse to humiliate and ruin the lovers' lives. And the mother of the child, surviving on heart-breaking glimpses of her son as he passed by the shop with a parent or grandparent.

Finally, around D-Day, they made their plans; plans to escape to the other side of the world where their secret would be safe and their love could be free, but sadly without the product of their tryst, the son they abandoned. They had prayed constantly that his wife would somehow find compassion for the lad, something she'd yet to demonstrate in his first five years, a compassion that could maybe grow into a bond once it was just the two of them.

But no; Wilfred Bunce, with whom Henry had kept in touch throughout his life in Australia, via his trusted solicitor (Lily, already demonstrating an early propensity for steaming open envelopes and not be trusted) sent Henry regular letters, telling of the boy's unhappiness and isolation from society, apart from the job he plodded off to every day in London, until the day the

Australian millionaire returned to see the young man for himself just before Christmas 1971.

Soon after this visit, Wilfred died and the contact was lost. From this Henry deduced the reason for his father posting the letter direct to him, a fateful mistake to think that this wouldn't be intercepted by the woman who saw the post long before him each weekday and would know from whom it came by the postmark and handwriting. Why did his father not send it to David Bodger, he wondered? Perhaps believing it may fall into the hands of Archibald Snapes. Oh, such a tangled web.

Finally Henry read of his parents' sincere intention, in the early years, to come back for him some way or another, but time passed and with it the weight of their shame grew heavier. Yet never did his mother go to sleep at night without kissing the photo of her day old son and offering up a silent prayer.

At the end of the letter he had signed 'Your Ever Loving Father and Mother', and below in brackets 'If you can ever find forgiveness in your heart to call us those names.'

And beneath this a postscript.

*'I am sending the wills of your mother and me, to a man whom I trust with my life, David Bodger of Bodger and Snapes, whose father was the most honourable of men and a good friend. The wills my wife, Irma, and I made in the presence of Mr Bodger Snr. were prepared but never signed or witnessed. Somehow I never got round to it. That was life at the time. Therefore, everything I own, which you will find is a considerable amount in money, business and property here in Australia, will go to the woman who is still, through my own stupidity, my legal wife, and this must not be. YOU are our only heir. The new wills leave everything to you. The 'new' man in the business, Archibald Snapes, is not to be trusted. Wilfred Bunce has assured me of this, so it is important he plays no part in it. David Bodger will be in touch with you as soon as he receives copies of the wills from my solicitor here in Queen Street, Brisbane. I cannot stress how much Archibald Snapes is not included in anything to do with this.'*

These wills, Henry now knew had been opened by Snapes without his partner's knowledge of their existence, the hulking epitome of corruption awaiting his chance to use the original unsigned ones for his own greedy ends. But David Bodger had later discovered them and confronted his partner.

It all confirmed what he already knew, damning evidence contained in the documents that Dorothy Bodger had given him the night before the final confrontation with his 'mother'; damning evidence which her husband David had vowed to disclose, an admission that helped seal his own death warrant and which would now cost his killer his liberty.

Having this knowledge was one thing, but now reading it in his father's hand Henry could hold back no more and all the sadness of his life and the suppression of his deepest feelings broke loose. The night before, he could not hold back the tears through feelings of sheer waste as he cradled the head of Irma Scroggins, but at this moment - as on the night he discovered the truth of Millicent's past - his body erupted into sobbing convulsions that grew and grew in intensity. And there, on his knees, in his crimson boxer shorts, his life truly began. Desensitised for forty years, the real man was all but complete.

No thoughts of anger or regret, no feelings of a wasted forty years and what might have been. Just relief; pure, unfettered relief and overwhelming love for three people who until six months ago he knew not existed; a father, a mother, a lover.

Henry Scroggins, once wandering lonely and miserable through life until he decided to attend his office Christmas party for the first time; Henry Scroggins, maker of such a tiny gesture of rebellion of the oppressed against the oppressor, had proved - like the butterfly's wing flapped in one part of the world that can cause a hurricane in a faraway region - that repercussions can sometimes get 'a little bit out of hand.'

He looked around at the bedroom of Irma Scroggins. The bed was unmade where she had probably been sitting in wait for Snapes' arrival, shocked at Henry's forced entry and in a state of panic as 'mother' and son confronted each other at the foot of the stairs. Her tea cup and saucer, with a half nibbled biscuit beside it, sat on her bedside table. It all looked as if she could walk straight back in and start demanding fresh tea at the right temperature.

His thoughts returned to that morning, the 23rd December, when the weather raged outside and he announced on the very spot where he stood at that moment that he was going to be late home. It was hard to imagine that Millicent was no part of his life then, not even in 'existence', just one of the millions who crowded the streets of London and who meant nothing to him. Seven short months in the life of a simple man; seven short months.

He took out a ring from the pocket of his shorts and polished it on the red silk. He peered inside at the initials H.S. and placed it on his wedding finger. He'd found it at the bottom of the tin box in the wardrobe; his father's wedding ring he'd decided.

'Wonderful. A perfect fit. Thank you Father. Now you'll be with me forever.'

And off he walked out of the room and down the stairs to make tea, proudly admiring his outstretched left hand.

## Chapter Forty Two

# OH, WHAT A LOVELY WEDDING!
## 29TH JULY 1981

There can be few more magnificent sights in the world than Sir Christopher Wren's cathedral masterpiece in the heart of London's great City, especially when set against a royal blue sky on a glorious summer's day in the searing heat of royal fever and fervour.

Festoon every London street, shop, office, balcony, window, tree, lamppost, horse, dog, vehicle and all other animate and inanimate objects with bunting, union jacks and banners; jam every corner, foot of pavement and elevated viewing space with cheering bodies all as one in glorious ecstasy with smiling police and other forms of benevolent officialdom, and then present the worshipping mass with a newly married beautiful princess and a handsome prince emerging onto the balcony of Buckingham Palace to rapturous applause, providing for the crowds the kiss they'd been longing to see, and you have a day to lift the spirits and warm the cockles of the dullest and most pessimistic members of humanity.

Not a negative word was heard, not a voice raised that didn't swell the giant wave of goodwill and bonhomie seeping from every human pore on this most glorious of summer's days. Indeed, if there had been any dissenters making their unwelcome voices heard within hearing of the joyous, jostling crowds, they might well have found themselves doing so hanging from one of the many lampposts readily available from Buckingham Palace to St. Paul's. No room for heresy today! The Tower was but a stone's throw from the cathedral and no shortage of couriers would have been found willing to dispatch the traitors there forthwith!

Some twenty-five miles south-south east of this historic spectacle, in a picturesque village that exuded 'quintessential' from its every fibre, brick, building, bush and blade of grass, a cluster of some twenty people stood in various poses concentrating their eyes on a television set propped on the bar of The King's Head public house. It was a village so unspoilt down the ages that the famous royal ancestor of the newly-wed prince, (the ancestor having had a certain penchant for royal weddings) would have no difficulty recognising it from the days some five hundred years previously when he was courting his soon to be second wife at her home in a nearby castle; a pretty more than grandiose structure still standing and renovated to its former glory for the patronage of many a tourist.

At the rear of this enthusiastic gathering stood a man looking casual and dapper in a crisp white collarless cotton shirt, sleeves rolled to just below the elbows, cream cotton trousers and a straw boater with a maroon and blue band, the hat sitting a little too rakishly over one eye, denoting he wasn't as yet quite attuned to hat angles, or the wearing of hats at all come to that, the hat only recently having been acquired from the gift shop at Lords Cricket Ground and having hardly left the head of its owner for some three weeks apart from sleeping, eating in several restaurants, and on particularly overcast days. The man, who looked as sporting as it's possible to look when one doesn't have a sporting bone in one's body, happened by chance to own the same Christian name as the ancestral king aforementioned.

Henry Scroggins looked up from beneath the rim of his boater, smiled impishly at his own sweet princess, radiant in a long, flowing white dress with thin straps over her tanned shoulders; a dress so graceful in its simplicity that the perfect figure it covered was shown to the greatest advantage, exuding class, chic and a rather difficult to ignore sexuality; not unlike sweet Tess dancing in the fields, little aware at the time that she was of the 'historic' D'Urberville dynasty.

She took the hat off Henry's head and handed it to him.

'I can't see you properly Henry.'

Henry looked down at his hat and brushed away a tiny fly.

'I'm trying to create an air of mystique before the ceremony, to drive you crazy with desire.'

Millicent grinned self-consciously, aware that several heads had turned slightly at Henry's words, and cupped her hand to whisper in his ear.

'Little bit late for that after we've spent the last month in the same bed.'

'True, true, my dear,' chuckled Henry, putting his finger to his lips as another head turned.

'How long before we've got to be in church?'

Henry glanced at his watch. 'It's one-fifteen, so another thirty minutes yet. No sign of any guests. Hope they find us okay.'

Millicent's smile turned to one of quizzical examination as she watched a close-up of the newly-weds on the screen.

'I wish he looked a bit surer of things,' said Millicent stretching her neck for a better view over the two or three heads between her and the screen. Henry raised himself on tiptoe and peered nonchalantly over a woman's shoulder.

'Doesn't look terribly comfortable does he, poor chap.'

'Poor girl I think,' mused Millicent, lost in thought.

'It's a fairytale wedding Millicent. Everyone says so, so it must be true. But who cares?' He leant towards her. 'Not as fairytale as ours - just a little sideshow before the main event.'

Millicent surprised him with a sudden peck on the nose which tickled and had to be scratched by a short rub with the brim of his hat. Then someone caught her eye behind Henry and a tall, good-looking, deeply-tanned man strode into the bar and lifted a hand to her in recognition. He was wearing a close-fitted short-sleeved denim shirt and light tan trousers, the overall effect somewhat spoilt by razor-sharp vertical creases down the trousers and a pair of complimentary horizontal ones across the shirt front, denoting that it might have been bought on the journey and just plucked from the box minutes before entering the pub. His brown Cuban-heeled boots clomped across the bar and having just left the hot street gave the scene a momentary air of 'High Noon' about it until Millicent's face broke into a broad smile and the man's eyes brightened and hands reached out in greeting. Henry turned to see who it was.

'Sean. How lovely to...' Her face fell. 'But where's....'

Before she could finish, another man dressed in a bright pink shirt, yellow trousers and soft white leather shoes poked his head round the door with a grin to match his companion's. The head, with blonde hair permed, tweaked and highlighted with brown tips, then introduced the rest of its body to the bar which induced thirty seconds of hugging and handshaking and general celebration causing a momentary distraction for the twenty something people in the bar, away from what they, together with six hundred thousand people on the streets of London and an estimated global audience of seven hundred and fifty million imagined (in their ignorance) was something more important happening some twenty-five miles due north-north-west.

It may be wondered what Sean Swadely and Gavin, the concierge from The Grand Hotel - for that's who the other gaily dressed gentleman was - were doing at the wedding of Henry and Millicent but then again it doesn't really take too much contemplation. When the chips are down in life, whether it be in a muddy war-ravaged trench or the awful abyss of loneliness and despair, it is people who come to the rescue. Good people; kind, decent, and more often than not - everyday people. We may walk amongst them all our lives and never need them but when we do, they surface quietly and unconditionally, expecting nothing in the belief they are giving little.

In Henry's case the two men who had just arrived through the pub door had saved his life. No question about it, they had saved his life. Henry knew it, Millicent knew it and the two men had both been told it by the matrimonial couple and asked to be witnesses at the registry office two days previously and honoured guests at the church blessing.

The Australian affairs of Henry's father were now almost completely transferred to his name under the smooth guidance of Dorothy Bodger - a qualified solicitor herself who had decided to continue the business in the name of Bodger & Bodger - and Dean Mansfield, an honest man whom his father had rightly and finally put his trust in; as much as Henry Scoggins senior ever completely trusted anyone, apart from his Betty. This taken care of and 52 Viola Street also under his ownership, Henry's life was irreversibly changed beyond any vague recognition to that when Millicent first 'found' him, lost and bewildered in a police station.

He had his own 'Betty' now of course, and who better to take care of a business such as his father's than the highly experienced Millicent Scroggins, late of *The Carter Consultancy* who was accustomed, more than just about anyone in London, to dealing with men in high places who had a particular, specialised usage for the female species. What Henry's father had created in Australia was, after all, not that far removed from *The Carter Consultancy* which although now only a nominal business name, was poised willing and able to flourish again and represent the UK office of the Scroggins Australian empire.

Henry and Millicent had, as wished, visited Brighton for two days of stone-skimming the week following the death of Irma Scroggins and the arrest of Archibald Snapes, during which time the concierge had expressed a long held desire of his and partner Eric to start a new life in Australia, preferably in the sub-tropics. It therefore hadn't taken long for the ideal jobs to be organised for them, running a small beachside hotel in Palm Bay just south of Surfers Paradise. It was one of Henry senior's favourite properties of the many up and down the Queensland coast he owned, and urgently required new management. So Gavin and Eric had given The Grand Hotel a week's notice and were leaving next week for a new life - flights and all expenses paid. Their excitement and gratitude knew no bounds.

Soon, the bar of The King's Head had been swelled by two more couples and a small squat lady, all of an age where nothing less than Sunday best would do for such an occasion. They joined the wedding party and were introduced to each other, with more handshaking and a certain degree of kissing wrong parts of faces, and shaking hands when maybe kissing was required and kissing when shaking hands would probably have been preferable, as often happens in these nervy circumstances.

By the time it came to stroll across the road for the church blessing, Millicent's father, Sean Swadely and Reginald Wilmot, cricket fanatics all, had analysed every detail of the remarkable Third Test Match at Headingly the previous week when Ian

397

Botham had placed himself and the match firmly into the annals of cricketing immortality by smashing one hundred and forty nine runs to snatch an 'impossible' victory for England.

In fact they are still discussing this memorable topic as they cross the road, enter the peace and serenity of the churchyard (slightly quieter voices) and stroll into the magnificent twelfth century church where their now whispered discussion seems beyond abating until the vicar appears smiling, gently coughing and handing out sheets of paper. Seconds behind them, having stayed to pay the drinks bill, wander Henry and Gavin in their own discussion about business down under, for Henry had already taken on his father's entrepreneurial mantle with consummate ease, as if born to it; as indeed he was.

Lily Bunce, resplendent in a fitted lavender dress and matching shoes - the dress rather too fitted perhaps, and the shoes rather too lavender - had travelled down with the Wilmots in their car, nervous the whole journey in anticipation of meeting Millicent's posh parents and other folk with whom she wasn't accustomed to rubbing shoulders. But Lily need not have worried one jot for she and Sally Carter soon discovered they were born in the same hospital in Canning Town, and in the very same year of nineteen-nineteen! Just three months apart! Goodness gracious! Incredible! Who'd have thought it possible!

The instant bonding that resulted from Lily discovering that behind the plum tones of this attractive, elegant lady was a true East End girl, threw the two ladies into paroxysms of sheer delight and recollections of numerous people and places - so much so that Millicent and Maureen Wilmot could only stand back and smile at each other at the sight of the two incessantly chattering 'firm friends' locked in conversation, the more elegant of the two in blissful ignorance of Lily's masterful skill with letters, kettle and steam.

Henry and Millicent were booked to fly to Australia two weeks after the concierge in order for the staff to meet their new boss who, by virtue of having the same name as his father, was going to make things nice and easy for those with bad memories. But at this stage he had made it perfectly clear to one and all that he was happy for Dean Mansfield and team to manage affairs whilst he kept loosely in touch from his new home with Millicent and George overlooking Regent's Park - the 'office' of a once leading firm of 'solicitors.'

Henry's welcome back to the office in Whitehall to officially pass over the reins to John Deighton, newly-appointed Department Manager, was one of mutual magnanimity and a general vowing to stay well in touch. Richard Gaines, having thrown Peregrine Spencer out of his house on learning that the destitute man had told Millicent of their erstwhile plot against Henry, was still to be found in The Carpenter's Arms defaming the names of good people for his own sick pleasure but finding few listeners to his vile tirades and presenting something of a sad, lonely figure at the bar, growing lonelier by the day.

With the short service conducted and the vicar joining the wedding party in the garden of The King's Head - quite at ease blessing an atheist with a quaint analogy of 'always keeping the net wide open for fresh fish' - the champagne was brought out and toasts made to one and all, the very last being from Henry who, having thanked everyone and flourished his wedding ring - even out-flourishing the simple white gold band with diamond that Millicent had chosen - stood up above the seated throng, once more kissed his 'beautiful, nay, *stunning* bride!' declared himself the luckiest man in the world for the hundredth time that day - and turned to Lily Bunce.

'Now Lily, I need to know - how are you getting on with our new tenant in the house?'

Lily smiled and looked around at everyone, a little coy and fumbling with the stem of her champagne glass.

'Well all I can say 'Enry is that ee's a real proper gen'l'man. And what ee's done to that 'ouse is nobody's business. You might out of the kindness of yer 'art 'ave allowed him to live there for nuffin', but I tell you ee's more than paying 'is way that man is. 'Ain't he Maureen? (Maureen nods vehemently). Every room decorated as you and Millicent had requested, the ceiling in your room fixed - gawd knows 'ow that didn't kill you before now! - and all done immaculate, nuffin' shoddy. And now 'ees on the garden which is looking like a minicher Kew - not that I've ever been there but that's what 'ee said was the effect 'ee was after. I've 'elped 'im plant out the borders mind, and loaned 'im my Wilfred's tools from the shed - gawd rest 'is soul if you'll excuse me vicar (benign smile from vicar with eyes closed) - in fact 'ee keeps 'old of the shed key now as it's easier. And you'll never guess what 'Enry...'

'Please, do tell us Lily.'

She put her hand to her mouth to stifle what looked like a laugh but could easily have been false teeth escaping, and glancing up at Henry's enquiring expression like a primary schoolgirl being tempted into her first playground kiss, spluttered:

'We're on first name terms now, and, and - don't laugh, ee's only invited me in f'dinner next week ain't ee! What d'yer fink o' that 'Enry!'

By now, all those gathered were in various states of mirth from silent shoulder shaking to Reginald's outright loud guffaw, when Henry exclaimed, steadying himself with one hand lightly resting on his bride's shoulder.

'Lily and *Peregrine*! I think that's wonderful! Simply wonderful! Now that *has* made my day Lily! That really has!'